DIANA PALMER

THE MEN OF MEDICINE RIDGE

HQN™

ISBN 0-373-77066-9

THE MEN OF MEDICINE RIDGE

Copyright © 2004 by Harlequin Books S.A.

The publisher acknowledges the copyright holder of the individual works as follows:

THE WEDDING IN WHITE
Copyright © 2000 by Diana Palmer

CIRCLE OF GOLD
Copyright © 2000 by Diana Palmer

Printed in U.S.A.

CONTENTS

THE WEDDING
IN WHITE

Chapter 1

"I'll never get married!" Vivian wailed. "He won't let me have Whit here at all. I only wanted him to come for supper, and now I have to call him and say it's off! Mack's just hateful!"

"There, there," Natalie Brock soothed, hugging the younger girl. "He's not hateful. He just doesn't understand how you feel about Whit. And you have to remember, he's been totally responsible for you since you were fifteen."

"But he's my brother, not my father," came the sniffling reply. Vivian dashed tears off on the back of her hand. "I'm twenty-two," she added in a plaintive tone. "He can't tell me what to do anymore, anyway!"

"He can, on Medicine Ridge Ranch," Natalie reminded her wryly. Medicine Ridge Ranch was the largest spread in this part of Montana—even the town was named after it. "He's the big boss."

"Humph!" Vivian dabbed at her red eyes with a handkerchief. "Only because Daddy left it to him."

"That isn't quite true," came the amused rejoinder. "Your father left him a ranch that was almost bankrupt, on land the bank was trying to repossess." She waved her hand around the expensive Victorian furnishings of the living room. "All this came from his hard work, not a will."

"And so whatever McKinzey Donald Killain wants, he gets," Vivian raged.

It was odd to hear him called by his complete name. For years, everyone around Medicine Ridge, Montana, which had grown up around the Killain ranch, had called him Mack. It was an abbreviation of his first name, which few of his childhood friends could pronounce.

"He only wants you to be happy," Natalie said softly, kissing the flushed cheek of the blond girl. "I'll go talk to him."

"Would you?" Bright blue eyes looked up hopefully.

"I will."

"You're just the nicest friend anybody ever had, Nat," Vivian said fervently. "Nobody else around here has the guts to say anything to him," she added.

"Bob and Charles don't feel comfortable telling him what to do." Natalie defended the younger brothers of the household. Mack had been responsible for all three of his siblings from his early twenties. He was twenty-eight now, crusty and impatient, a real hell-raiser whom most people found intimidating. Natalie had teased him and picked at him from her teens, and she still did. She adored him, despite his fiery temper and legendary impatience. A lot of that ill humor came from having one eye, and she knew it.

Soon after the accident that could as easily have killed him as blinded him, she told him that the rakish patch over his left eye made him look like a sexy pirate. He'd told her to go home and mind her own damned business. She ignored him and continued to help Vivian nurse him, even when he'd come home from the hospital. That hadn't been easy. Natalie was a senior in high school at the time. She'd just gone from the orphanage where she'd spent most of her life to her maiden aunt's house the year before the accident occurred. Her aunt, old Mrs. Barnes, didn't approve of Mack Killain, although she respected him. Natalie had had to beg to get her aunt to drive her first to the hospital and then to the Killain ranch every day to look after Mack. Her aunt had felt it was Vivian's job—not Natalie's—but Vivian couldn't do a thing with her elder brother. Left alone, Mack would have been out on the northern border with his men helping to brand calves.

At first, the doctors feared that he'd lost the sight in both eyes. But later, it had become evident that the right one still functioned. During that time of uncertainty, Natalie had attached herself to him and refused to go away, teasing him when he became despondent, cheering him up when he wanted to quit. She wouldn't let him give up, and soon there had been visible progress in his recovery.

Of course, he'd tossed her out the minute he was back on his feet, and she hadn't protested. She knew him right down to his bones, and he realized it and resented it. He didn't want her for a friend and made it obvious. She didn't push. As an orphan, she was used to rejection. Her aunt hadn't taken her in until the dignified lady was diagnosed with heart failure and needed someone to take care of her. Natalie had gone willingly, not only because she was tired of the orphanage, but also because her aunt lived on Killain's southern border. Natalie visited her new friend Vivian most every day after that. It wasn't until her aunt had died unexpectedly and left her a sizeable nest egg that she'd been able to put herself through college and keep up the payments on the little house she and her aunt had occupied together.

She lived frugally, and she'd managed all by herself. The money was almost gone now, but she'd made good grades and she had the promise of a teaching position at the local elementary school when she graduated. Life at the age of twenty-two looked much better than life at age six, when a grieving child had been taken from her family home and placed in the orphanage after a fire had killed both her parents. Like Mack, she'd had her share of tragedy and grief.

But teaching was wonderful. She loved first graders, so open and loving and curious. That was going to be her future. She and Dave Markham, a sixth-grade teacher at the school, had been dating for several weeks. No one knew that they were more friends than a romantic couple. Dave was sweet on the clerk at the local insurance agency, who was mooning over one of the men she worked with. Natalie wasn't interested in marriage anytime soon. Her only taste of love had been a crush on an older teenager when she was in her senior year. He'd just started noticing her when he was killed in a wreck while driving home from an out-of-town weekend fishing trip with his cousin. Losing her parents, then the one love of her short life, had taught her the danger of loving. She wanted to be safe. She wanted to be alone.

Besides that, she was far too fastidious for the impulsive leap-into-bed relationships that seemed the goal of many modern young women. She had no interest in falling in love, or in a purely physical affair. So until Dave came along, she hadn't dated at all. Well, that wasn't quite true, she conceded.

There was the dance she'd coaxed Mack into taking her to, but he'd been far older than the boys at the local community college who had attended. Nevertheless, he'd made Natalie the belle of the ball just by escorting her. Mack was a dish, by anybody's standards, even if he did lack social graces. By the time they left, he'd put more backs up than a debating team. She hadn't asked him to take her anywhere else, though. He seemed to dislike everybody these days. Especially Natalie.

Natalie hadn't really minded his abrasive company. She admired his penchant for telling the truth even when it wasn't welcome, and for saying what he thought, not what was socially acceptable. She tended to speak her own mind, too. She'd learned that from Mack. He'd forced her to fight back soon after she became friends with his sister. He put her back up and kept it up, refusing to let her rush off and cry. He taught her to stand her ground, to have the courage of her convictions. He made her strong enough to bear up under almost anything.

She remembered that they had an argument the night she'd coaxed him to the dance. He'd left her at her front door with one poisonous remark too many, his black eye narrow and no smile to ease the hard, lean contours of his face. There was too much between them to let a disagreement keep them apart, though.

Mack looked much older than twenty-eight. He'd had so much responsibility on his broad shoulders that he'd been robbed of a real childhood. His mother had died young, and his father had succumbed to drink, and then became abusive to the kids. Mack had stood up to him, many times taking blows meant for the other three. In the end, their father had suffered a stroke and been placed in a nursing home while Mack kept the younger Killains together and supported them by working as a mechanic in town. When Mack was twenty-one, his father had died, leaving Mack with three teenagers to raise.

Meanwhile, he'd invested carefully, bought good stock and started breeding his own strain of Red Angus. He was successful at everything he touched. His only run of real bad luck had been when he'd been thrown from his horse in the pasture with a big Angus bull. When the bull had charged him and he'd tried to catch it by the horns to save himself, he'd been gored in the face. He'd lost his sight, but fortunately only in one eye. The rest of him was still pure, splendid male, and women found him very appealing physically. He was every woman's secret desire, until he opened his mouth. His lack of diplomacy kept him single.

Natalie left Vivian crying in the living room and went to find Mack. He was on one knee in a stall on the cobblestones of the spacious, clean barn, ruffling the fur of one of his border collies. He was a kind man, for the most part, and he did love animals. Every stray in Baker County made a beeline for the Killain place, and there were always furry friends around to pet. The border collies were working dogs, of course, and used to help herd cattle on the vast plains. But Mack adored them, and it was mutual.

Natalie leaned against the doorway of the barn with her arms folded and smiled at the picture he made with the pup.

As if he sensed her presence, his head rose. She couldn't see his eyes under the shadow of his wide-brimmed hat, but she knew he was probably glaring at her. He didn't like letting people see how very human he was.

"Slumming, Miss Educator?" he drawled, rising gracefully to his feet.

She only smiled, used to his remarks. "Seeing how the other half lives, Mr. Cattle Rancher," she shot back. "Vivian says you won't let the love of her life through the front door."

"So what are you, a virgin sacrifice to appease me?" he asked, approaching her with that quick, menacing stride that made her heart jump.

"You aren't supposed to know that I'm a virgin," she pointed out when he stopped just an arm's length away.

He let out a nasty word and smiled mockingly, waiting to see what she'd say.

She ignored the bad language, refusing to rise to the bait. She grinned at him instead.

That disconcerted him, apparently. He pushed his hat over his jet black hair and stared at her. He had Lakota blood two generations back. He could speak that language as fluently as French and German. He took classes from far-flung colleges on the Internet. He was a great student; everything fascinated him.

His bold gaze roamed down her slender body in the neat, fairly loose jeans and soft yellow V-neck sweater she wore. She had short dark hair, very wavy, and emerald green eyes. She wasn't pretty, but her eyes and her soft bow mouth were. Her figure drew far more attention than she was comfortable with, especially from Mack.

"Viv's would-be boyfriend got the Henry girl pregnant last year," he said abruptly.

Her gasp made his eye narrow.

"You didn't have a clue, did you?" he mused. "You and Viv are just alike."

"I beg your pardon?"

"Pitiful taste in men," he added.

She gave him a look of mock indignation. "And I was just going to say how very sexy you were!"

"Pull the other one," he said with amazing coldness.

Her eyebrows arched. "My, we're touchy today!"

He glared at her. "What do you want? If it's an invitation to supper for Viv's heartthrob, he can't come unless you do."

That surprised her. He usually couldn't wait to shoo her off the place. "Three's a crowd?" she murmured dryly.

"Four. I live here," he pointed out. He frowned. "More than four," he continued. "Vivian, Bob and Charles and me. You and the would-be Romeo make six."

"That's splitting hairs," she pointed out. "You're suggesting that I come over to make the numbers even, of course," she chided.

His face didn't betray any emotion at all. "Wear a dress."

That really surprised her. "Listen, you aren't planning any pagan sacrificial rites at a volcano?" she asked, rubbing in the virgin sacrifice notion.

"Something low-cut," he persisted, his gaze narrow and faintly sensual on her pert breasts under the sweater.

"Stop staring at my breasts!" she burst out indignantly, crossing her arms over them.

"Wear a bra," he returned imperturbably.

Her face flamed. "I am wearing a bra!"

His black eye twinkled. "Wear a thicker bra."

She glared at him. "I don't know what's gotten into you!"

He lifted an eyebrow and his eye slid down her body appraisingly. "Lust," he said matter-of-factly. "I haven't had sex for so long, I'm not even sure I remember how."

She couldn't handle a remark like that. They shared such intimate memories for two old sparring partners. She couldn't fence with him verbally when he let his voice drop like that, an octave lower than normal. It was so sensuous that it made her knees weak. So was the memory of that one unforgettable night they'd shared. Warning signals shot to her brain.

He sighed theatrically when her cheeks turned pink. "So much for all that sophistication you pretend to have," he mused.

She cleared her throat. "I wish you wouldn't say things like that to me," she said worriedly.

"Maybe I shouldn't," he conceded. His hand went out and pushed a strand of hair behind her small ear. She jerked at his touch, and he moved a step closer. "I'd never hurt you, Natalie," he said quietly.

She managed a nervous smile. "I'd like that in writing," she said, trying to move away without making it look as if she was intimidated, even though she was.

The barn door was at her back, though, and there was no way to escape. He knew that. She could see it on his face as he slid one long arm beside her head and rested his hand by her ear.

Her heart jumped into her throat. She looked at him with all her darkest fears reflecting in her emerald eyes.

He searched them without speaking for a long moment. "Carl would never have made you happy," he said suddenly. "His people had money. They wouldn't have let him marry an orphan with no assets."

Her eyes darkened with pain. "You don't know that."

"I *do* know that," he returned sharply. "They said as much at the funeral, when someone mentioned how devastated you were. You couldn't even go to the funeral."

She remembered that. She remembered, too, that Mack had come looking for her in her aunt's home the night Carl had died. Her aunt was out of town shopping over the weekend, and she'd been all alone. Mack found her in a very sexy pink satin gown and robe, crying her eyes out. He'd picked her up, carried her to the old easy chair by the bed, and he'd held her in his lap until she couldn't cry anymore. After a close call that still made her knees weak, even in memory, he'd stayed with her that whole long, anguished night, sitting in the chair beside the bed, watching her sleep. It was a mark of the respect he commanded in the community that even Natalie's aunt hadn't said a word about his presence there when she found out about it on her return. Natalie inspired defense in the strangest quarters. Her tenderness made even the toughest people oddly vulnerable around her.

"You held me," she recalled softly.

"Yes." His face seemed to tauten as he looked at her. "I held you."

She felt him so close that it was like being lifted and carried away. Little twinges of pleasure shot through her when she met his searching gaze. The sensation was so intense as they looked at each other, she could almost feel his bare chest against hers. Five years had passed since that night, but it seemed like yesterday. It was like stepping into space.

"And when I lost my sight," he continued, "you held me."

She bit her lower lip hard to stop it from trembling. "I wasn't the only one who tried to nurse you," she recalled.

"Vivian cried when I snapped at her, and the boys hid under their beds. You didn't. You snapped right back. You made me want to go on living."

She lowered her eyes to his chest. He had the build of a rodeo cowboy, broad-shouldered and lean-hipped. His checked shirt was open at the neck, and she saw the thick, curling hair that covered him from his chest to his belt. He wasn't a hairy man, but he was devastating without a shirt. She'd seen him like that more often than she was comfortable remembering. He was beautiful under his clothing, like a sculpture she'd seen in pictures of museum exhibits. She even knew how he felt, there where the hair was thick over his breastbone....

"You were kind to me when Carl died," she returned.

There was a new tension between them after she spoke. She sensed a steely anger in him.

"Since we're on the subject of your poor taste in men, what

do you see in that Markham man?'' he asked curtly. ''He's as prissy as someone's maiden aunt, and in a stand-up fight, he'd go out in seconds.''

She lifted her face. ''Dave's my friend,'' she said shortly. ''And certainly he's no worse than that refugee from the witch trials that you go around with!''

His firm lips pursed. ''Glenna's not a witch.''

''She's not a saint, either,'' she assured him. ''And if you're going without sex, I can guarantee it's not *her* fault!'' she added without thinking. But once the words left her stupid mouth, and she saw the unholy light in the eye that wasn't covered by the black eye patch, she could have bitten her tongue in two.

''Will you two keep your voices down?'' young Bob Killain groaned, as he peered around the barn door to stare at them. ''If Sadie Marshall hears you all the way in the kitchen, she'll tell everybody in her Sunday school class that you two are living in sin out here!'' he exclaimed, naming the Killain housekeeper.

Natalie looked at him indignantly, both hands on her slender hips. ''It's Glenna you'd better worry about, if he gets involved with her!'' she assured Mack's youngest brother, a redhead. ''Her name is written in so many phone booths, she could qualify as a tourist attraction!''

Mack tried not to laugh, but he couldn't help himself. He pulled his hat across his eyes at a slant and turned into the barn. ''Oh, hell, I'm going to work. Haven't you got something to do?'' he asked his brother.

Bob cleared his throat and tried desperately not to laugh, either. ''I'm just going over to Mary Burns's house to help her with her trigonometry.''

''Carry protection,'' Mack's droll voice came back to him.

Bob turned as red as his hair. ''Well, we don't all stand around talking about sex all day!'' he muttered.

''No,'' Natalie agreed facetiously. She looked at Mack deliberately. "Some of us go looking for names in phone booths and call them up for dates!"

"Can it, Nat," Mack said as he opened a stall and led a horse out. He proceeded to saddle it, ignoring Natalie and Bob.

"I'll be back by midnight!" Bob called, seeing an opportunity to escape.

"You heard what I said," Mack called after him.

Bob made an indignant sound and stomped out of the barn.

"He's just sixteen, Mack," she said, regaining her composure enough to join him as he fastened the cinch tight.

He glanced at her. "You were just seventeen when you were dating the football hero," he reminded her.

She stared at him curiously. "Yes, but except for a few very chaste kisses, there wasn't much going on."

He gave her an amused glance before he went back to his chore. He tested the cinch, found it properly tight and adjusted the stirrups.

"What does that look mean?" Natalie asked curiously.

"I had a long talk with him when I found out you'd accepted a date for the Christmas dance from him."

Her lips fell open. "You what?"

He slid a booted foot into the stirrup and vaulted into the saddle with easy grace. He leaned over the pommel and looked at Natalie. "I told him that if he seduced you, he'd have me to contend with. I told his parents the same thing."

She was horrified. She could hardly breathe. "Of all the interfering, presumptuous—"

"You were raised in an orphanage by spinster women, and then you lived with your aunt, who couldn't even talk about kissing without going into a swoon," he said, and he didn't smile. "You knew nothing about men or sex or hormones. Someone had to protect you, and there wasn't anybody else to do it."

"You had no right!"

His dark eye slid over her with something like possession.

"I had more right than I'll ever tell you," he said quietly. "And that's all I'll say on the subject."

He turned the horse, deaf to her fury.

"Mack!" she raged.

He paused and looked at her. "Tell Viv she can have her friend over for supper Saturday night, on the condition that you come, too."

"I don't want to come!"

He hesitated for a minute, then turned the horse and came back to her. "You and I will always disagree on some things," he said. "But we're closer than you realize. I know you," he added in a tone that made her knees wobble. "And you know me."

She couldn't fight the emotions that made her more confused, more stirred, than she'd ever been before. She looked at him with eyes that betrayed her longing for him.

He drew in a long, slow breath, and his face seemed to lose its rigor. "I won't apologize for looking out for you."

"I'm not part of your family, Mack," she said huskily. "You can tell Viv and Bob and Charles what to do, but you can't tell me!"

He studied her angry face and smiled gently, in a way that he rarely smiled at anyone. "Oh, I'm not telling, baby," he replied softly.

"And don't call me baby, either!"

"All that fire and fury," he mused, watching her. "What a waste."

She was so confused that she could hardly think. "I don't understand you at all today!"

"No," he agreed, the smile fading. He looked straight into her eyes, unblinking. "You work hard at it, too."

He turned the horse, and this time he kept riding.

She wanted to throw things. She couldn't believe that he'd said such things to her, that he'd come so close in the barn that for an instant she'd thought that he meant to kiss her. And not a chaste brush on the cheek, like at Christmas parties under the mistletoe, either. But a kiss like ones she'd seen in movies, where the hero crushed the heroine against the length of his body and put his mouth so hard against hers that she couldn't breathe at all.

She tried to picture Mack's hard, beautiful mouth on her lips, and she shivered. It was bad enough remembering how it had been that rainy night that Carl had died, when one thin strap on her nightgown had slid down her arm and...

Oh, no, she told herself firmly. Oh, no, none of that! She wasn't going to start daydreaming about Mack again. She'd gone down that road once already, and the consequences had been horrible.

She went back into the house to tell Viv the bad news.

"But that's wonderful!" her friend exclaimed, all smiles instead of tears. "You'll come, won't you?"

"He's trying to manipulate me," Natalie said irritably. "I won't let him do that!"

"But if you don't come, Whit can't come," came the miserable reply. "You just have to, Nat, if I'm your friend at all."

Natalie grumbled, but in the end, she gave in.

Vivian hugged her tight. "I knew you would," she said happily. "I can hardly wait until Saturday! You'll like him, and so will Mack. He's such a sweet guy."

Natalie hesitated, but if she didn't tell her friend, Mack certainly would, and less kindly. "Viv, did you know that he got a girl in trouble?"

"Well, yes," she said. "But it was her fault," she pointed out. "She chased him and then when they did it, she wouldn't let him use anything. He told me."

Natalie blushed for the second time that day, terribly uncomfortable around people who seemed content to speak about the most embarrassing things openly.

"Sorry," Viv said with a kind smile. "You're very unworldly, you know."

"That's just what your brother said," Natalie muttered.

Vivian studied her curiously for a long time. "He may not

like the idea of Whit, but he likes the idea of your friend Dave Markham even less," she confided.

"He's one to criticize *my* social life, while he runs around with the likes of Glenna the Bimbo. Stop laughing, it isn't funny!"

Vivian cleared her throat. "Sorry. But she's really very nice," she told her friend. "She just likes men."

"One after the other," Natalie agreed, "and even simultaneously, from what people say. Your brother is going to catch some god-awful disease and it will be his own fault. Why are you still laughing?"

"You're jealous," Vivian said.

"That'll be the day!" Natalie said harshly. "I'm going home."

"He's only gone out with her twice," her best friend continued, unabashed, "and he didn't even have lipstick on his shirt when he came home. They just went to a movie together."

"I'm sure your brother didn't get to his present age without learning how to get around lipstick stains," she said belligerently.

"The ladies seem to like him," Vivian said.

"Until he speaks and ruins his image," Natalie added. "His idea of diplomacy is a gun and a smile. If Glenna likes him, it's only because she's taped his mouth shut!"

Vivian laughed helplessly. "I guess that could be true," she confessed. "But he is a refreshing change from all the politically correct people who are afraid to open their mouths at all."

"I suppose so."

Vivian stood up. "Natalie?"

"What?"

She stared at her friend quietly. "You're still in love with him, aren't you?"

Natalie turned quickly toward the door. She wasn't going to answer. "I really have got to go. I have exams next week, and

I'd better hit the books hard. It wouldn't do to flub my exams and not graduate,'' she added.

Vivian wanted to tell Natalie that she had a pretty good idea of what had happened between her and Mack so long ago, but it would embarrass Natalie if she came right out with it. Her friend was so repressed.

"I don't know what happened," she lied, "but you have to remember, you were just seventeen. He was twenty-three."

Natalie turned, her face pale and shocked. "He...told you?"

"He didn't tell me anything," Vivian said softly and honestly. She hadn't needed to be told. Her brother and her best friend had given it away themselves without a word. She smiled. "But you walked around in a constant state of misery and wouldn't come near the place when he was home. He wouldn't be at home if he knew you were coming over to see me. I figured he'd probably said something really harsh and you'd had a terrible fight."

Natalie's face closed up. "The past is best left buried," she said curtly.

"I'm not prying. I'm just making an observation."

"I'll come Saturday night, but only because he won't let Whit come if I don't," Natalie said a little stiffly.

"I'll never mention it again," Vivian said, and Natalie knew what she meant. "I'm sorry. I didn't mean to dredge up something painful."

"No harm done. I'd long since forgotten." The lie slid glibly from her tongue, and she smiled one last time at Vivian before she went out the door. Pretending it didn't matter was the hardest thing she'd done in years.

Chapter 2

Natalie sat in the elementary school classroom the next morning, bleary-eyed from having been up so late the night before studying for her final exams. It was imperative that she read over her notes in all her classes every night so that when the exam schedule was posted, she'd be ready. She'd barely had time to think, and she didn't want to. She never wanted to remember again how it had been that night when she was seventeen and Mack had held her in the darkness.

Mrs. Ringgold's gentle voice, reminding her that it was time to start handwriting practice, brought her to the present. She apologized and organized the class into small groups around the two large class tables. Mrs. Ringgold took one and she the other as they guided the children through the cursive alphabet, taking time to study each effort and offer praise and corrections where they were necessary.

It was during lunch that she met Dave Markham in the line.

"You look smug today," he said with a smile. He was tall and slender, but not in the same way that Mack was. Dave was an intellectual who liked classical music and literature. He couldn't ride or rope and he knew next to nothing about agriculture. But he was sweet, and at least he was someone Natalie could date without having to worry about fighting him off after dessert.

"Mrs. Ringgold says I'm doing great in the classroom," she advised. "Professor Bailey comes to observe me tomorrow. Then, next week, finals." She made a mock shiver.

"You'll pass," he said, smiling. "Everybody's terrified of exams, but if you read your notes once a day, you won't have any trouble with them."

"I wish I *could* read my notes," she confided in a low tone. "If Professor Bailey could flunk me on handwriting, I'd already be out on my ear."

"And you're teaching children how to write?" Dave asked in mock horror.

She glared at him. "Listen, I can tell people how to do things I can't do. It's all a matter of using authority in your voice."

"You do that pretty well," he had to admit. "I hear you had a good tutor."

"What?"

"McKinzey Killain," he offered.

"Mack," she corrected. "Nobody calls him McKinzey."

"Everybody calls him Mr. Killain, except you," he corrected. "And from what I hear, most people around here try not to call him at all."

"He's not so bad," she said. "He just has a little problem with diplomacy."

"Yes. He doesn't know what it is."

"In his tax bracket, you don't have to." She chuckled. "Are you really going to eat liver and onions?" she asked, glancing at his plate and making a face.

"Organ meats are healthy. Lots healthier than that," he returned, making a face at her taco. "Your stomach will dissolve from jalapeño peppers."

"My stomach is made of cast iron, thanks."

"How about a movie Saturday night?" he asked. "That new science fiction movie is on at the Grand."

"I'd love to…oh, I'm sorry, I can't," she corrected, grimacing. "I promised Vivian I'd come to supper that night."

"Is that a regular thing?" he wanted to know.

"Only when Vivian wants to bring a special man home," she said with a rueful smile. "Mack says if I don't come, her boyfriend can't come."

He gave her an odd look. "Why?"

She hesitated with her tray, looking for a place to sit. "Why? I don't know. He just made it a condition. Maybe he thought I wouldn't show up and he could put Viv off. He doesn't like the boy at all."

"Oh, I see."

"Where did all these people come from?" she asked, curious because there were hardly any seats vacant at the teachers' table.

"Visiting committee from the board of education. They're here to study the space problem," he added amusedly.

"They should be able to see that there isn't any space, especially now."

"We're hoping they may agree to budget an addition for us, so that we can get rid of the trailers we're presently using for classrooms."

"I wonder if we'll get it."

He shrugged. "Anybody's guess. Every time they talk about adding to the millage rate, there's a groundswell of protest from property owners who don't have children."

"I remember."

He found them two seats at the very end of the teachers' table and they sat down to the meal. She smiled at the visiting committee and spent the rest of her lunch hour discussing the new playground equipment the board of education had already promised them. She was grateful to have something to think about other than Mack Killain.

Natalie's little house was just on the outskirts of the Killain ranch, and she often complained that her yard was an afterthought. There was so little grass that she could use a Weed Eater for her yard work. One thing she did have was a fenced-in back yard with climbing roses everywhere. She loved to sit on the tiny patio and watch birds come and go at the small bird feeders hanging from every limb of her one tree—a tall cottonwood. Beyond her boundary, she could catch occasional glimpses of the red-coated Red Angus purebred cattle the Killains raised. The view outside was wonderful.

The view inside was another story. The kitchen had a stove and a refrigerator and a sink, not much else. The living-room-dining-room combination had a sofa and an easy chair—both second-hand—and a used Persian rug with holes. The bedroom had a single bed and a dresser, an old armchair and a straight chair. The porches were small and needed general repair. As homes went, it was hardly the American dream. But to Natalie, whose life had been spent in an orphanage, it was luxury to have her own space. Until her junior year, when she moved into her aunt's house to become a companion/nurse/house-keeper for the two years until her aunt died suddenly, she'd never been by herself much.

She had one framed portrait of her parents and another of Vivian and Mack and Bob and Charles—a group shot of the four Killains that she'd taken herself at a barbecue Vivian had invited her to on the ranch. She picked up the picture frame and stared hard at the tallest man in the group. He was glaring at the camera, and she recalled amusedly that he'd been so busy giving her instructions on how to take the picture that she'd caught him with his mouth open.

He was like that everywhere. He knew how to do a lot of things very well, and he wasn't shy with his advice. He'd walked right into the kitchen of a restaurant one memorable day and taught the haughty French chef how to make a proper barbecue sauce. Fortunately, the two of them had gone into the back alley before anything got broken.

She put the picture down and went to make herself a sandwich. Mack said she didn't eat right, and she had to agree. She could cook, but it seemed such a waste of time to go to all that trouble just for herself. Besides, she was usually so tired when she got home from her student teaching that she didn't have the energy to prepare a meal.

Ham, lettuce, cheese and mayonnaise on bread. All the essentials, she thought. She approved her latest effort before she ate it. Not bad for a single woman.

She turned on the small color television the Killains had given her last Christmas—a luxury she'd protested, for all the good it did her. The news was on, and as usual, it was all bad. She turned on an afternoon cartoon show instead. Marvin the Martian was much better company than anything going on in Washington, D.C.

When she finished her sandwich, she kicked off her shoes and curled up on the sofa with a cup of black coffee. There was nothing like having a real home, she thought, smiling as her eyes danced around the room. And today was Friday. She'd traded days with another checkout girl, so she had Friday and Saturday off from the grocery store she worked at part-time. The market was open on Sunday, but with a skeleton crew, and Natalie wasn't scheduled for that day, either. It would be a dream of a weekend if she didn't have to dress up and go over to the Killains' for supper the following night. She hoped Vivian wasn't serious about the young man she'd invited over. When Mack didn't approve of people, they didn't usually come back.

Natalie only had one good dress, a black crepe one with spaghetti straps, that fell in a straight line to her ankles. There was a lacy shawl she'd bought to go with it, and a plain little pair of sling-back pumps for her small feet. She used more makeup than usual and grimaced at her reflection. She still didn't look her age. She could have passed for eighteen.

She got into her small used car and drove to the Killain ranch, approving the new paint job Mack's men had given the fences around the sprawling Victorian home with its exquisite gingerbread woodwork and latticed porches. It could have slept ten visitors comfortably even before Mack added another wing to accommodate his young brothers' desire for privacy. There was a matching garage out back where Mack kept his Lincoln and the big double-cabbed Dodge Ram truck he used on the ranch. There was a modern barn where the tractors and combine and other ranch equipment were kept, and an even bigger stable where Mack lodged his prize bulls. A separate stable housed the saddle horses. There was a tennis court, which was rarely used, and an Olympic-size indoor swimming pool and conservatory. The conservatory was Natalie's favorite place when she visited. Mack grew many species of orchids there, and Natalie loved them as much as he did.

She expected Vivian to meet her at the foot of the steps, but Mack came himself. He was wearing a dark suit and he looked elegant and perturbed with his hands deep in his pockets as he waited for her to mount the staircase.

"Don't you have another dress?" he asked irritably. "Every time you come over here, you wear that one."

She lifted her chin haughtily. "I work six days a week to put myself through college, pay for gas and utilities and groceries. What's left over wouldn't buy a new piece of material for a mouse suit."

"Excuses, excuses," he murmured. His eyes narrowed on the low cleavage. "And I still don't like that neckline," he said shortly. "It shows too much of your breasts."

She threw up both hands, almost flinging her small evening bag against the ceiling. "Listen, what's this hang-up you have about my breasts lately?" she demanded.

He was frowning as he stared at her bodice. "You're flaunting them."

"I am *not!*"

"It's all right to do it around me," he continued flatly, "but I don't want Vivian's sex maniac boyfriend to start drooling over you at my supper table."

"I don't attract that sort of attention," she muttered.

"With a body like that, you'd attract attention from a dead man," he said shortly. "Just looking at you makes me ache."

She didn't have a comeback. He'd taken the sense right out of her head with that typically blunt remark.

"No sassy reply?" he taunted.

Her eyes ran over him in the becoming suit. "You don't look like a man with an ache."

"How would you know?" he asked. "You don't even understand what an ache is."

She frowned. "You're very difficult to understand."

"It wouldn't take an experienced woman five seconds to know what I meant," he told her. "You're not only repressed, you're blind."

Both eyebrows lifted. "I beg your pardon?"

He let out an angry breath. "Oh, hell, forget it." He turned on his heel. "Are you coming in or not?"

"You're testy as all get out tonight," she murmured dryly, following him. "What's wrong with you? Can't Glenna get rid of that…ache?"

He stopped and she cannoned into his back, almost tripping in the process. He spun around and caught her by the waist, jerking her right against him. He held her there, and one lean hand went to the small of her back and ground her hips deliberately into his.

He held her gaze while his body tautened and swelled blatantly against her stomach. "Glenna can't get rid of it because she doesn't cause it," he said with undeniable mockery.

"McKinzey Donald Killain!" she gasped, outraged.

"Are you shocked?" he asked quietly.

She tried to move back, but his hand contracted and he groaned sharply, so she stood very still in the sensual embrace.

"Does it hurt you?" she whispered huskily.

His breathing was ragged. "When you move," he agreed, a ripple running through his powerful frame.

She stared at him curiously, her body relaxing into the hard curve of him as both his hands went to her hips and held her there very gently.

He returned her quiet stare with his good eye narrowed, intent, searching her face. "I've never let you feel that before," he said huskily.

She was fascinated, not only with the intimacy of their position, but also with the strange sense of belonging it gave her to know that she could arouse him so easily. It didn't embarrass her, really. She felt possessive about him. She always had.

"Do you have this effect on Markham?" he asked, and he didn't smile.

"Dave is my friend," she replied. "It would never occur to him to hold me...like this."

"Would you let him, if he wanted to?"

She thought about that for a few seconds and she frowned again, worried. "Well, no," she confessed reluctantly.

"Why not?"

Her eyes searched his good one. "It would be...repulsive with him."

She felt his heartbeat skip. "Would it?" he asked. "Why?"

"It just would."

His lean hands spread blatantly over her hips and drew her completely against him. He shivered a little at the pleasure it sent careening through his body. His teeth ground together, and he closed his eyes as he bent to rest his forehead against hers.

Natalie felt her breasts go hard at the tips. Her arms were under his now, her hands flat against the rough fabric of his jacket. Her small evening bag lay somewhere on the wooden floor of the porch, completely forgotten. She felt, saw, heard nothing except Mack. Her whole body pulsated with delight at the feel of him so close to her. She could feel his minty breath on her lips while the sounds of the night dimmed to insignificance in her ears.

"Natalie," he whispered huskily, and his hands began to move her hips in a slow, sweet rotation against him. He groaned harshly.

She shivered with the pleasure. Her body rippled with delicious, dangerous sensations.

"Mack?" she whispered, lifting involuntarily toward him in a sensuous little rhythm.

His hands slid to her hips, her waist and blatantly over the thin fabric that covered her breasts in the lacy little long-line bra she wore under the dress. As she met his searching gaze, his hands went inside the deep V neckline and down over the silky skin of her breasts. She caught her breath at the bold caress.

"This," he said softly, "is a very bad idea."

"Of course it is," she agreed unsteadily. Her body was showing a will of its own, lifting and shifting to tease his lean hands closer to the hard tips that wanted so desperately to be caressed.

"Don't," he murmured quietly.

"Mack?"

His forehead moved softly against hers as he tried to catch his breath. "If I touch you the way you want me to, I won't be able to stop. There are four people right inside the house, and three of them would pass out if they saw us like this."

"Do you really think they would?" she asked in a breathless tone.

His thumbs edged down toward the tiny hardnesses inside the long-line and she whimpered.

"Do you want me to touch them?" he whispered at her lips.

"Yes!" she choked.

"It won't be enough," he murmured.

"It will. It will!"

"Not nearly enough," he continued. His mouth touched her eyelids and closed them while his thumbs worked their way lazily inside the lacy cups. "You have the prettiest little breasts, Natalie," he whispered as he traced the soft skin tenderly. "I'd give almost anything right now to put my mouth over them and suckle you."

She cried out, shocked at the delicious images the words produced in her mind.

"I ache," he breathed into her lips, even as his thumbs finally, *finally,* found her and pressed hard against the little peaks.

She sobbed, pushing her face against him as she shivered in the throes of unbelievable sensation.

He made a rough sound and maneuvered her closer to the dark end of the porch, away from the door and windows. His hands cupped her, caressed her insistently while his hot mouth pressed hungrily against her throat just where her pulse throbbed.

"Yes," she choked, lifting even closer into his hands. "Yes, Mack, yes, please, oh, please!"

"You crazy little fool!" he moaned.

Seconds later, he'd unzipped the dress and his mouth was where his hands had been, hot and feverish in its urgency as it sought the soft skin of her breast and finally forced its way into the lacy cup to fasten hungrily on the hard peak.

Her nails bit into the nape of his neck like tiny blades, pulling his mouth even closer as she fed on the exquisite demands it made on her innocence. She lifted against him rhythmically while he suckled her in the warm darkness, his arms contracted to bring her as close as he could get her.

The suddenness with which he pushed her away left her staggering, so weak that she could hardly stand. He'd moved away from her to lean against the wall, where one big hand pressed hard to support him. He was breathing as if he'd been running a race, and she could see the shudders that ran through his tall body. She didn't know what to say or what to do. She was overwhelmed. She couldn't even move to pull up her dress.

After a few seconds he took a harsh, deep breath and turned to look at her. She hadn't moved a step since he'd dragged himself away from her. He smiled ruefully. She was, he thought, painfully innocent.

"Here," he said in a husky tone, moving to pull up her dress and fasten it. "You can't go inside like that."

She looked at him like a curious little cat while he dressed her, as if it was a matter of course to do it.

"Natalie," he laughed harshly, "you have to stop looking like an accident victim."

"Do you do that with her?" she asked, and her pale green eyes flashed.

He mumbled a curse as he fastened the hook at the top of the dress. "Glenna is none of your business."

"Oh, I see. You can ask me about my social life, and I can't ask you about yours, is that how it works?"

He frowned as he held her by both shoulders and looked at her. "Glenna isn't a fuzzy little peach ripening on a tree limb," he muttered. "She's a grown, sophisticated woman who doesn't equate a good time with a wedding ring."

"Mack!" Natalie exclaimed furiously.

"I don't even have to look at you to know you're blushing," he said heavily. "Twenty-two, and you haven't really aged a day since I held you in your bedroom the night of Carl's wreck."

"You looked at me," she whispered.

His hands tightened. "Lucky you, that looking was all I did."

Her eyes searched his face in the dim light. "You wanted me," she said with sudden realization.

"Yes, I did," he confessed. "But you were seventeen."

"And now I'm twenty-two."

He sighed and smiled. "There isn't much difference," he murmured. "And there still isn't any future in it."

"Not for a man who just wants to have a little fun occasionally," she said sarcastically.

"You certainly don't fall into that category," he agreed. "I've got two brothers and a sister to take care of here. There isn't room for a wife."

"Okay. Just forget that I proposed."

His fingers trailed gently across her soft, swollen mouth. "Besides the responsibilities, I'm not ready to settle down. Not for years yet."

"I'm sure they'll take back the engagement ring if I ask them nicely."

He blinked. "Are we having the same conversation?"

"I only bought you a cheap engagement ring, anyway," she continued outrageously. "It probably wouldn't have fit, so don't worry about it."

He started laughing. He couldn't help it. She really was a pain in the neck. "Damn it, Natalie!" He hugged her close and hard, an affectionate hug with bare overtones of unsatisfied lust.

She hugged him back with a long sigh, and her eyes closed. "I think it's like baby ducks," she murmured absently.

"What is?"

"Imprinting. They follow the first moving thing they see when they hatch, assuming it's their mother. Maybe it's like that with men and women. You were the first man I was ever barely intimate with, so I've imprinted on you."

His heart jumped wildly and his arms tightened around her. "The world is full of men who want to get married and have kids."

"And I'll find one someday," she finished for him. "Have it your own way. But if you really want me to find someone else to fixate on, I have to tell you that dragging me into dark corners and pulling my dress half off isn't the way to go about it."

He was really laughing now, so hard that he had to let her go. "I give up," he said helplessly.

"It's too late now," she returned, going to fetch her purse from the floor. "You've said you don't want the ring."

"Let's go inside while there's still time," he replied as he moved toward the door.

"Not yet," she said quickly. She moved into a patch of light and looked into her compact mirror, taking time to replace her lipstick and fix her hair.

He watched her calmly, his gaze narrow and intense.

She put the compact in her evening bag and moved toward him. "You'd better do some quick repairs of your own," she murmured after she examined his face. "That shade of lipstick definitely doesn't suit you."

He gave her a glare, but he pulled out his handkerchief and let her remove the stains from his cheek and neck. Fortunately, the lipstick had missed his white collar or there wouldn't be any disguising it.

"Next time, don't put on six layers of it before you come over here," he advised coolly.

"Next time, keep your hands in your pockets."

He chuckled dryly. "Fat chance, with your dress showing off your breasts like that."

She unfastened her lacy shawl and draped it across her bodice and over her shoulder. She gave him a haughty glance and waited for him to open the front door.

"The next dress I buy will have a mandarin neckline, you can bet on that," she told him under her breath.

"Make sure it doesn't have buttons, then," he whispered outrageously as he stood aside to let her pass.

"Lecher," she whispered.

"Temptress," he whispered back.

She walked past him and into the living room before he could think up any more smart remarks to throw at her. She looked calm, but inside, she was rippling with tiny fears and remnants of pleasure from his touch. It occurred to her that, over the years, she'd been more intimate with him than any other man she'd ever known, but he'd never kissed her.

Thinking about that didn't help her situation, so she smiled warmly at Bob and Charles as they rose to their feet, and then at Vivian and the tall, blond man who stood up from his seat on the sofa beside her.

"Natalie, this is Whit," Vivian introduced them. Her blue

eyes looked at the blond man with total possession. Whit, in turn, looked at Natalie as if he'd just discovered oil.

Oh, boy, Natalie thought miserably as she registered the gleam in Whit's blue eyes when they shook hands. He held hers for just a few seconds too long, and she grimaced. Here was a complication she hadn't counted on.

Chapter 3

It didn't help matters that Whit was a graduate of the same community college Natalie attended and had taken classes with some of the professors who taught her. Vivian had never wanted to go to college, and was unsure what she wanted to do with her life. Just recently, Mack had put his foot down and insisted that she get either a job or a degree. Vivian had been horrified, but she'd finally agreed to try a course in computer programming at the local vocational school. That was where she'd met Whit, who taught English there.

As they ate dinner, Natalie carefully maneuvered the conversation toward the vocational school, so that Vivian could join in. Vivian was livid and getting more upset by the minute. Natalie could have kicked Mack for putting her in this position. If only he'd let Vivian invite Whit over unconditionally!

"Why didn't you go to college to study computer programming?" Whit asked Vivian, and managed to make it sound condescending.

"The classes were already full when I decided to go," Vivian said with a forced smile. "Besides, I'd never have met you if I'd gone to college instead of the vocational school."

"I suppose not." He smiled at her, but his attention went immediately back to Natalie. "What grade do you plan to teach?"

"First or second," Natalie said. "And I have to leave very soon, I'm afraid. I have exams next week, so I expect to be up very late tonight studying."

"You can't even stay for dessert?" Whit asked.

"Nope...sorry."

"What a shame," Whit said.

"Yes, what a shame." Vivian echoed the words, but the tone was totally different.

"I'll walk you out to your car," Mack said before Whit could volunteer.

Whit knew when he was beaten. He smiled sheepishly and asked Vivian if she'd pour him a second cup of coffee.

It was pitch black outside. Mack held Natalie's arm on the way down the steps, but not in any affectionate way. He was all but cutting off the circulation.

"Well, that was a disaster," he said through his teeth.

"It was your disaster," she pointed out irritably. "If you hadn't insisted that I come over, too—"

"Disaster is my middle name lately," he replied with half-hearted amusement.

"He isn't a bad man," she told him. "He's just normal. He likes anything with a passable figure. Sooner or later, Viv is going to realize that he has a wandering eye, and she'll drop him. *If,*" she added forcibly, "you don't put her back up by disapproving of him. In that case, she'll probably marry him out of spite!"

He stopped at the driver's side of her car and let her arm fall. "Not if you're around, she won't."

"I won't be around. He gives me the willies," she said flatly. "If I hadn't had this shawl on, I'd have pulled the tablecloth over my head!"

"I told you not to wear anything low-cut."

"I only did that to spite you," she admitted. "Next time,

I'll wear an overcoat." She dug in her evening bag for her car keys. "And I thought you said he was a boy. He isn't. He's a teacher."

"He's a boy compared to me."

"Most men are boys compared to you," she said impatiently. "If Viv used you as a yardstick, she'd never date anybody at all!"

He glared at her. "That doesn't sound very much like a compliment."

"It isn't. You expect anything male to be just like you."

"I'm successful."

"Yes, you're successful," she conceded. "But you're a social disaster! You open your mouth, and people run for the exits!"

"Is it my fault if people can't do their jobs properly?" he shot back. "I try not to interfere unless I see people making really big mistakes," he began.

"Waitresses who can't get the coffee strong enough," she interrupted, counting on her fingers. "Bandleaders who don't conduct with enough spirit, firemen who don't hold the hoses right, police officers who forget to give turn signals when you're following them, little children whose shoelaces aren't tied properly—"

"Maybe I interfere a little," he defended himself.

"You're a walking consumer advocate group," she countered, exasperated. "If you ever get captured by an enemy force, they'll shoot themselves!"

He started to smile. "Think so?"

She threw up her hands. "I'm going home."

"Good idea. Maybe the English expert will follow suit."

"If he doesn't, you could always correct his grammar," she suggested.

"That's the spirit."

She opened the door and got into the car.

"Don't speed," he said, leaning to the open window, and

he wasn't smiling. "There's more than a little fog out here.
Take your time getting home, and keep your doors locked."

"Stop nursemaiding me," she muttered.

"You do it to me all the time," he pointed out.

"You don't take care of yourself," she replied quietly.

"Why should I bother, when you're so good at doing it for
me?" he queried.

She was losing the battle. It did serve to keep her mind off
the way he'd held her earlier, the touch of those strong hands
on her bare flesh. She had to stop thinking about it.

"Keep next Friday night open," he said unexpectedly.

She frowned. "Why?"

"I thought we might take Vivian and the professor over to
Billings to have dinner and see a play."

She hesitated. "I don't know..."

"What's your exam schedule?"

"One on Monday, one on Tuesday, one on Thursday and
one on Friday."

"You'll be ready to cut loose by then," he said confidently.
"You can afford one new dress, surely?"

"I'll buy myself some chain mail," she promised.

He grinned. It changed him, made him look younger, more
approachable. It made her tingle when he looked like that.

"We'll pick you up about five."

She smiled at him. "Okay."

He moved away from the car, waiting until she started it
and put it in gear before he waved and walked toward the
porch. She watched him helplessly for several seconds. There
had been a shift in their relationship. Part of her was terrified
of it. Another part was excited.

She drove home, forcing herself not to think about it.

That night, Natalie had passionate, hot dreams of herself
and Mack in a big double bed somewhere. She woke sweating
and couldn't go back to sleep. She felt guilty enough to go
to church. But when she got home and fixed herself a bowl

of soup for lunch, she started thinking about Mack again and couldn't quit.

The rain was coming down steadily. If the temperature had been just a little lower, it might have turned to snow, even this late in the spring. Montana weather was unpredictable at best.

She got out her biology textbook and grimaced as she tried to read her notes. This was her second course on the subject, and she was uncomfortable about the upcoming exam. No matter how hard she studied, science just went right through her head. Genetics was a nightmare, and animal anatomy was a disaster. Her professor warned them that they'd better spend a lot of time in the lab, because they were going to be expected to trace blood flow through the various arteries and veins and the lymphatic system. Despite the extra hours she'd put in with her small lab study group, she was tearing her hair out trying to remember everything she'd learned over the course of the semester.

She'd been hard at it all afternoon when there was a knock at the front door. It was almost dark, and she was hungry. She'd have to find something to eat, she supposed. Halfway expecting Vivian, she went to the door barefooted, in jeans and a loose button-up green shirt with no makeup on and her hair uncombed. She opened the door and found Mack there, dressed in jeans and a yellow knit shirt, carrying a bag of food.

"Fish and chips," he announced.

"For me?" she asked, surprised.

"For us," he countered, elbowing his way in. "I came to coach you."

"You did?" She was beginning to feel like a parrot.

"For the biology exam," he continued. "Or don't you need help?"

"I'm considering around-the-clock prayer and going to class on crutches for a sympathy concession from my professor."

"I know your professor, and he wouldn't feel sorry for a dismembered kitten if it was trying to get out of his exam," he returned. "Do I get to stay?"

She laughed softly. "Sure."

He went into the kitchen and started getting down plates.

"I'll make another pot of coffee," she volunteered. She felt a little shy of him after the night before. They had such intimate memories for two old sparring partners. She glanced at him a little nervously as she went about the ritual of making coffee. "Wasn't your science fiction show on tonight?" she asked, because she knew he only watched one, and this was the night it ran.

"It's a rerun," he said smoothly. "Have you got any ketchup?"

"You're going to put ketchup on fish?" she asked in mock surprise.

"I don't eat things I can't put ketchup on," he replied.

"That lets out ice cream."

He tossed her a grin. "It's good on vanilla."

"Yuck!"

"Where's your sense of adventure?" he taunted. "You have to experience new things to become well rounded."

"I'm not eating ketchup on ice cream, whether it rounds people out or not."

"Suit yourself." He put fish and chips onto the plates, fished out two napkins and put silverware at two places on the small kitchen table.

"I gather we're eating in here," she murmured dryly.

"If we eat in the living room, you'll want to watch television," he pointed out. "And if you can find a movie you like, the studying will be over."

"Spoilsport."

"I want you to graduate. You've worked too hard, too long to slack off at the eleventh hour."

"I guess you know all about genetics?" she sighed, seating herself while the coffee finished dripping.

"I breed cattle," he reminded her. "Of course I do."

She grimaced. "I love biology. You'd think I'd be good at it."

"You're good with children," he said, smiling gently at her. "That's what matters the most."

She shrugged. "I suppose you're right." She studied his lean, dark face with its striking black eye patch. "Are you still half buried in Internet college courses?"

"Yes. It's forensic archaeology this semester. Bones," he clarified. His eye twinkled. "Want to hear all about it?"

"Not over fish and chips," she said distastefully.

"Squeamish, are you?"

"Only when I'm eating," she replied. She glanced at the coffeemaker, noted that the brewing cycle was over and got up to fill two thick white mugs with black coffee. She put his in front of him and seated herself. Neither of them took cream or sugar, so there was no sense in putting them on the table.

"How's Viv?" she asked as they started on the fish.

"Fuming. Lover boy went home without asking her for another date." He gave her a curious look. "She thought he might have phoned you."

"Not a chance," she said easily. "Besides, he's not my type."

"What is? The Markham man?" That was pure venom in his deep voice.

"Dave is nice."

"Nice." He finished a bite of fish and washed it down with coffee. "Am I nice?" he persisted.

She met his teasing glance and made a face at him. "You and a den of rattlesnakes."

"That's what I thought." He munched on a chip, leaning back in his chair to give her a long, steady scrutiny. "You're the only woman I know who improves without makeup."

"It's too much work when I'm home alone. I wasn't expecting company," she added.

He smiled. "I noticed. How old is that blouse?"

"Three years," she said with a sigh, noting the faded pattern. "But it's comfortable."

His gaze lingered on it just a little too long, narrow and vaguely disturbing.

"I am wearing a bra!" she blurted.

His eyebrows lifted. "Are you really?" he asked in mock surprise.

"Don't stare."

He only smiled and finished his fish, oblivious to her glare.

"Tell me about blood groups," he said when they were on their second cup of coffee.

She did, naming them and describing which groups were compatible and which weren't.

"Not bad," he said when she was through. "Now, let's discuss recessive genes."

She hadn't realized just how much material she'd already absorbed until she started answering questions on those topics. It was only when they came to the formulae for the various combinations and the descriptions of genetic populations and gene pools that she foundered.

They went into the living room. She handed him the book. He stretched out on the sofa, slipping off his boots so that he could sprawl while she curled up in the big armchair across from him.

He read the descriptions to her, made her recite them, then formulated questions to prompt the right answers. She couldn't remember being drilled so competently on a subject before.

Then he took her lab report and had her point out the various circulation patterns of blood through the body of a lab rat the class had dissected. He drew her onto the floor with him and put the book in front of them, so that she could see the diagram and label the various organs as well as the major arteries and veins.

"How does he do this on the exams?" he asked. "Does he lay out a diagram and have you fill in the spaces?"

"No. He usually just sticks a pin in the organ or vein or artery he wants us to identify."

"Barbarian," he muttered.

She grinned. "That's what we call him when he isn't listening," she admitted. "Actually, we have a much more thorough course of study in biology than most of the surrounding colleges, because most of our students go on to medical school or into nursing. Biology is a real headache here, but none of our students ever have to take remedial courses later on."

"That says a lot for the quality of teaching."

She smiled. "So it does."

He went over the anatomy schematic with her until she knew the answers without prompting. But it was ten o'clock when she started to yawn.

"You're tired," he said. "You need a good night's sleep, so you can feel up to the exam in the morning."

"Thanks for helping me."

He shrugged. "What are neighbors for?" he asked with a chuckle. "How about a cup of hot chocolate before I go home?"

"I'll make it."

He stretched lazily on the carpet. "I was hoping you'd offer. I can't make it unless I have something you just stir into hot milk. As I recall, you can do it from scratch."

"I can," she said smugly. "Won't take a jiffy."

She got down the ingredients, mixed them, heated the milk in her used microwave oven and took two steaming mugs into the living room. He was still sprawled on the carpet, so she sprawled with him, both of them using the sofa for a backrest while they drained the warm liquid.

"Just the thing to make me sleep," she murmured drowsily. "As if I needed help!"

"Do you think you know the material now?" he asked.

"Inside out," she agreed. "Thanks."

"You'd do the same for me."

"Yes, I would."

He finished his drink and put the mug on the side table, taking hers when she emptied it and placing it beside his.

"How do you feel about the other exams?" he asked.

"That material, I do know," she told him. "It was just a question of reviewing my notes every day. But this biology was a nightmare. I never thought I'd grasp it. You have a knack for making it sound simple. It isn't."

"I use a lot of it in my breeding program," he said on a lazy stretch. He flexed his shoulders. "You can't get good beef cattle unless you breed for specific qualities."

"I guess not." Her eyes went involuntarily to his high cheekbones, his straight nose, and then down to that disciplined, very sensuous mouth. It made her tingle to look at it.

"You're staring," he murmured.

"I was just thinking," she replied absently.

"Thinking what?"

She shifted a little and lowered her eyes, smiling shyly. "I was thinking that you've never kissed me."

"That's a lie," he returned amusedly. "I kissed you last Christmas under the mistletoe."

"That was a kiss?" she drawled.

"It was the only sort of kiss I felt comfortable with, considering that my brothers and my sister were staring at us the whole time," he said with a twinkle in his dark eye.

"I guess they'd run you ragged if you made a serious pass at someone."

"I've made several serious passes at you," he replied, and he didn't smile. "You don't seem to notice them."

She colored, and her voice felt choked. "I notice them, all right."

"You run," he corrected. His gaze fell to her soft mouth and lingered there. "I'd enjoy kissing you, Nat," he added quietly. "But a kiss is a stepping-stone. It leads down a road you may not want to walk right away."

She frowned, puzzled. "What sort of road?"

"I don't want to get married," he said simply. "And you don't want to have intercourse."

"McKinzey Killain!" she exclaimed, outraged, sitting straight up.

"There's another word for it." He grinned wickedly. "Want to hear it?"

"You say it, and I'll brain you with your own boot!" she threatened, making a grab for one of the highly polished pair lying just past his hip.

He was too quick for her. He caught her arm as it reached his abdomen and jerked her down on the other side of him, turning her under a long, powerful leg and arm with speed and grace.

She found herself flat on her back looking into his taut, somber face. She'd expected laughter, amusement, even mocking good humor. None of those emotions was evident. He was very still, and his good eye held an intimidating expression.

She could feel the powerful muscle of his thigh across hers, the pressure vaguely arousing. She could feel the hard, heavy beat of his heart against her breasts in their light covering. She could taste his breath on her mouth as he stared at her from point-blank range. She began to feel hot and swollen all over from the unfamiliar proximity. She didn't know whether to try to laugh it off or fight her way off the carpet.

He seemed to sense her internal struggle, because that long leg moved enough to pin her in a position that was just shy of intimate.

She jerked and moved her hips. He caught them with one big, lean hand and held her down hard.

"Don't do that," he said huskily, "unless you're in a reckless mood."

She stilled, curious.

He let go of her hip and slid his hand into her hair, tugging off the band that held it in place behind her ears. He smoothed her hair over the carpet and looked into her face with an expression that bordered on possession.

His fingers trailed down the side of her neck to the opening of her blouse and lingered there, tracing a deliberate pattern on the soft skin that provoked a shiver from her responsive body.

His long leg moved, just barely, and her lips parted on an audible sound as her body arched involuntarily.

His hips shifted, pinning her, and his face hardened. "Do you know what that does to me? Or are you experimenting?"

She swallowed, and her eyes searched his. "I don't know what it does," she confessed huskily. "I feel very odd."

"Odd how?"

His intent gaze made her heartbeat quicken. "I feel swollen," she whispered, as if she were telling him a secret.

His gaze dropped to her parted mouth. "Where?" he breathed. "Here?" And his hand slid under her hips and lifted her right into the blatant contours of his aroused body.

She did gasp then, but she didn't try to get away. She looked straight at him, enthralled.

"I want you," he said in a rough whisper. "And now you know what happens when I want you." His hand contracted, grinding her against him. "You'd better be sure what *you* want, before I go over the edge."

Her body seemed to dissolve under him. She made a husky little sound deep in her throat and shivered as delicious sensations rippled through her body.

He groaned. His hand moved into the thick fall of her hair and pinned her head as he bent down. "I should be shot," he ground out against her parted lips.

"Why?" she moaned, lifting her arms around his neck.

"Nat..."

The sound went into her mouth. He kissed her with a barely leashed hunger that made every secret dream of her life come true. She relaxed under him, reached up to hold him tight, moved her legs to admit the harsh downward thrust of his hips. She moaned again, a sound almost of anguish, as the kiss grew harder and slower and more insistent. He tasted of hot chocolate and pure man as he explored her soft, willing mouth. She'd been kissed, but never like this. He knew more about women than she ever expected to learn about men. She matched his hunger with enthusiasm rather than experience, and he knew immediately that she was in over her head.

He lifted his mouth, noticing with reluctant pleasure that she followed its ascent, trying to coax it back over her lips.

"No," he whispered tenderly, holding her down with a gentle arm right across her hard-tipped breasts.

"Why not?" she asked miserably. "Don't you like kissing me?"

He drew in an unsteady breath and ground his hips against hers. "Does that feel as if I like it?" he asked with black humor.

She just looked at him, a little shy but totally without understanding.

He shifted so that he was beside her on the carpet, arched across her yielding, taut body. "I don't keep anything in my wallet to use," he said bluntly. "If you want to make love, I have to go to town and buy something to keep you from getting pregnant. Does that make it any clearer?"

Her eyes seemed to widen impossibly for a few seconds. "You mean...have sex?"

"A man has sex with a one-night stand. You're not one."

She studied him quietly, with open curiosity. "I'm not?"

He traced her mouth with a lean forefinger, watching it open hungrily. "I want you very badly," he whispered. "But your conscience would beat you to death, with or without precautions."

She still hesitated. "Maybe..."

He put his finger across her lips. "Maybe not," he said

with returning good humor. "I came over to teach you biology, not reproduction."

"You don't want babies," she said, and she sounded sad.

He grimaced. "I don't want them right now," he corrected. "One day, I'd like several." He traced her thin eyebrows lazily. "You haven't had much experience with men."

"I'm doing my best to learn," she murmured dryly.

His fingers trailed into her hair and speared into its softness. "I'll tell you what to do, when the time comes. This isn't it," he added only half humorously.

She eyed him mischievously. "Are you sure?" She moved deliberately and smiled as he shuddered.

He caught her hip and held her down. "I'm sure," he resigned.

"Okay." She sighed and relaxed into the carpet. "I guess I can live on dreams if I have to."

He pursed his lips. "Do you dream about me?"

"Emphatically," she confessed.

"Should I ask how you dream about me?"

"I'll spare you the blushes," she told him, and moved away so that she could sit up. She pushed back her disheveled hair.

"So they're that sort of dreams, are they?" he asked, chuckling.

"I don't suppose you dream about me," she fished.

He didn't say anything for a long moment. Finally, he sat up and got to his feet gracefully. "I'm leaving while there's still time," he said, and he grinned at her.

"Craven coward," she muttered. "You'd never make a teacher. You have no patience with curious students."

"You've got enough curiosity for both of us," he told her. "Walk me to the door."

"If I must."

He paused with the door open and looked down at her with open possession. "One step at a time, Nat," he said softly. "Slow and easy."

She blushed at the tone and the soft insinuation.

He bent and brushed his mouth briefly against hers. "Get some sleep. I'll see you Friday."

"We're still going to Billings?"

"I wouldn't miss it for the world," he said gently. "Good night."

Frustrated and weak in her knees, she watched him stride to his car. She didn't know how it was going to work out, but she knew that there was no going back to the old easy friendship they'd once enjoyed. She wasn't sure if she was glad or not.

Chapter 4

There were plenty of nervous faces and anxious conversations when Natalie sat in the biology classroom to wait for the professor to hand out the written test questions. She'd assumed that the lab questions would require everyone to file into the lab with another sheet of paper and identify the labeled exhibits there. But the professor announced that the dissection questions were on a separate sheet included with the exam. Everybody was on edge. It was common knowledge that many people failed the finals in this subject and had to retake the course. Natalie prayed that she wouldn't. She couldn't graduate with her class if she flubbed it.

When the papers were handed out, the professor gave the go-ahead. Natalie read each question carefully before she began to fill in the tiny circles of the multiple choice questions. As she studied the drawing of the dissected rat and noted the placement of the various marks, she found that she remembered almost every single one. She was certain that she was going to pass the course. Mack had made sure of it. She almost whooped for joy when she turned in her paper and pencil. There was one more thing required—she had to fill out a rating sheet for the professor and the course, a routine part of finals.

She loved the class and respected the professor, so her answers were positive. She turned in that sheet, too, and left the room. There were still fifteen people huddled over their papers when she went out the door, with only five minutes left for completion.

She almost danced to her car. One down, she thought delightedly. Three to go. And then, graduation! She could hardly wait to share her good news with Mack.

The week went by very quickly. Natalie was almost certain to graduate, because she knew she did well on her finals. The only real surprise would be her final grade, and it would include the marks she received for her practice teaching. She hoped her scores would be good enough to satisfy the school where she would begin her career next term.

When Friday rolled around, she breathed a sigh of relief as she left the English classroom where she'd finished her final round of questions. It was like being freed from jail, she reflected. Although she would miss her classmates and her professors, it had been a long four years. She was ready to go out into the world.

She hadn't heard from Mack all week. Vivian called her Thursday night to ask if she was still planning to go out with them. She didn't sound very enthusiastic about the double date. Natalie tried to smooth it over, but she knew that her friend was jealous, and she didn't know what to do about it. She must discuss it with Mack, she decided.

She tried his cell phone, and he answered with a voice that held both terse authority and irritation.

"Mack?" she asked, surprised by the tone, which he never used with her.

"Nat?" The impatience was gone immediately. "I thought you'd have forgotten this number by now," he added in a slow, smooth tone that sounded amused. "What do you want?"

"I need to talk to you."

There was a pause. She heard him cover the mouthpiece and

talk to someone in the tone she'd heard when he first answered the phone. Then his voice came back to her. "Okay. Go ahead."

"Not over the phone," she said uncomfortably.

"All right. I'll come over."

"But I'm ready to leave," she protested. "I have to drive to town to buy a dress for tonight."

There was a pause. "Good for you."

"It's your fault. You keep making fun of the only dress I've got."

"I'll pick you up in ten minutes," he said.

"I told you, I'm going—"

"I'm going with you," he said. "Ten minutes."

The line went dead. Oh, no, she thought, foreseeing disaster. He'd have the women in the clothing store standing on their heads, and before he was through, the security guards would probably carry him out in a net.

But she realized it wasn't going to be easy to thwart him. Even if she jumped in her car and left, he knew where she was going. He'd simply follow her. It might be better to humor him. After all, she didn't have to buy a dress today. She could wear the one he didn't like.

He drew up in front of the door exactly ten minutes later, pushing the passenger door open when she came out of the house and locked it.

His dark gaze traveled over her neat figure in gray slacks and a gray and white patterned knit top. He wasn't wearing chaps or work boots. She assumed he'd been instructing his men on how to work cattle instead of helping with roundup. He looked clean and unruffled. She was willing to bet his men didn't.

"How many of your men have quit since this morning?" she asked amusedly after she'd fastened her seat belt.

He gave her a quick glare before he pulled the big, double-cabbed truck out of her driveway and into the ranch road that led to the highway. "Why do you think anyone quit?"

"It's roundup," she pointed out. She leaned against the door and studied him with a wicked grin. "Somebody always quits. Usually," she added, "it's the man who thinks he knows more than you do about vaccinations and computer-chip ear tags."

He made an uncomfortable movement and gave her a piercing glance before his foot went down harder on the accelerator. She noticed his boots. Clean and nicely polished.

"Jones quit," he confessed after a minute. "But he was going to quit anyway," he added immediately. "He thinks he knows too much about computer technology to waste it on a cattle ranch."

"You corrected him about the way he programmed your computer," she guessed.

He glared at her. "He did it wrong," he burst out. "What the hell was I supposed to do, let him tangle my herd records so that I couldn't track weight-gain ratios at all?"

She chuckled softly. "I get the picture."

He took off his gray Stetson and stuck in into the hat carrier above the visor. Impatient fingers raked his thick, straight black hair. "He was lumping the calves with the other cattle," he muttered. "They have to be done separately, or the data's no use to me."

"Had he ever worked on a ranch?"

"He worked on a pig farm," he said, and looked absolutely disgusted.

She hid a smile. "I see."

"He said the sort of operation didn't matter, that he knew enough about spreadsheet programs that it wouldn't matter." He glanced at her. "He didn't know anything."

"Ah, now I remember," she teased. "You took the computer programming courses *last* semester."

"I passed with honors," he related. "Something *he* sure as hell didn't do!"

"I hope you never take a course in teaching," she said to herself.

"I heard that," he shot at her.

"Sorry."

He paused at the highway to make sure it was clear before he turned onto it. "How did exams go?"

"Much better than I expected," she said with a smile. "Thanks for helping me with the biology test."

He smiled. "I enjoyed it."

She wasn't sure how to take that, and when he glanced at her with a sensuous smile, she flushed.

"What sort of dress are you going to buy?" he asked.

She gave him a wary look. "I want a simple black one."

"Velvet's in this season," he said carelessly. "You'd look good in green velvet. Emerald green."

"I don't know..."

"I like the feel of it in my hands."

Her eyes narrowed and she glared at him. "Oh, does Glenna wear it?" she asked before she thought.

"No." He studied her for as long as he dared take his gaze off the highway. He smiled. "I like that."

"You like what?" she asked irritably.

"You're jealous."

Her heart skipped a beat. She stared out the window, searching for a defense.

"It wasn't a complaint," he said after a minute.

"I still don't want to be anyone's mistress, in case you were wondering," she said blatantly, hoping to distract him. She was jealous—she just didn't want to admit it.

He chuckled. "I'll keep that in mind."

It was a short drive. She told him where she wanted to go, and he pulled the truck into a parking space near the door of the small boutique.

"You don't have to come in, too," she protested when he joined her on the sidewalk.

"Left to your own devices, you'll come out carrying a black sack with shoulder straps. Where you go, I go," he said imperturbably. "Think of me as a fashion consultant."

She glared at him, but he didn't budge. "All right," she

gave in. "But don't you start handing out advice to the sales-lady! If you do, I'm leaving."

"Fair enough."

He followed her into the shop, where a young woman and an older one were browsing through dresses on a sale rack.

As Natalie headed in that direction, he caught her hand gently in his and maneuvered her to the designer dresses.

"But I can't..." she began.

He put his forefinger across her soft mouth. "Come on."

He gave her a considering look and moved hangers until he found a mid-calf-length velvet dress with cape sleeves and a discreet V neckline. He pulled it out, holding it up to Natalie's still body. "Yes," he said quietly. "The color does something for your eyes. It makes them change color."

"Why, yes, it does," an elderly saleslady said from behind him. "And that particular model is on sale, too," she added with a smile. "We ordered it for a young bride who became unexpectedly pregnant and had to bring it back."

Natalie looked at the dress and then at Mack with uncertainty in her face.

"It's okay," he murmured drolly. "Pregnancy isn't contagious."

The saleslady had to turn away quickly. The younger woman across the shop couldn't help herself and burst out laughing.

"Try it on," he coaxed. "Just for fun."

She clasped it to her chest, turned and followed the saleslady to the back of the store where the fitting rooms were located.

How Mack had judged the size so correctly, she didn't want to guess. But it was a perfect fit, and he was absolutely right about the way it changed her eyes. It made her look mysterious, seductive, even sexy. Despite her lack of conventional beauty, it gave her an air of sophistication. She looked pretty, she thought, surprised.

"Well?" he asked from outside the fitting room.

She hesitated. Oh, why not, she asked herself. She opened the stall door and walked into the shop.

Mack didn't say anything. He didn't have to. His whole face seemed to clench as he studied her seductive young body in the exquisite garment that fit her like a custom-made glove.

"Well?" she asked, echoing his former query.

His gaze went up to collide with hers. He didn't say a word. His hands were in his pockets, and he didn't remove them. He couldn't seem to stop looking at her.

"It was made for you, my dear," the saleslady said with a sigh.

"We'll take it," Mack said quietly.

"But, Mack, I'm not sure…" she began. There hadn't been a price tag on the garment, and even on sale, it might be more than her budget could stand.

"I am." He turned on his heel and followed the saleslady out of the fitting room.

Natalie looked after them wistfully. She could protest, but Mack and the saleslady had just formed a team that the Dallas Cowboys couldn't defeat. She gave in.

By the time Natalie changed into her slacks and shirt and tidied her hair with a small brush from her purse, Mack was signing a sales slip. He handed it to the saleslady along with the pen, and turned as Natalie emerged with the dress over her arm.

"Let me have it, dear, and I'll hang it for you."

Natalie gave it up, watching blankly as the saleslady put it on a hanger, draped a bag over it and tied the bag at the bottom.

"I hope you enjoy it," the saleslady said with a smile as she handed the hanger to Mack.

"Thank you," Natalie said, uncertain if she was thanking the saleslady or her determined escort.

Mack led her out of the store and put her in the truck after he'd hung her new dress on the hook in the back seat.

"Do you need shoes to go with it?" he asked.

"I have some nice black patent leather ones, and a purse to match," she said. "Mack, how could you pay for it? Everyone will think—"

His hand caught hers and curled into it hungrily. "Nobody will know you didn't buy it yourself unless you tell them," he said curtly. His head turned and he looked at her intently. "It really was made for you."

"Well…"

His fingers curled intimately into hers. "You can wear it to Billings," he said. "And when we go nightclubbing."

Her heart raced madly, as much from the caressing touch of his strong fingers as from what he said. "Are we going nightclubbing?"

"We're going lots of places," he said casually. "You don't start teaching until fall. That means, you'll have plenty of spare time. We can go on day trips and picnics, too."

Her body tingled from head to toe. She looked at the big, beautiful hand holding hers. "All four of us?" she asked, wondering if he wasn't taking this chaperon thing a little too seriously.

"You and me, Nat."

"Oh."

He turned off the highway onto a dirt track that led under an enormous pecan tree. He stopped and cut off the engine. The dark eye that met hers was somber and intent on her face.

"Are you serious about Markham?" he asked at once.

"I told you before, he's my friend."

"What sort of friend?" he persisted. "Do you kiss him?"

She frowned worriedly. "Well, no…"

"Why not?"

She sighed angrily. "Because I don't like kissing him. Mack…"

"You like kissing me," he continued quietly.

"You're making me nervous," she blurted. "I don't understand why you're asking so many questions all of a sudden."

He unfastened his seat belt and then hers before he pulled her across his body, her back to the steering wheel and her head resting on his left shoulder. He looked at her for a long moment before he spoke.

"I want to know if you have any long-range plans that involve your teaching colleague," he said finally.

"Not the sort you mean," she confessed.

His lean hand traced her shoulder and then slid down sensuously right onto her soft, firm breast. She gasped and caught his wrist, but he wouldn't budge.

"You don't have to pretend to be outraged," he said gently. "I've touched you like this before."

"You shouldn't," she whispered, flustered.

"Why not?" His hand spread in a slow, sensuous caress that made her nipples go immediately hard. "Your body likes it, even if your mind doesn't."

"My body is stupid," she muttered.

"No, it isn't. It has excellent taste in men," he mused, tongue in cheek.

"Will you be reasonable? It's broad daylight. What if someone drives down this way?" she asked, exasperated.

"We'll tell them a bee got in your blouse and I stopped to take it out," he murmured as his head lowered. "Now stop worrying about slim possibilities and kiss me."

She tried to tell him that it wasn't a good idea, but his mouth was already firmly on her soft lips before she could get a word out. He nibbled at her upper lip in a lazy, sensual rhythm that made it difficult for her to think. When his hand slid inside the blouse and under the strap of the flimsy lace bra, she stopped thinking altogether.

She heard the soft moan of the wind outside and the closer sound of her heartbeat in her ears. She curled a hand into Mack's cotton shirt and lifted herself closer to him.

He bit her lower lip gently while his fingers felt for buttons and moved them out of buttonholes before he coaxed her soft hand inside his shirt and against warm, hard muscle and thick black hair.

It brought back memories of the rainy night he'd come to sit with her after Carl was killed. He'd held her close in his arms that night, too, and he'd pulled her hands inside his shirt, against his bare chest. She remembered his sudden, frightening loss of control….

Her hand stilled against him as she drew her mouth from under his and looked at him with traces of apprehension in her drowsy eyes.

"What's wrong?" he asked.

She swallowed. "I don't want to…to make things difficult for you," she said finally.

"They're already difficult." He shifted her in his arms so that her head lay in the crook of his arm, and his hand went under her blouse and around her to unfasten the hooks on her bra.

"We shouldn't," she tried to protest.

He lifted his head and looked around for a few seconds before his gaze came back to her. "There isn't a car in sight," he said. "And I'm not planning to ravish you within sight of a major highway."

"I knew that."

"Tell me you don't want this and I'll let you go," he said bluntly, hesitating.

She wanted to. She really did. He looked impossibly arrogant with his shirt half unbuttoned and his mouth swollen from the long, hard contact with her lips. His hair was mussed by her fingers, and he looked somber and dangerous. She should tell him to let her go. But his fingers were tracing under her arm, and her traitorous body was writhing in an attempt to get his hand where she really wanted it. She could barely breathe as she twisted helplessly against him.

"That's what I thought," he said quietly, and he shifted her again, just enough to give him room to pull the blouse and bra up, baring her breasts to his intent scrutiny.

Natalie couldn't get enough breath to make a token protest. She loved letting him look at her. She loved the slow, gentle tracing of his fingertips on her delicate skin. She loved the way he looked at her, as if she were a work of art. It wasn't possible to be ashamed.

"Nothing to say?" he teased softly.

"Nothing at all," she whispered, her breath jerking with the little bites of pleasure he gave her with his tender exploration of her breasts.

His thumb moved roughly over her nipple, and she bit her lower lip as pure delight arched her against him.

"I've never felt with anyone the things I feel with you," he breathed as his head lowered. "Some nights, I think I'll go stark raving mad from just the dreams."

She barely heard him. His mouth suddenly covered her breast, and he suckled her, hard.

The cry she made was audible. She trembled as he fed on her soft, smooth skin. It was cool in the cab of the truck, but she was burning all over. Her arms looped around his neck, and she hid her hot face in his neck as the pressure of his mouth increased until it almost made her weep with pleasure.

She pulled at his head, trying to get his mouth even closer, but he pulled back, his eye stormy as it met hers.

"Don't," he said gently. "You'll make me hurt you."

"It won't hurt me." She shivered. Her eyes were as turbulent as the emotions that were overwhelming her. "Don't stop," she whispered unsteadily.

His fingers traced the curve of her breast, and he looked down to watch her body lift up against them.

"Your skin is like silk," he said huskily. "I can't get enough of it." He bent again, his hard mouth smoothing over her in a caress that made her moan.

She arched up, totally without inhibitions, loving his warm lips on her body.

The sound of a car in the distance brought his head up reluctantly. He glanced at the highway, grimaced and helped her sit. "I thought we were alone on the planet," he murmured with a forced laugh. "I suppose it was wishful thinking. Need any help?" he asked as she fumbled behind her for catches.

"I can do it." She glanced at the car as it whizzed past. So much for isolation, she thought, and flushed when she realized how embarrassed she would have been if the car had pulled in behind them and stopped instead of going on its way.

He watched her loop her seat belt across her chest and fasten it. He did the same with his before he cranked the truck.

"A woman like you could make a man conceited," he said with a tender smile.

"It isn't my fault that I can't resist you," she pointed out. "And if you'd stop undressing me—"

"I can't do that," he interrupted. "I'd have nothing left to live for." He backed up until he could pull onto the highway. "Besides," he added with a grin, "how would you ever get any practical experience?"

"I think I may be getting too much," she replied. Her eyes slipped over him possessively, but she looked away before he noticed.

"Don't worry," he said. "I won't push you into doing something you don't really want."

"Do you think you could?"

"I know I could," he replied quietly. "But you'd hate me for it. Maybe I'd hate myself. Whatever happens, it has to be honest and aboveboard. No sneak attacks or seduction."

"I won't sleep with you," she said defensively.

"You would, but I'm not going to let it go that far between us. I've got as much responsibility as I can handle already." His face seemed to harden before her eyes. "The boys can take care of themselves, but Viv can't. She seems to get less mature by the day." He glanced at her. "And she's poisonously angry at you right now."

"Because Whit paid me too much attention, I gather," she said miserably.

"Exactly."

"But that wasn't my fault," she muttered.

"I know that. Vivian won't believe it. Have you forgotten how she was just after Carl was killed?" he added. "She never considered you his girlfriend. She swore he only dated you to get near her. I love my sister, but she has enough conceit for two women."

"Vivian is really beautiful," she pointed out. "I'm not."

He looked at her and smiled slowly. "You're worth any ten beauty queens, Nat," he said in a tone that was like being stroked with a velvet glove. "You have a big heart and you're kind. Too kind, sometimes. You can't refuse people, and they take advantage of you."

"Yes, I noticed," she said pointedly. "Just because I let you kiss me—"

"Stop while you're ahead," he cautioned with a bland look. "That was as mutual a passion as any two people ever shared. You love having my mouth on your body. You can't even hide it."

She crossed her legs and glared out the window with her arms folded. "I don't know beans about men, so I'm a pushover."

"Really? Then why won't you let the fellow teacher touch you?"

She gave him a hard glare, which he ignored. "You came along when I was at an impressionable age," she reminded him. "Remember what I said about baby ducks and imprinting?"

"You're no baby duck."

"I'm imprinted, just the same," she said angrily. "Seventeen years old, and spoiled for other men in the course of a night. You should never have come near me while I was in such a vulnerable state!"

"I couldn't leave you by yourself to grieve," he pointed out. "And you may have been vulnerable, but you didn't protest very much."

"You didn't leave me enough breath to protest with," she reminded him. "I may have been stupid about men, but you were no novice! I was outflanked and outgunned!"

"I'm sorry about Carl, but you were no match for him. He liked a more flighty sort of girl altogether, and he had no plans to marry until he finished college. You'd have broken your heart over him."

"It was my heart to break."

He stopped at a traffic light and turned to meet her angry eyes. "For an intelligent woman, you are unbelievably naïve. Did you really think he took you out because he was in love with you?"

"He was," she said. "He told me he was!"

"He told his friends that he dated you because his brother bet him he couldn't get you to go out with him. There was more to it than that," he added somberly, "but I'll spare you the rest."

"How do you know what he was planning?" she demanded, outraged.

"His younger brother and Bob were good friends," he reminded her. "When Bob got wind of it, he came to me. That's why I had words with Carl and his parents before he tried anything with you."

She was devastated. She'd mourned Carl for months when she was seventeen, and now it turned out that he'd only dated her on a dare. He hadn't loved her. He'd been playing a game. She leaned her head against her window and bit back tears. She was a bigger fool than she'd realized. Why hadn't she guessed? And why hadn't Mack told her years ago?

Chapter 5

Mack saw the glitter of tears in her eyes and he grimaced. "I'm sorry," he said tersely. "I should never have told you."

She pushed back a wisp of hair and dug in her purse for a tissue so she could wipe her eyes. "You should have told me years ago," she corrected. "What an idiot I was!"

"You were naïve," he said gently. "You saw what you wanted to see."

His face was grim, and she realized belatedly that he was angry. She wondered what else Carl had said to his brother, but she was leery of asking.

He glanced at her and tapped his fingers on the steering wheel. "You were seventeen and bent on putting him on a pedestal for life. It would have been a waste."

That note in his voice was almost defensive. She turned in the seat and looked at him openly. She was seeing things she didn't want to see. "What you did...that night," she faltered. "It was deliberate."

"It was," he confessed quietly. "I wanted to give you something to think about, at least something to compare with what you'd already experienced." His jaw tensed. "I didn't realize how innocent you were until it was too late."

"Too late?"

He slowed for a turn and he looked so formidable that she didn't say another word. A tense silence lay between them for several long seconds.

"Maybe it really was like imprinting," he said heavily. "I should never have touched you. You were far too young for what happened."

She felt her face coloring. The hungry passion they'd shared today and the night at his house was almost as explosive as what they'd shared all those years ago. Even in memory, her body burned as she relived her first experience of Mack.

"Do you think I blame you?" she asked finally, but she didn't look at him.

"I blame myself. You've lived like a recluse ever since."

She leaned her face against the glass of the window and smiled. "You were a pretty hard act to follow," she said huskily.

His hands tightened on the steering wheel. "So were you." He sounded as if the words were dragged out of him, and she turned her head to encounter a stare that stopped her heart.

It was as if she could see right into his mind, and she ached at the images that flashed at her, memories they shared.

"I didn't really expect that you'd be inexperienced just because I warned your boyfriend off," he added after a minute. "I got the shock of my life when I realized that you'd never experienced even the mildest form of intimacy."

"Men always say they know, but how do they?" she asked irritably.

He forced his gaze to the road. "Because of the way you reacted," he said tersely. "A sophisticated woman gives as much as she gets, Nat," he told her bluntly. "You were wide-eyed and fascinated by everything I did, and I got in over my head long before I expected to. I dreamed about that night for years."

"If we're making confessions, so did I," she admitted without looking at him.

He grimaced. "I should have gone home before I gave in to temptation."

Her pale eyes touched his face like loving hands. She'd never known anyone like him. She didn't think there was anyone else like him. He'd colored her dreams, become her world, in the years since that one incredible night.

She didn't answer him. He glanced at her and laughed hollowly. "Which doesn't change the past or bring us any closer to a solution," he mused. "You're not liberated, and I'm a confirmed bachelor."

She toyed with her seat belt. "Are you really? I used to think that your father made you wary of marriage. He and your mother were totally unsuited, from what everybody says."

"Everybody being my sister, Vivian," he guessed. "She doesn't remember our mother."

"Neither do you, really, do you?" she wondered aloud.

"She died and left him with four kids," he told her. "He wasn't up to raising even one. I've always thought that the pressure of it started him drinking, and then he couldn't stop."

His face hardened with the words, and she knew he was remembering the bad times he'd had with his father.

"Mack, do you really think you're like him?" she asked softly.

"They say abused kids become abusive parents," he replied without thinking, and then could have bitten his tongue right through for the slip.

She only nodded, as if she'd expected that answer. "So they say. But there are exceptions to every rule. If you were going to be abusive, Vivian and Bob and Charles would have been sitting in the school counselor's office years ago. They could have asked to go into foster care any time they wanted to."

"Vivian would never have given up shopping sprees," he pointed out.

She swiped gently at his sleeve. "Stop that. You know she loves you. So do the boys. You're the kindest human being I've ever known."

A ruddy color ran up his high cheekbones. He didn't look at her. "Flattery?"

"Fact," she countered. Her fingers smoothed over his sleeve lazily. "You're one of a kind."

He moved his shoulder abruptly. "Don't do that."

She pulled her fingers back. "Okay. Sorry." She laughed it off, but her face flushed.

"Don't get your feelings hurt," he said irritably, glancing at her. "I want you. Don't push your luck."

Her eyes widened.

"You still haven't got the least damned notion of what it does to me when you touch me, do you?" he asked impatiently. "This stoic exterior is a pose. Every time I look at you, I see you in that velvet dress, and I want to stop the truck and..." He ground his teeth together. "It's been a long dry spell. Don't make it worse."

"What about Glenna?" she chided.

He hesitated for a minute and then glanced at her with a what-the-hell sort of smile and said, "She can't fix what she didn't break."

Her eyebrows reached for the ceiling. "You don't look broken to me."

"You know what I mean. She's pretty and responsive, but she isn't you."

Her face brightened. "Poor Glenna."

"Poor Dave What's-his-name," he countered with a mocking smile. "Apparently he doesn't get any further with you than she does with me."

"Everyone says he's very handsome."

"Everyone says she's very pretty."

She shook her head and stared out the window, folding her arms. "Vivian is barely speaking to me," she said, desperate to change the subject. "I know she's jealous of the way Whit flirts with me. I just don't know how to stop him. It almost seems as if he's doing it deliberately."

"He is," he said, his expression changing. "It's an old ploy, but it's pretty effective."

"I don't understand."

He pulled up at a stop sign a few miles outside Medicine Ridge and looked at her. "He makes her think he isn't interested so that she'll work harder to attract his attention. By that time, she's so desperate that she'll do anything he wants her to do." His eye narrowed angrily. "She's rich, Nat. He isn't. He makes a good salary, for a teacher, but I had him investigated. He spends heavily at the gambling parlors."

She bit her lower lip. "Poor Viv."

"She'd be poor if she married him," he agreed. "That's why I object to him. He did get a girl in trouble, but that's not why I don't want him hanging around Viv. He's a compulsive gambler and he doesn't think he has a problem." He looked genuinely worried. "I haven't told her."

She whistled softly. "And if you do tell her..."

"She won't believe me. She'll think I'm being contrary and dig in her heels. She might marry him out of spite." He shrugged. "I'm between a rock and a hard place."

"Maybe I should encourage him," she began.

"No."

"But I could—"

"I said no," he repeated, his tone full of authority. "Let me handle it my way."

"All right," she said, giving in.

"I know what I'm doing," he told her as he pulled the truck onto the highway. "You just be ready at five."

"Okay, boss," she drawled, and grinned at his quick glare.

Natalie was on pins and needles waiting for five o'clock. She was dressed by four. She'd topped her short hair with a glittery green rhinestone hair clip that brought out the emerald of her eyes and made the green velvet dress look even more elegant. When the Lincoln pulled up in her front yard and

Mack got out to meet her on the porch, she fumbled trying to lock her door.

He took her hand in his and held it tight. "Don't start getting flustered," he chided gently, looking elegant in his dinner jacket and matching slacks. The white shirt had only the hint of ruffles down the front, with its black vest and tie. He was devastating dressed up. Apparently he found her equally devastating, because his glance swept over her from the high heels to the crown of her head. He smiled.

"You look nice, too," she said shyly.

His fingers locked into hers. "I'm rather glad we aren't going to be alone tonight," he murmured dryly as they walked toward the car. "In that dress, you'd tempt a carved statue."

"I'm not taking it off for you," she told him. "You're a confirmed bachelor."

"Change my mind," he challenged.

Her heart jumped and she laughed. "That's a first."

"Tonight is a first," he pointed out as they paused beside the passenger door. He looked at her with slow, sensuous appraisal. "Our first date, Natalie."

She colored. "So it is."

He opened the door. In the back seat, Vivian and Whit broke apart quickly, and Vivian laughed in a high-pitched tone, pushing back her short blond hair.

"Hi, Nat!" Vivian said cheerfully, sounding totally unlike the very stressed woman who'd phoned her the day before. "You look terrific."

"So do you," Natalie said, and her friend really was a knockout in pale blue silk. Whit was wearing evening clothes, like Mack, but he managed to look slouchy just the same. Vivian didn't notice. She was clinging to Whit's arm as if he was a treasure she was fearful of losing.

"I have a black velvet dress, but I wanted something easier to move around in," Vivian said.

"Velvet's very nice," Natalie agreed.

"Very expensive, too," Vivian added, as if she knew that Natalie hadn't paid for the dress.

"They do have charge accounts, even for penniless college students," Natalie pointed out in a tone she rarely used.

Vivian flushed. "Oh. Of course."

"We aren't all wealthy, Vivian," Whit added in a cooler tone. "It's nice for you, if you can pay cash for things, but we lesser mortals have to make do with time payments."

"I said I'm sorry," Vivian said tightly.

"Did you? It didn't sound very much like it," Whit said and moved away from her.

Vivian's teeth clamped shut almost audibly, and she grasped her evening bag as if she'd like to rip it apart.

"Which play are we going to see?" Natalie asked quickly, trying to recover what was left of the evening.

"Arsenic and Old Lace," Mack said. "The Billings community college drama classes are presenting it. I've heard that they are pretty good."

"Medicine Ridge College has a strong drama department of its own, doesn't it, Natalie?" Whit asked conversationally. "I took a class in dramatic arts, but I was always nervous in front of an audience."

"So was I," Natalie agreed. "It takes someone with less inhibitions than I have."

"I had the lead in my senior play," Vivian said coldly.

"And you were wonderful," Natalie said with a smile. "Even old Professor Blake raved about your portrayal of Stella."

"Stella?" Whit asked.

"In Williams's play *A Streetcar Named Desire*," Natalie offered.

"One of my favorites," Whit said, turning to Vivian. "And you played the lead. You never told me that!"

Vivian's face lit up magically, and for the next few minutes, she regaled Whit with memories of her one stellar performance. In the front seat, Natalie and Mack exchanged sly smiles. With any luck, Natalie's inspiration could have saved the evening.

The play was hilarious, even if Natalie did find herself involuntarily comparing the performances with those of Cary Grant and Raymond Massey in the old motion picture. She chided herself for that. The actors in the play might be amateurs, but they were very good and the audience reacted to them with hysterical laughter.

Afterward, they went to a nightclub for a late supper. Natalie and Mack ordered steak and a salad, while Whit and Vivian managed to pick the most expensive dishes on the menu.

There was dancing on the small floor with a live band, a Friday night special performance, and Natalie found herself in Mack's arms as soon as she finished the last spoonful of her dessert.

"This is worth waiting all day for," he murmured in her ear as he held her close on the dance floor. "I knew this dress would feel wonderful under my hands."

She snuggled closer. "I thought Viv was going to ask how I could afford it," she said with a sigh. She closed her eyes and smiled. "You really shouldn't have paid for it, you know."

"Yes, I should have." He made a turn, and her body was pushed even closer to his. She felt his body react with stunning urgency to the brush of hers. She faltered and almost fell.

"Sorry," she said shakily.

He only laughed, the sound rueful and faintly amused as they continued across the floor. "It's an unavoidable consequence lately with you," he murmured. "Don't worry. No one will notice. We're alone here."

She glanced past his chest at the dozen or so other couples moving lazily to the music and she laughed, too. "So I see."

"Just don't do anything reckless," he said softly. "With very little effort, we could become the scandal of the county."

She felt his lips at her forehead and smiled. "Think so?"

One lean hand was at the back of her head, teasing around her nape and her ears in a sensual exploration that made her tingle all over. "Do you remember what I told you the night of the wreck?" he asked huskily.

"You told me a lot of things," she hedged.

"I told you that, when you were old enough, I'd teach you everything you need to know about men." His hand slid to her waist and pulled her gently closer. "You're old enough, Nat."

She stiffened. "You stop that," she whispered urgently, embarrassed by his blatant capability.

"Sorry. It doesn't work that way. I'd need a cold shower, and that isn't going to happen here." His cheek brushed against hers and his lips touched just the corner of her mouth. "We could drop Vivian and the professor off at my house first," he said under his breath.

Her heart ran wild. "And then what?"

His lips traced her earlobe. "We could do what we did that night. I've spent years dreaming about how it felt."

Her knees threatened to collapse. "Mack Killain," she groaned. "Will you please stop?"

"You can't stop an avalanche with words," he whispered roughly. "You burn in me like a fever. I can't eat, sleep, think, work, because you're between me and every single thing I do."

She swallowed. "It's just an ache," she said firmly. "Once you satisfied it, where would we be?"

He drew back a little and looked into her eyes evenly. "I don't think it can be satisfied," he said through his teeth.

She stood very still, like a doe in the glare of bright headlights, looking at him.

"And you still don't know what it feels like," he said gruffly, in a tone that was just short of accusation. "You like being kissed and touched, but you don't know what desire is."

She averted her eyes. "You're the one who always pulls back," she said huskily.

His arm contracted roughly, pinning her to him. "I have

to,'' he said impatiently. ''You have no idea what it would be like if I didn't.''

''I'm twenty-two,'' she reminded him. ''Almost twenty-three. No woman reaches that age today, even in a small town, without knowing something about relationships.''

''I'm talking about physical relationships. They aren't something you have and walk away from. They're addictive.'' He drew in a harsh breath as the music began to wind down. ''They're dangerous. A little light lovemaking is one thing. What I'd do to you in a bed is something else entirely.''

The tone, as much as the content, made her uneasy. She stared at him, frowning. ''I don't understand.''

He groaned. ''I know. That's what's killing me!''

''You're not being rational,'' she murmured.

The hand at her waist contracted and moved her in a rough, quick motion against the rock-solid thrust of his body. He watched her blush with malicious pleasure. ''How rational does that feel to you?'' he asked outrageously.

She forced her eyes to his drawn face. ''It isn't rational at all. But you keep trying to save me from anything deep and intimate. It has to happen someday,'' she said.

His jaw tautened even more. ''Maybe it does. But I told you, I'm not a marrying man. That being the case, I'd have to be out of my mind before I'd take you to bed, Natalie.''

''Dave wouldn't,'' she taunted. ''In fact, Whit wouldn't,'' she added, glancing at Vivian's partner, who was watching her as much as he was watching his partner.

His hand tightened on her waist until it hurt. ''Don't start anything with him,'' he said coldly. ''Vivian would never forgive you. Neither would I.''

''I was just kidding.''

''I'm not laughing,'' he told her, and his face was solemn.

''You treat me like a child half the time,'' she accused, on fire with new needs. She felt reckless, out of control. His body, pressed so close to hers, was making her ache. ''And then you accuse me of tempting you, when you're the one with the experience.''

He let her go abruptly and moved back. ''You aren't old enough for me,'' he said flatly.

''I'm six years younger than you are, not twenty,'' she pointed out.

His eye narrowed, glittering at her. ''What do you want from me?''

In his customary blunt way, he'd thrown the ball into her court and stood there arrogantly waiting for an answer she couldn't give.

''I want you to be my friend,'' she said finally, compromising with her secret desires.

''I am.''

''Then where's the problem?''

''You just felt it.''

''Mack!''

He caught her hand and tugged her toward their table. ''What's that song—one step forward and two steps back? That's how I feel lately.''

She felt churned up, frustrated, hot with desire and furious that he was playing some sort of game with her hormones. She knew she was flushed and she couldn't quite meet Vivian's eyes when they went to the table.

''Don't sit down,'' Whit drawled, catching Natalie by the wrist before she could be seated. ''This one's mine.''

He drew her on the dance floor to the chagrin of brother and sister and wrapped her tight as the slow dance began.

''If you want to keep that arm, loosen it,'' Natalie told Whit with barely contained rage.

He did, at once, and grinned at her. ''Sorry. That's the way big brother was holding you, though. But, then, he's almost family, isn't he? Vivian says the two of you went through high school together.''

''Yes, we did. We've been friends for a long time.''

''She's jealous of you,'' he said.

"That's a hoot," she replied, laughing. "She's a beauty queen and I'm plain."

"That isn't what I mean," he corrected. "She envies you your kind heart and intelligence. She has neither."

"That's a strange way to talk about a girl you care for," she chided.

"I like Vivian a lot," he said. "But she's like so many others, self-centered and spoiled, waiting for life to serve up whatever she wants. I'll bet there hasn't been a man in years who's said no to her."

"I don't think anyone's ever said no to her," she replied with a smile. "She's pretty and sweet, whatever else she is."

He shrugged. "Pretty and rich. I guess that's enough for most men. When do you start teaching?"

"In the fall, if I passed my exams. If I don't graduate, it will be another year before I can get a teaching job around here."

"You could go farther afield," he told her. "I was surfing the Internet the other night, browsing for teachers' jobs. There are lots of openings in north Texas, especially in Dallas. I always thought I'd like to live in Texas."

"I don't really want to live that far from home," she said.

"But you don't have a home, really, do you?" he asked. "Vivian said you were orphaned when you were very young."

"My mother was born here," she said. "So was her mother, and her mother's mother. I have roots."

"They can be a trap as much as a safety cushion," he cautioned. "Do you really want to spend the rest of your life out here in the middle of nowhere?"

"That's an odd question for someone who came here from Los Angeles," she pointed out.

He averted his gaze. "Nevada, actually," he said. "I got tired of the rat race. I wanted someplace quiet. But it's just a little too quiet here. A year of it is more than I expected to do."

"Do you like teaching?"

He made a face. "Not really. I wanted to do great things. I had all these dreams about building exotic houses and making barrels of money, but I couldn't get into architecture. They said I had no talent for it."

"That's a shame."

"So I teach," he added with a cold smile. "English, of all things."

"Viv says you're very good at it."

"It doesn't pay enough to keep me in decent suits," he said in a vicious tone. "When I think of how I used to live, how much I had, it makes me sick."

"What did you do before you were a teacher?" she asked, fishing delicately.

"I was in real estate," he said, but he didn't meet her eyes. "It was a very lucrative business."

"Couldn't you get a license here in Montana and go back into it?"

"Nobody wants to buy land in Montana these days," he muttered. "It's not exactly hot real estate."

"I suppose not."

The music ended and he escorted her to the table, where Mack and Vivian sat fuming.

Vivian got to her feet at once. "And now it's my turn," she said pertly and with a smile that didn't quite reach her eyes.

"Sure," Whit said easily, and smiled as he led her onto the dance floor.

"What was all the conversation about?" Mack wanted to know.

"I was trying to draw him out about his former profession. He said he was in real estate in Nevada," she said, with a wary glance toward Viv and Whit, who were totally involved with each other for the moment.

"And I'm the tooth fairy," Mack said absently.

Natalie laughed helplessly.

"What?" he demanded.

"I was picturing you in a pink tutu."

That eye narrowed. "You'll pay for that one."

"Okay. A white tutu."

He shook his head. "Finish your drink. We have to leave pretty soon. I have an early appointment in town tomorrow."

"Okay, boss," she drawled, and ignored his stormy expression.

As it turned out, Mack took Natalie home first and walked her to her front door.

"Try to stay out of trouble," he cautioned. "I may see you at the grocery store tomorrow."

"Sadie shops. You don't."

"I can shop if I want to," he said. He searched her bright face. "Just for the record, I wanted to take them home first."

She smiled. "Thanks."

One shoulder lifted and fell. "It isn't the right time. Not yet." He bent and brushed a soft kiss against her forehead. "This is to throw them off the track," he whispered as he stood straight again. "A little brotherly peck should do the trick."

"Yes, it should."

His gaze fell to her soft mouth for an instant. "Next time, I'll make sure I take you home last. Good night, angel."

"Good night."

He winked and walked to the car, whistling an off-key tune on the way. Natalie waved before she went into the house. She'd wanted Mack to kiss her again, but maybe he'd had enough kissing that afternoon. She hadn't. Not by a long shot. She didn't want to feel this way about Mack, but she couldn't help herself. She wondered how it would eventually work out between them, but it was too disturbing to torture herself like that. She cleaned her face, got into her gown and went to bed. And she dreamed of Mack all night long.

Chapter 6

The phone rang on the one morning during the week when Natalie could sleep late. It was Mack, and he sounded worried.

"It's Viv," he said at once, not bothering with a greeting. "I had to take her to the emergency room early this morning. She's got the flu and it's complicated with pneumonia. She refused to let me put her in the hospital, and I've got to fly out to Dallas this morning on business. My plane leaves in less than an hour and a half. The boys are off on a hunting trip. I hate to ask you, but can you come over and stay with her until I get home?"

"Of course I can," she replied. "How long are you going to be away?"

"With luck, I'll be back by midnight. If not, first thing tomorrow."

"I don't have to go in to the grocery store to work until tomorrow afternoon. I'll be glad to stay with her. Did the doctor give you prescriptions for her, and have you been to the pharmacy to pick up her medicine?"

"No," he said gruffly. "I'll have to do that—"

"I'll pick them up on my way over," she said. "You go

ahead and catch your flight. I'll be there in thirty minutes if they have her prescriptions ready.''

"They should be," he said. "I dropped them off before I brought her home. I'll phone and give them my credit card number, so they'll already be paid for.''

"Thanks.''

"Thank *you*," he added. "She feels pretty bad, so she shouldn't give you much trouble. Oh, and there's a little complication," he said irritably. "Whit's here.''

"That should cheer her up," she reminded him.

"It will, as long as you don't look at him.''

She laughed. "No problem there.''

"I know you don't like him, but she won't believe it. If there was anybody else I could ask, I wouldn't bother you. I just don't like the idea of leaving her alone with him, even if she does have pneumonia.''

"I don't mind. Honest. You be careful.''

"The plane wouldn't dare crash," he chuckled. "I've got too much work to do.''

"Keep that in mind. I'll see you when you get back.''

"You be careful, too," he said. "And wear your raincoat. It's already sprinkling outside.''

"I'll wear mine if you wear yours.''

He chuckled again. "Okay. You win. I'll be home as soon as I can.''

She said goodbye and hung up, rushing to get her bag packed so that she could get over to the ranch.

She walked into Viv's bedroom with a bag of medicine, a cold soft drink that she knew her friend liked and some cough drops.

Viv looked washed out and sick, but she managed a wan smile as Natalie approached the bed. Whit was sprawled in an armchair by the bed, looking out of sorts until he saw Natalie. His eyes ran over her trim figure in jeans and a button-up gray knit sweater with a jaunty gray and green scarf.

"Don't you look cute," he said with a smile.

Viv glared at him. So did Natalie.

"Why don't you make some coffee, Whit?" Viv asked angrily. "I could do with a cup."

He got out of the chair. "My pleasure. What do you take in yours, Nat?" he asked smoothly.

She turned and looked him right in the eye. "Nobody calls me Nat except Mack," she pointed out. "It isn't a nickname I tolerate from anyone else."

His cheekbones colored briefly. "Sorry," he said with a nervous laugh. "I'll just make that coffee. Be back as soon as I can."

Viv watched him go and then turned cold eyes on her friend. "You don't have to snap at him," she said curtly. "He was only being polite."

Natalie's eyebrows went up. "Was he?"

"Mack shouldn't have called you," she said tersely. "I'd have been just fine here with Whit."

Natalie felt uncomfortable and unwelcome. "He thought you needed nursing."

"He thought I needed a chaperone, you mean," she said angrily. "And I don't! Whit would manage just fine."

"All right, then," Natalie said with a forced smile. "I'll go home. There's your medicine and some cough drops. I guess Whit can pick up anything else you need. Sorry I bothered you."

She turned and walked to the door, almost in tears.

"Oh, Nat, don't go," Viv said miserably. "I'm sorry. You came all this way and even brought my medicine and I'm being horrible. Please come back."

Natalie had the door open. "You've got Whit...."

"Come back," Viv pleaded.

Natalie closed the door and went to the armchair by the bed, but her eyes were wounded and faintly accusing as she sat.

"Listen, Whit doesn't like me," Natalie told Viv. "He's only flirting with me to make you jealous. Why can't you see

that? What in the world could he see in me? I'm not pretty
and I don't have any money."

"In other words, he wouldn't like me if I didn't have a
wealthy background?" Viv asked pointedly.

"I said you were pretty, too," she replied. "I know you feel
bad, Viv, but you're being unreasonable. We've been friends
for a long time. I don't know you lately, you're so different."

Viv shifted against her pillows. "He talks about you, too,
even when you aren't here."

"It isn't what you think," Natalie said, exasperated. "He's
never said or done a thing out of line."

"He's very good-looking," Viv persisted.

"So are you," Natalie said. "But right now you're sick and
you don't need to upset yourself like this. Mack asked me to
take care of you, and that's what I'm going to do."

Viv studied her through fever-bright eyes. "Did you know
that Glenna was going with him to Dallas?" she asked with
undeniable venom.

Natalie forced herself not to react. "Why?" she asked carelessly.

"Beats me. I suppose she had something to do there, too.
Anyway, I don't think he'll come back tonight. Do you?"

Natalie glared at her. "You really are a horror," she said
through her teeth.

Viv flushed. "Yes, I guess I am," she agreed after a minute.
"Mack said he wouldn't wish the boys and me on a wife. He
said it wouldn't be fair to expect anyone to have to take us on,
as well as him. I know Glenna wouldn't. She hates me."

"Your brother loves all three of you very much," Natalie
said, disquieted by what Viv had said.

"Well, he's not my father. Bob and Charles are in their last
two years of high school and then Bob wants to go into the
Army. Charles wants to study law at Harvard. That will get
them out of the way, and if I marry Whit, which I want to do,
Mack will have the house to himself." Her voice was terse

and cool. She didn't quite meet Natalie's eyes. "Would you marry him, if he asked you?"

"That won't happen," Natalie said quietly.

"Are you sure of that?"

"Yes," came the soft reply. "I'm sure. Mack's self-sufficient and he doesn't want to be tied down. He's said often enough that marriage wasn't for him. Probably he and Glenna will go on together for years," she added, aching inside but not letting it show, "since they both like being uncommitted."

"Maybe you're right." Viv studied her friend curiously. "But he's very protective of you."

Natalie averted her eyes. "Why shouldn't he be? I'm like a second sister to him."

Vivian frowned. She didn't say anything. After a few seconds, she started coughing violently. Natalie handed her some tissues and helped her sit up with a pillow held to her chest to keep the pain at bay.

"Does that help?" Natalie asked gently when the spasm passed.

"Yes. Where did you learn that?" she asked.

"At the orphanage. One of the matrons had pneumonia frequently. She taught me."

Viv dropped her eyes. Occasionally in her jealousy, she forgot how deprived Natalie's life had been until the Killains had come along. She knew how Nat felt about Mack, and she didn't understand her sudden need to hurt a woman who'd been nothing but kind to her ever since their friendship began. She was fiercely jealous that Whit seemed to prefer Natalie, which didn't help her burgeoning resentment toward her best friend. She was confused and envious and so miserable that she could hardly stand herself. She didn't know what she was going to do if Whit made a serious pass at Natalie. She was sure that she'd do something desperate, and that it would be the end of her long friendship with the other woman.

The hours dragged after that tense exchange. Natalie kept out of Vivian's bedroom as much as she could, busying herself

with tidying up around the living room. Whit paused to flirt
with her from time to time, but she managed to keep him away
by reminding him of Viv's condition. He was getting on her
nerves, and Viv was getting more unbearable by the minute.

When eight o'clock rolled around, it was all Natalie could
do to keep from running for her life. Whit was still around,
and for the past fifteen minutes, he'd been coming on to Natalie. She was on the verge of assault when Mack walked in
unexpectedly.

He gave Natalie and Whit a speaking glance. They were
standing close together and Whit was leaning over her. It
looked as if he'd just broken up something, and his eye flashed
angrily.

"Why don't you make another pot of coffee, Whit?" she
asked quickly.

"As soon as I get back," he promised. "I need to run to
the convenience store and get some cigarettes. I'm dying for a
smoke."

"Okay," Natalie said.

Mack didn't say a word. With bridled fury, he watched the
other man go. But when he shook off his raincoat, he smiled
at Natalie as she took it and hung it on the rack for him.

"Did it rain all the way home?" she asked.

"Just about. How's Viv?"

"She's doing fine."

"Good." He caught her hand, pulled her into the study with
him and closed the door. "You can sit with me while I get
these papers sorted. Then we'll go up and see Viv."

"Whit won't know where we are when he comes back."

He lifted an eyebrow. "It's my house."

"Point taken." She sat in the chair across from his big desk
and watched him sort through a briefcase before he sat down
with several stacks of papers and began putting them into files.

As she watched his hands, she thought back to the night
Carl had been killed in the wreck...

* * *

It was a stormy night, with lightning flashes illuminating everything inside and outside the house where Natalie was living with her aunt, old Mrs. Barnes. It was her seventeenth birthday, and she was spending it alone, in tears, mourning the death of the only boy she'd ever loved. His death that night in a wreck, driving home from an out-of-town weekend fishing and camping trip with a cousin was announced on the late news. The cousin lived. Carl had died instantly, because he wasn't wearing a seat belt. The official cause of the one-car accident was driving too fast for conditions in a blinding rain. The car had veered off the highway at a high speed and crashed down a hill. One of her friends from school had called, almost distraught with grief, to tell Natalie before she had to find out from the news.

Carl Barkley had been the star quarterback of their high school football team. Natalie had been his date, and the envy of the girls in the senior class, for the Christmas dance. She was to be his date for the senior prom, as well. Handsome, blond, blue-eyed Carl, who was president of the Key Club, vice president of the student council, an honor student with a facility for physics that had gained him a place at MIT after graduation. Carl, dead at eighteen. Natalie couldn't stop crying.

At times like these, she ached for a family to console her. Old Mrs. Barnes, who'd given her a home during her junior year of high school and with whom she would live while she attended the local community college, was away for the weekend. She wasn't due back until the next morning. There was Vivian Killain, of course, her best friend. But Vivian had also been a friend of Carl, and she was too upset to drive. The only fight Natalie and Vivian had ever had was over Carl, because Vivian had started dating him first. Carl had only gone out with her once before he and Natalie ended up in English class together. It had been love at first sight for both of them, but Vivian only saw it as Natalie tempting her boyfriend away. It wasn't like that at all.

The thunder shook the whole house, and it wasn't until the

rumble died down that Natalie heard someone knocking on the front door. Slipping a matching robe over a thin pink satin nightgown with spaghetti straps, she went to see who it was.

A tall, lean man in a raincoat and broad-brimmed Stetson stared at her.

"Vivian said your aunt was out of town and you were alone," Mack Killain said quietly, surveying her pale, drenched face. "I'm sorry about your boyfriend."

Natalie didn't say a word. She simply lifted her arms. He picked her up with a rough sound and kicked the door shut behind him. With her wet face buried in his throat, he carried her easily down the hall to the open door that was obviously her bedroom. He kicked that door shut, too, and sat her gently on the armchair beside the bed.

He took off his raincoat, draping it over the straight chair by the window, and placed his hat over it. He was wearing work clothes, she saw through her tears. He hadn't even stopped long enough to change out of his chaps and boots and spurs. His blue-checked long-sleeve shirt was open halfway down his chest, disclosing a feathery pattern of thick, black curling hair. His broad forehead showed the hat mark. A lock of raven-black straight hair fell over the thin black elastic of the eye patch over his left eye.

He stared at Natalie for a few seconds, taking in her swollen eyes and flushed cheeks, the paleness of the rest of her oval face.

"I didn't even get to say goodbye, Mack," she managed huskily.

"Who does?" he replied. He bent and lifted her so that he could drop down into the armchair with her in his lap. He curled her into his strong, warm body and held her while she struggled through a new round of tears. She clung to him, grateful for his presence.

She'd always been a little afraid of him, although she was careful not to let it show. She'd been the one who nursed him, over the objections of the orphanage, when he was gored in the face by one of his own bulls. His sister, Vivian, was no good at all with anyone who was hurt or sick—she simply went to pieces. And his brothers, Bob and Charles, were terrified of their big brother. Natalie had known that he stood to lose his sight in both eyes instead of just one, and she'd held him tight and told him over and over again that he mustn't give up. She'd stayed out of classes for a whole week while the doctors fought to save that one eye, and she hadn't left him day or night until he was able to go home.

Even then, she'd stopped by every day to check on him, having presumed that he'd have his family standing on its ear trying to keep him in bed for the prescribed amount of time. Sure enough, the boys had walked wide around him and Vivian just left him alone. Natalie had made sure that he did what the doctor told him to. It amused and amazed his siblings that he'd let her boss him around. Killain gave orders. He didn't take them from anybody—well, except from Natalie, when it suited him.

"We were going to the senior prom together," she said huskily, wiping her eyes with the back of her hand. "This morning, I was deciding what sort of dress to wear and how I was going to fix my hair…and he's dead."

"People die, Nat," he said, his voice deep and quiet and comforting at her ear. "But I'm sorry he did."

"You didn't know him, did you?"

"I'd spoken to him a time or two," he said with deliberate carelessness.

"He was so handsome," she said with a ragged sigh. "He was smart and brave and everybody loved him."

"Of course."

She shifted into a more comfortable position on his lap, and as she did, her hand accidentally slid under the fabric of his cotton shirt, to lie half buried in thick hair. Odd, how his powerful body tensed when it happened, she thought with confusion. She was aware of other things, too. He smelled of horses and soap and leather. His breath pulsed out just above her nose, and she could smell coffee on it. Her robe was open, and the tiny straps that held her gown up had slipped in her relaxed position. One of her breasts was pressed against Mack's chest, and she could feel warm muscle and prickly hair against it just above the nipple. Her body felt funny. She wanted to pull the gown away and press herself closer, so that his skin and hers would touch. She frowned, shocked by the longing she felt to be held hungrily by him.

She tensed a little. "You're still wearing your work clothes," she said. Her voice sounded as odd as she felt. "Why?"

"We had a fence down and we didn't know it until the sheriff called and said we had cattle strung up and down the highway," he told her. "It's taken two hours to get them back in and fix the fence. That's why it took me so long to get here. Vivian had been calling me on my cell phone since dark, but I was out of the truck."

"Don't you have a flip phone as well as the one installed in your truck?" she wondered aloud.

He chuckled. "Sure. It's at home recharging."

She smiled drowsily. "Thank you for coming over. I'm sure you didn't feel like it after all that."

His broad shoulders lifted and fell. "I couldn't leave you here alone," he said simply. "And Vivian was in no sort of shape to come." His lean hand smoothed her wavy dark hair. "She thinks you cut her out with Carl, but that's just the way she is."

"I know." She sighed. "She's so pretty that she takes it for granted that the boys all want her. Most of them do, too."

"She's spoiled," he replied. "I was hard on Bob and Charles, but I've made a lot of allowances for Viv, simply because she was the only girl in the family. Maybe that was a mistake."

"It's not a mistake to care for people," she pointed out.

"So they say." His fingers tangled in her soft hair. "Want something to drink?"

"No, thanks," she replied. Her fingers spread involuntarily in the thick hair over his breastbone, and his intake of breath was sharp and audible.

His body tensed again. She and Carl had kissed, but she'd been careful not to let things go very far. In fact, she hadn't felt any sort of strong physical attraction to the football star, which was strange, considering how much he meant to her. With Mack, she experienced sensations she'd never felt before. She felt hot and swollen in the most unusual places, and it puzzled her. The sudden tension she noticed in the man holding her puzzled her, as well. Mack didn't say a word, but she could feel his heartbeat increase, hear the rough sound of his breathing.

She let her face slide down his muscular arm, and her curious eyes met his good one. It was narrow and unblinking and vaguely intimidating. Even as she watched, his gaze went to where her robe was open and one of her breasts in its lace-trimmed satin lay soft and warm against his chest.

Involuntarily, she followed his intense scrutiny and saw what she hadn't realized before—the gown had slipped so far down that her nipple, hard and tight, was visibly pressing into the thick hair over his chest.

He looked into her stunned eyes, and the hand in her hair tightened. "Didn't you do this with your boyfriend?" he asked bluntly.

"No," she said shakily.

"Why not, if you loved him?" he persisted.

She frowned worriedly. It was becoming increasingly hard to think at all. "I didn't feel like this with him," she confessed in a whisper.

Mack's face changed. His hand in her hair arched her face to his and tugged it into the crook of his arm. He shifted, so that the bodice came completely away from one pert little breast, and his arm tightened, moving her skin sensuously against him.

She gasped. Her nails bit into his chest, and her lips parted in shock and delight. Involuntarily, she arched closer, so that her breast dragged roughly against his skin.

The hand in her hair began to hurt. His body tensed, and a faint shudder rippled through him.

His jaw clenched, and he fought his hunger. She realized that he wanted to feel her against him without the fabric between them, and it was what she wanted, as well. She forgot about wrong and right, about decency, about everything except the pleasure they were giving each other here, in the quiet room with the silence only broken by the sound of the rain outside the window and their breathing.

"I should be shot for doing this, and you should be shot for letting me," he said through his teeth. But even as he spoke, his free hand was stripping the robe and gown to her waist. His gaze fell to her naked breasts, and he shuddered again, violently, as his arm suddenly tightened and dragged her breasts against his hair-roughened chest in a feverish caress.

She moaned harshly. Her nails bit into the hard muscles of his upper arms as he crushed her against him and buried his face in the thick hair at her ear. He held her, rocked her, in an aching excess of desire.

Both arms were around her now. She slid her arms around his neck and clung for dear life. She couldn't catch her breath at all. It was the most intense pleasure she'd ever known. She trembled with desire.

The embrace was fierce. They held each other in a tense silence that seemed to throb with need. Her fingers tangled in the hair at the nape of his strong neck, and her eyes closed as she lay against him, unafraid and unashamed of the growing intimacy of the embrace.

He could feel his body growing harder by the second. If he moved her any closer, she'd be able to feel it. He didn't want that. It was years too soon for the sort of intimacy they were leading up to. He could barely think at all, but the part of his brain that still worked was flashing with red warning lights. She was seventeen, just barely, and he was twenty-three. She wasn't old enough or experienced enough to know what was about to happen. He was. He couldn't take advantage of her like this. He had to pull away and stop while he still could.

Abruptly, he shot to his feet, taking her with him. He held her, swaying on her feet, just in front of him. For one long, tense moment, his gaze went to her taut, bare breasts and his face seemed to clench. Then he pulled the straps up and replaced them on her shoulders, easing the robe into place. He tied it with swift, sharp movements of his big hands.

She stared at him, too overwhelmed by the intimacy and its abrupt end to think clearly. "Why did you stop?" she asked softly. "Did I do something wrong?"

Her pale green eyes made him ache as they searched his face. He caught her by the waist and took a slow, deliberate breath before he spoke. "Didn't they teach sex education at the orphanage?" he asked bluntly.

Her face flamed scarlet. Her eyes, like saucers, seemed to widen endlessly.

He shook his head. She was so deliciously naïve. He felt a generation apart from her instead of only six years. "A man can't take much of that without doing something about it, Nat," he said gently. "Looking isn't enough."

She was embarrassed, but she didn't drop her eyes. "I never could have done that with Carl," she said, feeling vaguely guilty about it. "I enjoyed kissing him, but I never wanted him to do anything else. I didn't like it when he tried to."

He ached to his boots. His hands contracted on her shoulders. "You're only seventeen," he reminded her. "I know Carl was special to you, but you aren't really old enough for a physical relationship with anyone."

"My mother was just eighteen when she had me," she pointed out.

"This is a different world than hers," he countered. "And even for an innocent woman, you're remarkably backward."

"Weren't you, at my age?" she asked in a driven tone.

He pursed his lips and studied her face. "At your age, I'd

already had my first woman. She was two years my senior and pretty experienced for a place like Medicine Ridge. She taught me.''

She felt her heartbeat racing madly in her chest. She hadn't expected him to be innocent, but it was shocking to have him speak about it so bluntly.

His lean fingers brushed over her cheek. ''And when you're old enough,'' he said in a strange, caressing tone, ''I'll teach you.''

Those shocking words from the past resonated in her mind as she looked at him in the dimly lit study. *I'll teach you. I'll teach you.*

While she was reliving the past, he'd gotten out of his chair and moved around the desk. He was propped against it, his jacket and tie off, his arms folded, watching her.

''Oh,'' she said, blinking. ''Sorry. I was lost in thought. Literally.'' She laughed softly.

He didn't smile. ''Come here, Nat.''

She measured the distance to the door and then laughed inwardly at her cowardice. She'd adored this man for so many years that she couldn't imagine letting anyone else touch her, ever. Besides, she assured herself, he had Glenna to satisfy those infrequent urges he'd once spoken of so bluntly. He wanted to talk without being overheard by Whit in case he came back unexpectedly, that was why he wanted her closer.

With a self-mocking smile she came to a stop less than arm's length away and looked at him.

He let his gaze encompass her, from her flat moccasins to the thrust of her breasts against the thin sweater. The top two buttons were undone, hinting at the cleavage below.

''I shouldn't leave Viv alone too long,'' she began.

He ignored the hint. His fingers spread along her cheek and his gaze dropped to her soft mouth. ''Viv can wait,'' he replied quietly. His thumb abruptly moved roughly across her lips, sensitizing them in a shock of desire.

His good eye narrowed. "Go and lock the door," he said in a tone he hadn't used with her since the night Carl had died.

She wasn't going to be dictated to, she told herself. Even Mack wasn't going to be allowed to tell her what to do!

So it came as a surprise that she closed the door and locked it, her back to him. She was almost shaking with desire. She leaned her hot forehead against the cold wood of the door, hearing the jerk of her breath in her throat.

She didn't hear him approach, because the thick carpet muffled the sound of his footsteps. But she felt him at her back, felt the heat of his powerful body as both arms went past her to the door. He moved deliberately close, so that his body made contact with hers from her shoulders to her thighs. The contours of his body changed instantly, and she knew, even in her innocence, that what they shared was something rare.

"And now you know why I put you away so quickly that night, don't you?" he asked quietly.

She swallowed, her body involuntarily responding to his need by arching toward him. "Yes. I do now."

His hands slid to her flat belly and pulled her closer to him.

"You felt this way all those years ago?" she said, realizing.

"Yes." His hands smoothed to her rib cage and hesitated. "I accumulated a fair share of experience when I was younger," he continued. "But in recent years, sex has become a more serious matter to me. I've gone hungry. You were innocent and curious, and I almost lost control with you. I didn't feel comfortable letting you see how tempted I was—especially under the circumstances."

"I'm still innocent," she reminded him without turning.

"And just as curious," he concluded for her. His hands flattened over her rib cage and became possessive. "But tonight, I'm going to satisfy your curiosity. Completely." And he turned her around.

Chapter 7

Natalie caught her breath at the look on Mack's face. The naked hunger in that one beautiful dark eye was almost frightening.

His big, lean hands framed her face as he searched her eyes. "Don't be afraid of me," he said softly. "I'd cut off my arm before I'd ever hurt you."

"I know that." She studied him worriedly. "But I can't—"

His lips caught the words and stopped them. She felt his hands drop to her throat and then to her shoulders, smoothing up and down the skin left bare by her short-sleeve sweater. He was slow and tender and sensual. It was like a dance in slow motion, a poem, a symphony.

The door was hard at her back as he moved closer, trapping her between his body and the wood. One long leg inserted itself confidently between both of hers with a lazy movement that was as arousing as the kiss they were sharing.

She gasped, and his mouth lifted away. He looked at her, breathing a little jerkily. "This is perfectly natural," he said quietly. "Don't fight it."

Her eyes were wild and a little frightened by the overwhelming desire she felt. "You went away...with Glenna," she whispered.

"She went on the plane," he corrected. "She didn't go with me." His mouth traced her eyelids and closed them. His hands were under her arms, lifting her closer. They moved slowly, gently, onto her breasts and caressed them with lazy delight.

She felt her legs go weak underneath her. It was unlike any other time she'd been in his arms. He handled her as if she belonged to him, as if she were precious to him, cherished by him.

Her eyes opened when he lifted his head, and they were full of wonder, wide with breathless hunger and delight. Her heart was in them.

He searched them quietly, and a faint smile touched his hard mouth. "I've waited years for that expression," he said under his breath. "Years."

He bent again, and this time her arms lifted slowly around his neck, cradling his head as his mouth covered her parted lips. They clung to each other, letting the kiss build, feeling its power. She moaned when it became fierce and hungry, but she didn't try to get away. Involuntarily, her body pressed hard against his.

She felt him shiver. He pushed down, his hands lifting her suddenly into the hard thrust of him and holding her there with a slow, sensual rhythm that made her tremble and gasp into his mouth.

"Sweetheart!" he whispered roughly.

The kiss grew harder. She felt him move and lift her clear off the floor in his arms. He walked to the sofa and spread her lengthwise on the leather, easing his body down to cover hers in a silence that was heated and tense.

He was fiercely aroused, and she wanted him at that moment more than she'd ever wanted anything in her life. She followed where he led, even when she felt him shifting her so that his lean hips were pressed squarely against hers, between her legs, in an intimacy that was suddenly urgent and feverish with dark pleasure. She couldn't have pushed him away if her survival had depended on it. Presumably he felt the same, because his arms held her relentlessly as he began to move against her.

She shuddered with the riptide of pleasure the movement produced, and her eyes flew open, locking with his dark, passionate gaze as he lifted his head to look at her.

With his hands at her head, taking most of his weight, he moved deliberately, watching her as she lifted to meet him and gasped at the sensations the contact produced. Her nails bit into his hard arms, but she wasn't fighting. She was melting into the leather, flying up into the sky, burning, burning!

The intimacy became so torturous, so fierce, that it was almost too late to draw back when he realized what was happening to them. His hands caught her hips in a bruising clasp and he pulled her over him, holding her still, with her cheek on his pounding chest as he fought to breathe and stop all at the same time.

"No!" She choked, trying to return to the intimacy of their former embrace.

His hands forced her to be still. His breath at her forehead was hot and shaky, audible in the stillness of the study. "Don't," he bit off. "Don't move. For God's sake, don't!"

Her mouth pressed into the cotton of his shirt, hot and hungry. "I want to," she choked.

"God, don't you think I want to?" he demanded huskily. His hands hurt in their fight to keep her still. "I want you to the point of madness. But not like this, Natalie!"

Belatedly, she realized that he was trying to save her from her own hunger for him. It wasn't a thought she cherished at the moment, when her whole body was burning with a passion she'd never felt before. But slowly, the trembling eased and she began to breathe normally, if a little fast.

His hands smoothed over her hair, bunching it at her nape as he held her cheek to his chest.

"Why?" she whispered miserably when she was able to speak.

"Because I can't marry you," he explained. "And because you can't live with sleeping with me if I don't."

All her dreams vanished in a haze. As the room came into focus across his broad chest, she realized just how far gone they were and how intimate their position on the sofa had become. If he hadn't stopped, they'd be lovers already. She hadn't even protested. But he'd had the presence of mind to stop.

So much for her willpower and her principles, she thought sadly. It seemed that her body had a will of its own, and it was much stronger than her mind.

Tears poured from her eyes, and she didn't even notice until she felt his shirt become damp under her cheek.

His hand laced into her hair and soothed her scalp. "If I thought it would help matters, I'd cry, too," he murmured dryly.

She hit his shoulder with her fist. "How could you do that to me?" she demanded.

"How could you do it to me?" he shot back. "You know how I feel about commitment. I've said so often enough."

"You started it," she raged.

He sighed. "Yes, I did," he admitted after a minute. "This is all I've been able to think about since we went nightclubbing," he confessed. "That was probably the most misguided thing I've done in recent years. It's hard to put out a brushfire once it's started. Or didn't you notice?"

She moved experimentally and felt him help her move away to a healthy distance, lying beside him on the long leather couch with her cheek on his shoulder. She looked at him quietly, curiously. His face was a little flushed, and his mouth was swollen from the hard, hungry kisses they'd shared. His shirt was open at the throat. His hair was disheveled. He looked as though he'd been making love, and probably so did she. She didn't really mind. He looked sensual like that.

"You'd better leave town," he suggested with a wry smile. "You just went on the endangered list."

Her fingers spread on his shirt, but he caught and stilled them. "Stop that. I'm barely a step away from ravishment."

"How exciting," she murmured.

"You wouldn't think so for the first few minutes," he murmured skeptically. "And you wouldn't be able to live with your conscience even if you did enjoy it eventually."

She grimaced. "I guess not. I'm not really cut out for passionate affairs."

"And I'm not cut out for happily ever after," he said without looking at her.

"Because of your family?" she asked.

He drew in a long breath. She felt his chest rise and fall under her hand. "We could make a list. It wouldn't change anything." He looked at her rapt, soft face, and his hardened. "Despite everything," he whispered huskily, "I would give everything I own to have you, just once."

She managed a faint smile. "Maybe you'd be disappointed."

He traced her mouth with a lazy finger. "Maybe you would, too."

"So it's just as well, isn't it?"

"That's what my mind says," he agreed.

She nuzzled against his shoulder and closed her eyes. "Isn't there a poem about hopeless attraction?"

"Hundreds," he said.

She felt his hand smoothing her hair, almost in a comforting gesture. She smiled. "That feels nice."

"You feel nice, lying against me like this," he whispered. He bent and kissed her closed eyelids with breathless tenderness. "It was like this, the night of the wreck," he added in a hushed tone. "I held you and comforted you, and wanted you until I ached."

"But I was seventeen."

"But you were seventeen." He pressed a kiss on her forehead and put her aside so that he could get to his feet. "You haven't changed much," he added as he helped her up.

"I'm older," she pointed out.

He laughed, and it had a hollow sound. "If you were a modern woman, we'd have fewer problems."

"But I'm not modern," she replied sadly. "And that says it all."

A door opened and shut, and he glanced toward the closed door of the study. "That'll be Romeo, I reckon," he drawled with a glittery look at Natalie. "I don't like the way he hangs around you."

"He likes me," she said carelessly. "I like him, too. What's wrong with that?"

"He belongs to Vivian," he returned, and he didn't smile.

She searched his hard face. "You can't own people."

The eyebrow that wasn't under the string of the eye patch lifted sardonically. "She won't thank you for making a play for him."

She ached all over with frustration and misery, and she hated him for arousing her and pushing her away at the same time. It wasn't logical, but then, she wasn't thinking clearly. She didn't mean what she said next, but she was so angry she couldn't help herself. "What would you care if I did? You don't like him. Maybe it would open her eyes."

"Don't do it," he warned in a low, threatening tone.

"Or you'll do what?" she challenged icily.

He didn't answer. They were enemies in the blink of an eye. He was furious, and it showed. He went to the door and opened it with a jerk, waiting for her to leave.

She hesitated, but only for an instant. If that was the way he wanted it, all right! She went out the door without looking at him, without speaking, without knowing that she'd just altered the whole pattern of her life.

Mack closed the door sharply behind her, and she grimaced before she went to the kitchen to see if Whit was there. He was. He'd just made coffee, in one of the expensive modern coffee machines that did it in seconds. He'd poured two cups, one for himself and one for Vivian.

"Where's the tray?" he asked, looking around.

"I haven't got a clue," she admitted. She looked in cupboards, but she couldn't find one.

"Never mind," he said. "I take mine black and she takes hers with cream. I can carry both cups if you'll bring the cream, and we'll forget the tray."

"Okay," she said.

He was gazing at her with an experienced eye, and it suddenly occurred to her that she must look pretty disheveled. She thought about taking a minute to repair her makeup before she went upstairs, but Whit was already out the door.

She followed him up the staircase and into Vivian's room. It hadn't dawned on her, either, that Whit had been out in the wind and his hair was disheveled. When the two of them entered the room, Vivian put together Natalie's swollen mouth and mussed hair and Whit's mussed hair and came up with infidelity.

"Go home," she told Natalie in a vicious tone. "Go right now and don't ever come back!"

"Viv! What's wrong?" she asked.

"As if you don't know!"

Whit didn't say anything, but he had a very strange look in his eyes. "You'd better go," he said gently. "I'll look after Viv."

Natalie looked at Vivian, but she turned her face away and refused to say another word. With resignation and bitter sadness, Natalie put down the cream and left the room.

Nobody was around when she went out the front door. She'd made a clean sweep tonight. Mack and Vivian were both furious at her over Whit when she hadn't meant to cause trouble. She hoped it would all blow over.

For the moment, all she could think about was the close call she'd had in Mack's arms on the sofa, and she wished with all her heart that things had been different between them. For better or worse, she loved him with her whole heart. But he had nothing to offer her.

She went home and fell, exhausted, into bed.

Whit was left alone with Vivian, who was in tears. "You were making love to her!" she accused, her blue eyes shooting sparks at him. "My boyfriend and my best friend! How could you?"

He hesitated before he spoke, with both hands in his pockets. He'd seen Vivian as a nice, biddable little source of gambling money and light lovemaking. But she'd become jealous and possessive of him, and he was getting tired of it. There were other women.

"So what?" he asked, not denying her charge. "She's not as pretty or rich as you are, but she's sweet and she doesn't question every move I make."

Vivian stared at him, almost purple with rage and frustration and hurt pride. "Then go with her," she spat at him. "Get out. And don't come back!"

"That," he replied, "will actually be a pleasure. You're no man's idea of the perfect woman, Viv. In fact, you're a spoiled little rich girl who wants to own people. It's not worth it."

"Worth what?" she choked.

He looked at her with world-weary cynicism and contempt. "I like to gamble. You had money. We made a handsome couple. I thought we'd be a match made in heaven. But there are other rich girls, honey."

He laughed mockingly and walked out, closing the door behind him. Vivian went wild, throwing things and weeping horribly until Mack came into the room minutes later and helped her off the floor and into bed.

"What in God's name is wrong with you?" he demanded, surveying the destruction of her bedroom.

"Whit and Natalie," she choked. "They were...making love.... Whit said she was everything I'm not." Sobs choked the words for several seconds while her brother stood by the bed, frozen. "Oh, I hate them so. I hate them both! My boy-friend and my best friend! How could they do this to me?"

"How do you know they were making love?" he asked in a hollow tone.

"I saw them," she lied viciously. "And Whit admitted it. He even laughed about it!"

Mack's face became a mask. He drew the covers over Vivian with a strange, frightening silence.

Vivian wasn't making connections. She was just short of hysteria. "They won't come here again. I told them not to. I'm through with them!"

"Yes." His voice sounded strained. "Try to calm down. You'll make yourself sicker."

"If either of them call," Vivian added coldly, "I won't speak to them."

"Don't worry about that," he told her. "I'll handle it."

"I already handled it," she shot back. "And don't tell Bob and Charles. Nobody else needs to know!"

"All right, Viv. Try to get some sleep. I'll have Sadie come in tomorrow and clean up in here."

"Thanks, Mack," she managed through her tears. "You really are a dear."

He didn't answer her. He went out and closed the door quietly, and the life seemed to drain out of him. Natalie, with Vivian's boyfriend. He'd told her not to flirt with the man, and she'd been angry with him. Was that why? Did it explain why she'd go from his arms into another man's in less than ten minutes?

Well, if her idea was to make him jealous, it had failed. He had nothing but contempt for her. Like Vivian, he didn't want her in the house, in his life. He went downstairs to his study and immersed himself in paperwork, trying not to see that long leather couch where they'd lain together in the sweetest interlude of his life.

Maybe it was just as well. He couldn't marry her. There

were too many strikes against them. But he didn't like the idea of her with that gambler. Or any other man...

He cursed his hateful memory and put the pencil down. Natalie ran like a golden thread through so much of his life. In recent years, she'd been involved in just about everything that went on at the ranch. She rode with him and Vivian, she came to parties, barbecues, cattle sales. She was always around. Now he wouldn't see her come running up the steps, laughing in that unaffected way she had. She wouldn't flirt with him, chide him, lecture him. He was going to be alone.

He got up and went to the liquor cabinet. He seldom drank, but he kept a bottle of aged Scotch whiskey for guests. He poured himself a shot and threw it down, enjoying the hot sting of it as it washed down his throat. He couldn't remember a time when he'd felt so powerless. He looked at the bottle and carried it to the desk. As an afterthought, he locked the door.

Vivian couldn't sleep. She got up and washed her face, careful of the broken objects she'd dashed against walls in her rage. She kept remembering Mack's face when she'd told him about Natalie and Whit. She'd never seen such an expression.

It bothered her enough to go looking for him. He wasn't in his room or anywhere upstairs. Walking slowly, because it was difficult to walk and breathe at the same time despite the antibiotic, she made it to the door of his study. She tried to open the door, but it was locked. Mack never locked the door.

She hesitated, but only for a moment. She combined the look on his face with his strange behavior and the way he'd held Natalie when they'd danced at the nightclub, and with trembling hands she went to the intercom panel and called the foreman.

"I want you to come up here right now," she said after identifying herself. "Haven't we got a man who does locksmithing part-time?"

"Yes, ma'am," he said.

"Bring him, too. And hurry!"

"Yes, ma'am!"

She sat down in the hall chair, biting her lip. It had been a lie that she'd seen Natalie and Whit together, but they both looked as if they'd been kissing. And Whit hadn't denied it. But if Mack was in love with Natalie, which was becoming a disturbing possibility, she might have caused a disaster. Despite Glenna's persistence, Mack had never behaved as if he couldn't live without her. But the way he watched Natalie, the way he'd held her on the dance floor, the way his gaze followed her...oh, God, let those men hurry!

It seemed like an eternity before the doorbell sounded. She went as quickly as she could to answer it.

"I want you to unlock this door," she told the man beside the foreman.

"Can't you use the key?" he asked, clearly hesitant.

"I don't have the key. Mack does, and he's locked himself in there." She wrapped her arms over her thick bathrobe. "Please," she said in an uncharacteristic request for help. Gone was the autocratic manner. "There's been some...some trouble. He's in there. He won't answer me."

Without a word, the locksmith took out his leather packet of tools and went to work. In short order, he had the door unlocked.

"Wait," she said when they started to open it. "Wait here. I'll call you if I need you." She didn't want to expose her brother to gossip if there was no need.

She went inside and closed the door. The sight that met her eyes was staggering. It made her shiver with guilt. Mack was lying facedown on the desk, a nearly empty whiskey bottle overturned at his hand. Mack never drank to excess; the memory of his father's alcoholism stopped him.

She went to the door and opened it just a crack. "He's just asleep. Thank you for your trouble. You can go."

"Are you sure, Miss Killain?" the foreman asked.

"Yes," she said confidently. "I'm sure."

"Then, good night. We'll come back if you need us."

Both men left. Vivian curled up in the big chair beside the desk and sat there all night with her brother. For the first time in her life, she realized how self-absorbed she'd become.

In the morning, very early, he woke up. He sat, dizzy, and scowled when he saw his sister curled in her robe in the big chair by the desk. He swept back his hair and surveyed the remains of the whiskey.

"Viv?" he called roughly. "What the hell do you think you're doing down here?"

She opened her eyes, still very sick. "I was worried about you," she said. "You never drink."

He held his head. "I never will again, I can promise you," he said wryly.

She uncurled and got slowly to her feet. "Are you all right?"

His shoulder moved jerkily. "I'm fine. How about you?"

She managed a smile. "I'll get by."

His face locked up tight. "We were both bad judges of character," he said.

"About what I said last night," she began earnestly. "I ought to tell you—"

He held up a big hand, and his face was hard with distaste. "They deserve each other," he said flatly. "You know I go around with Glenna," he added. "I don't want a long-term relationship, least of all with a penniless, fickle, two-timing orphan!"

She felt two inches high. She did blame Natalie, but she had a terrible feeling that Mack would never recover. It would take her a while to get over Whit's betrayal, as well. But she felt guilty and ashamed for making matters worse.

"Maybe they couldn't help it," she said heavily.

"Maybe they didn't want to," he returned. He got to his feet. "And that's all I'll ever say on the matter. I don't want to hear her name mentioned in this house ever again."

"All right, Mack."

He looked at the whiskey bottle with cold distaste before he dropped it into the trash can by the desk.

"Let's get you back upstairs," he told Viv with a smile. "I'm supposed to be taking care of you."

She slid her arm around his waist. "You're my brother. I love you."

He kissed her forehead and hugged her close. "Thanks."

She shrugged. "We're Killains. We're survivors."

"You bet we are. Come on."

He put her back to bed and went to see about the animals in the barn. He didn't think about the night before. And when Bob and Charles came home, nothing of what had happened was mentioned. But Vivian managed to get them alone long enough to warn them not to talk about Natalie at all in front of Mack.

"Why not?" Bob wanted to know, puzzled. "She's like family."

"Sure she is," Charles emphasized. "We all love her."

Vivian couldn't meet their eyes. "It's a long story. She's done something to hurt me and Mack. We don't want to talk about it, okay?"

They were reluctant, but she persuaded them. If she could only persuade her conscience that she was the wronged party. She couldn't forget what Whit had said to her. Natalie had been her only best friend for years. Was it realistic that Natalie would make a play for her boyfriend? She had for Carl, all those years ago, Vivian thought bitterly, and then she remembered that Carl had only been dating Natalie for a bet. She'd known, and she hadn't told Natalie because she was jealous of her relationship with Carl. In hindsight, she began to see how painfully unfair she'd been. Her whole life had been one of pampered security. Natalie hadn't had the advantages Vivian had, but she'd never been envious or jealous of Vivian. Remembering that made Vivian feel even more guilty. But it was too late to undo the damage. If Whit was telling the truth, everyone would know it soon, because Natalie would be seen going around with him. Then, Vivian told herself, she'd be vindicated.

But it didn't happen. In fact, Whit was seen with the daughter of a local contractor who had plenty of money and liked to gamble. They were the talk of the town, so soon after Whit's visible break with Vivian.

As for Natalie, she'd gone home the night of the uproar and, surprisingly, slept all night and most of the morning after she cried herself to sleep. She barely made it to the grocery store in time to work her shift. She was grateful for the job, because it took her mind off the painful argument with Mack and the vicious tongue-lashing Vivian had given her. For the first time in years, she really did feel like an orphan. She was worried about how her exams would be graded, as well, and about graduation. It seemed that the weight of the world had fallen on her over the weekend. Worst of all, of course, was Mack's anger. Perhaps she'd provoked it, but the pain was terrible.

Chapter 8

Natalie received her grades from the registrar the following week, and she laughed out loud with relief when she saw that she'd passed all her subjects. She would graduate, after all.

But as her classmates placed their orders for tickets to the baccalaureate service and the graduation exercises, Natalie realized with a start that she had no one to get tickets for. None of the Killains were speaking to her, and she had no family. She would have nobody to watch her graduate.

It was a painful realization. She went through the rehearsals and picked up her cap and gown, but without much enthusiasm. No one would have known from her bright exterior that she was unhappy. Even at work, she pretended that she was on top of the world.

She saw Dave Markham briefly before her big day. They hadn't had much contact since her student teaching stint had been over, and she'd missed his pleasant company.

"I hear through the grapevine that you're graduating," he told her, tongue in cheek, as he waited at the grocery store for her to check out his groceries.

She grinned. "So they say. It's really a relief. I wondered during exams if I was going to pass everything."

"Everyone goes through that," he assured her. "Finals in your senior year are enough to cause a nervous breakdown." He studied her quietly as she bent over the computer keyboard after she'd scanned his purchases into the machine. "There's another rumor going around."

She stopped, her head lifting. "Which is?"

He grimaced. "That you've had a split with the Killains," he continued. "I didn't believe it, though. You and Vivian have been friends for years."

"Sadly," she said, "it's true." She drew in a long breath as she gave him his total, then waited for him to count out the amount and give it to her.

He waited while she finalized the transaction before he spoke again, taking the sales slip automatically. "What happened? Can you tell me?"

She called for one of the grocery boys to come and help her bag his purchases before she turned to him. "I'd rather not, Dave," she said honestly. "It hurts to talk about it."

"That's why it hurts, because you haven't opened up." His eyes narrowed. "I hear Whit Moore's going around with a new girl and Vivian's quit taking classes at the vocational school."

That was news. "Did she?" She couldn't really blame her former best friend for that decision, of course. It wouldn't have been easy for her to go back into one of Whit's classes after they'd broken up in such a terrible way. She wondered if he'd ever been honest with Vivian about what had happened that night and decided that he probably hadn't. It was a major misunderstanding that might never be cleared up, and Natalie missed not only her former friend, but the boys, as well. She missed Mack most of all. She supposed that he'd heard all about it from Vivian. She'd hoped that he wouldn't believe his sister, but that was a forlorn hope. Natalie had never, in her acquaintance with the other girl, known her to tell Mack a deliberate lie.

"Mrs. Ringgold asks about you all the time," Dave added, trying to cheer her up. "She said she hopes you'll come and teach at our school in the fall, if there's an opening. So do I. I miss having you to talk to.''

She remembered his hopeless love and smiled with fellow feeling. ''Maybe I'll do just that,'' she said.

The bag boy came to sack his groceries, another customer pushed a cart up behind him, and the brief conversation was over. He left with a promise to call her and she went back to work, trying to put what she'd learned out of her mind. She wished Mack would call, at least, to give her a chance to explain the misunderstanding. But he didn't. And after Vivian's fierce hostility, she was nervous about phoning the house at all. She hoped that things would work themselves out, if she was patient.

Late afternoon on the Thursday before baccalaureate exercises Friday night, she walked out of the bank after depositing her paycheck and ran right into Mack Killain.

It was the first time she'd seen him since the day she'd had the falling out with Vivian. He moved away from her, and the look he gave her was so contemptuous, so full of distaste, that she felt dirty. That was when she realized that Vivian must have told Mack what she thought Natalie and Whit had done. It was painfully obvious that Mack wasn't going to listen to an excuse. She'd never imagined that he would look at her like that. The pain went all the way to her soul.

''How could you do that to Vivian, to your best friend?'' he asked coldly.

''Do...what?'' she faltered.

''You know what!'' he thundered. ''You two-timing, lying, cheating little flirt. He must be crazy. No man in his right mind would look twice at you.''

Her mouth fell open. Her heart raced. Her mouth was dry as cotton. ''Mack...''

''You had us all fooled,'' he continued, raising his voice and not minding who heard. Several people did. ''Vivian trusted you! And while she was in bed with pneumonia, you were making out with the man she loved!''

Natalie wanted to go through the sidewalk. Her eyes brimmed over with tears. ''I didn't!'' she tried to defend herself, almost choking on the words.

''There's no use denying it. Vivian saw you,'' he said with magnificent contempt. ''She told me.''

It was a lie, but he believed it. Maybe he wanted to believe it. He'd said that they had no future together, and this would make the perfect excuse for him to push her out of his life. Nothing she said was going to make any difference. He simply did not want her, and he was making it clear.

She'd thought the pain was bad before. Now it was unbearable.

''All of us trusted you, made you part of our family. And this is how you repaid us, by betraying Vivian, who never did anything to hurt you.'' His tone was vicious, furious. ''Not only that, Natalie, you didn't even try to apologize for it.''

She lifted her face defiantly. ''I have nothing to apologize for,'' she said in a husky, hoarse tone.

''Then we have nothing to say to each other, ever again,'' he replied harshly.

''Mack, if you'd just let me try to explain,'' she said, hoping for a miracle. ''Calm down and talk to me.''

''I am calm,'' he said in an icy tone. ''What did you expect, anyway? A proposal of marriage?'' He laughed bitterly. ''You know where I stand on that issue. And even if I were in the mood for it, it wouldn't be with a woman who'd sell me out the minute the ring was on her finger. You went to him afterward,'' he gritted, ''and you as much as told me you were going to. But if you think I'm jealous, honey, you're dead wrong. You were Vivian's friend, but I never wanted you hanging around my house. I tolerated you for Vivian's sake.''

''I see.'' Her face was white and she was aware of pitying, embarrassed looks around her, because he was eloquent.

He hardened his heart, bristling with wounded pride as he

looked at her, furious at his own weakness. Well, never again. "Which reminds me, Natalie," he added coldly, "I suppose it goes without saying that you're not welcome at the ranch anymore."

She lifted her eyes to his hard face and nodded slowly. "Yes, Mack," she said in a subdued tone. "It does go without saying."

Her heart was breaking. She turned away from that accusing, contemptuous gaze and walked briskly down the street to get away from him. She didn't know how she was going to bear this latest outrage of Vivian's. It had cost her Mack, whom she loved more than her own life. And he hated her. He hated her!

The bystanders were still staring at Mack when she was out of sight, but he didn't say a word. He stalked into the bank, noticing that people almost fell over trying to get out of his way. He was furious. After going right out of his arms into Whit's, she'd had the gall to try and deny it, even when Vivian had seen her with Whit! He would never trust his instincts about women again, he decided. If he could be fooled that easily, for that long, he was safer going around with Glenna. She might not be virtuous, but at least she was loyal—in her fashion.

Natalie went home with her heart around her knees. She made supper but couldn't eat it. She'd assumed that Mack was making assumptions. It hadn't occurred to her that Vivian would tell such a lie, or that Mack would believe it. But she'd helped things along by making those remarks to Mack in frustration when he'd put her out of the office after their tempestuous interlude. She hadn't wanted Whit, ever. But nobody would believe that now. She'd lost not only Mack, but the only family she'd known for years. She went to bed and lay awake most of the night, wretched and alone.

She wondered how she could go on living in the same town with the Killains and see Mack and Vivian and the boys week after week. Did Bob and Charles hate her, too? Was it a wholesale contempt? Vivian had lied. That a woman she'd considered her best friend could treat her so callously hurt tremendously. Perhaps she was doomed to a life without affection. God knew that her aunt, old Mrs. Barnes, had only brought her from the orphanage to be a housekeeper and part-time nurse until the old lady died. No one had ever loved her. She'd wanted Mack to. She'd even thought at odd moments that he did, somehow. But the hatred in his eyes was damning. If he'd loved her, he'd have at least given her the benefit of the doubt.

But he hadn't. He'd believed Vivian without hesitation. So all her dreams of love eternal had gone up in smoke. There was nothing left except to make a decision about what she was going to do with the rest of her life. She knew immediately that she couldn't stay in Medicine Ridge. She would have to leave. Next week, after graduation, she was going to talk to one of her instructors who'd told her she knew of a job opening in a Dallas school where a relative was principal. Dallas sounded like a nice place to live.

Natalie marched in with her class to the baccalaureate service, trying not to notice how many of her classmates' whole families had come to see them in their caps and gowns. It was a brief service, held in the college chapel with a guest speaker who was some sort of well-known political figure. Natalie barely heard what went on around her because she was so heartbroken.

When the service was over, she greeted classmates she knew and drove herself home. The next morning, she got up early to go to the college with her gown for the graduation exercises. She felt very proud of her accomplishment as she marched into the chapel along with her class and waited for her name to be called, for her diploma to be handed out. It would have been one of the best days of her life, if the Killains hadn't been angry with her. As it was, she went through the motions like a zombie, smiling, looking happy for the cameras. But inside, she was so miserable that she only wanted to be alone. The minute the service was over, she went to look for the teacher who'd offered to help her get the Dallas job. And she told her she was interested.

The Killains were somber at the dinner table on Sunday. It was the first time in days they'd all been together, with the boys home, as well. It was more like a wake than a meal.

"Natalie graduated yesterday," Bob said coolly, glaring at Mack and Vivian, who wouldn't look at him. "My friend Gig's sister was in her class. She said that Natalie didn't have one single person of her own in the crowd for baccalaureate or graduation. Viv?"

Vivian had burst into tears. She pushed away from the table and went upstairs as fast as her healing lungs would allow.

Mack threw down his napkin, leaving his supper untouched, and stalked out of the room, as grim as death itself.

Bob looked at his brother and grimaced. "I guess I should have kept my mouth shut."

"I don't see why," Charles replied irritably. "Natalie belongs to us, to all of us. But the two of them behave as if she's at the top of the FBI's most-wanted list. It's that damned Whit, you mark my words. He did something or said something that caused this. He's going around with old Murcheson's daughter now, and she's grubstaking his gambling habit. Everybody knows it. He even said that our sister was only a means to an end, so if Natalie was the cause of that breakup, good for her! She saved Viv from something a lot worse than pneumonia. Not that anybody but us cares, I guess," he muttered as he attacked his steak.

In the hall, Mack overheard and scowled. He'd thought Whit had left Vivian for Natalie, so why was he going around with the Murcheson girl? First Natalie's impassioned denial, now Viv's hysterical retreat. Something was wrong here.

He followed Vivian upstairs to her room. She was sitting in the chair by her bed, tears rolling down her pale cheeks. He sank down on the bed facing her.

"Why don't you tell me why you're crying, Viv," he invited gently.

She wiped at her red eyes with a tissue to catch the tears. "I lied," she whispered.

His whole body stiffened. "I beg your pardon?"

"I mean, Natalie was pretty disheveled and Whit's hair was ruffled. They looked like they'd been making out," she said defensively. "I didn't actually see them, though. But there was nobody else in the house except the two of them and they were down there for almost an hour." Her face hardened as she said it, so she missed the sudden pallor of her brother's face.

"I was down there," he snapped. "Whit went out to get cigarettes. He'd just come back and made coffee when he and Natalie went up to your room."

She gaped at him. Her jaw fell. Horror claimed her face. "Oh, no," she whispered. "Oh, dear God, no!"

"She did nothing. With Whit," he added, averting his gaze to the window. He looked, at that moment, as if he'd never smiled in his life. He was hearing himself accuse Natalie on the street in front of half a dozen bystanders of being a faithless tease.

Now it made sense. Mack had gotten drunk because he thought Natalie had gone straight from his arms to Whit's. Vivian had told him so, believing that Natalie and Whit had been alone for that hour. Whit had admitted it. And all the time...

"I'll go to her," Vivian said at once. "I'll apologize, on my knees if I have to!"

"Don't bother," he said, getting to his feet. "She won't let you past the porch. I told her she wasn't welcome here ever again." His fists clenched at his hips. "And several other things that were...overheard," he added through his teeth. "She went to her graduation all alone." He had to stop because he was too choked to say another word. He went out without looking at Vivian, and the door closed with a jerk behind him.

Vivian put her face in her hands and bawled. Out of her own

selfishness, she'd destroyed two lives. Mack loved Natalie. And she knew—she *knew*—that Natalie loved Mack, had always loved him! It wasn't Natalie who'd betrayed them. It was Vivian herself. Her pride had been hurt because Whit preferred Natalie, but she'd been done a huge favor. She was besotted enough with the man to have given him all the money he'd asked for. She'd had a narrow escape, for which she had Natalie to thank. But they weren't friends anymore. They'd pushed Natalie out of their lives. It was wishful thinking to suppose she'd forgive them or ever give them a chance to hurt her again. She'd never really been loved, unless it was by the parents who'd been so tragically killed in her childhood. She was alone in the world, and she must feel it now more than ever before. Vivian took a deep breath and dried her eyes. Surely there was some way, something she could do, to make amends. She had to.

Mack went off on a prolonged business trip the next day. He barely spoke to Vivian on his way out, and he looked like death warmed over. She could only imagine how he felt, after the way he'd behaved. Natalie might forgive him one day, but she'd probably never be able to forget.

It took her two days to get up enough courage to drive over to Natalie's house and knock on the door. She got a real shock when the door was opened, because there were two suitcases sitting on the floor, and Natalie was dressed for travel.

"Natalie, could I speak to you for a minute?" Vivian asked hesitantly.

"A minute is all I have," came the cool, distant reply. "I thought you were my cab. I have to get to the airport. One of my college professors is letting me fly with her to Dallas."

"What's in Dallas?" Vivian asked, shocked.

"My new job." Natalie looked past her at a cab that was just pulling into the driveway. She checked to make sure she had her purse and all the documents she needed before she lifted her suitcases and put them on the porch. She locked the door while Vivian stood nearby, speechless.

"I've put the house on the market," she continued. "I won't be coming back."

"Oh, Nat," Vivian whispered miserably. "I lied. I lied to Mack. I thought... You were downstairs and so was Whit, for an hour or more. Whit didn't deny what I accused him of doing with you. But I didn't know Mack had come home."

Natalie looked straight at her. In that instant she looked as formidable as Vivian's taciturn brother. "Mack believed you," she said. That was all. But it was more than a statement of fact. It meant that he didn't even suspect that Natalie might be innocent. She was tarred and feathered and put on a rail without qualm.

"I'm his sister. I've never lied to him before," she added. "Nat, I have to tell you something. You have to listen!"

"Are you the lady who wants to go to the airport?" the cabdriver asked.

"Yes, I am," Natalie said, carrying her bags down the steps without another word to Vivian.

"Don't go!" Vivian cried. "Please don't go!"

"There's nothing left in Medicine Ridge for me, and we both know it, Vivian," she told the other woman without meeting her eyes as the cabdriver put both her bags in the trunk and then went to open the back door for Natalie to get into the cab. "You've finally got what you wanted. Aren't you happy? I'll never be even an imagined potential rival for any of your boyfriends again."

"I didn't know," Vivian moaned. "I jumped to conclusions and hurt everybody. But please, Natalie, at least let me apologize! And don't blame Mack for it. It's not his fault."

"Mack doesn't want me," Natalie said heavily. "I suppose I knew it from the beginning, but he made it very clear the last time I saw him. He'll date Glenna and be very happy. Maybe you will, too. But I'm tired of being the scapegoat. I'm going to find a new life for myself in Dallas. Goodbye, Vivian,'' she said tersely, still without looking in Vivian's direction.

Vivian had never felt so terrible in all her life. She stood on the steps, alone, and watched the best friend she'd ever had leave town because of her.

"I'm sorry," she whispered to the retreating cab. "Oh, Natalie, I'm so very sorry!"

She had to tell Mack that Natalie had gone, of course. That was almost as hard as watching Natalie leave. She found him in his study, at the computer, making decisions about restocking. He looked up when he saw her at the door.

"Well?" he asked.

She went into the room and closed the door behind her. She looked washed out, miserable, defeated.

"I went to apologize to Natalie," she began.

His face tautened, and he looked a little paler. But he gathered himself together quickly and only lifted an eyebrow as he dropped his gaze to the computer screen. "I gather that it didn't go well?"

She fingered her wristwatch nervously. This was harder than she'd dreamed. "I was just in time to see her leave."

He frowned as he lifted his head. "Leave?"

She nodded. She sat in the chair beside the desk, where she'd sat and watched him the night he got drunk. She hated telling him what happened. He'd had so much responsibility in his life, so much pain. He'd never really had anyone to love, either, except for his siblings. He'd loved Natalie. Vivian had cost him the only woman who could have made him happy.

"Leave for where?" he demanded shortly.

She swallowed. "Dallas."

"Dallas, Texas? Who the hell does she know in Texas?" he persisted, still not understanding what Vivian was saying.

"She's got a job there," she said reluctantly. "She's...selling her house. She said she wouldn't be coming back."

For a few seconds, Mack didn't speak. He stared at his sister as though he hadn't understood her. Then, all at once, the life seemed to drain out of him. He stared at the dark paneling of the wall blindly while the truth hit him squarely in the gut. Natalie had left town. They'd hurt her so badly that she couldn't even stay in the same community. Probably the gossip had been hard on her, too, because Mack had made harsh accusations in front of everyone. And how did you stop gossip, when it was never spoken in public?

He sank down into his chair without a word.

"I tried to explain," she continued. "To apologize." She swallowed hard. "She wouldn't even look at me. I don't blame her. I've ruined her life because I was selfish and conceited and obsessed with jealousy. Now that I look back, I realize that it wasn't the first time I saw Nat as a rival and treated her accordingly. I've been an idiot. And I'm sorry, Mack. I really am."

His chest rose and fell. He toyed with the pencil on the desk, trying to adjust to a world without at least the occasional glimpse of Natalie. Now that he'd lost her for good, he knew how desperately he loved her. It was a hell of an irony.

"I could go to Dallas and try to make her listen," Vivian persisted, because he looked so defeated. Her brother, the steel man, was melting in front of her.

His shoulders seemed to slump a little. He shook his head. "Let her go," he said heavily. "We've done enough harm."

"But you love her!"

His eyes closed briefly and then opened. He turned to the computer and moved the mouse to reopen his file, his face drawn and remote. He didn't say another word.

After a minute of painful silence, Vivian got up and left him there. She loved her brother. It devastated her to realize how much she'd hurt him lately. And that was nothing to what she'd done to Natalie. She could never make up for what she'd cost Natalie and her brother. But she wished she had the chance to try.

*   *   *

Natalie, meanwhile, had settled into a small apartment near the school. She'd interviewed for the position and after a few days, she was notified that she had the job. The teaching roster had been filled for the year, but one of the teachers had come down with hepatitis and couldn't continue, so there was a vacancy. Natalie was just what they wanted for the third graders, a bilingual teacher who could understand and communicate with the Hispanic students. She was glad she'd opted for Spanish for her language sequence instead of German, which had been her first choice. It had been one of only a few good moves she'd made in her life.

She thought about Vivian's painful visit and the admission that she'd lied to Mack about Natalie and Whit. So Mack knew, but he hadn't tried to stop her. He hadn't phoned or written. Apparently she didn't even mean that much to him. He must have meant all the terrible things he'd said to her on the street, where everyone could hear him.

Part of her realized that it was for the best. He'd said that he didn't want marriage or an affair, which could only have led to more misery for both of them. It was just as well that the bond was broken abruptly. But their history went back so far that she couldn't even conceive of life without Mack. And when Vivian was herself, they'd had such wonderful times together, along with Bob and Charles. Natalie had felt as if she belonged to the Killains, and they to her. Now she was cut adrift again, without roots or ties. She had to adjust to being alone.

At least she had a job and a place to live. She'd found work with a temporary agency for the summer so that she could save up for a few additions to her meager wardrobe for the beginning of school in August. She would survive, she promised herself. In fact, she would thrive!

But she didn't. The days turned to weeks, and although she adjusted to her new surroundings, she still felt like an outsider. When she began teaching, she was nervous and uncertain of herself, and the children knew it and took advantage of her tentative style. Her classroom was a madhouse. It wasn't until one of the other teachers, a veteran of first days on the job, came to restore order that she could manage to teach.

She was taken gently aside and taught how to handle her exuberant students. The next day was a different story. She kept order and began to learn the children's names. She learned to recognize other members of the staff, and she enjoyed her work. But at night, she lay awake remembering the feel of Mack Killain's strong arms around her, and she ached for him.

By the second week of school, she was beginning to fit in. But on the way home she passed a small basketball court and noticed two boys who looked barely high-school age pushing and shoving each other and raging at each other in language that was appalling even in a modern culture. On a whim, she went toward them.

"Okay, guys, knock it off," she said, pushing her way between them. Unfortunately she did it just as the hand of one boy went inside his denim shirt and came out with a knife. She saw a flash of metal and felt a pain in her chest so intense that it made her fall to the ground.

"You've killed her, you fool!" one of them cried.

"It was your fault! She just got in the way!"

They ran away, still arguing. She lay there, feeling a wetness on the concrete around her chest. She couldn't get air into her lungs. She heard voices. She heard traffic. She saw the blue sky turn a blinding, painful white....

Mack Killain was downloading a new package of software into his computer when the phone rang. It had been a busy summer, and the unwelcome bull roundup was under way, along with getting fattened calves ready for market and pulling out herd members that were unproductive. He'd worked himself half to death trying not to think about Natalie. He still did. She haunted him, waking and sleeping.

He picked up the receiver absently on impulse, instead of

letting the answering machine take over, still loading his program while he said, "Hello?"

"Mack Killain?"

"Yes?"

"This is Dr. Hayes at the Dallas Medical Center," came a voice from the other end of the line.

Mack's heart stopped. "Natalie!" he exploded with a sense of premonition.

There was a pause. "Well, yes, I am calling about a Miss Natalie Brock. Your name and number were on an accident card in her purse. I'm trying to locate a member of her family."

"What happened? Is she hurt?" Mack demanded.

"She needs immediate surgery or she's going to die," the doctor said frankly, "but I have to have written authorization for it, and she can't sign anything. She's unconscious. I have to have a member of her family."

Mack felt his heart stop. He gripped the receiver tightly. "I'm her cousin," Mack lied glibly. "I'm the only relative she has. I'll sign for her. I can be there in two hours."

"She'll be dead in two hours," came the sharp reply.

Mack closed his eyes, praying silently. "I've got a fax machine," he said. "I can write out a permission slip on my letterhead and sign it and fax it to you. Will that do?"

"Yes. But quickly, please. Here's our fax number."

Mack jotted it down. "I'll have it there in two minutes," he promised. "Don't let her die," he added in a tone as cold as ice before he hung up.

His hands shook as he stopped the loading process and pulled up his word processor instead. He typed a quick permission note, printed it out on ranch letterhead, whipped out two pens before he found one with ink, signed it, and rushed it into the fax machine. In the time he'd promised, he had it on the way.

He cut off the computer and picked up the phone, calling a charter service in a nearby city. "I want a Learjet over here in ten minutes to take me to Dallas. Don't tell me you can't do it," he added shortly. "I'll be waiting at the local airport." He gave the location and hung up.

There was no time to pack. He went barreling out of the office just as Bob and Charles came in behind a stunned Vivian.

"What's going on?" Vivian asked in concern, because Mack's face was white.

"I have no idea. But Natalie's in a Dallas hospital about to undergo emergency surgery. I had to sign for her, so if anybody calls here and asks, we're her cousins."

"Where are you going?" Bob asked.

"To Dallas, of course," Mack said impatiently, pushing past them.

"Not without us, you aren't," Charles told him bluntly. "Natalie belongs to all of us. I'm not staying here."

"Neither am I," Bob seconded.

"Where one goes, we all go," Vivian added. "I'm the one who caused all this in the first place. Natalie needs me, and I'm going. I'll make her listen to my apology when she's well."

"I don't have time to argue with you. Get in the car. I'll lock the door."

"How are we going to get there?" Vivian asked as she herded her tall brothers outside.

"I've got a charter jet on the way."

"Flying," Bob told his sibling. "That's cool."

"Yeah, I like flying," Charles agreed.

"Well, I don't," Vivian muttered. "But it's quicker than driving."

She piled into the front seat with Mack while the two boys got in back. All the way to the airport, Mack drove like a maniac. By the time they arrived, the three passengers had held their collective breaths long enough to qualify as deep-sea divers.

They spilled out in the parking lot at the small airport. The jet was already there, as the charter service had promised, gassed up and ready, with its door open and the ladder down.

Mack didn't say a word until he shook hands with the pilot and copilot and got into the back with his sister and brothers. Until now, he'd had the organization of the trip to keep his mind off the danger of the situation.

Now, with hours with nothing to do but think during the flight, he recalled what the surgeon had said to him—that Natalie could die. He had no idea what had happened. He had to know. He pulled the cell phone he always carried from his pocket and, after checking with the pilot that it was safe to use once they were in the air, he got the number of the Dallas hospital and bullied his way verbally to a resident in the emergency room. He explained who he was, asked if the fax had been received and was told that Miss Brock was in surgery. They had no report on her condition, except that there was at least one stab wound and one of her lungs had collapsed. The resident was sorry, but he had no further information. Mack told him an approximate arrival time and hung up.

"A knife wound?" Bob exclaimed. "Our Nat?"

"She's a teacher," Vivian said miserably. "Some students are very dangerous these days."

"She teaches grammar school," Mack said disgustedly. "How could a little kid stab her?"

"It might have been someone related to one of the little kids," Charles offered.

Vivian brushed back her blond hair. "It's my fault if she dies," she said quietly.

"She's not going to die," Mack said firmly. "Don't talk like that!"

She glanced at him, saw his expression and put her hand over his. "Okay. I'm sorry."

He averted his face, but he didn't shake off her hand. He was terrified. He'd never been so frightened in all his life. If he lost Natalie, there was nothing in the world to live for. It would be the end, the absolute end of everything.

Chapter 9

When Natalie regained consciousness, there was a smell of antiseptic. Her side ached. Her lung hurt. She had a tube up her nose, and it was irritating her nasal passages. She felt bruised and broken and sick. Her eyes opened slowly to a white room with people in green gowns, moving around a room that only she seemed to occupy.

She blinked hard, trying to get her eyes to focus. Obviously, she was in a recovery room. She couldn't remember how she got there.

A deep voice, raised and urgent, was demanding access to her, and a nurse was threatening to call security. It didn't do any good. He was finally gowned and masked and let in, because a riot was about to ensue in the corridor.

There was a breeze and then a familiar face with a black eye patch hovered just above her. She couldn't quite focus. Her mind was foggy.

A big, warm hand spread against her cheek, and the one eye above her was much brighter than she remembered it. It seemed to be wet. Impossible, of course. She was simply dreaming.

"Don't you die, damn it!" he choked huskily. "Do you hear me, Natalie? Don't you dare!"

"Mr. Killain," one of the nurses was trying to intervene.

He ignored her. "Natalie, can you hear me?" he demanded. "Wake up!"

She blinked again. Her eyes barely focused. She was drifting in and out. "Mack," she whispered, and her eyes closed again.

He was raving mad. She heard him tossing orders around as if he were in charge, and she heard running feet in response. She would have smiled if she'd been able. Every woman's dream until he opened his mouth...

She didn't know that she'd spoken aloud, or that the smile had been visible.

Mack had one of her small hands in his with a death grip. Now that he could see her, touch her, he was breathing normally again. But she looked white, and her chest was barely moving. He was scared to death, and it displayed itself in venomous bad temper. Somebody would probably run him out any minute, maybe arrest him for causing a disturbance. But he'd have gone through an armed camp to get to her, just to see her, to make sure that she was alive. He couldn't have imagined himself like this not so long ago.

Neither could his siblings, who stood in awe of him as he broke hospital rules right and left and sent veteran health-care workers running. This was a Mack they'd never seen before. It was obvious that he was in love with the woman lying so still and quiet in the recovery room. All of them looked at each other, wondering why they hadn't realized it a long time ago.

The surgeon—presumably the one who'd spoken to him on the telephone—came into the recovery room still wearing his operating clothes. He looked like a fire-eater himself, tall and dark-eyed and taciturn.

"Killain?" he asked.

"Yes." Killain let go of Natalie's limp hand long enough to shake the surgeon's. "How is she?"

"Lost a lower lobe of her lung," he said. "There was some

internal bleeding and we'll have to keep her here for a while. The danger now is complications. But she'll make it," he added confidently.

Mack felt himself relax for the first time in hours. "I want to stay with her," he said bluntly.

The doctor raised an eyebrow and chuckled. "I think that's fairly obvious to the staff," he mused. "Since you're a relative, I don't have an objection. But we would prefer to have you wait until we can get her out of recovery and into a room. Meanwhile, it would help if you'd go to the business office and fill out some papers for her. She was brought in unconscious."

Mack hesitated, but Natalie was asleep. Perhaps it wouldn't hurt to leave her, just briefly. "All right," he said finally.

The surgeon didn't dare look as relieved as he felt. He pointed Mack toward the business office, noticing that three younger people fell in step behind him. The victim apparently had plenty of family to look after her. That lightened his step as he went toward the operating theater to start the next case.

Several hours later, Natalie opened her eyes again, groggy from the anesthetic and hurting. She groaned and touched her side, which was heavily bandaged.

A big, warm hand caught hers and lifted it away. "Be careful. You'll pull out the IV," a familiar voice said tenderly. It sounded like Mack. It couldn't be, of course.

She turned her head and there he was. She managed a smile. "I thought I was dreaming," she murmured drowsily.

"The nurses don't. They think they're having a nightmare," Bob said with a wicked glance at his brother.

"I saw an orderly run right out the front door," Charles added dryly.

"Shut up," Mack said impatiently.

"He just wants to make sure you're properly looked after, Nat," Vivian said, coming close enough to brush back Natalie's hair. "You poor baby," she added softly. "We're all going to take care of you."

"That's right," Bob agreed.

"You belong to us," Charles added firmly.

Mack didn't say anything.

Too groggy to understand much of what was going on, Natalie managed another weak smile and then grimaced. But after a minute she relaxed and went back to sleep.

Vivian studied the apparatus she was hooked to. "I think this has a painkiller unit that automatically injects her every few minutes. I'm going to ask someone."

Without another word, she went into the hall.

Bob and Charles shared a speaking glance and announced that they were going after coffee, offering to bring back a cup for their big brother.

Mack just nodded. He only had eyes for Natalie. It was like coming home after a long journey. He didn't want to do anything except sit there and look at her. Even in her weak, wan condition, she was beautiful to him. His hand curled closer around hers and gripped it securely.

All the things he'd said came back to haunt him. How could he ever have doubted her? She wouldn't lie to him. Somewhere deep inside he knew that. So only one reason for his immediate assumption of her guilt was left. He'd been fighting a rearguard action against her gentle presence with the last bit of willpower he possessed. He was blind in one eye. Someday, he might lose his sight in the other, as well. He had the responsibility for his two brothers and his sister until they could stand on their own. He hadn't felt that it was fair to inflict all that on a young woman like Natalie.

But ever since the crisis had developed, his family had been united behind him and shared his concern for Natalie. They loved her, too. He knew that there would inevitably be conflicts, hopefully small ones, but he'd seen what life without her would be like, and anything was preferable. He'd do whatever he could to make her happy, to keep her safe. Of course, when she was her old self again, she was going to want to knock him over the head with a baseball bat. He was resigned to even that.

The first order of business was to get her well. He was going to take her back to Montana if he had to wrap her in sheets tied at both ends. She might not like it, but she'd have to go. She didn't have anyplace else to recuperate, and she couldn't work. At the ranch, the four of them could take turns sitting with her.

While he was considering possibilities, Vivian came back. "It automatically injects painkillers," she announced with a smile. "I spoke with the duty nurses at their station. They have computers everywhere with records and charts...." She glanced at her brother with a self-conscious smile. "It fascinates me. I didn't realize nursing was so challenging, or so complicated."

"I haven't seen a lot of nurses in here," he remarked darkly.

She grinned at him. "You will when you leave," she said, tongue in cheek.

"Don't you start," he muttered.

She hugged him and sat in the chair on the other side of the bed. "Why don't you go and get something to eat? I'll sit with Nat."

He shook his head. He had her hand firmly in his and he wasn't letting go until he knew for certain that she wasn't trying to give up.

"Want some coffee?" she persisted.

"The boys went to bring some back."

"Okay. In that case, I think I'll walk down to the canteen and get a bag of potato chips and a soft drink."

"Good idea."

She smiled to herself as she went out. He hadn't spared her a glance. She could read him like a book. He was afraid that if he left, Natalie might not recover. He was going to keep her alive by sheer will, if he had to. Vivian couldn't blame him for being concerned. Natalie did look so white and thin lying there. Vivian blamed herself for Natalie's condition. If she hadn't been so horrible, none of this would have happened. She had yet to make her own apologies. But it was nice to know that Nat would be around to hear them.

She wandered down the corridor. Back in the room, Mack leaned forward to study Natalie's sleeping face. "Poor little scrap," he murmured softly, touching her cheek with a touch light enough not to disturb her. "How did I ever think I could manage without you?"

At some level, she was aware that he was speaking to her. But she was fighting the pain and the drugs, and her mind was foggy. She felt his touch, first on her cheek and then lightly brushing her mouth. He was whispering in her ear, words that sounded like the softest kind of endearments. At that point, she was sure she was dreaming. Mack never used endearments....

It was late that night before she returned to something approaching consciousness. She looked around the room with surprised amusement. Vivian was asleep in the chair by the radiator. Mack was sprawled, snoring faintly, in the chair beside her bed, with her hand still gripped in his. Beside him, on the floor, Bob and Charles were asleep sharing a blanket on the cold linoleum. She could only imagine the nursing staff's frustration trying to work around them. And wasn't there some rule about the number of visitors and how long they could stay? Then she remembered the uproar Mack had caused on his arrival, and she imagined he'd broken every rule they had already.

"Mack?" she whispered. Her voice barely carried. She tried again. "Mack?"

He stirred sleepily, and his eye opened at once. He sat up, increasing his firm hold on her hand. "What is it, sweetheart?"

The endearment was disconcerting. He stood and came closer, bending over her with evident concern. "Tell me," he asked softly. "What do you want?"

She searched his face with hungry eyes. It had been weeks since she'd seen him. There was something different....

"You've lost weight," she whispered.

His gaze fell to her hand in his. "So have you."

She wanted to tell him that she'd been only half alive without him, that it was the lack of him in her life that had aged her. But she couldn't say that. She'd been hurt and someone had called him. Probably her serious condition had caused Vivian to finally tell him the truth. He'd come out of guilt. Perhaps they all had.

She pulled her hand out of his and laid it across her chest. "I don't need anything," she said, averting her face. "Thank you," she added politely.

The effect of that cool, polite reply hit him hard. She was conscious again, and she'd be remembering their last meeting and what he'd said to her. He put his hands deep in his pockets and studied her for a long minute before he went to the chair and sat down. The breath he let out was audible.

She was still groggy enough that she went back to sleep at once. Mack didn't. He sat brooding, watching her, until the first rays of dawn filtered through the venetian blinds. Around him, the boys and Vivian began to stir.

Vivian got up and looked out the door, noticing the bustle of early-morning duty shifts. "Why don't you three go get us a nice hotel suite and have a bath. I'll stay here with Natalie while they get her bathed and fed. By the time you come back, she'll be ready for visitors."

Mack was reluctant. Vivian pulled him out of the chair. "You're absolutely dead on your feet, and you look fifty," she said. "You're not going to be any good to anybody until you get some rest. Have you slept at all?"

He grimaced. "She woke up in the night," he said, as if that explained it all. His face was drawn with worry and guilt. "She remembered what I said to her. It was in her eyes."

"She'll remember what I said, too," Vivian replied. "We'll

get through it. She's not a person who holds grudges. It will be all right."

He hesitated. "She isn't going to want to go home with us," he realized. His face began to tauten. "But she will, if I have to put her in a sack! If she wakes up before I come back, you tell her that!"

The loud tones woke Natalie. She winced as she moved, and her chest hurt, but her eyes lifted to Mack's hard face, and they began to sparkle. She struggled to sit up. "I'm not go-ing...anywhere with you, Mack Killain," she told him in as strong a tone as she could manage in her depleted condition. "I wouldn't walk to the...elevator with you!"

"Calm down," Vivian said firmly, easing her down on the pillows. "When you've gotten your strength back, I'll get you a frying pan and you can lay about him with it. In fact, I'll even bend over and give you a shot at me. But for now," she added softly, "you have to get well. You can only stay in the hospital until you're back on your feet. But full recuperation takes longer—and you can't stay by yourself."

Bob and Charles were awake and crowding around the bed with their siblings.

"Right," Charles said firmly, looking so much like his older brother that it was uncanny. "We'll all take care of you."

"I'll hook up my game system and teach you how to play arcade games," Bob offered.

"I'll teach you chess," Charles seconded.

"I'll teach you how to be a real pain in the neck," Vivian added, tongue in cheek. "I think I wrote the book on it."

Natalie wavered as her eyes went to Mack. His gaze was steady on her face, quiet, and he looked almost vulnerable. Maybe it was a trick of the light.

"You could teach her how to jump to conclusions," Vivian murmured dryly.

"I learned that from you," he shot right back. He turned to Natalie. "I'm not coaxing. You're coming back with us, one way or the other, and that's the end of it."

Natalie's eyes started flashing. "You listen here, Mack Killain!"

"No, you listen," he interrupted firmly. "I'm going to talk to the surgeon and find out what sort of care you need. I'll hire a private nurse and get a hospital bed moved in. Whatever it takes."

Natalie's small fist hit the bedcovers in frustration. That hurt her chest, and she grimaced.

"Temper, temper," Mack said mockingly. "That won't get you anywhere."

"I am not a parcel to be picked up and carried off," she raged. "I don't belong to you!"

He lifted one eyebrow. "In one way or another," he said very quietly, "you've belonged to me since you were seventeen." He turned to Vivian. "I'll take the boys to a hotel and come back in a couple of hours. I'll phone you as soon as we're settled and you can get in touch with us if you need to."

"Okay," Vivian said with a smile. "Don't worry," she added when he hesitated at the door. "I'll take good care of her."

He still hesitated, but after a minute he shot a last, worried look at a furious Natalie and followed the boys into the hall.

"I won't go!" Natalie choked out.

Vivian went close to the bed and gently smoothed Natalie's hair from her forehead. "Yes, you will," she said gently. "Mack and I have a lot to make up to you. I was so jealous of you that I couldn't stand it. I thought I'd die if I couldn't have Whit." She shook her head sorrowfully. "You know, he even lied to me that he'd been making out with you. You were both downstairs for almost an hour and I didn't have a clue that Mack had come home in the meantime," she added ruefully, watching Natalie blush as she recalled what she and Mack had been doing during that time. "Whit said he'd found you more receptive than I'd ever been. It was a major misunderstanding all around, and the lie I told Mack, that I'd seen you and Whit together, didn't do anything to help matters."

Her worried blue eyes met Natalie's green ones. "Can you forgive me, do you think?"

Natalie let out the anger in a slow breath. "Of course," she said. "We've been friends far too long for me to hold a grudge."

Vivian bent and kissed her cheek. "I haven't been much of a friend up until this point," she said. "But I'm going to do a better job from now on. And the first matter of business is to get you a sponge bath and some breakfast."

"Mack believed you," Natalie said.

Vivian paused on her way to the door. She came back and put a gentle hand over Natalie's where it lay on her stomach over the covers. "The night I told Mack that lie, he went into the office and locked the door and drank half a bottle of Scotch whiskey. I had to get the foreman and a locksmith to open it for me. When I finally got in, he'd passed out."

Her eyes were troubled. "He never loses control like that. That was when I knew how much I'd hurt him. And after your graduation, when Bob and Charles lit into us about not being there, he went off by himself and wouldn't even talk to us for days. I know what we did hurt you, Natalie," she concluded. "But it hurt us just as badly. I'm sorry. Mack was right about Whit all along. He's going around with another rich girl, but one who likes to gamble herself, and he's got all the money he wants for the time being. I was an idiot."

"You were in love," Natalie excused her. "It doesn't exactly make people lucid."

"Doesn't it?" Vivian asked pointedly, and with a curious smile.

"Don't ask me," the other woman replied, averting her face. "I was only seventeen when I had my first and last taste of it."

"I know," Vivian said disconcertingly. She smiled gently. "It was always Mack. And I knew it, and used it to hurt you. I regret that more than anything."

"That wasn't what I meant," Natalie ground out.

Vivian didn't press the issue. She patted her hand gently. "Everything's going to be all right. Believe that, if you don't believe another word I say."

Natalie shifted to a more comfortable position. "Did all of you come down here together?" she asked.

"Yes. Your surgeon phoned and told us you were fighting for your life and that somebody had to give permission for him to operate." She grimaced. "Mack had to fax a permission slip to him as next of kin, so if anyone asks, we're your cousins." She held up a hand when Natalie started to speak. "If he hadn't, you might have died, Nat."

"I had that accident card in my purse, the one you made me fill out with Mack's name and phone number on it," Natalie recalled. "I guess they found it when I was brought in."

Vivian hesitated. "Do you remember what happened?"

"Yes. I saw two boys fighting on a basketball court. Like an idiot, I went in to stop it." She smiled wryly. "One of them had a knife, and I was just in time to catch it in my chest. Fortunately it only cost me a little bit of one lung instead of my life."

"Next time, call the police," Vivian said firmly. "That's their job, and they do it very well."

"Next time, if there ever is one, I will." Natalie caught Vivian's hand as she moved it. "Thank you for coming all the way here. I never dreamed that any of you would—especially Mack."

"When the boys heard, the first thing they said was that you belonged to us," Vivian told her. "And you do. Whether you like it or not."

"I like it very much." Her lower lip became briefly unsteady. "I'm glad we're still friends," she managed shakily.

"Oh, Nat!" Vivian leaned down to hug her as gently as she could. "I'm sorry, I'm so sorry! I'll never, never be so selfish and horrible again, ever!"

Natalie hugged her with her good arm and sighed as the

tears poured out of her, therapeutic and comforting, hot on her pale face.

Vivian drew back and found tissues for both of them to wipe their wet eyes with, and they laughed while they did it.

"Mack still has his apologies to make," Vivian added. "I think he'll welcome the opportunity. But it's going to be hard for him, so meet him halfway, would you?"

Natalie looked worried. "He looks bad."

"He should. He's been driving himself for weeks. I won't even try to tell you how hard he's been to live with."

"That isn't anything unusual," Natalie said with her first glint of humor.

"This has been much worse than usual. If you don't believe it, try looking into the hall when he comes back. You'll see medical people running for the exits in droves." She chuckled. "We just stood and gaped at him when he walked into the recovery room and started throwing orders around. The army sure lost a great leader when he was mustered out after his tour of duty. He made captain, at that."

"Did…Glenna come, too?" she had to ask.

"He hasn't seen Glenna since you left town," Vivian said quietly. "He doesn't talk about her, either."

Natalie didn't comment. She was sure that Mack was trying to heal a guilt complex, although he had no reason to feel guilty. He'd made a wrong assumption and accused her of something she hadn't done, but he hadn't caused her to be stabbed. That had been her own lack of foresight in stepping into a situation she wasn't trained to handle. It could have happened anywhere.

For the moment, she nodded and lay back. Vivian left her to find the nurses.

Mack came back with the boys just after lunch. He looked rested. They all did. She supposed they'd taken the opportunity to catch a little sleep in a real bed.

The boys only stayed for a few minutes, having discovered

a mall near the hospital where they could look over the video games. Vivian went to the hospital cafeteria to get herself a salad for lunch. Mack sat in the chair beside the bed and looked at Natalie, who was much more animated than she had been the night before.

He reached out and caught her fingers in his, sending a wicked tingle of sensation through her, and he smiled at her gently. "You look better. How do you feel?"

"Like I've been buffaloed," she said. She was shy with him, as she'd never been. Amazing, considering their history. They knew each other so well, almost intimately, but she couldn't find anything to say to him.

He seemed to realize that. His fingers curled closer into hers and he leaned forward. "The surgeon says you can leave Friday," he told her. "I can take you back on the Learjet if you're not showing any bronchial symptoms."

"The Learjet?"

"I chartered one to bring us down here. The pilot and copilot are staying at my hotel until we're ready to leave."

"That must be costing a fortune," she blurted.

He smiled cynically. "What do you think I'm worth? In addition to a very successful cattle ranch and interests in several businesses, I own shares in half a dozen stocks that skyrocketed since I bought my first shares."

She averted her eyes. "I've got an apartment here," she began.

"You *had* an apartment here."

She stared at him, confused. "What?"

"I told your landlady you weren't coming back," he said flatly. "I had your stuff packed up, carefully, and shipped to Medicine Ridge. I even had your mail collected and filled out a form for it to be forwarded on to you back home."

"You can't!" she exclaimed. "Mack, I have a job here!"

"Oh, yes, I spoke to the principal about that," he continued, maddeningly calm. "They're sorry to lose you, but considering the length of your recovery, they have to have someone come in to replace you. You can reapply if you want to come back. But you won't want to.''

''Of course I'll want to come back!'' she exclaimed, stunned at the changes he'd created, the havoc he'd created in her nice new life. ''You can't do this!''

''I've already done it, Nat,'' he replied, standing to loom over her, still holding her hand. ''And when you have time to think about it, you'll realize that it was the only thing I could do,'' he added somberly. ''Leaving you here alone was never an option, not even if I'd hated you.''

She dropped her eyes to his big, lean hand holding hers. It was tanned, like his face, from the long hours he spent working on the ranch. ''I thought you did hate me, when I left.''

He laughed with pure self-contempt. ''I know you did. Viv was right, I could sure teach you how to jump to conclusions.'' His eye narrowed. He put a hand on the pillow beside her head and leaned close. ''But there are a lot of other things I'd rather teach you.''

''What things?'' she asked breathlessly.

''What I promised I would, when you were seventeen.'' His mouth brushed her lips as gently as a breath, lingering, tasting, arousing. ''Don't you remember, Natalie? I said that, when the time came, I was going to teach you how to make love.''

Chapter 10

Natalie couldn't believe she'd actually heard him say that, and in a tone so tender that she hardly recognized it. It was difficult to think, anyway, with his hard mouth making little tingles of excitement everywhere it touched her face.

"Do you think I'm joking?" he asked when she didn't answer him. He bent, his breath whispering against her parted lips. "All the teasing stopped when Dr. Hayes called me and said you were at the point of death," he added tautly. His head lifted, and he looked into her eyes. "From now on, it's totally serious."

She didn't understand. Her expression told him so.

He brushed his mouth softly over her lips, careful not to take advantage of the situation or cause her even more pain. "I should never have let you leave Medicine Ridge in the first place," he said gruffly.

"You told me I wasn't welcome at the ranch ever again," she admonished, her lower lip trembling.

He actually groaned. He kissed her with something that felt like utter desperation and visibly had to force himself to stop. His hand was faintly unsteady as it pushed back her disheveled hair and traced her oval face. "I thought you went from me to him," he confessed huskily. "I couldn't bear the thought."

Her expression lightened. Her heart seemed to lift. For the first time, she reached to touch his hard mouth. "As if I could," she said with wistful sadness.

He brought her palm to his lips and kissed it hungrily. "Weeks of misery," he said heavily, "all because Vivian and I jumped to conclusions."

"It's hard to trust people. I ought to know." She searched his one beautiful eye slowly. She was uncertain with him, hesitant. The medicine was still affecting her, and she was wary of his sudden affection. She didn't trust it. Worse, she was remembering her past. There had never been a person she loved that she didn't lose. First her parents and then Carl; even if Carl hadn't been in love with her, he'd been her first real taste of it.

"Such a somber expression," he said gently. "What are you thinking?"

"That I've lost everybody I ever loved," she whispered involuntarily, shivering.

His head lifted and he looked straight into her wide, worried eyes. "You won't lose me," he said quietly.

Her heart ran wild. Now she was certain that she was hearing things. She opened her mouth to ask him to say it again, but just as she did, the nurse came in to check her vitals. Mack only smiled at her frustration and went in the hall to stretch his legs.

When he came back, it was as if he hadn't said anything outrageous at all. He started outlining travel plans, and by the time he finished, Vivian and the boys were back and conversation remained general.

Natalie's lungs were clear by Friday morning, and the surgeon, Dr. Hayes, released her for travel home in the Learjet. Mack lifted her out of the wheelchair at the hospital entrance and into the hired car, which they took to the airport. Less than an hour later, they were airborne, and by late afternoon, they were landing in Medicine Ridge.

The foreman had driven the Lincoln to the airport and had another ranch hand follow him in one of the ranch trucks. That made enough room for the Learjet's weary passengers to ride in the car to the ranch house. There, Mack picked Natalie up in his arms and, holding her just a little too close, he mounted the front steps and carried her over the threshold.

He glanced at her with a faintly possessive smile as he stopped just briefly in the vestibule to search her soft eyes.

"You don't have to carry me," she whispered, aware that the boys had headed straight for the kitchen and Vivian had gone ahead of them upstairs to open the guest room door for them.

"Why not?" he mused, bending to brush her mouth lazily with his. "It's good practice."

Practice for what, she wondered wearily, but she didn't question the odd remark. She moved her arm and grimaced as her whole side protested. The wound was still painful.

"Sorry," he said gently. "I keep forgetting the condition you're in. We'll go right on up."

He carried her easily up the long, graceful staircase to the guest room that adjoined his bedroom. She gave him a worried look.

"I'm not having you at the other end of the house in this condition," he told her as he passed Vivian and went into the airy room with its canopied double bed, where he gently put her down. "I'm going to leave the connecting door open, as well. If you need me in the night, all you have to do is call me. I'm a light sleeper." He glanced at his sister with a speaking glance. "Something I can't say for anybody else in this family."

Vivian grimaced. "I do eventually wake up," she said defensively.

"I've got your pain medication in my pocket," he added.

"If you need it at bedtime, I'll make sure you get it. Vivian can help you into a gown."

"Something nice and modest," Vivian murmured, tongue in cheek, with a wicked glance at her brother.

"Good idea," he said imperturbably. He paused at the door and that good eye twinkled. "And I'll wear pajamas for a change."

Vivian chuckled at Natalie's flushed cheeks as Mack left them alone. "You're in no condition for any hanky-panky," she reminded her friend. "So stop worrying and just concentrate on getting well. You'll never convince me that you won't feel safer with Mack a few yards away in the night."

"I will," Natalie had to admit. "But I still feel like I'm imposing."

"Family doesn't impose," her friend shot right back. "Now let's get you into something light and comfortable, and then I'll go and see what's on the menu for supper. I don't know about you, but I'm starved!"

It came as a surprise when Mack brought a tray to her room and sat down to have his supper with her. But other surprises followed. Instead of going to work in the study, as was his habit, he read her a selection of first-person accounts of life in Montana before the turn of the century. History was her favorite subject, and she loved it. She closed her eyes and listened to his deep voice until she fell asleep.

She'd been heavily sedated in the hospital and she hadn't had nightmares. But her first night in a comfortable bed, she relived the stabbing. She was lifted close to a warm, comforting chest and held very gently while soothing endearments were whispered into her ear. At first it felt like a dream. But the heat and muscle of the chest felt very real, like the thick hair that covered it. Her hand moved experimentally in the darkness.

"Mack?" she whispered hesitantly.

"I hope you don't expect to wake up and find any other

man in your bed from now on,'' he murmured sleepily. His big hand smoothed her hair gently. "You had a nightmare, sweetheart. Just a nightmare. Try to go back to sleep.''

She blinked and lifted her face just enough to look around. It was her bedroom, but Mack was under the covers with her and had apparently been there for some time.

He pulled her down and held her as close as he dared. "Did you really think I meant to leave you alone in here after what you've been through?'' he asked somberly.

"But what will the family think?'' she asked worriedly.

"That I love you, probably.''

She was so drowsy that she couldn't make sense of the words. "Oh.''

"Which is why we're getting married, as soon as you're back on your feet.''

She wondered if painkillers could make people hallucinate. "Now I know I'm still asleep,'' she murmured to herself.

"No such luck. Try to sleep before I do something stupid. And for the record, my sister's idea of a modest nightgown is sick. Really sick. I can feel your skin through that damned thing!''

He probably could. She could certainly feel his chest against her breasts much better than she was comfortable doing. But she still wasn't quite awake. Her fingers curved into the thicket of hair that covered his breastbone. "What sort of stupid thing were you thinking of trying?'' she asked conversationally.

"This.'' His hand found the tiny buttons that held the bodice together and efficiently slipped them so that she was lying skin to skin against his chest.

She felt her nipples go hard at once, and she gasped with the heated rush of sensation that made her heart race.

"That's exactly how I feel,'' he murmured dryly, "a few inches lower.''

It took her a few seconds to realize what he was saying, and she was glad that the darkness hid her face. "You pig!'' she exclaimed.

He chuckled. "I can't resist it. You do rise to the bait like a trophy fish," he commented. "You'll get used to it. I've been blinder than I look, but a lot of things became clear when that surgeon phoned me. The main one was that you belong to me. I'm not a perfect physical specimen, and I've cornered the market on dependents, but you could do worse."

"There's nothing wrong with you," she said quietly. "You have a slight disability."

"We both know I could go blind eventually, Natalie," he said, speaking to her as he never had before. "But I think we could cope with that, if we had to."

"Of course we could," she replied.

His hand smoothed her hair. "The boys and Vivian love you, and you love them. We may have disagreements, but we'll be a family, just the same. A big family, if we all have children," he added, chuckling. "But children will be a bonus."

Her hand flattened on his chest. "I'd like to have a child with you," she said daringly. She felt his heart jump when she said it. "Would you like a son or a daughter?" she added.

"I'd like anything we get," he said quietly. "And so would you."

That sounded permanent. She smiled and couldn't stop smiling. Children meant a commitment.

"Yes. So would I," she said, closing her eyes with a long, heartfelt sigh of contentment.

His hand tensed on her hair. "I wouldn't do too much of that," he cautioned.

"What?"

"I can feel every cell of your body from the waist up, Nat," he said in a strained tone. "And I've gone hungry for a while. You aren't up to a passionate night. Not yet."

"That last bit sounds promising," she murmured.

"I'll make you a promise," he replied. "When you're in a condition to appreciate it, I'll make you glad you waited for me."

"I already am, Mack," she whispered. "I love you more than the air I breathe."

For a few seconds, he didn't say anything. Then he turned, and his mouth found hers in the darkness in a kiss that was hard and hungry and passionate but so tender that it touched her heart. But after a few seconds, when one of his legs slid against hers almost involuntarily, he stiffened and abruptly rolled over onto his back beside her, groaning as he laughed.

"I knew this was a bad idea," he sighed.

Her body was tingling with delicious sensations. She pulled herself into a sitting position, grimacing with discomfort. "Well, there goes that brilliant idea," she murmured, holding her rib cage as she eased back down.

"What brilliant idea?" he asked.

"I was going to see if I could—" She stopped dead when she realized what she was about to say. "I mean, I..."

There was a highly amused sound from beside her. "If you got on top, Nat, I'd still have to hold you there, and after the first few seconds, I wouldn't be gentle. We'd reopen that wound and the pain would be vicious."

She swallowed. "Just a thought. Forget I mentioned it."

He laughed tenderly, bending to kiss her briefly. "I'll try," he said softly. "Thanks for the thought, anyway. But this isn't the time or the place. First we get married," he continued. "And then we can make all sorts of discoveries about each other."

Her heart was still racing. "It's exciting to think about that."

"For both of us," he admitted. "But we'd better quit right now, while we're ahead." He bent and brushed his mouth softly over a hard nipple, lingering to taste it with his tongue.

She caught her breath and he lifted his head to look at her in the soft glow of the small night-light.

"I like that," she whispered.

"Me, too." He was hesitating. This was a bad idea. One of the worst he'd ever had. But he was bending to her body while he was thinking it. His mouth covered her breast again, very gently, and one lean hand smoothed down her body to ease her gown up. He traced her upper thigh with slow, expert movements, making lazy and exciting forays inside it under the gown.

She started trembling. Her hands hesitated on his shoulders while she let her mind go blank except for the pleasure he was giving her. It had been so long. While she was thinking it, she said it.

"So long," he breathed urgently. "Yes, Nat. Too long!"

Her hands went between them to his broad chest and caressed him with delight, enjoying the thickness of hair and the warm muscles under it.

She felt his body tense and his hand move to a much more intimate exploration. She tried to catch his wrist, but it was too sweet to deny. She gave in, moaning as she felt the most exquisite sensations pulse through her.

She was drowning in pleasure. It was so intense that she barely felt him take her hand and guide it down his body. He'd unsnapped his pajamas and she was inside them, discovering the major difference between men and women with a fascination that was going to make her die of embarrassment sooner or later. For the moment, though, it was exciting to touch him that way. She couldn't have dreamed of doing that with anyone else.

He shifted restlessly, enticing her slow tracing to grow in confidence as he groaned aloud at her breast.

"It won't hurt you, will it?" she whispered shakily.

"What you're doing?" He shivered and his mouth grew hungry at her breast, making her moan, as well. "I'm in agony. No, don't stop!" he said quickly, catching her hand before it withdrew. "Don't stop, baby," he whispered, moving to cover her mouth with his. "I love feeling you touch me! I love it!"

She opened her lips to speak, and he invaded them as his hand moved into a more intimate exploration, one that caused her whole body to spin off into a realm she'd never known existed.

She was moving in a helpless rhythm, helping him, enticing him to continue. Her eyes opened and his was there, seeing her pleasure, watching.

"This is how it feels when a man and a woman go all the way," he whispered huskily, and before she could question the blunt statement, his touch became urgent and invasive, and she seemed to explode into a thousand pulsating, white-hot fragments under his fascinated scrutiny.

She clutched his shoulders, shivering in the aftermath, her open mouth against his bare shoulder. Seconds later, she was crying. Her chest hurt again, but her whole body felt as if it had been caressed to heaven.

"Mack," she whimpered. "Oh, Mack!"

He was kissing her, soft, undemanding caresses all over her face and throat, down to her still taut breasts and back up again. She could feel his body against her without a stitch of clothing in the way. And only then did she realize that her gown was lying on the floor somewhere.

She didn't remember the clothes being removed. She only remembered the throbbing pleasure that even in memory made her tremble.

"When we have each other, we're going to set fires," he whispered into her ear.

"I want to," she breathed into his lips. Her hands smoothed his cheeks as she looked at him with caressing eyes. "I want to right now." Her hips moved against his, feeling the hard thrust of him that he made no effort to hide.

"So do I. More than you realize," he replied tersely. "But we're not going one step further than this until you're completely healed and we're married."

"Mack!" she groaned.

"You can't take my weight," he said. "Even if you lie over me, it would be more violent than this when I went into you. And once I started, I'd lose control."

Her gasp was audible. Word pictures formed in her mind and made her flush in the dim light.

"You're still a virgin," he continued huskily. "No matter how much I arouse you, it's probably going to be uncomfortable. But I want you to know what it's going to feel like when you adjust to me. I don't want you afraid of me on our wedding night."

"As if I could be...after that," she whispered, pushing her face into his throat. "Oh, it was...glorious!"

"Watching you was glorious," he said roughly. "But we have to stop. I won't take my pleasure at the expense of your pain."

He got up abruptly, pausing to help her into her gown before he picked up his pajama trousers. He turned toward her deliberately, watching her avert her eyes.

"Are you afraid to look at me?" he asked gently.

She grimaced. "I'm sorry. It's...difficult."

He laughed, but it wasn't mocking laughter. "All right, chicken." She heard his pajama trousers snap, unusually loud in the room, before he climbed into bed beside her and drew her demurely to his side.

"You're going to stay with me all night?" she whispered breathlessly.

"All night, every night, if I have to put a chastity belt on you to protect you until we're married," he said wickedly. "And I may. I want you excessively."

She nuzzled her face against his shoulder. "I felt like that, too. I didn't expect to. I've never known what it was to want someone until you started making passes at me."

"I couldn't help it," he sighed. "I'd reached the end of my patience."

"What do you mean?"

He kissed the tip of her nose. "Later. I've got work to do tomorrow. We both have to get some sleep. Okay?"

She sighed, as close to heaven as she'd ever dreamed of being. "Okay, Mack."

She let her sated body relax and curled into him, closing her eyes. He gathered her as close as he dared and pulled the covers up.

"And don't brood over what I just did to you," he murmured firmly. "It's part of the courtship ritual. We'll restrain ourselves until it's legal. In the meantime, you and Vivian can plan the wedding."

She moved drowsily. "Are you really serious?"

"Deadly," he said, and he wasn't laughing. "I wanted you when you were seventeen and I want you now. Somewhere in the middle, I fell in love without realizing it. These past few weeks have been the purest hell I've ever known. I don't want to go through them again."

"Neither do I." She touched his face in the darkness. "I'll be the best wife in the world, I promise I will. I'll take care of you until we die."

He swallowed hard. "I'll take care of you, too, Natalie," he whispered. "And I'll never stop loving you. Not even when they lay me down in the dark."

She pressed her mouth against his bare shoulder and her hands clung to him. "Not without me, you don't. Where you go, I go. No matter where."

He couldn't manage another word. He kissed her forehead with breathless tenderness and wrapped her close in the darkness.

The wedding took a lot of planning. It had to be small, because Natalie didn't recover as fast as she'd hoped to. But it had to be big enough to accommodate everyone who wanted to see them married, and that meant having it at church. They settled on the local Presbyterian church, and Natalie decided to have a traditional white wedding gown and to let Vivian be maid of honor. Mack decided to have two best men so that both his brothers could stand up with them. It was unconventional, but very much a family affair.

With Mack in a dark suit and Natalie in her elegant puffy-sleeved white silk dress with a long veil and a bouquet of white roses, they were married. They exchanged rings and when Mack lifted the veil to look at her for the first time as his wife, tears rained down her face as he bent and kissed her more tenderly than he ever had before. They looked at each other with expressions that brought tears to the eyes of some of the matrons in the congregation. Afterward, there was the mad dash out the door—done leisurely to accommodate Natalie's still slow pace—and the rice and ribbons. It was traditional in that respect, at least, and in the reception in the fellowship hall with the cakes and punch.

"You made the most beautiful bride in the world, Nat," Vivian said as she kissed her warmly after the ceremony. "I'm so glad things worked out, in spite of me."

Natalie laughed warmly. "We both have a lot to learn about life. Besides," she added, "every bad experience has a silver lining. Look at what mine has produced. And not only for me," she added wryly.

Vivian wrinkled her nose as she smiled. "Imagine me, in nursing school," she chuckled. "But the nurses in Dallas said I was a natural, and I think I am. I love the work, the equipment, everything. I daresay if I study hard, I'll make a decent nurse."

"You could make a decent doctor, if you wanted to," Mack added as he joined them to slip a possessive arm around his new wife. "We can afford medical school."

"I know that," Vivian said. "But I'm not really keen on spending ten years in school, just the same. Besides," she said with a grin, "everyone knows that the nurses are the real power in hospitals!"

Natalie laughed. "You certainly would be."

Mack kissed his sister's cheek. "You've changed a lot in the past few months," he pointed out. "I'm very proud of you."

Vivian flushed with pleasure. "I'm proud of you, too, big brother. Even though it took you so long to realize that marriage isn't a trap."

He searched her face quietly. "I was afraid that it might be too much responsibility for Natalie to take on. But uncertainty is part of life. Families band together and get through the bad times."

"Indeed they do," Vivian seconded. "I'm so glad we all had a second chance. Look what wonderful things we've done with it!"

"And the most wonderful is only a few hours away," Mack whispered in Natalie's ear a few minutes later as they were preparing to leave on their brief honeymoon to Cancún.

Natalie pressed her hand against his cheek and felt him lift and turn it to press his lips to the palm. "I've waited a long time for you," she said cheekily. "You said you'd be worth it."

He chuckled. "Wait and see."

They had Vivian and the boys drive them to the Medicine Ridge airport, where they took the Learjet to Cancún. They were booked into a luxury hotel on the long island just off the mainland, with one of the most beautiful sugary white beaches in the world. It looked like paradise to Natalie.

"It's so beautiful," she kept repeating after they'd checked in and were standing on their private balcony. "It looks like a picture postcard!"

"You can't swim just yet," he reminded her. "But would you like to go and walk on the beach?"

She turned to him and smiled softly. "Would you?"

He pursed his lips and gave her lithe body in the peach silk dress a long and ardent scrutiny. "I think we both know what *I'd* like to do," he mused. "But I'll humor you."

"It would be nice to look for shells," she said. "And besides, it's not dark yet."

He blinked. "I beg your pardon?"

"It's not dark. I mean, it's broad daylight." She hesitated, because he wasn't getting it at all. She flushed a little. "I couldn't possibly take off my clothes in the light and do... that...in bed with you looking at me!"

Chapter 11

He stared at her with utter astonishment. "My God!"

He looked as if she'd thrown a pie in his face. She put her hands on her hips. "My God, what?" she demanded. He sure was acting funny.

He took the tourist booklet out of her hands and put it on the round table inside the sliding door. He pulled her to him, very gently, and bent to her mouth.

It was the first time he'd kissed her with intent, as a lover instead of a fiancé. Despite their intimacy her first night back at the Killain house, she hadn't dreamed there were such deep levels of intimacy in a simple kiss, until she felt her knees buckle and her body begin to burn with sensations she'd never felt.

She held onto his arms as his big, warm hands began a slow, teasing exploration of her figure that rose to just under her breasts, and around them, without touching them at all. After a few seconds, her body began to follow them, to entice them and finally to plead for the teasing touch that he denied her. When it came, when she felt his hands close around them, she moaned harshly and caught his wrists to hold his hands there.

It was like that night he'd touched her so intimately and

taught her the sensations her untried body could feel with him. He'd taken her to heights that she'd dreamed about and moaned hungrily over in the time before the wedding. He hadn't come very close to her in the meantime, apparently dead serious about abstaining until the rings were in place. He had continued to share her bed, but with the hall door cracked open and a resistance to all her flirting that made her reel. He was affectionate, gentle, even tender—but there was nothing indiscreet or urgent. Until now.

She never felt him ease her down on the bed. Each caress was followed by one that was more enticing, more teasing, more provocative. Her world narrowed to the needs of her body. She'd gone hungry for him in recent days. She ached to have him against her. She wanted his hands on her bare skin. She wanted his eyes on her. She wanted utter, absolute possession. She arched her back and ground her mouth into his, her hands trembling as they locked behind his head and guided those expert lips to her breasts. They were bare, although she didn't realize it until his mouth fastened hard onto a taut nipple and began to suckle it. She made a sound that she didn't recognize and twisted up to prolong the sweet agony of the contact. It had been so long. Too long. Ages too long!

In the tense, lazy minutes that followed, she was all too eager to shed her clothing, because her body was hungry for his mouth and his hands. They felt warm in the faint chill of the air conditioner, but she was blind to the light that flowed in through the venetian blinds as he ripped the cover off the bed and pushed the pillows after it. His body moved lazily against hers between urgent unfastening and unbuttoning. He managed to get the fabric out of the way and follow it with two pairs of shoes in a blind, throbbing heat that had both of them out of their minds with desire.

"I thought I'd go mad before the ceremony," he said against her breasts. "I ached like a boy before his first time. All I could think about was that night we lay naked together in your bed, and you let me satisfy you!"

"I thought about it, too," she groaned, clinging to him. "I want it again. I want you!"

"I want you, too," he said huskily, suckling her a little roughly in his ardor. "More than you realize!"

He lifted away from her for a minute, his expression barely controlled, tense. He looked at her nudity with raging desire while he gauged her readiness for what was to come. He traced a torturous path down her taut body and touched her blatantly, his eye narrow and glittery.

"Yes, you're ready," he breathed.

She wondered how he knew, but before she could ask, he was moving her closer to him with an expertise she couldn't begin to match.

He rolled onto his side, pulling her between his long, powerful legs. His hands settled on her slender hips, moving her against the hard thrust of him in an arousing rhythm as he played hungrily with her soft, parted lips.

One of his long legs eased between both of hers in a teasing motion that was even more arousing than the play of his warm hands on her bare skin. She shivered and tried to get closer.

"Don't rush it," he said tenderly. "I have to be slow, so that I don't hurt you too much. Let me show you what I want you to do."

He guided her with his hips until she was right up against him in an intimacy they'd never shared unclothed. Her eyes widened as she felt him in the most intimate place of all. She jerked a little at the unfamiliar closeness.

"That's it, sweetheart," he coaxed, both hands on her hips, drawing her over him tenderly so that he moved slowly against the faint barrier she could feel.

Her hands bit into his hard arms. She stared at him, fascinated at the play of expressions on his taut features as his body began to invade hers with the advent of a sharp, unexpected pain. He hesitated, and his hand went between them, working magic on her tense muscles.

She began to shiver with the onrush of pleasure, diverted

from the pain. He was so blatant with his ardor that she lost the last vestiges of fear and began to move with him, hungry, greedy for more of the fierce pleasure he was teaching her.

"It won't hurt for long," he promised as he began to move closer. "I'll be careful with you."

"I don't care," she choked, pushing against him in an agony of need. Her eyes closed on a sob. "Oh, please, Mack! It aches so!"

"Natalie," he groaned, losing his patience in the heated brushing of her thighs against his. He brought her against him hard while his mouth ground into hers. He felt her body open to him completely, hesitate, flinch briefly.

His eye opened and looked into both of hers, but she wasn't hesitating, she wasn't protesting. Her eyes were blind with passion, her face flushed with desire.

His hands contracted while he watched her face. She gasped at the slow, deep, sweet invasion and moaned sharply as her body adjusted to this new and wonderful intimacy.

"Don't tense," he whispered.

"I'm not!" she whispered back, swallowing hard. "It feels..." Her eyes closed and she gasped. "So good, Mack! So...good! So good!"

She was sobbing with every fierce movement of his hips, her hands clutching at him, her body following the quick, hard dance of his in the silence of the room. Spirals of pleasure were running through her like flames, lifting her, turning her against him. She felt him inside her and the pleasure began to pulse, like the quick, sharp beat of her heart as he moved in a deep, throbbing rhythm. She had a glimpse of his face going taut, and she heard his breath become torturous as the movement increased in fury and insistence.

She was reaching for some incredibly sweet peak of pleasure. It was there, it was...there. If only she could find the right position, the right movement, the right...yes! She lifted to him in an arch, gasping.

"There?" he whispered. "All right. Here we go. Don't fight it...don't fight it...don't...Natalie!"

His voice throbbed like her body, like the pulse that was beating in her eyes, her brain, her body, a heat that was as close to pain as it was to pleasure. And all at once, it became an unbearably wonderful tension that pulled and pulled and suddenly snapped, throwing her against him in an agony of pleasure. She shivered and felt him shiver as they clung together in the most delicious ecstasy she'd ever experienced in her life.

She heard his voice at her ear, harsh and deep, as his body clenched one last time and finally relaxed, pressing her into the mattress with the weight of him. Her arms curled around his long back and her eyes closed and she smiled, achingly content as she held him like that, heavy and damp and warm, vulnerable in his satiation, on her heart.

All too soon, he leaned up, his gaze holding on her rapt face. He smiled gently. "Well?"

She knew what he was asking. She smiled shyly and hid her face in his warm, damp throat.

He rolled over, still joined to her, holding her close. "How's the rib cage?"

"It's fine," she whispered.

"And what do you think about lovemaking, Mrs. Killain?" he whispered wickedly.

"I think it's wonderful," she blurted. "I never would have believed it could be so sweet. And I was afraid!" she added, laughing.

"I noticed." He kissed her nose. "Are you ready for a shock?"

She looked at him, puzzled. "A shock?"

"Uh-huh."

While she was trying to work it out, he lifted her away from him, and she looked down. Her face went scarlet.

"Now you know, don't you?" he asked with a worldly wisdom she couldn't match. He put her down and got out of bed, magnificently naked and not a bit inhibited. He went to the small icebox and pulled out a bottle of beer, which he took to bed, sprawling on top of the sheets against the headboard.

"Come on," he coaxed, opening his arm to gather her beside him. "You'll get used to it. Marriage is an adventure. You have to expect startling discoveries."

"This is one," she murmured, still shy of him like this.

He chuckled. "I'm just flesh and blood. The mystery will get less mysterious as we go along. We're through the worst of the honeymoon shocks, though."

"Think so?" she mused. "You haven't seen me with my hair in curlers and no makeup yet."

He bent and kissed the tip of her nose. "You're beautiful to me. It won't matter what you wear. Or how you look. I love you. Now more than ever."

He opened the beer and took a sip, putting the bottle to her lips. She made a face.

"It isn't good beer," he agreed. "But it's cold and good for the sort of thirst we've worked up." He took another sip and let his eyes run down the length of her soft body, lingering on the places he'd touched and kissed until she flushed. "You really are a knockout," he murmured. "I knew you were nicely shaped, Mrs. Killain, but you're more than I ever expected."

"That goes for me, too," she said.

He kissed her lips tenderly. "Feel like doing that again?" he whispered. "Or is it going to be uncomfortable?"

She rolled onto her side and slid one of her legs to the inside of his. "It won't be uncomfortable," she whispered. She rubbed her body against him and felt him tense with a sense of pride and accomplishment. "I want you."

The beer bottle barely made it to the table without overturning as he pulled her to him and kissed her with renewed passion. He really shouldn't have been capable of this much desire this soon, but he wasn't going to question a nice miracle. His mouth opened on her eager one, and he forgot the rest of his questions.

                              * * *

That evening, they sat on the balcony after a light supper, drinking cola and watching the moon rise over the Gulf of Mexico. They sat side by side, holding hands and glancing at each other every few seconds to make sure that it was all real.

"In all my dreams, it was never like this," she confessed softly.

"Not in mine, either," he replied gently. "I don't like to leave you even long enough to take a shower." His gaze went hungrily to her face. "I never thought it could be like this, Natalie," he breathed. "Not so that I feel as if we're sewn together by invisible threads."

She drew the back of his big hand to her lips. "This is what they say marriage should be," she said dreamily. "But it's more than I hoped for."

His fingers curled into hers. "I know." He glanced at her hungrily. "You'll never know how I felt when Vivian confessed that she'd lied. I couldn't bear the thought that I'd almost lost you."

"It's all in the past," she said tenderly. "Speaking of your sister, Vivian phoned while you were showering," she said suddenly. "She said that Bob and Charles have gone hunting with that Marlowe man and she was going to spend the weekend cramming for her first test."

"I told the boys not to go off and leave her alone," he said grimly.

"Stop that," she chided. "Vivian's grown, and the boys practically are. You have to stop dictating every move they make."

He glared at her. "Wait until we have kids that age, and tell me that then!" he chided.

She sighed over him, her eyes full of wonderful dreams. "I'd like one of each," she mused. "A boy to look like you, and a girl who'll spend time with me when I'm working in the kitchen or the garden, or who'll be old enough for school when I go back to teaching."

"Planning to?" he asked comfortably.

"Not until the children are old enough to go, too," she said. "We can afford for me to stay home with them while they're small, and I will. When they're old enough to go to school, I'll go back to work."

He brought her hand to his mouth and smiled. "Sensible," he agreed. "And I'll change diapers and give bottles and teach them how to ride."

She studied his handsome face and thought back over all the long years they'd known each other, and the trials they'd faced together. "It's the bad times that bring us close," she commented softly.

"Yes," he said. "Like fire tempering steel. We've seen the best and worst of each other, and we have enough in common that even if we didn't have the best sex on two continents, we'd still make a good marriage."

She pursed her lips. "As it is," she said, "we'll make an extraordinary one."

"I couldn't agree more." He lifted his can of soda and she lifted hers, and they made a toast.

Out on the bay, a cruise ship was just coming into port, its lights making a fiesta of the darkness, a jeweled portrait in the night. Natalie felt like that inside, like a holiday ship making its way to a safe harbor. The orphan finally had a home where she belonged. She clasped her husband's hand tight in her own and sighed with pure joy.

* * * * *

CIRCLE OF GOLD

Chapter 1

Kasie Mayfield was excited. Her gray eyes were brimming with delight as she sat in the sprawling living room at the Double C Ranch in Medicine Ridge, Montana. There was a secretarial position available on the mammoth Double C, and she had the necessary qualifications. She was only twenty-two, but she had a certificate from secretarial school and plenty of initiative. Besides all that, the position was secretary to John Callister, the second son of the well-known family that headed not only a publishing empire in New York City, but a cattle empire out West.

There was a very interesting story about the ranch in a magazine that Kasie was reading while she waited her turn to be interviewed. The elder Callisters lived in New York, where they published, among others, a famous sports magazine. When they weren't in the city, they lived in Jamaica on an ancestral estate. The Callister who had founded the American branch of the family had been a British duke. He bought an obscure little magazine in New York City in 1897 and turned it into a publishing conglomerate. One of his sons had emigrated to Montana and founded the ranch. It eventually passed to Douglas Callister, who had raised the boys, Gilbert and

John. Nobody talked about why the uncle had been given custody of both boys and left them the ranch when he died. Presumably it was some dark family secret. Apparently there
wasn't a lot of contact between the boys and their parents.

Gilbert, the eldest at thirty-two, had been widowed three
years ago. He had two young daughters, Bess, who was five,
and Jenny, who was four. John had never married. He was a
rodeo champion and did most of the traveling that accompanied showing the ranch's prizewinning pedigree black Angus
bulls. Gil was the power in the empire. He was something of
a marketing genius, and he dealt with the export business and
sat on the boards of two multinational corporations. But mostly
he ran the ranch, all thirty thousand acres of it.

There was a photograph of him in the magazine, but she
didn't need it to know what he looked like. Kasie had gotten
a glimpse of him on her way into the house to wait for her
turn to be interviewed. One glimpse had been enough. It
shocked her that a man who didn't even know her should glare
at her so intently.

A more conceited woman might have taken it for masculine
interest. But Kasie had no ego. No, that tall, lanky blond man
hadn't liked her, and made no secret of it. His pale blue eyes
under that heavy brow had pierced her skin. She wouldn't get
the job. He'd make sure of it.

She glanced at the woman next to her, a glorious blonde
with big brown eyes and beautiful legs crossed under a thigh-
high skirt. Then she looked at her own ankle-length blue
jumper with a simple gray blouse that matched her big eyes.
Her chestnut hair was in a long braid down her back. She wore
only a little lipstick on her full, soft mouth, and no rouge at
all on her cheeks. She had a rather ordinary oval face and a
small, rounded chin, and she wore contact lenses. She wasn't
at all pretty. She had a nice figure, but she was shy and didn't
make the most of it. It was just as well that she had good office
skills, she supposed, because it was highly unlikely that anybody would ever want to actually marry her. She thought of

her parents and her brother and had to fight down tears. It was so soon. Too soon, probably. But the job might keep her from thinking of what had happened....

"Miss Mayfield!"

She jumped as her name was called in a deep, authoritative tone. "Yes?"

"Come in, please."

She put a smile on her face as she clutched her small purse in her hands and walked into the paneled office, where plaques and photos of bulls lined the walls and burgundy leather furniture surrounded the big mahogany desk. A man was sitting there, with his pale eyes piercing and intent. A blond man with broad shoulders and a hard, lean face that seemed to be all rocky edges. It was not John Callister.

She stopped in front of the desk with her heart pounding and didn't bother to sit down. Gil Callister was obviously doing the interviews, and now she was sure she wouldn't get the job. She knew John Callister from the drugstore where she'd worked briefly as a stock clerk putting herself through secretarial courses. John had talked to her, teased her and even told her about the secretarial job. He'd have given her a chance. Gil would just shoot her out the door. It was obvious that he didn't like anything about her.

He tossed a pen onto the desk and nodded toward the chair facing it. "Sit down."

She felt vulnerable. The door was closed. Here she was with a hungry tiger, and no way out. But she sat anyway. Never let it be said that she lacked courage. They could throw her into the arena and she would die like a true Roman... She shook herself. She really had to stop reading the Plinys and Tacitus. This was the new millennium, not the first century A.D.

"Why do you want this job?" Gil asked bluntly.

Her thin eyebrows lifted. She hadn't expected the question. "Because John is a dish?" she ventured dryly.

The answer seemed to surprise him. "Is he?"

"When I worked at the drugstore, he was always kind to

me," she said evasively. "He told me about the job, because he knew I was just finishing my secretarial certificate at the vocational-technical school. I got high grades, too."

Gil pursed his lips. He still didn't smile. He looked down at the résumé she'd handed him and read it carefully, as if he was looking for a deficiency he could use to deny her the job. His mouth made a thin line. "Very high grades," he conceded with obvious reluctance. "This is accurate? You really can type 110 words a minute?"

She nodded. "I can type faster than I can take dictation, actually."

He pushed the résumé aside and leaned back. "Boyfriends?"

She was nonplussed. Her fingers tightened on her purse. "Sir?"

"I want to know if you have any entanglements that might cause you to give up the job in the near future," he persisted, and seemed oddly intent on the reply.

She shifted restlessly. "I've only ever had one real boyfriend, although he was more like a brother. He married my best friend two months ago. That was just before I moved to Billings," she added, mentioning the nearby city, "to live with my aunt. So, I don't date much."

She was so uncomfortable that she almost squirmed. He didn't know about her background, of course, or he wouldn't need to ask such questions. Modern women were a lot more worldly than Kasie. But she'd said that John was a dish. She flushed. Good grief, did he think she went around seducing men or something? Was that why he didn't want her in his house? Her expression was mortified.

He averted his eyes. "You have some odd character references," he said after a minute, frowning at them. "A Catholic priest, a nun, a Texas Ranger and a self-made millionaire with alleged mob ties."

She only smiled demurely. "I have unique friendships."

"You could put it that way," he said, diverted. "Is the millionaire your lover?"

She went scarlet and her jaw dropped.

"Oh, hell, never mind," he said, apparently disturbed that he'd asked the question and uncomfortable at the reaction it drew. "That's none of my business. All right, Kasie..." He hesitated. "Kasie. What's it short for?"

"I don't know," she blurted out. "It's my actual name."

One eye narrowed. "The millionaire's name is K.C.," he pointed out. "And he's at least forty."

"Thirty-seven. He saved my mother's life, while she was carrying me," she said finally. "He wasn't always a millionaire."

"Yes, I know, he was a professional soldier, a mercenary." His eyes narrowed even more. "Want to tell me about it?"

"Not really, no," she confided.

He shook his head. "Well, if nothing else, you'll be efficient. You're also less of a distraction than the rest of them. There's nothing I hate more than a woman who wears a skirt up to her briefs to work and then complains when men stare at her if she bends over. We have dress codes at our businesses and they're enforced—for both sexes."

"I don't have any skirts that come up to my...well, I don't wear short ones," she blurted out.

"So I noticed," he said with a deliberate glance at her long dress.

She fumbled with her purse while he went over the résumé one last time. "All right, Kasie, you can start Monday at eight-thirty. Did John tell you that the job requires you to live here?"

"No!"

His eyebrows arched. "Not in his room, of course," he added just to irritate her, and then looked satisfied when she blushed. "Miss Parsons, who has charge of my daughters, lives in. So does Mrs. Charters who does the cooking and housekeeping. We have other part-time help that comes infrequently. Board and meals are provided by us, in addition to your sal-

ary.'' He named a figure that made Kasie want to hold on to
something. It was astronomical compared to what she'd made
working at the drugstore part-time. ''You'll be a private secretary,'' he added. ''That means you may have to travel with
us from time to time.''

''Travel?'' Her face softened.

''Do you like to travel?'' he asked.

''Oh, yes. I loved it when I was little.''

She wondered by the look he gave her if he assumed that
her parents had been wealthy. He could not know, of course,
that they were both deceased.

''Do you want the job?'' he asked.

''Yes,'' she said.

''All right. I'll tell the others they can leave.'' He got to his
feet, elegant and lithe, moving with a grace that was unequaled
in Kasie's circle of acquaintances. He opened the office door,
thanked the other young women for coming and told them that
the position had been filled. There was a shuffle of feet, some
murmuring, and the front door closed.

''Come on, Kasie,'' Gil said. ''I'll introduce you to...''

''Daddy!'' came a wail from the end of the hall. A little girl
with disheveled long blond hair came running and threw herself at Gil, sobbing.

He picked her up, and his whole demeanor changed. ''What
is it, baby?'' he asked in the most tender tone Kasie had ever
heard. ''What's wrong?''

''Me and Jenny was playing with our dollies on the deck
and that bad dog came up on the porch and he tried to bite
us!''

''Where's Jenny?'' he demanded, immediately threatening.

A sobbing little voice answered him as the younger girl
came toddling down the hall rubbing her eyes with dirty little
fists. She reached up to Gil, and he picked her up, too, oblivious to her soiled dress and hands.

''Nothing's going to hurt my babies. Did the dog bite either
of you?'' Gil demanded.

"No, Daddy," Bess said.

"Bad doggie!" Jenny sobbed. "Make him go away!"

"Of course I will!" Gil said roughly, kissing little cheeks with a tenderness that made Kasie's heart ache.

A door opened and John Callister came down the hall, looking very unlike the friendly man Kasie knew from the drugstore. His pale eyes were glittering in his lean, dark face, and he looked murderous.

"Are they all right?" he asked Gil, pausing to touch the girls' hair. "It was that mangy cur that Fred Sims insisted on bringing with him when he hired on. I got between it and the girls and it tried to bite me, too. I called Sims up to the house and told him to get rid of it and he won't, so he's fired."

"Here." Gil handed his girls to his brother and started down the hall with quick, measured steps.

John stared after him. "Maybe Sims will make it to his truck before Gil gets him," he murmured. "But I wouldn't bet on it. Are my babies all right?" he asked, kissing their little damp cheeks as the girls clung to either shoulder.

"Bad old doggie," Bess sobbed. "Our Missie never bites people!"

"Missie's a toy collie," John explained to a silent Kasie with a smile. "She lives indoors. Nothing like that vicious dog Sims keeps. We've had trouble from it before, but Sims was so good with horses that we put up with it. Not any more. We can't let it endanger the girls."

"If it would come right up on the porch and try to bite them, it doesn't need to be around children," Kasie agreed.

The girls looked at her curiously.

"Who are you?" Bess asked.

"I'm Kasie," she replied with a smile. "Who are you?"

"I'm Bess," the child replied. "That's Jenny. She's just four," she added, indicating the smaller child, whose hair was medium-length and more light brown than blond.

"I'm very glad to meet you both," Kasie said, smiling

warmly. "I'm going to be Mr. Callister's secretary," she added with an apologetic glance at John. "Sorry."

"Why are you sorry?" John asked amusedly. "I only flog secretaries during full moons."

Her eyes crinkled with merriment and she grinned.

"Gil won't let me hire secretaries because I have such a bad track record," John confessed. "The last one turned out to be a jewel thief. You, uh, don't like jewels?" he added deliberately.

She chuckled. "Only costume jewelry. And unless you wear it, we shouldn't have a problem."

There was a commotion outside and John grimaced. "He'll come back in bleeding, as usual," he muttered. "I just glare at people. Gil hits." He gave Kasie a wicked grin. "Sometimes he hits me, too."

The girls giggled. "Oh, Uncle Johnny," Bess teased, "Daddy never hits you! He won't even hit us. He says little children shouldn't be hitted."

"Hit," Kasie corrected absently.

"Hit," Bess parroted, and grinned. "You're nice."

"You're nice, too, precious," Kasie said, reaching out to smooth back the disheveled hair. "You've got tangles."

"Can you make my hair like yours?" Bess asked, eyeing Kasie's braid. "And tie it with a pink ribbon?"

The opening of the back door stopped the conversation dead. Gil came back in with his shirt and jeans dusty and a cut at the corner of his mouth. As he came closer, wiping away the blood, his bruised and lacerated knuckles became visible.

"So much for that little problem," he said with cold satisfaction. His eyes were still glittery with temper until he looked at the little girls. The anger drained out of him and he smiled. "Dirty chicks," he chided. "Go get Miss Parsons to clean you up."

John put them down and Bess looked up at her father accusingly. "Miss Parsons don't like little kids."

"Go on. If she gives you any trouble, come tell me," Gil told the girls.

"Okay, Daddy!"

Bess took Jenny's hand and, with a shy grin at Kasie, she drew the other child with her up the winding staircase.

"They like Kasie already," John commented. "Bess said..."

"Miss Parsons takes care of the kids," Gil said shortly. "Show Kasie the way we keep records. She's a computer whiz in addition to her dictation skills. She should be able to get all those herd records onto diskettes for you. Then we can get rid of the paper clutter before we end up buried in it."

"Okay," John said. He hesitated. "Sims get off okay?"

"Sure," Gil said easily. "No problem." He wiped the blood away from his mouth with a wicked look at his brother before he turned and went up the staircase after the children.

John just shook his head. "Never mind. Come on, Kasie. Let's get you started."

Kasie moved into the house that weekend. Most of her parents' things, and her own, were at Mama Luke's, about ten miles away in Billings, Montana, to whom she'd come for refuge after losing her family. She had only the bare necessities of clothing and personal items; it barely filled one small suitcase. When she walked into the ranch house with it, Gil was on the porch with one of his men. He gave her a curious appraisal, dismissing the man.

"Where's the rest of your stuff?" he asked, glancing past her at the small, white used car she drove, which she'd parked beside the big garage. "In the trunk?"

"This is all the stuff I have," she said.

He looked stunned. "Surely you have furniture...?"

"My other things are at my aunt's house. But I don't have much stuff of my own."

He stepped aside to let her go inside, his face curious and

his eyes intent on her. He didn't say a word, but he watched her even more closely from then on.

The first week on the job, she lost a file that Gil needed for a meeting he was flying to in the family Piper plane. It was an elegant aircraft, twin-engine and comfortable. Gil and John could both fly it and did, frequently, trucking the livestock they were showing from one state to the next with employees. Kasie wished she could go with the livestock, right now. Gil was eloquent about the missing file, his deep voice soft and filled with impatience.

"If you'll just be quiet for a minute, Mr. Callister, I'll find it!" she exclaimed finally, driven to insubordination.

He gave her a glare, but he shut up. She rustled through the folders on her desk with cold, nervous hands. But she did find the file. She extended it, sheepishly, grimacing at the look in his eyes.

"Sorry," she added hopefully.

It didn't do any good. His expression was somber and half-angry. His eyes glittered down at her. She thought absently that he looked very nice in a gray vested suit. It suited his fair hair and light eyes and his nice tan. It also emphasized the excellent fitness of his tall, muscular body. Kasie thought idly that he must have women practically stalking him when he went to dinner meetings. He was striking just to look at, in addition to that very masculine aura that clung to him like his expensive cologne.

"Where's John?" he asked.

"He had a date," she said. "I'm trying to cope with the new tax format."

His eyes narrowed. "Surely they taught tax compilation at your school?"

She grimaced. "Well, actually, they didn't. It's a rather specialized skill."

"Buy what you need from the bookstore or the computer

store and have them send me the bill," he said shortly. "If you can't cope, tell me that, too."

She didn't dare. She wouldn't have a job, and she had to support herself. She couldn't expect Mama Luke to do it. "I can cope, sir," she assured him.

His eyes narrowed as he stared down at her. "One thing more," he added curtly. "My girls are Miss Parsons's responsibility, not yours."

"I only read them a story," she began, blushing guiltily.

His eyebrows arched. "I was referring to the way you braided Bess's hair," he said. "I thought it was an isolated incident."

She swallowed. Hardly isolated. The girls were always somewhere close by when Kasie stopped for lunch or her breaks. She shared her desserts with the children and frequently read to them or took them on walks to point out the various sorts of flowers and trees around the ranch house. Gil didn't know that and she'd hoped the girls hadn't said anything. Miss Parsons was curt and bullying with the children, whom she obviously disliked. It was inevitable that they'd turn to Kasie, who adored them.

"Only one story," she lied.

He seethed. "In case you didn't get the message the first time, Kasie, I am not in the market for a wife or a mother for my daughters."

The insult made her furious. She glared up at him, forgetting all her early teachings about turning cheeks and humility. "I came to work here because I need a job," she said icily. "I'm only twenty-two, Mr. Callister," she added. "And I don't have any interest in a man almost old enough to be my father, with a ready-made family to boot!"

His reaction was unexpected. He didn't fire back. He grew very quiet. He turned and went out of the room without another word. A minute later, she heard the front door close and, soon, an engine fire up.

"So there," she added to herself.

* * *

Gil came home from his trip even quieter than when he'd left. There was tension between him and Kasie, because she hadn't forgotten the insulting remark he'd made to her before he left. As if she'd come to work here just so she could chase him. Really! But there was another complication now, as well. Kasie was a nervous wreck trying to keep him from seeing how much time she actually spent with his little girls. She didn't need to worry when he was off on his frequent business trips, but they suddenly stopped. He started sending Brad Dalton, his manager, to seminars and conferences. He stayed home on the pretext of overseeing massive improvements on the property.

It was just after roundup, when the cattle business was taking up a little less of his time. But there were new bunkhouses being built, as well as new wells being dug in the pastures and new equipment brought in for tagging and vaccinations of new calves. The trucks were being overhauled, along with the other farm machinery such as tractors and combines that harvested the grain crops. The barns were repaired, a new silo erected. It was a busy time.

Kasie found herself involved unexpectedly with Gil when John went out of state to show two new bulls at a pedigree competition and Gil's secretary, Pauline Raines, conveniently sprained her thumb and couldn't type.

"I need these yesterday," he said without preamble, laying a thick sheaf of papers beside Kasie's neat little hand on the desk. "Pauline can't do them. She missed the tennis ball and hit her thumb with the tennis racket."

She managed not to make a disparaging comment—barely. She didn't like Pauline any more than Gil's daughters did. The woman was lazy and seductive, and always hanging on Gil like a tie. What little work she actually did was of poor quality and she was pitifully slow as well. She worked at the ranch office near the front of the house three days a week, and Kasie had already inherited a good deal of her work. Pauline spent her time by the pool when Gil wasn't watching. Now, Kasie thought miserably, she was going to end up doing not only John's paperwork, including the unbelievably complex taxes that she was still struggling to understand, but Gil's as well.

"I don't guess she could type with her toes?" she murmured absently.

There was an odd sound, but when she looked up, Gil's hard face was impassive. "How long will it take?" he persisted.

She looked at the pages. They weren't data, as she'd first thought, but letters to various stock producers. They all had different headings, but the same basic body. "Is this all?" she asked with cool politeness.

He glowered at her. "There are fifty of them. They'll have to be done individually..."

"No, they won't," she said gently. "All you have to do—" she opened a new file, selected the option she needed and began typing "—is type the body of the letter once and then just type the various addresses and combine them. An hour's work."

He looked as if he'd been slapped. "Excuse me?"

"This word processor does all that for you," she explained. "It's very simple, really."

He looked angry. "I thought you had to type all fifty individually."

"Only if you're using a prehistoric typewriter and carbon system," she pointed out.

He was really angry now. "An hour?" he repeated.

She nodded. "Maybe less. I'll get right on it," she added quickly, hoping to appease him. Heaven only knew what had set him off, but she recognized that glitter in his eyes.

He left her and went to make some phone calls. When he came back, Kasie was printing the letters out, having just finished the mailing labels. There was a folding machine that made short work of folding the letters. Then all she had to do was stuff, lick, stamp and mail the envelopes.

Gil put on the stamps for her. He watched her curiously. Once, when she looked up into his eyes, it was like an electric shock. Surprised, she dropped her gaze and blushed. Really, she thought, he had a strange effect on her.

"How do you like your job so far?" he asked.

"Very much," she said. "Except for the taxes."

"You'll get used to doing them," he assured her.

"I suppose so."

"Can you manage John's load and mine as well, or do you want me to get a temporary to help you?"

"There isn't a lot," she pointed out. "If I get overwhelmed, I'll say so."

He finished stamping the envelopes and stacked them neatly to one side. "You're very honest. It's unusual in most people." He touched a stamp with a floral motif. "My wife was like that." He smiled. "She said that lies were a waste of time, since they got found out anyway." His eyes were far away. "We were in grammar school together. We always knew that we'd marry one day." The smile faded into misery. "She was a wonderful rider. She rode in the rodeo when she was younger. But a gentle horse ran away with her and a low-lying limb ended her life. Jenny was only a year old when Darlene died. Bess was two. I thought my life was over, too."

Kasie didn't know what to say. It shocked her that a man like Gil would even discuss something so personal with a stranger. Of course, a lot of people discussed even more personal things with Kasie. Maybe she had that sort of face that attracted confidences.

"Do the girls look like her?" she asked daringly.

"Bess does. She was blond and blue-eyed. She wasn't beautiful, but her smile was." His eyes narrowed in painful memory. "They had to sedate me to make me let go of her. I wouldn't believe them, even when they swore to me that no means on earth could save her..." His fingers clenched on top of the envelope and he moved his hand away at once and stood up. "Thanks, Kasie," he said curtly, turning away, as if it embarrassed him to have spoken of his wife at all.

"Mr. Callister," she said softly, waiting until he turned to continue. "I lost…some people three months ago. I understand grief."

He hesitated. "How did they die?"

Her face closed up. "It was…an accident. They were only in their twenties. I thought they had years left."

"Life is unpredictable," he told her. "Sometimes unbearable. But everything passes. Even bad times."

"Yes, that's what everyone says," she agreed.

They shared a long, quiet, puzzling exchange of sorrow before he shrugged and turned away, leaving her to her work.

Chapter 2

Kasie was almost tearing her hair out by the next afternoon. John's mail was straightforward, mostly about show dates and cancellations, transportation for the animals and personal correspondence. Gil's was something else.

Gil not only ran the ranch, but he dealt with the majority of the support companies that were its satellites. He knew all the managers by first names, he often spoke with state and federal officials, including well-known senators, on legislation affecting beef production. Besides that, he was involved in the scientific study of new grasses and earth-friendly pesticides and fertilizers. He worked with resource and conservation groups, even an animal rights group; since he didn't run slaughter cattle and was rabidly proconservation, at least one group was happy to have his name on its board of directors. He was a powerhouse of energy, working from dawn until well after dark. The problem was, every single task he undertook was accompanied by a ton of paperwork. And his part-time secretary, Pauline Raines, was the most disorganized human being Kasie had ever encountered.

John came home late on Friday evening, and was surprised to find Kasie still at work in the study.

He scowled as he tossed his Stetson onto a rack. "What are you doing in here? It's almost ten o'clock! Does Gil know you're working this much overtime?"

She glanced up from the second page of ten that she was trying to type into the computer. None of Pauline's paperwork had ever been keyed in.

She held up the sheaf of paperwork in six files with a sigh. "I think of it as job security," she offered.

He moved around beside the desk and looked over what she was doing. "Good God, he's not sane!" he muttered. "No one secretary could handle this load in a week! Is he trying to kill you?"

"Pauline hurt her thumb," she said miserably. "I get to do her work, too, except that she never put any of the records into the computer. It's got to be done. I don't see how your brother ever found anything in here!"

"He didn't," John said dryly, his pale eyes twinkling. "Pauline made sure of it. She's indispensable, I hear."

Kasie's eyes narrowed. "She won't be for long, when I get this stuff keyed in," she assured him.

"Don't tell her that unless you pay up your life insurance first. Pauline is a girl who carries grudges, and she's stuck on Gil."

"I noticed."

"Not that he cares," John added slowly. "He never got over losing his wife. I'm not sure that he'll ever remarry."

"He told me."

He glanced down at her. "Excuse me?"

"He told me specifically that he didn't want a mother for the girls or a new wife, and not to get my hopes up." She chuckled. "Good Lord, he must be all of thirty-two. I'm barely twenty-two. I don't want a man I'll have to push around in a wheelchair one day!"

"And I don't rob cradles," came a harsh, angry voice from the doorway.

They both jumped as they looked up to see Gil just coming

in from the barn. He was still in work clothes, chaps and boots and a sweaty shirt, with a disreputable old black Stetson cocked over one eye.

"Are you trying to make Kasie quit, by any chance?" John challenged. "Good God, man, it'll take her a week just to get a fraction of the information in these spreadsheets into the computer!"

Gil frowned. He pulled off his hat and ran a hand through his sweaty blond hair. "I didn't actually look at it," he confessed. "I've been too busy with the new bulls."

"Well, you'd better look," John said curtly.

Gil moved to the desk, aware of Kasie's hostile glare. He peered over her shoulder and cursed sharply. "Where did all this come from?" he asked.

"Pauline brought it to me and said you wanted it converted to disk," she replied flatly.

His eyes began to glitter. "I never told her to land you with all this!"

"It needs doing," she confessed. "There's no way you can do an accurate spreadsheet without the comparisons you could use in a computer program. I've reworked this spreadsheet program," she said, indicating the screen, "and made an application that will work for cattle weight gain ratios and daily weighing, as well as diet and health and so forth."

"I'm impressed," Gil said honestly.

"It's what I'm used to doing. Taxes aren't," she added sheepishly.

"Don't look at me," John said. "I hate taxes. I'm not learning them, either," he added belligerently. "Half this ranch is mine, and on my half, we don't do tax work." He nodded curtly and walked out.

"Come back here, you coward!" Gil muttered. "How the hell am I supposed to cope with taxes and all the other routine headaches that you don't have, because you're off somewhere showing cattle!"

John just waved his hand and kept walking.

"Miss Parsons knows taxes inside out," Kasie ventured. "She told me she used to be an accountant."

He glared at her. "Miss Parsons was hired to take care of my daughters." He kept looking at Kasie, and not in any friendly way. It was almost as if he knew...

She flushed. "They couldn't get the little paper ship to float on the fish pond," she murmured uneasily, not looking at him. "I only helped."

"And fell in the pond."

She grimaced. "I tripped. Anybody can trip!" she added in a challenging tone, her gray eyes flashing at him.

"Over their own feet?" he mused.

Actually it had been over Bess's stuffed gorilla. The thing was almost her size and Kasie hadn't realized it was there. The girls had laughed and then wailed, thinking she'd be angry at them. Miss Parsons had fussed for hours when Bess got dirt on her pretty yellow dress. But Kasie didn't scold. She laughed, and the girls were so relieved, she could have cried. They really didn't like Miss Parsons.

He put both hands on his lean hips and studied her with reluctant interest. "The girls tell me everything, Kasie," he said finally. He didn't add that the girls worshiped this quiet, studious young woman who didn't even flirt with John, much less the cowboys who worked for the family. "I thought I'd made it perfectly clear that I didn't want you around them."

She took her hands off the keyboard and looked up at him with wounded eyes. "Why?"

The question surprised him. He scowled, trying to think up a fair answer. Nothing came to mind, which made him even madder.

"I don't have any ulterior motives," she said simply. "I like the girls very much, and they like me. I don't understand why you don't want me to associate with them. I don't have a bad character. I've never been in trouble in my life."

"I didn't think you had," he said angrily.

"Then why can't I play with them?" she persisted. "Miss

Parsons is turning them into little robots. She won't let them play because they get dirty, and she won't play with them because it isn't dignified. They're miserable.''

"Discipline is a necessary part of childhood," he said curtly. "You spoil them."

"For heaven's sake, somebody needs to! You're never here," she added shortly.

"Stop right there, while you still have a job," he interrupted, and his eyes made threats. "Nobody tells me how to raise my kids. Especially not some frumpy little backwoods secretary!"

Frumpy? Backwoods? Her eyes widened. She stood up. She was probably already fired, so he could just get it from the hip. "I may be frumpy," she admitted, "and I may be from the backwoods, but I know a lot about little kids! You don't stick them in a closet until they're legal age. They need to be challenged, made curious about the world around them. They need nurturing. Miss Parsons isn't going to nurture them, and Mrs. Charters doesn't have time to. And you aren't ever here at bedtime, even if you're not away on business," she repeated bluntly. "Whole weeks go by when you barely have time to tell them good-night. They need to be read to, so they will learn to love books. They need constructive supervision. What they've got is barbed wire and silence."

His fists clenched by his side, and his expression darkened. She lifted her chin, daring him to do anything.

"You're an expert on children, I guess?" he chided.

"I took care of one," she said, her eyes darkening. "For several months."

"Why did you quit?"

He was assuming that she'd meant a job. She didn't. The answer to his question was a nightmare. She couldn't bear to remember it. "I wasn't suited to the task," she said primly. "But I won't corrupt your little girls by speaking to them."

He was still glowering. He didn't want Kasie to grow close to the girls. He didn't want her any closer to him than a desk and a computer was. His eyes went involuntarily to the desk piled high with Pauline's undone work. The files were supposed to have been converted to computer months earlier, when he'd hired the woman. He'd assumed that it had been done, because she was always ready with the information he needed. He felt suddenly uneasy.

"Check out Black Ribbon's growth information for me," he said suddenly.

She hesitated, but apparently she was still working for him. She sat down and pulled the information up on the computer. He went to his desk and pulled a spreadsheet from a drawer. He brought it to Kasie and had her compare it with the figures she'd just put into the computer. There was a huge difference, to his favor.

He said a word that caused Kasie's face to grow bright red. That disturbed him, but he didn't allude to it. "I've made modifications to improve what seemed like a deficiency in diet. Now it looks as if it wasn't even necessary. How long will it take you to get the breeding herd information transcribed?"

"Well, I've done about a third of it," she said. "But John has letters and information to be compiled for this new show…"

"You're mine until we get this information on the computer. I'll make it all right with John."

"What about Pauline?" she asked worriedly.

"Pauline is my concern, not yours," he told her.

"Okay, boss. Whatever you say."

He made an odd gesture with one shoulder and gave her a long scrutiny. "I told you to let me know if there was too much work. Why didn't you?"

"I thought I could keep up," she said simply. "I wouldn't have complained as long as I could do it within a couple of weeks, and I can."

"Working fourteen-hour shifts," he chided.

"Well, work is work," she said. "I don't mind. It's not as if I have an active social life or an earthshaking novel to write or anything. And I get paid a duke's ransom as it is."

He frowned. "Why don't you have a social life?"

"Because cowboys stink," she shot right back.

He started to speak, burst out laughing and walked to the door. "Stop that and go to bed. I'll have you some help by morning. Good night, Kasie."

"Good night, Mr. Callister."

He hesitated, turned, studied her, but he didn't speak. He left her tidying up and went upstairs to change out of his work clothes and have a shower.

The next morning, when she went into the office, Pauline was there and so was Gil. They stopped talking when Kasie walked in, so she assumed that they'd been talking about her. Apparently it hadn't been in a friendly way. Pauline's delicate features were drawn in anger and Gil's eyes were narrow and glittery.

"It's about time you got down here!" Pauline said icily.

"It's eight twenty-five," Kasie said, taken aback. "I'm not supposed to be in here until eight-thirty."

"Well, let's get started, then," Pauline said, flopping down at the computer.

"Doing what, exactly?" Kasie asked, disconcerted.

"Teach her how to put information on the computer," Gil said in a voice that didn't invite argument. "And while she's doing that, you can tackle John's work."

Kasie grimaced. Her pupil didn't look eager or willing. It was going to be a long morning.

It was, too. Pauline made the job twice as tedious, questioning every keystroke twice and grumbling—when Gil was out of the office—about having to work with Kasie.

"Look, this wasn't my idea," Kasie assured her. "I could do it myself if Mr. Callister would just let me."

Pauline didn't soften an inch. "You're trying to get his attention, playing up to those kids," she accused. "You want him."

Kasie just looked at her. "I love children," she said quietly. "But I don't want to get married."

"Who said anything about marriage?" Pauline chided.

Kasie averted her eyes. "I needed a job and John needed a secretary," she murmured as she turned a spreadsheet page.

"Funny. You call him John, but Gil is 'Mr. Callister.' Why?"

The younger woman blinked. "John is just a few years older than I am," she replied.

Pauline frowned. "How old are you?"

"Twenty-two."

There was a long pause. "Well!" she said finally. She pursed her lips and entered a number into the computer. "You think Gil is old, do you?"

"Yes." She didn't, really, but it seemed safer to say so. She did, after all, have to work with this perfumed barracuda for the immediate future.

Pauline actually smiled. But only for a minute. "What do I do now?" she asked when she finished entering the last number.

Kasie showed her, faintly disturbed by that smile. Oh, well, she'd figure it out later, maybe.

Pauline went home at five o'clock. By now, she had a good idea of how to use the computer. Practice would hone her skills. Kasie wondered why Gil, who had the lion's share of the work, only had a part-time secretary.

When he came back in, late Saturday night, dressed in evening clothes with a black tie and white ruffled shirt, Kasie was still in the office finalizing the spreadsheets. She looked up, surprised at how handsome he was dressed like that. Even if he wasn't really good-looking, he had a natural authority and grace of carriage that made him stand out. Not to mention a physique that many a Hollywood actor would have coveted.

"I thought I told you to give up this night work," he said curtly.

She spared him a glance while she saved the information onto a diskette. "You won't let me play with the girls. I don't have anything else to do."

"Watch television. We have all the latest movies on pay-per-view. You can watch any you like. Read a book. Take up knitting. Learn Dutch. But," he added with unnatural resentment, "stay out of the office after supper."

"Is that an order?" she asked.

"It damned well is!"

He was absolutely bristling, she thought, frowning as she searched his pale blue eyes. She closed the files and shut down the program, uneasy because he was glowering at her.

She got up, neat and businesslike in her beige pantsuit, with her chestnut hair nicely braided and hanging down her back.

But when she went around the desk to go to the door, he blocked her path. She wasn't used to men this close and she backed up a step, which only made things worse. He was so tall that she wished she were wearing high heels. The top of her head barely came up to his nose.

His pale eyes glittered even more. "Old age isn't contagious," he said with pure venom in his deep voice.

"Sir?"

"And don't call me sir!"

She swallowed. He was spoiling for a fight. She couldn't bear the thought of one. Her early life had been in the middle of a violent battleground, and loud noises and voices still upset her. "Okay," she agreed immediately.

He slammed his hands into his pockets and glared more. "I'm thirty-two. Ten years isn't a generation and I'm not a candidate for Social Security."

"Okay," she repeated uneasily.

"For God's sake, stop agreeing with me!" he snapped.

She started to say "Okay" again, and bit her tongue. She was as rigid as a ruler, waiting for more explosions with her breath trapped in her throat.

He took his hands out of his pockets and they clenched at

his sides as he looked down at her with more conflicting emotions than he'd ever felt. She wasn't beautiful, but there was a tenderness in her that he craved. He hadn't had tenderness in his life since Darlene's untimely death. This young woman made him hungry for things he couldn't grasp. He didn't understand it, and it angered him.

Kasie was wavering between a dash for the door or backing up again. "Do you want me to quit?" she blurted out.

His teeth ground together. "Yes."

She swallowed. "All right. I'll leave in the morning." She moved around him to the door, trying not to take it personally. Sometimes people just didn't like other people.

"No!"

His voice stopped her with her hand on the doorknob.

There was a long pause. Kasie turned, surprised by his indecision. From what she already knew of Gil Callister, he wasn't a man who had trouble making decisions. But he seemed divided about Kasie.

She went toward him, noticing the odd expression on his face when she stopped within arm's length and folded her hands at her waist.

"I know you don't like me," she said gently. "It's all right. I'll really try hard to stay away from the girls. Once Pauline learns how to input the computer files, you won't even have to see me."

He seemed troubled now. Genuinely troubled. He sighed as if he were carrying the weight of the world on his shoulders. At that moment, he looked as if he needed comforting.

"Bess would love it if you took her and Jenny to one of those cartoon movies," she said out of the blue. "There's a Sunday matinee at the Twin Oaks Cinema."

He still didn't speak.

She searched his cold eyes. "I'm sorry that I've gone behind your back to spend time with them. It's not what you think. I mean, I'm not trying to worm my way into your family, even if Pauline does think so. The girls...remind me...of my own little niece.'' Her voice almost broke but she controlled it quickly.

"Does she live far away?'' he asked abruptly.

Her eyes darkened. "Very...far away...now,'' she managed. She forced a smile. "I miss her.''

She had to turn away then, or lose control of her wild emotions.

"You can stay for the time being,'' he said finally, reluctantly. "It will work out.''

"That's what my aunt always says,'' she murmured as she opened the door.

"I didn't know you had family. Your parents are dead, aren't they?''

"They died years ago, when I was little. My aunt was in charge of us until we started school.''

"Us?''

She couldn't say it, she couldn't, she couldn't. "I ha...have a twin brother,'' she corrected quickly.

She lifted her head, praying for strength. "Good night, Mr. Callister.''

She heard the silence of his disapproval, but she was too upset to care. She went up the staircase with no hesitation at all, straight to her room. She locked the door and lay down on the covers, crying silently so that no one would hear.

There was a violent storm that night. The lightning lit up the whole sky. Kasie heard engines starting up and men's voices yelling. The animals must be unsettled. She'd read that cattle didn't like lightning.

She got up to look out the window, and then she heard the urgent knocking at her door.

She went to it, still in her neat thick white cotton gown that concealed the soft lines of her body. Her hair was loose down her back, disheveled, and she was barely awake.

She opened the door, and looked down. There were Bess

and Jenny with tears streaming down their faces. Bess was clutching a small teddy bear, and Jenny had her blanket.

"Oh, my babies, what's wrong?" she asked softly, going down on her knees to pull them close and cuddle them.

"The sky's making an awful noise, Kasie, and we're scared," Bess said.

She threw caution to the winds. She was already in so much trouble, surely a little more wouldn't matter.

"Do you want to climb in with me?" she asked softly.

"Can we?" Bess asked.

"Of course. Come on."

They climbed into bed with her and under the covers, Jenny on one side and Bess on the other.

"Want a story," Jenny murmured.

"Me, too," Bess seconded.

"Okay. How about the three bears?"

"No, Kasie, that's scary," Bess said. "How about the mouse and the lion?"

"Aren't you scared of lions?" she asked the girls.

"We like lions," Bess told her contentedly, cuddling closer. "Daddy took us to the zoo and we saw lions and tigers and polar bears!"

"The lion it is, then."

And she proceeded to tell them drowsily about the mouse who took out the thorn in the lion's paw and made a friend for life. By the time she finished, they were both asleep. She kissed their pretty little sleeping faces and folded them close to her as the lightning flashed and the thunder rolled. She wondered just before she fell asleep how much trouble she'd be in if their father came home and found them with her, after she'd just promised not to play with them. If only, she thought, Gilbert Callister would get a thorn in his paw and she could pull it out and make friends with him....

It was almost two in the morning when Gil and John got back from the holding pens. There had been a stampede, and two hundred head of cattle broke through their fences and spilled out into the pasture that fronted on a highway. The brothers and every hand on the place were occupied for three hours working in the violent storm to round them up and get them back into the right pasture and fix the fence. It helped that the lightning finally stopped, and in its wake came a nice steady rain. But everyone was soaked by the time they finished, and eager for a warm, dry bed.

Gil stripped off his wet clothes and took a shower, wrapping a long burgundy silk robe around his tall body before he went to check on the girls. He opened the door to the big room they shared and his heart skipped a beat when he realized they were missing.

Where in hell was Miss Parsons and where were his children? He went along to her room and almost knocked at the door, when he realized suddenly where the girls were most likely to be.

With his lips making a thin line, he went along the corridor barefoot to Kasie's room. Without knocking, he opened the door and walked in. Sure enough, curled up as close as they could get to her, were Bess and Jenny.

He started to wake them up and insist that they go back to bed, when he saw the way they looked.

It had been a long time since he'd seen their little faces so content. Without a mother—despite the housekeeper and Miss Parsons—they were sad so much of the time. But when they were around Kasie, they changed. They smiled. They laughed. They played. He couldn't remember the last time he'd seen them so happy. Was it fair to deny them Kasie's company just because he didn't like her? On the other hand, was it wise to let them get so attached to her when she might quit or he might fire her?

The question worried him. As he pondered the situation, Kasie moved and the cover fell away from her sleeping form. He moved closer to the bed in the dim light from the security lights outside, and abruptly he realized that she was wearing the sort of gown a dowager might. It was strictly for utility, plain and white, with no ruffles or lace or even a fancy border. He scowled. Kasie was twenty-two. Was it normal for a woman her age to be so repressed that she covered herself from head to toe even in sleep?

She moved again, restlessly, and a single word broke from her lips as the nightmare came again.

"Kantor," she whispered. "Kantor!"

Chapter 3

Without thinking, Gil reached down and shook Kasie's shoulder. "Wake up, Kasie!" he said firmly.

Her eyes opened on a rush of breath. There was horror in them for a few seconds until she came awake and realized that her boss was standing over her. She blinked away the sleepiness and pulled herself up on an elbow. Her beautiful thick chestnut hair swirled around her shoulders below the high neck of the gown as she stared at him.

"You were having a nightmare," he said curtly. "Who's Kantor?"

She hesitated for a few seconds. "My brother," she said finally. "My twin." She noticed that he was wearing a long robe and apparently nothing under it. Thick dark blond hair was visible in the deep vee of the neckline. She averted her eyes almost in panic. It embarrassed her to have him see her in her nightgown; almost as much as to see him in a robe.

"Why do you have nightmares about him?" he asked gently.

"We had an argument," she said. She pushed back her hair. "I don't want to talk about it."

His eyes narrowed. Apparently it was a painful subject. He

let it drop. His eyes went to the girls and not without misgiving. "Why are they in here with you?"

"The storm woke them up. They got scared and came to me," she said defensively. "I didn't go get them."

He was studying them quietly. His expression was hard, grave, wounded.

"I'm sure they went to look for you first," she began defensively.

His eyes glittered down into hers. "We've had this conversation before. Miss Parsons is supposed to be their governness," he emphasized.

"Miss Parsons is probably snoring her head off," she said curtly. "She sleeps like the dead. Bess had a fever week before last, and she didn't even get up when I woke her and told her about it. She said that a fever never hurt anybody!"

"That was when she had strep and I took her to the doctor," he recalled. "Miss Parsons said she was sick. I assumed that she'd been up in the night with her."

"Dream on."

He glared at her. "I'll excuse it this time," he said, ignoring the reference he didn't like to Miss Parsons and her treatment of Bess. He'd have something to say to the woman about that. "Next time, come and find me if you can't wake Miss Parsons."

She just stared back, silent.

"Did you hear me, Kasie?" he demanded softly.

"All right." She glanced from one side of her to the other. "Do you want to wake them up and carry them back to their own beds?"

He looked furious. "If I do, we'll all be awake the rest of the night. We had cattle get out, and we got soaked trying to get them back in. I'm worn-out. I want to go to sleep."

"Nobody here is stopping you," she murmured.

His pale eyes narrowed. "I should have let you go when you offered to resign," he said caustically.

"There's still time," she pointed out, growing more angry by the minute.

He cursed under his breath, glared at her again and walked out.

The next morning, Kasie woke to soft pummeling little hands and laughing voices.

"Get up, Kasie, get up! Daddy's taking us to the movies today!"

She yawned and curled up. "Not me," she murmured sleepily. "Go get breakfast, babies. Mrs. Charters will feed you."

"You got to come, too!" Bess said.

"I want to sleep," she murmured.

"Daddy, she won't get up!" Bess wailed.

"Oh, yes, she will."

Kasie barely had time to register the deep voice before the covers were torn away and she was lifted bodily out of the bed in a pair of very strong arms.

Shocked, she stared straight into pale blue eyes and felt as if she'd been electrified.

"I'll wake her up," Gil told the girls. "Go down and eat your breakfast."

"Okay, Daddy!"

The girls left gleefully, laughing as they went to the staircase.

"You look like a nun in that gown," Gil remarked as he studied his light burden, aware of her sudden stillness. Her face was very close. He searched it quietly. "And you've got freckles, Kasie, just across the bridge of your nose."

"Put...put me down," she said, unnerved by the proximity. She didn't like the sensations it caused to feel his chest right against her bare breasts.

"Why?" he asked. He gazed into her eyes. "You hardly weigh anything." His eyes narrowed as he studied her face thoroughly. "You have big eyes," he murmured. "With little flecks of blue in them. Your face looks more round than oval, especially with your hair down. Your mouth is—'' he searched for a word, more touched than he wanted to be by its vulnerability ''—full and soft. Half-asleep you don't come across as a fighter. But you are, aren't you?''

Her hands were resting lightly around his neck and she stared at him disconcertedly while she wondered what John or Miss Parsons would say if they walked in unexpectedly to find them in this position.

''You should put me down,'' she said huskily.

''Don't you like being carried?'' he murmured absently.

She shivered as she remembered the last time she'd been carried, by an orderly in the hospital...

She pushed at him. ''Please.''

He set her back down, scowling curiously at the odd pastiness of her complexion. ''You're mysterious, Kasie.''

''Not really. I'm just sleepy.'' She folded her arms over her breasts and flushed. ''Could you leave, please, and let me get dressed?''

He watched her curiously. ''Why don't you date? And don't hand me any bull about stinking cowboys.''

She was reluctant to tell him anything about herself. She was a private person. Her aunt, Mama Luke, always said that people shouldn't worry others with their personal problems. She didn't.

''I don't want to get married, ever.''

He really scowled then. ''Why?''

She thought of her parents and then of Kantor, and her eyes closed on the pain. ''Love hurts too much.''

He didn't speak. For an instant, he felt the pain that seemed to rack her delicate features, and he understood it, all too well.

''You loved someone who died,'' he recalled.

She nodded and her eyes met his. ''And so did you.''

For an instant, his hard face was completely unguarded. He was vulnerable, mortal, wounded. ''Yes.''

''It doesn't pass away, like they say, does it?'' she asked softly.

"Not for a long time."

He moved a step closer, and this time she didn't back up. Her eyes lifted to his. He slid his big, lean hand into the thick waves of her chestnut hair and enjoyed its silkiness. "Why don't you wear your hair down, like this?"

"It's sinful," she whispered.

"What?"

"When you dress and wear your hair in a way that's meant to tempt men, to try to seduce them, it's sinful," she repeated.

His lips fell open. He didn't know how to answer that. He'd never had a woman, especially a modern woman, say such a thing to him.

"Do you think sex is a sin?" he asked.

"Outside of marriage, it is," she replied simply.

"You don't move with the times, do you?" he asked on an expulsion of breath.

"No," she replied.

He started smiling and couldn't stop. "Oh, boy."

"The girls will be waiting. Are you really taking them to a movie?" she asked.

"Yes." One eye narrowed. "I need to take you to one, too. Something X-rated."

She flushed. "Get out of here and stop trying to corrupt me."

"You're overdue."

"Stop or I'll have Mama Luke come over and lecture you."

He frowned. "Mama Luke?"

"My aunt."

"What an odd name."

She shrugged. "Our whole family runs to odd names."

"I noticed."

She made a face. "I work for you. My private life is my own business."

"You don't have a private life," he said, and smiled tenderly.

"I'm a great reader. I love Plutarch and Tacitus and Arrian."

"Good God!"

"There's nothing wrong with ancient history. Things were just as bad then as they are now. All the ancient writers said that the younger generation was headed straight to purgatory and the world was corrupt."

"Arrian didn't."

"Arrian wrote about Alexander the Great," she reminded him. "Alexander's world was in fairly good shape, apparently."

"Arrian wrote about Alexander in the distant past, not his own present." His eyes became soft with affection as he looked at her. "Why don't I like you? There isn't a person in my circle of acquaintances who would even know who Arrian was, much less what he wrote about."

"I don't like you much, either," she shot right back. "But I guess I can stand it if you can."

"I'll have to," he mused. "If I let you walk out, the girls will push me down the staircase and call you back to support them at my funeral."

She shivered abruptly and wrapped her arms around herself. Funeral. Funeral...

"Kasie!"

Her somber eyes came up. She was barely breathing. "Don't...joke about things like that."

"Kasie, I didn't mean it that way," he began.

She forced a smile. "Of course not. I have to get dressed."

He lifted an eyebrow. "You might as well come as you are. I haven't seen a gown like that since I stayed with my grandmother as a child." He shook his head. "You'd set a lingerie shop back decades if that style caught on."

"It's a perfectly functional gown."

"Functional. Yes. It's definitely functional. And about as seductive as chain mail," he added.

"Good!"

He burst out laughing. "All right, I'm leaving."

He went out, sparing her a last, amused glance before he closed the door.

Kasie dressed in jeans and a dark T-shirt. She put her long hair in a braid and pulled on sneakers. She felt a twinge of guilt because she'd missed so many Sunday sermons in past months. But she couldn't reconcile her pain. It needed more time.

The whole family was at the table when she joined them for breakfast. John gave her a warm smile.

"I hear you had visitors last night," he told Kasie with a mischievous glance at the two little girls, who were wolfing down cereal.

"Yes, I did," Kasie replied with a worried glance that encompassed both Gil and Miss Parsons.

"You should have called me, Miss Mayfield," Miss Penny Parsons said curtly and glanced at Kasie with cold dark eyes. "I take care of the children."

Kasie could have argued that point, but she didn't dare. "Yes, Miss Parsons," she said demurely.

Gil finished his scrambled eggs and lifted his coffee cup to his firm lips. He was wearing slacks and a neat yellow sports shirt that emphasized his muscular arms. He looked elegant even in casual wear, Kasie thought, and remembered suddenly the feel of those strong arms around her. She flushed.

He noticed her sudden color and caught her gaze. She couldn't seem to look away, and he didn't even try to. For a space of seconds, they were fused in some sort of bond, prisoners of a sensual connection that made Kasie's full lips part abruptly. His gaze fell to them and lingered with unexpected hunger.

Kasie dropped her fork onto her plate and jumped at the noise. "Sorry!" she said huskily as she fumbled with the fork.

"Didn't get much sleep last night, did you?" John asked with a smile. "Neither did any of us. About midnight, I thought seriously about giving up cattle ranching and becoming a door-to-door vacuum cleaner salesman.''

"I felt the same way," Gil confessed. "We're going to have to put a small line cabin out at the holding pens and keep a man there on stormy nights."

"As long as I'm not on your list of candidates," John told his brother.

"I'll keep that in mind. Bess, don't play with your food, please," he added to the little girl, who was finished with her cereal and was now smearing eggs around the rim of her plate.

"I don't like eggs, Daddy," she muttered. "Do I gotta eat 'em?"

"Of course you do, young lady!" Miss Parsons said curtly. "Every last morsel."

Bess looked tortured.

"Miss Parsons, could you ask Mrs. Charters to see me before she plans the supper menu, please?" Gil asked.

Miss Parsons got up. "I will. Eat those eggs, Bess."

She left. Gil gave his oldest daughter a sign by placing his forefinger across his mouth. He lifted Bess's plate, scraped the eggs onto his, and finished them off before Miss Parsons returned.

"Very good," she said, nodding approvingly at Bess's plate. "I told you that you'd grow accustomed to a balanced breakfast. We must keep our bodies healthy. Come on, now, girls. We'll have a nice nap until your father's ready to go to the movies."

Bess grimaced, but she didn't protest. She got up with Jenny and was shepherded out by the governess.

"Marshmallow," John chided the older man, poking the air with his fork. "You should have made her eat them herself."

"When you start eating liver and onions voluntarily, I'll make Bess eat eggs," Gil promised. "Want to come with us to the movies?" He named the picture they were going to see.

"Not me," John said pleasantly. "I'm going to Billings to

see a man about some more acreage.'' He glanced at Kasie speculatively. ''Want to tag along, Kasie?''

The question surprised her. While she was trying to think of a polite way to say she didn't, Gil answered for her.

''Kasie's going with us to the movies,'' he replied, and his pale eyes dared her to argue. ''The girls will have conniptions if we leave her behind. Besides, she likes cartoons. Don't you, Kasie?''

''I'm just crazy about them, Mr. Callister,'' she agreed with a tight smile, angry because he'd more or less forced her into agreeing to go.

''Mr. Callister was our father,'' Gil said firmly. ''Don't use it with us.''

She grimaced. ''I work for you. It doesn't seem right.''

John was gaping at her. ''You're kidding.''

''No, she isn't,'' Gil assured him. ''When you have a free minute, get her to tell you why she braids her hair. It's a hoot.''

She glared at Gil. ''You cut that out.''

He wiped his mouth with a white linen napkin and got to his feet. ''I've got some phone calls to make before we go. We'll leave at one, Kasie.''

''Phone calls on Sunday?'' she asked John when his brother had left them alone.

''It's yesterday in some parts of the world, and tomorrow in some other parts,'' he reminded her. ''You know how he is about business.''

''Yes,'' she agreed.

''What amazes me,'' he mused, watching her, ''is how much he grumbles about you. He loves women, as a rule. He's always doing little things to make the job easier for Mrs. Charters. He lets Pauline get away with only working three days of the week, when he needs a full-time secretary worse than I do. But he's hard on you.''

''He doesn't like me,'' she said quietly. ''He can't help it.''

''You don't like him, either.''

She smiled sheepishly. ''I can't help it, either.'' She picked up on something he'd said earlier. "How can Pauline make ends meet with only a part-time job?" she asked curiously.

"She's independently wealthy," John told her. "She doesn't need a job at all, but she caught Gil at a weak moment. He doesn't have many of them, believe me. I think she attracted him at first. Now things have cooled and he's stuck with her. She's tenacious."

"Why would she need to work?" she wondered aloud.

"Because Gil needed a secretary, of course. She hasn't had any business training, and I don't doubt that the files are in a hellacious mess."

"Couldn't he get somebody else?"

"He tried to. Pauline cried all over him and he gave up."

"He doesn't look like a man who'd even notice tears," she said absently.

"Appearances are deceptive. You saw how he was when the dog threatened the girls," he reminded her. "He's not immune to tears."

"I'd need convincing," she said and grinned wickedly.

He leaned back in his chair with his coffee cup in his hand and studied her. "You're good with the kids," he said. "You must have spent a lot of time around children."

She lowered her eyes to her empty plate. "I did. I'm not formally taught or anything, but I do know a few things."

"It shows. I've never seen Bess respond to any of her various governesses. She liked you on sight."

"How many governesses has she had?" she asked curiously.

"Four. This year," he amended.

Her eyebrows arched. "Why so many?"

"Are you afraid of spiders, garter snakes, or frogs?" he asked.

She shook her head. "Why?"

"Well, the others were. They got downright twitchy about opening drawers or pulling down bedcovers," he recalled with a chuckle. "Bess likes garter snakes. She shared them with the governesses."

"Oh, dear," Kasie said.

"You see the point. That's why Miss Parsons was hired. She's the next best thing to a Marine DI, as you may have noticed."

Her face lightened. "So that's why he hired her. I did wonder."

John sighed. "I wish he'd hired her to do the tax work on the payroll instead. She's a natural, and since she's a retired accountant that experience would make her an asset. We have a firm of C.P.A.'s to do yearly stuff, but our bookkeeper who did payroll got married and moved to L.A. just before we hired you."

"And Miss Parsons got hired to look after the girls. She really dislikes children," she added.

"I know. But Gil refuses to believe it. He's been lax about work at the ranch for a while. He stayed on the road more and more, avoiding the memories after Darlene died. I felt bad for him, but things were going to pot here. I have to travel to show the bulls," he added, "because the more competitions we win, the higher the prices we can charge for stud fees or young bulls. The ranch can't run without anybody overseeing it." He pursed his lips as he studied her. "I gather that you said something to him about neglecting the girls. I thought so," he mused when she shifted uncomfortably. "I've told him, too, but he didn't listen to me. Apparently he listens to you."

"He's already tried to fire me once," she pointed out.

"You're still here," he replied.

"Yes. But I can't help but wonder for how much longer," she murmured, voicing her one real fear. "I could go back and live with my aunt, but it isn't fair to her. I have to work and support myself. This was the only full-time job that I was qualified for. Jobs are thin on the ground, regardless of the reports coming out about how great the economy is."

"How did you end up in Medicine Ridge in the first place?" he wondered.

"I was living with my aunt in Billings when I saw the ad

for this job in the local paper. I'd already been all over Billings hoping for a full-time job and couldn't find one. This one seemed tailor-made for me.''

"I'm glad you applied for it," he said. ''There were a lot of candidates, but we ruled out most of them in less than five minutes each. You were the only woman out there who could even type.''

"You're kidding.''

"No. They thought I wanted beauty instead of brains. I didn't.'' He smiled. ''Not that you're bad on the eyes, Kasie. But I wasn't running a pageant.''

"I was surprised that your brother hired me," she confessed. ''He seemed to dislike me on sight. But when he found out how fast I could type, he was a lot less antagonistic.''

He wasn't going to mention what Gil had said to him after he hired Kasie. It had been against Gil's better judgment, and he'd picked her appearance and her pert manner to pieces. It was interesting that Gil was antagonistic toward her. Very interesting.

"You're a whiz at the computer," John said. ''A real asset. I didn't realize what you could do with a spreadsheet program until you modified ours. You're gifted.''

"I love computers," she said with a smile. ''Pauline is going to enjoy them, too, when she learns just a little more. Once she discovers the Internet, she'll be even more efficient. There are all sorts of Web sites dedicated to the cattle industry. It would be great for comparisons—even for buying and selling bulls. You could have your own Web site.''

John let out a low whistle. ''Funny, I hadn't even considered that. Kasie, it might revolutionize the way we do business, not to mention cutting down on the amount of travel we have to do every year.''

"That's what I thought, too," she said, smiling at him.

"Mention it to Gil when you go to the movies," he coaxed. ''Let's see what he thinks.''

"He might like the idea better if it came from you," she said.

"I think he'll like it, period. I already do. Can you make a Web site?"

She grimaced. "No, I can't. But I know a woman who can," she added. "She works out of Billings. I met her when we were going to secretarial school. She's really good, and she doesn't charge an arm and a leg. I can get in touch with her, if you like."

"Go ahead. We do a lot of communication by e-mail, but neither of us even thought about putting cattle on our own site. It's a terrific idea!"

"You sound like Bess," Gil said from the doorway. "What's terrific?"

"We're going on the Internet," John said.

His big brother frowned. "The Internet?"

"Kasie can tell you what she's proposed. It could open new doors for us in marketing. It's international."

Gil was quick. He caught on almost at once. "You mean, get a Web site and use it to buy and sell cattle," he said.

"It will save you as much time as sending e-mail back and forth between potential buyers and sellers already does," she added.

"Good idea." Gil studied her with a curious smile. "Full of surprises aren't you, Miss Mayfield?"

"She's gifted," John said, grinning at his brother. "I told you so. Now maybe you can stop talking about firing her, hmm?"

Gil pressed his lips together and refused to rise to the bait. "It's almost one o'clock. If we're going to the movies, let's go. Kasie, fetch the girls."

She almost saluted, but he looked vaguely irritated. It looked as though nothing she suggested was ever going to please him. She wondered why she didn't just walk out and leave him to it. The thought was painful. She went up to get the little girls, more confused than ever.

Chapter 4

The girls chattered like birds all the way to town in Gil's black Jaguar. Kasie sat in front and listened patiently, smiling, while they told her all about the movie they were going to see. They'd seen the previews on television when they watched their Saturday morning cartoons.

It was a warm, pretty day, and trees and shrubs were blooming profusely. It should have been perfect, but Kasie was uneasy. Maybe she shouldn't have mentioned anything about Web sites, but it seemed an efficient way for Gil and John to move into Web-based commerce.

"You're brooding," Gil remarked. "Why?"

"I was wondering if I should have suggested anything about Internet business," she said.

"Why not? It's a good idea," he said, surprising her. "John told me about the Web site designer. Tomorrow, I want you to get in touch with her and get the process started."

"She'll need you to tell her what you want on the site."

"Okay."

She glanced in the back seat where the girls were sharing a book and enthusing over the pop-up sections.

"I brought it home for them yesterday," he commented, "and forgot to give it to them. They love books."

"That's the first step to getting them to love reading," she said, smiling at the little heads bowed over the books. "Reading to them at night keeps it going."

"Did your mother read to you?" he asked curiously.

"She probably did," she mused, smiling sadly. "But Kantor and I were very young when she and our father...died. Mama Luke read to us, when we were older."

"I suppose you liked science fiction," he murmured.

"How did you know?" she asked.

"You love computers," he said with a hint of a smile.

"I guess they do fit in with science fiction," she had to admit. She eyed him curiously. "What sort of books did you like to read?"

"Pirate stories, cowboy stories. Stuff like that. Now, it's genetics textbooks and management theory," he added wryly. "I hardly ever have time to read just for fun."

"Do your parents help you with the ranch?"

He seemed to turn to ice. "We don't talk about our parents," he said stiffly.

That sounded odd. But she was already in his bad books, so she didn't pursue it. "It's nice of you to take the girls to the movies."

He slowed for a turn, his expression taut. "I don't spend enough time with them," he said. "You were right about that. It isn't a lack of love. It's a lack of delegation. You'd be amazed how hard it is to find good managers who want to live on a cattle ranch."

"Maybe you don't advertise in a wide enough range," she suggested gently.

"What?"

She plunged ahead. "There are all sorts of trade magazines that carry ads with blind mailboxes," she said. "You can have replies sent to the newspaper and nobody has to know who you are."

"How do you know about the trade magazines?" he asked.

She grinned sheepishly. "I read them. Well, I ought to know something about cattle, since I work for a ranch, shouldn't I?"

He shook his head. "You really are full of surprises, Kasie."

"Kasie, what's this big word?" Bess asked, thrusting the book at her. Kasie took it and sounded the word out phonetically, coaching the little girl in its pronunciation. She took the book back and began to teach the word to Jenny.

"You're patient," Gil remarked. "I notice that Miss Parsons doesn't like taking time to teach them words."

"Miss Parsons likes numbers."

"Yes. She does." He pulled into the theater parking lot, which was full of parents and children. He got everyone out and locked the door, grimacing as they walked past several minivans.

"They're handy for little kids," Kasie said wickedly. "Mothers love them, I'm told."

"I love my kids, but I'm not driving a damned minivan," he muttered.

She grinned at his expression. The little girls ran to get in line, and struck up a conversation with a child they knew, whose bored mother perked up when she saw Gil approaching.

"Hi, Gil!" she called cheerily. "We're going to see the dinosaur movie! Is that why you're here?"

"That's the one," he replied, pulling bills out of his wallet. He gave one to each of the little girls, and they bought their own tickets. Gil bought his and Kasie's as they came to the window. "Hi, Amie," he called to the little girl with Bess and Jenny, and he smiled. She smiled back. She was as dark as his children were fair, with black eyes and hair like her mother's.

"We're going to sit with Amie, Daddy!" Bess said excitedly, waving her ticket and Jenny's.

"I guess that leaves me with you and…?" the other woman paused deliberately.

"This is Kasie," Gil said, and took her unexpectedly by the

arm, with a bland smile at Amie's mom. "You're welcome to join us, of course, Connie."

The other woman sighed. "No, I guess I'll sit with the girls. Nice to have seen you," she added, and moved ahead with the girls, looking bored all over again.

Gil slid his hand down into Kasie's. She reacted nervously to the unexpected touch, but his fingers clung, warm and strong against her own. He drew her along to the line already forming alongside the velvet ropes as the ticket takers prepared to let people through to the various theaters.

"Humor me," he said, and it looked as though he were whispering sweet nothings into her ear. "I'm the entrée, in case you haven't noticed."

Kasie glanced around and saw a number of women with little children and no man along, and two of them gave him deliberate, wistful glances and smiled.

"Single moms?" she whispered back, having to go on tip-toe.

He caught her around the waist and held her against his hip. "No. Get the picture?"

Her breath caught. "Oh, dear," she said heavily.

He looked down into her wide eyes. "You're such a child sometimes," he said softly. "You don't see ugliness, do you? You go through life looking for rainbows instead of rain."

"Habit," she murmured, fascinated by the pale blue lights in his eyes.

"It's a rather nice habit," he replied. The look lasted just a few seconds too long to be polite, and Kasie felt her heart begin to race. But then, the line shifted and diverted him. He moved closer to the ticket-taker, keeping the girls ahead carefully in sight while his arm drew Kasie along with him.

She liked the protectiveness of that muscular arm. He didn't look like a body-builder, all his movements were lithe and graceful. But he worked at physical labor from dawn until dusk most days. She'd seen him throw calves that had to be doctored. She'd seen him throw bulls, too. He was strong. Involuntarily she relaxed against him. It was delicious, the feeling of security it gave her to be close to him, to the warm strength of him.

The soft movement caught him off guard and sent a jolt of sensation through him that he hadn't felt in a long time. He looked down at her with curious, turbulent eyes that she didn't see. She was smiling and waving at the girls, who were darting off down into the theater with the little girl and her mother.

"They like you," he said.

"I like them."

He handed their tickets to the uniformed girl, who smiled as she handed back the stubs and pointed the way to the theater that was showing the cartoon movie.

Gil caught Kasie's hand in his and drew her lazily along with him through the crowd of children and parents until they reached the theater. But instead of going down to the front, he drew Kasie to an isolated double-seat in the very back row and sat down beside her. His arm went over the back of the chair as the theater darkened and the previews began showing.

Kasie was electrified by the shift in their relationship. She felt his lean fingers on her shoulder, bringing her closer, and his cheek rested against her temple. She hadn't ever been to a movie with a man. There had been a blind double date once, and the boy sat on his own side of the seat and looked nervous until they got home again. This was worlds away from that experience.

"Comfortable?" he asked at her ear, and his voice was like velvet.

"Yes," she said unsteadily.

His chest rose and fell and he found himself paying a lot more attention to the feel of Kasie's soft hair against his skin than the movie. She smelled of spring roses. Her hair was soft, and had a faint herbal scent of its own. Twenty-two. She was twenty-two. He was thirty-two, and she'd already said that he was too old for her.

He scowled as he thought about that difference. She needed

someone as young as she was, with that same vulnerable, kind, generous spirit. He had two little girls and a high-pressure business that gave him little free time. He was still grieving, in a way, for Darlene, whom he'd loved since grammar school. But there was something about Kasie that made him hungry. It wasn't desire, although he was aware of heady sensations when she was close to him. No, it was the sort of hunger a man got when he was standing outside in the snow with a wet coat and soaked jeans, looking through the window at a warm, glowing fireplace. He couldn't really explain the feelings. They made him uneasy.

He noticed that she was still a little stiff. He touched a curl at her ear. "Hey," he whispered.

She turned her head and looked up at him in the semidarkness.

"I'm not hitting on you," he whispered into her ear. "Okay?"

She relaxed. "Okay."

The obvious relief in her voice made him feel guilty and offended. He moved his arm back to the chair and forced himself to watch the movie. He had to remember that Kasie worked for him. It wasn't fair to use her to ward off other women. But...was it really that?

The dinosaur movie was really well-done, Kasie thought as she became involved in the storyline and the wonder of creatures that looked really alive up there on the screen. It was a bittersweet sort of cartoon, though, and she was sorry for the little girls. Because when it was over, Bess and Jenny came to them crying about the dinosaurs that had died in the film.

"Oh, sweetheart, it was only a movie," Kasie said at once, and bent to pick up Bess, hugging her close. "Just a movie. Okay?"

"But it was so sad, Kasie," cried the little girl. "Why do things have to die?"

"I don't know, baby," she said softly, and her eyes closed

for an instant on a wave of remembered pain. She'd lost so many people she loved.

Gil had Jenny up in his arms, and they walked out of the theater carrying the children. Behind them, other mothers were trying to explain about extinction.

"There, there, baby," he cooed at Jenny and kissed her wet eyes. "It was only make-believe. Dinosaurs don't really talk, you know, and they had brains the size of peas." He shifted her and smiled. "Hey, remember what I told you about chickens, about how they'll walk right up to a rattlesnake and let it strike them? Well, dinosaurs didn't even have brains that big."

"They didn't?" Bess asked from her secure hold on Kasie.

"They didn't," Gil said. "If a meteor had struck them, they'd be standing right in its path waiting for it. And they wouldn't be discussing it, either."

Kasie laughed as she looked at Gil, delighted at the way he handled the sticky situation. He was, she thought, a marvelous parent.

"Can we get some ice cream on the way home?" Bess asked then, wiping her tears.

"You bet. We'll stop by the yogurt place."

"Thanks, Daddy!" Bess cried.

"You're the nicest daddy," Jenny murmured against his throat.

"You really are, you know," Kasie agreed as they strapped the little girls into the back seat.

His eyes met hers across the children. "I'm a veteran daddy," he told her dryly.

"Is that what it is?" Kasie chuckled.

"You get better with practice, or so they tell me. Do you like frozen yogurt? I get them that instead of ice cream. It's healthy stuff."

"I like it, too," Kasie said as she got into the front seat beside him.

"We'll get some to take home for Mrs. Charters and Miss

Parsons,'' he added, ''so that we don't get blamed for ruining their appetites for supper.''

''Now that's superior thinking,'' Kasie had to admit.

He started the engine and eased them out of the crowded parking lot.

The yogurt shop was a few miles from home. They stopped and got the treat in carryout cups, because Gil was expecting a phone call from a buyer out of state.

''I don't like to work on Sundays,'' he remarked as they drove home. ''But sometimes it's unavoidable.''

''Do you ever take the girls to church?''

He hesitated. ''Well...no.''

She was watching him with those big, soft gray eyes, in which there wasn't condemnation or censure. It was almost as if she knew that his faith had suffered since the death of his wife. No, for longer than that. It had suffered since childhood, when his parents had...

''I haven't gone for several months, myself,'' Kasie remarked quietly. She twisted her purse slowly in her hands. ''If I...start back, I could take them with me, if you didn't mind.''

''I don't mind,'' he replied.

Her eyes softened and she smiled at him.

He tore his gaze away from that warm affection and forced it back to the road. His hands tightened on the steering wheel. She really was getting to him. He wished he knew some way to head off trouble. He found her far too attractive, and she continued to make her lack of receptiveness known. He didn't want to do something stupid and send her looking for another job.

''I enjoyed today,'' he said after a minute. ''But you remember that Miss Parsons is supposed to be responsible for the girls,'' he added with a stern glance. ''You have enough to do keeping John's paperwork current. Understand?''

''Yes, I do. I'll try very hard to stop interfering,'' she promised.

"Good. Pauline is out of town for the next week, but she'll be home in time for the pool party we're giving next Saturday. She'll be in the office the following Monday morning. You can give her another computer lesson."

She grimaced. "She doesn't like me."

"I know. Don't let it worry you. She's efficient."

She wasn't, but apparently she'd managed to conceal it from Gil. Kasie wondered how he'd managed not to notice the work Pauline didn't do.

"Did John have a secretary before me?" she asked suddenly.

"He did, and she was a terrific one, too. But she quit with only a week's notice."

"Did she say why?" she fished with apparent unconcern.

"Something about being worked to death. John didn't buy it. She didn't have that much to do."

She did, if she was doing John's work and having Gil's palmed off on her as well. Kasie's eyes narrowed. Well, she wasn't going to get away with it now. If Pauline started expecting Kasie to do her job for her, she was in for a surprise.

"Funny," Gil murmured as he turned onto the black shale ranch road that led to the Double C. "Pauline said she couldn't use the computer, but she always had my herd records printed out. Even if they weren't updated properly."

Kasie didn't say a word. Surely he'd work it out by himself one day. She glanced back at the girls, who were still contentedly eating frozen yogurt out of little cups. They were so pretty and sweet. Her heart ached just looking at them. Sandy had been just Bess's age...

She bit down hard on her lip. She mustn't cry. Tears were no help at all. She had to look ahead, not backward.

Gil pulled up in front of the house and helped Kasie get the girls out.

"Thanks for the movie," Kasie told him, feeling shy now.

"My pleasure," he said carelessly. "Come on, girls, let's

get you settled with Miss Parsons. Daddy's got to play rancher for a while."

"Can't we play, too?" Bess asked, clinging to his hand.

"Sure," he said. "Just as soon as you can compare birth weight ratios and compute projected weaning weight."

Bess made a face. "Oh, Daddy!"

"I'll make a rancher out of you one day, young lady," he said with a grin.

"Billy's dad said he was sure glad he had a son instead of girls. Daddy, do you ever wish me and Jenny was boys?" she asked.

He stopped, dropped to one knee and hugged the child close. "Daddy loves little girls," he said softly. "And he wouldn't trade you and Jenny for all the boys in the world. You tell Billy I said that."

Bess chuckled. "I will!" She kissed his cheek with a big smack. "I love you, Daddy!"

"I love you, too, little chick."

Jenny, jealous, had to have a hug, too, and they ended up each clinging to a strong, lean hand as they went into the house.

Kasie watched them, feeling more lost and alone than she had in months. She ached to be part of a family again. Watching Gil with the girls only emphasized what she'd lost.

She went up onto the porch and up the staircase slowly, her hand smoothing over the silky wood of the banister as she tried once again to come to grips with her loss.

She was curled up in her easy chair watching an old movie on television when there was a soft knock at the door just before it opened. Bess and Jenny sneaked in wearing their gowns and bathrobes and slippers, peering cautiously down the hall before they closed the door.

"Hello," Kasie said with a smile, opening her arms as they clambered up into the big chair with her and cuddled close. "You smell nice."

"We had baths," Bess said. "Miss Parsons said we was covered with chocolate sauce." She giggled. "We splashed her."

"You bad babies," she chided softly and kissed little cheeks.

"Could you tell us a story?" they asked.

"Sure. What would you like to hear?"

"The one with the bears."

"Okay." She started the story, speaking in all the different parts, while they snuggled close and listened with attention.

Just to see if they were really listening, she added, "And then the wolf huffed and puffed..."

"No, Kasie!" Bess interrupted. "That's the pig story!"

"Is it?" she exclaimed. "All right, then. Well, the bears came home..."

"Huffing and puffing?" came a deep, amused query from the doorway. The little girls glanced at him, looking guilty and worried. "Miss Parsons is looking for you two fugitives," he drawled. "If I were you, I'd get into my beds real fast. She's glowering."

"Goodness! We got to go, Kasie!" Bess said, and she and Jenny scrambled to their feet and ran past their father down the hall, calling good-nights as they went.

Gil studied Kasie from the doorway. She was wearing her own white gown, with a matching cotton robe this time, and her long hair waved around her shoulders. She looked very young.

"You weren't reading from a book. What did you do, memorize the story?" he asked curiously.

"I guess so," she confided, smiling. "I've told it so many times, I suppose I do have it down pretty well."

"Who did you tell it to?" he asked reasonably.

The smile never faded, but she withdrew behind it. "A little girl who stayed with us sometimes," she replied.

"I see."

"They came in and asked for a story," she explained. "I hated telling them to go away..."

"I haven't said a word."

"You did," she reminded him worriedly. "I know that Miss Parsons looks after them. I'm not trying to interfere."

"I know that. But it's making things hard for her when they come to you instead," he said firmly.

She grimaced. "I can't hurt their feelings."

"I'll speak to them." He held up a hand when she started to protest. "I'll speak to them nicely," he added. "I won't make an issue of it."

She hesitated. "Okay."

"You have your own duties," he continued. "It isn't fair to let you take on two jobs, no matter how you feel about it. I don't pay Miss Parsons to sit and read tax manuals."

Her eyes widened. "You're kidding," she said, sitting up straight. "She reads tax manuals? What for? Did you ask her?"

"I did. She says she reads them for pleasure," he said. "Apparently she didn't really want to retire from the accounting business, but she was faced with a clerical position or retirement," he added with a droll smile.

"Oh, dear."

He pushed away from the door facing. "Don't stay up too late. John needs to get an early start. He'll be away for a week showing Ebony King on the road."

"He's the new young bull," Kasie recalled. "He eats corn out of my hand," she added with a smile. "I never thought of bulls as being gentle."

"They're a real liability if they're not," he pointed out. "A bull that size could trample a man with very little difficulty."

"I guess he could." She stood up, with her hands in the pockets of the cotton robe. "I'm sorry about the girls coming in here."

"Oh, hell, I don't mind," he said on a rough breath. "But it isn't wise to let them get too attached to you, Kasie. You know it, and you know why."

"They think you're going to marry Pauline," she blurted out, and then flushed at having been so personal with him.

"I haven't thought a lot about remarrying," he replied quietly. His eyes went over her with a suddenly intent appraisal. "But maybe I should. They're getting to the age where they're going to need a woman's hand in their lives. I love them, but I can't see things from a female point of view."

"You've done marvelously with them so far," she told him. "They're polite and generous and loving."

"So was their mother," he remarked and for a few seconds, his face was lined with grief before he got it under control. "She loved them."

"You said Bess was like her," she reminded him.

"Yes," he said at once. "She had long, wavy blond hair, just that same color. Jenny looks more like me. But Bess is more like me."

She smiled. "I've noticed. She has a very hard head when she doesn't want to do something."

He shrugged. "Being stubborn isn't always a bad thing. Persistence is the key to most successes in life."

"Yes." She searched his hard face, seeing the years of work and worry. It was a good, strong face, but it wasn't handsome.

He was looking at her, too, and something stirred inside him, a need that he had to work to put down. He moved out the door. "Sleep well, Kasie," he said curtly.

"You, too."

He closed the door behind him, without looking at her again. She went back to her movie, but with much less enthusiasm.

Chapter 5

The week went by slowly, and the girls, to Kasie's dismay, became her shadows. She worried herself sick trying to keep Gil from noticing, especially after the harsh comments he'd made about her job responsibilities. It didn't help that she kept remembering the feel of his arm around her at the movie theater, and the warm clasp of his big lean hand in her own. She was afraid to even look at him, because she was afraid her attraction to him might show.

Saturday came and the house was full of strangers. Kasie found it hard to mix with high society people, so she stuck to Miss Parsons and the girls. Miss Parsons took the opportunity to sneak back inside the house while Kasie watched the girls. Everything went well at first, because Gil was too busy with guests to notice that Miss Parsons was missing. But not for long. Kasie had given the girls a beach ball to play with, which was her one big mistake of the morning.

It wouldn't have been so bad if she'd just let the children's beach ball fly into the swimming pool in the first place. The problem was that, if she didn't stop it, Pauline was going to get it in the mouth, which wouldn't improve the already-bad situation between her and Kasie. Bess and Jenny didn't like

Gil Callister's secretary. Neither did Kasie, but she loved the little girls and didn't want them to get into trouble. So she gave in to an impulse, and tried valiantly to divert the ball from its unexpecting target.

Predictably, she overreached, lost her footing and made an enormous splash as she landed, fully clothed, in the deep end. And, of course, she couldn't swim...

Gil looked up from the prospectus he'd been reading when he heard the splash. He connected Kasie's fall, the beach ball, and his two little blond giggling daughters at once. He shook his head and grimaced. He put aside the prospectus and dived in to save Kasie, Bermuda shorts, Hawaiian shirt and all.

Her late parents had lived long enough to see the irony of the second name they'd given her. Her middle name was Grace, but she wasn't graceful. She was all long legs and arms. She wasn't pretty, but she had a lovely body, and the thin white dress she was wearing became transparent in the water. It was easily noticed that she was wearing only the flimsiest of briefs and a bra that barely covered her pert breasts. Just the thing, she thought miserably, to wear in front of the Callisters' business partners who were here for a pool party on the big ranch. Feline blond Pauline Raines was laughing her head off at Kasie's desperate treading of water. Just you wait, lady, she fumed. Next time I'll give Bess a soccer ball to bean you with and I won't step in the way...!

Her head went under as her arms gave out. She took a huge breath as powerful arms encircled and lifted her clear of the deep water. It would have to be Gil who rescued her, she thought miserably. John wasn't even looking their way. He'd have dived in after her in a minute, she knew, if he'd seen her fall. But while he was nice, and kind, he wasn't Gil, who was beginning to have a frightening effect on Kasie's heart. She glanced at Pauline as she spluttered. Kasie wished that she was beautiful like Pauline. She looked the very image of an efficient secretary. Kasie had great typing speed, dictation skills and organizational expertise, but she was only ordinary-looking. Besides, she was a social disaster, and she'd just proved it to Gil and all the guests.

Gil had been unexpectedly kind to her at the theater when he'd taken her with the girls to see the movie. She still tingled, remembering his hand holding hers. This, however, was much worse. Her breasts were almost bare in the thin blouse, and she felt the hard muscular wall of his chest with wonder and pleasure and a little fear, because she'd never felt such heady sensations in her body before. She wondered if he'd fire her for making a scene at his pool party, to which a lot of very wealthy and prominent cattlemen and their wives had been invited.

To give him credit, she hadn't exactly inspired confidence on the job in the past few weeks. Two weeks earlier, she tripped on the front steps and landed in a rosebush at the very feet of a visiting cattleman from Texas who'd almost turned purple trying not to laugh. Then there had been the ice-cream incident last week, which still embarrassed her. Bess had threatened Kasie with a big glop of chocolate ice cream. While Kasie was backing away, laughing helplessly, Gil had come into the house in dirty chaps and boots and shirt with his hat jerked low over one blue eye and his mouth a thin line, with blood streaming from a cut on his forehead. Bess had thrown the ice cream at Kasie, who ducked, just in time for it to hit Gil right in the forehead. While he was wiping it off, Kasie grabbed the spoon from Bess and waited for the explosion as her boss wiped the ice cream away and looked at her. Those blue eyes could cut like diamonds. They actually glittered. But he hadn't said a word. He'd just looked at her, before he turned and continued down the hall to the staircase that led up to his room.

Now, here she was half-drowned from a swimming pool accident, having made a spectacle of herself yet again.

"I wonder if I could get work in Hollywood?" she sputtered as she hung on for dear life. "There must be a market for terminal clumsiness somewhere!"

Gil raised an eyebrow and gave her a slow, speaking glance before he pulled her close against his chest and turned toward the concrete steps at the far end. He walked up out of the pool, streaming water, and started toward the house. "Don't struggle, Kasie," he said at her temple, and his voice sounded odd.

"Sorry," she coughed. "You can put me down, now. I'm okay. I can walk."

"If I put you down, you're going to become the entertainment," he said enigmatically at her ear. He looked over his shoulder. "John, look after the girls until I get back!" he called.

"Oh, I'll watch them, Gil!" Pauline interrupted lazily. "Come over here, girls!" she called, without even looking in their direction.

"John will watch them," Gil said emphatically and didn't move until his lean, lanky brother jumped up and went toward his nieces, grinning.

Gil went up the staircase with Kasie held close to his chest. "Why can't you swim?" he asked.

His deep, slow voice made her feel funny. So did the close, almost intimate contact with him. She nibbled on her lower lip, feeling soggy and disheveled and embarrassed. "I'm afraid of the water."

"Why?" he persisted.

She wouldn't answer him. It would do no good, and she didn't want to remember. Probably he'd never seen anyone drown. "Sorry I messed up the pool party," she murmured.

He shook her gently as they passed the landing and paused at her bedroom door. "Stop apologizing every second word," he said curtly as he put her down. He held her there with two big, lean hands on her upper arms and studied her intently in the dim light of the wall sconces.

The feel of all that warm strength against her made her giddy. She'd never been so close to him before. He was ten years older than Kasie, and he had an authority and maturity that must have been apparent even when he'd been her age.

She had tried to think of him as Bess and Jenny's daddy, but after their closeness at the movie theater, it was almost impossible to think of him as anything but a mature, sexy man.

"I can't seem to make you understand that the girls are Miss Parsons's responsibility, not yours!" He saw her faint flush and scowled down at her. "Speaking of Miss Parsons, where in hell is she?"

She cleared her throat and pushed back a soggy strand of dark hair. "She's in the office."

"Doing what?"

She shifted, but he didn't let go of her arms. That unblinking, ferocious blue stare robbed her of a smart retort. "All right," she said heavily. "She's doing the withholding on John's tax readout." He didn't speak. She looked up and grimaced. "Well, I'm not up on tax law, and she is."

"So you traded duties without permission, is that it?"

She hesitated. "Yes. I'm sorry. But it's just for today! You already know that she doesn't…well, she doesn't like children very much, really, and I hate taxes…"

"I know."

"I shouldn't have given them the beach ball. I thought they were going into the shallow part of the pool with it. And then Bess threw it…"

"Right at Pauline's expensive new coiffure," Gil finished for her. He pursed his sensuous lips and searched her face. "You won't tell on them, of course. You took the blame for the ice cream, too. And when one of Jenny's toys tripped you on the front steps and you went into the rosebush, you blamed that on clumsiness."

"You knew?" she asked, surprised.

"I've been a father for five years," he mused. "I know all sorts of things." His pale blue eyes slid very slowly down Kasie's wet dress and narrowed on what was showing. She had the most delicious body. Every line and curve of it was on view where the thin dress was plastered to her body. Her breasts were perfectly shaped and the nipples were dusky. The feel of her against his chest, even through her wet blouse and his cotton shirt, had almost knocked the breath out of him. It upset him that he was noticing these things about her. He was beginning to react to them, too. He had to get out of here. She was so young...

He cursed under his breath. "You'd better change," he said curtly. He turned on his heel and went toward the staircase.

"About Miss Parsons...!" she called after him, in one last attempt to ward off retribution.

"You might as well consider the girls your job from now on," he said angrily. "I can see that it's a losing battle to keep you away from them. I'll give Miss Parsons to John. He won't enjoy the view as much, but keeping out of prison because we can't figure out tax forms might sweeten the deal," he said, without breaking stride. "When you have some spare time, you can continue giving Pauline computer lessons. That includes Monday morning. Mrs. Charters can watch the girls while you work with Pauline."

"But I'm not a trained governess. I'm a secretary!" she insisted.

"Great. You can let Bess dictate letters to you for her dolls."

"But...!"

It was too late. He never argued. He just kept walking. She threw up her hands and went back into her room. She started toward the bathroom to change out of her wet things when she got a look at herself in the mirror. The whole outfit was transparent. She remembered Gil's intent stare and blushed all the way to her toes. No wonder he'd been looking at her. Everything she had was on view! She wondered how she'd ever be able to look him in the eye again.

She changed and went back to the pool party, dejected and miserable. It was hard to believe that she'd not even had a mild crush on John when she first went to work for the Callisters. He was handsome, and very sexy, but she just didn't feel that way about him. Fortunately he'd never felt that way about her, either. John had some secret woman in his past, and now he didn't get serious about anyone. Kasie had heard that from Mrs. Charters, who was a veritable storehouse of information about it. John didn't look to Kasie like a man with a broken heart. But maybe he played the field to camouflage it.

Kasie had never really been in love. She'd had crushes on TV celebrities and movie stars, and on boys at school—and one summer she'd had a real case on a boy who lived near Mama Luke, her aunt, in Billings. But those had all been very innocent, limited to kisses and light caresses and not much desire.

All that had changed when Gil Callister held her hand at the movies. And when Gil had carried her up the staircase this morning, she was on fire with pleasure. She was still shivery with new sensations, which she didn't understand at all. Gil was her boss and he disliked her. She'd been spending more time with the girls than the grown-ups because John didn't like to do paperwork and he was always dodging dictation. He could usually be found out with the men on the ranch, helping with whatever routine task was going on at the time. Gil did that, too, of course, but not because he didn't like paperwork. Gil rarely ever sat still.

Mrs. Charters said it was because he'd loved his wife and had never gotten over her unexpected death from a freak horse-back-riding accident. She was only twenty-six years old.

That had been only three years ago. Since then, Gil had hired a succession of nurses, at first, and then motherly governesses to watch over the girls. Old Mrs. Harris had retired and then Gil had hired Miss Parsons in desperation, over a virtual flood of young marriageable women who had their eye on either Gil or John. Kasie remembered Gil saying that he had no interest in marriage ever again. At that time, she couldn't have imagined feeling attracted to a widowed man with two children who had the personality of a spitting cobra.

For her first few weeks on the job, he'd watched Kasie. He

hadn't wanted his children around Kasie, and made it plain. Amazing, how much that had hurt.

They were such darling little girls.

At least, she thought, now she could spend time with them and not have to sneak around doing it. Gil might not like her, but he couldn't deny that his daughters did. Probably he felt that he didn't have a choice.

Kasie was going to miss the secretarial work, and she wondered how Gil would manage with Pauline, who absolutely hated clerical duties. The woman only did it to be near Gil, but he didn't seem to realize it. Or if he did, he didn't care.

She tried to picture Gil married to Pauline and it wounded her. Pauline was shallow and selfish. She didn't really like the girls, and she'd probably find some way to get them out of her hair when she and Gil married, if they did. Kasie hated the very idea of such a marriage, but she was a little nobody in the world and Gil Callister was a millionaire. She couldn't even tease him or flirt with him, because he might think she was after him for his wealth. It made her self-conscious, so she became uneasy around him and tongue-tied to boot.

That made him even more irritable. Sunday afternoon there was another storm and he and the men had to go out and work the cattle. He came in just after dark, drenched, unfastening his shirt on the way into the office. His hair was plastered to his scalp and his spurs jingled as he walked, his leather bat-wing chaps making flapping noises with every stride of his long, powerful jean-clad legs. His boots were soaked, too, and caked with mud.

"Mrs. Charters will be after you," Kasie remarked as she lifted her eyes from the badly scribbled notes John had left, which Miss Parsons had asked her to help decipher. Miss Parsons had already gone up to bed, anticipating a very early start on work the next morning.

"It's my damned house," he shot at her irritably, running a hand through his drenched hair to get it off his forehead. "I can drip wherever I please!"

"Suit yourself," Kasie replied. "But red mud won't come out of Persian wool carpets."

He gave her a hard glare, but he sat down in a chair and pulled off the mud-caked boots, tossing them onto the wide brick hearth of the fireplace, where they wouldn't soil anything delicate. His white socks were soaked as well, but he didn't take them off. He sat down behind his desk, picked up the telephone and made a call.

"Where are the girls?" he asked while he waited for the call to be answered.

"Watching the new *Pokémon* movie up in their room," Kasie said. "Miss Parsons can't read John's handwriting, so I'm deciphering this for her so she can start early tomorrow morning on the payroll and the quarterly estimated taxes that are due in June. If that's all right," she added politely.

He just glared at her. "Hello, Lonnie?" he said suddenly into the telephone receiver he was holding. "Can you give me the name of that mechanic who worked on Harris's truck last month? Yes, the one who doesn't need a damned computer to tell him what's wrong with the engine. Got his number? Just a minute." He fished in the drawer for a pen, grabbed an envelope and wrote a number on it. "Sure thing. Thanks." He hung up and dialed again.

While he spoke to the mechanic, Kasie finished transcribing John's terrible handwriting neatly for Miss Parsons.

Gil hung up and got to his feet, retrieving his boots. "If you've got a few minutes free, I need you to take some dictation for me," he told Kasie.

"I'll be glad to."

He gave her a narrow appraisal. "I've got a man coming over to look at my cattle truck," he added. "If he gets here while I'm in the shower, show him into the living room and don't let him leave. He can listen to an engine and tell you what's wrong with it."

"But it's Sunday," she began.

"I need the truck to haul cattle tomorrow. I'm sure he went

to church this morning, so it's all right," he assured her dryly. "Besides…"

The ringing of the phone interrupted him. He jerked up the receiver. "Callister," he said.

There was a pause, during which his face became harder than Kasie had ever seen it. "Yes," he replied to a question. "I'll talk to John when he gets back in, but I can tell you what the answer will be." He smiled coldly. "I'm sure that if you use your imagination, you can figure that out without too much difficulty. No, I don't. I don't give a damn. Do what you please with them." There was a longer pause and Kasie thought she'd never seen such coldness in a man's eyes. "I don't need a thing, thanks. Yes. You do that."

He hung up. "My parents," he said harshly. "With an invitation to come and bring the girls to their estate on Long Island next week."

"Are you going?"

He looked briefly sardonic. "They're hosting a party for some people who are interested in seeing what a real cattleman looks like," he said surprisingly. "They're trying to sell them on an advertising contract for their sports magazine and they think John and I might be useful." He sounded bitter and angry. "They try this occasionally, but John and I don't go. They can make money on their own. I'll be upstairs if the mechanic comes. Tell him the truck's in the barn with one of my men. He can go right on out."

"Okay."

He walked out and Kasie stared after him. The conversation with his parents hadn't been pleasant for him. He seemed to dislike them intensely. She knew that they were never mentioned around the girls, and John never spoke of them, either. She wondered what they'd done to make their sons so hostile. Then she remembered what Gil had said, about their being used by their parents only to make money, and it all began to make sense. Perhaps they didn't really want children at all. What a pity, that their sons were nothing more than sales incentives to them.

The mechanic did come while Gil was upstairs. Kasie went with him onto the long porch and showed him where the barn was, so that he could drive on down there and park his truck. The rain had stopped, though, so he didn't have to worry about getting wet. There was a pleasant dripping sound off the eaves of the house, and the delicious smell of wet flowers in the darkness.

Kasie sat down in the porch swing and rocked it into motion. It was a perfect night, now that the storm had abated. She could hear crickets, or maybe frogs, chirping all around the flowering shrubs that surrounded the front porch. It reminded her, for some reason, of Africa. She vaguely remembered sitting in a porch swing with her mother and Kantor when their father was away working. There were the delicious smells of cooking from the house, and the spicy smells drifting from the harbor nearby, as well as the familiar sound of African workers singing and humming as they worked around the settlement. It was a long time ago, when she still had a family. Now, except for Mama Luke, she was completely alone. It was a cold, empty feeling.

The screen door suddenly opened and Gil came out onto the porch. His blond hair was still damp, faintly unruly at the edges and tending to curl. He was wearing a blue checked Western shirt with clean jeans and nice boots. He looked just the way a working cowboy should when he was cleaned up, she thought, trying to imagine him a century earlier.

"Is the mechanic here?" he asked abruptly when he spotted Kasie in the swing.

"Yes, I sent him on down to the barn."

He went down the steps gracefully and stalked to the barn. He was gone about five minutes and when he came out of the barn, so did the mechanic. They shook hands and the mechanic drove off.

"A fuse," he murmured, shaking his head as he came up

the steps and dropped into the swing at Kasie's side. "A damned fuse, and the whole panel went down. Imagine that."

"Sometimes it's the little things that give the most trouble," she murmured, shy with him.

He put an arm behind her and rocked the swing into motion. "I like the way you smell, Kasie," he said lazily. "You always remind me of roses."

"I'm allergic to perfume," she confided. "The florals are the only ones I can wear without sneezing my head off."

"Where are my babies?" he asked.

"Mrs. Charters is baking cookies with them in the kitchen," she said, smiling. "They love to cook. So do I. We've all learned a lot from Mrs. Charters."

He looked down at her in the darkness. One lean hand went to the braid at the back of her head, and he tugged on it gently. "You're mysterious," he murmured. "I don't really know anything about you."

"There's not much to tell," she told him. "I'm just ordinary."

He shifted, and she felt his powerful thigh against her leg. Her body came alive with fleeting little stabs of pleasure. She could feel her breath catching in her throat as she breathed. He was too close.

She started to move, but it was too late. His arm curled her into his body, and the warm, hard pressure of his mouth pushed her head back against the swing while he fed hungrily on her lips.

Part of her wanted to resist, but a stronger part was completely powerless. She reached up and put her arms around his neck and opened her lips for him. She felt him stiffen, hesitate, catch his breath. Then his mouth became rough and demanding, and he dragged her across his legs, folding her close while he kissed her until her mouth was swollen and tender.

He nibbled her upper lip, fighting to breathe normally. "Don't let me do this," he warned.

"You're bigger than I am," she murmured breathlessly.

"That's no excuse at all."

Her fingers trailed over his hard mouth and down to his chest where they rested. She stared at the wide curve of his mouth with a kind of wonder that a man like this, good-looking and charming and wealthy, would look twice at a chestnut mouse like Kasie. Perhaps he needed glasses.

He touched her oval face, tracing its soft lines in a warm, damp darkness that was suddenly like an exotic, faraway place. Kasie felt as if she'd come home. Impulsively, she let her head slide down his arm until it rested in the crook of his elbow. She watched his expression harden, heard his breathing change. His lean fingers moved down her chin and throat until they were at the top button of her shirtwaist dress. They hesitated there.

She lay looking up at him patiently, curiously, ablaze with unfamiliar longings and delight.

"Kasie," he whispered, and his long fingers began to sensually move the top button out of its buttonhole. As it came free, he heard her soft gasp, felt the jerk of her body, and knew that this was new territory for her.

His hand started to slide gently into the opening he'd made. He watched Kasie, lying so sweetly in his embrace, giving him free license with her innocence, and he shivered with desire.

But even as he felt the soft warmth of the skin at her collarbone, laughing young voices came drifting out onto the porch as the front door opened.

Gil moved Kasie back into her own seat abruptly and stood up.

"Daddy's home!" Bess cried, and she and Jenny ran to him, to be scooped up and kissed heartily.

"I'll, uh, just go and get my pad so that you can dictate that letter you mentioned," Kasie said as she got up, too.

"You will not," Gil said, his voice still a little husky. "Go to bed, Kasie. It can wait. In the morning, you can tutor Pauline on the computer, so that she can take over inputting the cattle records. John won't be in until late tonight, and he leaves early tomorrow for the cattle show in San Antonio. There's nothing in the office that can't wait."

She was both disappointed and relieved. It was getting harder to deny Gil anything he wanted. She couldn't have imagined that she was such a wanton person only a few weeks ago. She didn't know what to do.

"Okay, I'll call it a night," she said, trying to disguise her nervousness. "Good night, babies," she told Bess and Jenny with a smile. "Sleep tight."

"Will you tell us a story, Kasie?" Bess began.

"I'll tell you a story tonight. Kasie needs her rest. All right?" he asked the girls.

"All right, Daddy," Jenny murmured, laying her sleepy head on his shoulder.

They all went upstairs together. Kasie didn't quite meet his eyes as she went down the hall to her own room. She didn't sleep very much, either.

Chapter 6

Pauline Raines was half an hour late Monday morning. Gil had already gone out to check on some cattle that was being shipped off. John had left before daylight to fly to San Antonio, where the cattle trailer was taking his champion bull, Ebony King, for the cattle show. While the girls took their nap, Kasie helped Miss Parsons with John's correspondence and fielded the telephone. Now that it was just past roundup, things weren't quite as hectic, but sales reports were coming in on the culled cattle being shipped, and they weren't even all on the computer yet. Neither were most of the new calf crop.

Miss Parsons had gone to the post office when Pauline arrived wearing a neat black suit with a fetching blue scarf. She glared at Kasie as she threw her purse down on the chair.

"Here I am," she said irritably. "I don't usually come in before ten, but Gil said I had to be early, to work on this stupid computer. I don't see why I need to learn it."

"Because you'll have to put in all the information we're getting about the new calves and replacement heifers," Kasie explained patiently. "It's backing up."

"You can do that," Pauline said haughtily. "You're John's secretary."

"Not anymore," she replied calmly. "I'm going to take care of the girls while Miss Parsons takes my place in John's office. She's going to handle all the tax work."

That piece of information didn't please Pauline. "You're a secretary," she pointed out.

"That's what I told Mr. Callister, but it didn't change his mind," Kasie replied tersely.

"So now I'll have to do all your work while Miss Parsons does taxes? I won't! Surely you'll have enough free time to put these records on the computer! Two little girls don't require much watching. Just put them in front of the television!"

Kasie almost bit her tongue right through keeping back a hot reply. "It isn't going to be hard to use the computer. It will save you hours of paperwork."

Pauline gave her a glare. "Debbie always put these things on the computer."

"Debbie quit because she couldn't do two jobs at once," Kasie said, and was vindicated for the jibe when she saw Pauline's discomfort. "You really will enjoy the time the computer saves you, once you understand how it works."

"I don't need this job, didn't anyone tell you?" the older woman asked. "I'm wealthy. I only do it to be near Gil. It gives us more time together, while we're seeing how compatible we are. Which reminds me, don't think you're onto a cushy job looking after those children," she added haughtily. "Gil and I are going to be looking for a boarding school very soon."

"Boarding school?" Kasie exclaimed, horrified.

"I've already checked out several," Pauline said. "It isn't good for little girls to become too attached to their fathers. It interferes with Gil's social life."

"I hadn't noticed."

Pauline frowned. "What do you mean, you hadn't noticed?"

"Well, Mr. Callister is almost a generation older than I am," she said deliberately.

"Oh." Pauline smiled secretively. "I see."

"He's a very kind man," Kasie emphasized, "but I don't think of him in that way," she added, lying through her teeth.

Pauline for once seemed speechless.

"Here, let's get started," Kasie said as she turned on the computer, trying to head off trouble. She hoped that comment would keep her out of trouble with Pauline, who obviously considered Gil Callister her personal property. Kasie had enough problems without adding a jealous secretary to them. Even if she did privately think Gil was the sexiest man she'd ever known.

Pauline seemed determined to make every second of work as hard as humanly possible for Kasie. She insisted on three coffee breaks before noon, and the pressing nature of the information coming in by fax kept Kasie working long after Pauline called it a day at three in the afternoon and went home. If Mrs. Charters hadn't helped out by letting Bess and Jenny make cookies, Kasie wouldn't have been able to do as much as she did.

She'd only just finished the new computer entries when Gil came in, dusty and sweaty and half out of humor. He didn't say a word. He went to the liquor cabinet and poured himself a scotch and water, and he drank half of it before he even looked at Kasie.

It took her a minute to realize that he was openly glaring at her.

"Is something wrong?" she asked uneasily.

"Pauline called me on the cell phone a few minutes ago. She said you're making it impossible for her to do her job," he replied finally.

Her heart skipped. So that was how the other woman was going to make points—telling lies.

"I've been showing her how to key in this data, and that's all I've done," Kasie told him quietly. "She hates the computer."

"Odd that she's done so well with it up until now," he said suspiciously.

"Debbie did well with it," Kasie replied bluntly, flushing a little at his angry tenseness. "She was apparently having to put her own work as well as Pauline's into the computer."

He took another sip of the drink. He didn't look convinced. "That isn't what Pauline says," he told her. "And I want to know why you suddenly want my girls in a boarding school, after you've spent weeks behind my back and against instructions winning them over, so they're attached to you." He added angrily, "I meant it when I said I have no plans to marry. So if that changes your mind about wanting to take care of them, say so and I'll give you a reference and two weeks severance pay!"

He really did look ferocious. Kasie's head was spinning from the accusations. "Excuse me?"

He finished the drink and put the glass down firmly on the counter below the liquor cabinet. His pale eyes were glittery. "John and I spent six of the worst years of our lives at boarding school," he added unexpectedly. "I'm not putting my babies in any boarding school."

Kasie felt as if she were being attacked by invisible hands. She stood up, her mind reeling from the charges. Pauline had been busy!

"I haven't said anything about boarding school," she defended herself. "Pauline said…"

He held up a hand. "I know Pauline," he told her. "I've known her most of my life. She doesn't tell lies."

Boy, was he in for a shock a little further on down the road, she thought, but she didn't say anything else. She was already in too much trouble, and none of it of her own making.

She didn't say a word. She just looked at him with big, gray, wounded eyes.

He moved closer, his mind reeling from Pauline's comments about Kasie. He didn't want to believe that Kasie was so two-faced that she'd play up to the girls to get in Gil's good graces and then want to see them sent off to boarding school. But what did he really know about her, after all? She had no family except an aunt in Billings, or so she said, and except for the information on her application that mentioned secretarial school, nothing about her early education was apparent. She was mysterious. He didn't like mysteries.

He stopped just in front of her, his face hard and threatening as he glared down at her.

"Where were you born?" he asked abruptly.

The question surprised her. She became flustered. "I, well, I was born in…in Africa."

He hadn't expected that answer, and it showed. *"Africa?"*

"Yes. In Sierra Leone," she added.

He frowned. "What were your parents doing in Africa?"

"They worked there."

"I see." He didn't, but she looked as if she hated talking about it. The mystery only deepened.

"Maybe you're right," she said, unnerved by his unexpected anger and the attack by Pauline, which made her look like a gold digger. "Maybe I'm not the best person to look after the girls. If you like, I'll hand in my notice…!"

He had her by both shoulders with a firm grip and the expression on his face made her want to back away.

"And just for the record, ten years isn't a generation!" he said through his teeth as he glared down at her. His gaze dropped to her soft, generous mouth and it was like lightning striking. He couldn't help himself. The memory of her body in his arms on the porch swing took away the last wisp of his willpower. He bent quickly and took that beautiful softness under his hard lips in a fever of hunger, probing insistently at her tight mouth with his tongue.

Kasie, who'd never been kissed in any intimate way, even by Gil, froze like ice at the skillful, invasive intimacy of his mouth. She couldn't believe what was happening. Her hands against his chest clenched and she closed her eyes tightly as she strained against his hold.

Slowly it seemed to get through to him that she was shocked at the insistence. He lifted his demanding mouth and looked at her. This was familiar territory for him. But, it wasn't for her, and it was apparent. After the way she'd responded to him the night before, he was surprised that she balked at a deep kiss. But, then, he remembered her chaste gowns and her strange attitude about wearing her beautiful hair loose. She wasn't fighting him. She looked...strange.

His lean hands loosened, became caressing on her upper arms under the short sleeve of her dress. "I'm sorry. It's all right," he breathed as he bent again. "I won't be rough with you. It's all right, Kasie..."

His lips barely brushed hers, tender now instead of demanding. A few seconds of tenderness brought a sigh from her lips. He smiled against her soft mouth as he coaxed it to part. He nibbled the full upper lip, tasting its velvety underside with his tongue, enjoying her reactions to him. He felt her young body begin to relax into his. She worked for him. She was an employee. He'd just been giving her hell about trying to trap him into marriage. So why was he doing this...? She made a soft sound under her breath and her hands tightened on the hard muscles of his upper arms. His brows began to knit as sensation pulsed through him at her shy response. What did it matter *why* he was doing it, he asked himself, and threw caution to the winds.

His arms went around her, gently smoothing her against the muscular length of him, while his mouth dragged a response under its tender pressure. He felt her gasp, felt her shiver, then felt her arms sliding around his waist as she gave in to the explosion of warm sensation that his hungry kiss provoked in her.

It was like flying, he thought dizzily. He lifted her against him, feeding on the softness of her mouth, the clinging wonder of her arms around him. It had been years since a kiss had been this sweet, this fulfilling. Not since Darlene had he been so hungry for a woman's mouth. Darlene. Darlene. Kasie was so much like her...

Only the need to breathe forced him to put her down and

lift his head. His turbulent eyes met her dazed ones and he had to fight to catch his breath.

"Why did you do that?" she asked unsteadily.

He was scowling. He touched her mouth with a lean fore-finger. "I don't know," he said honestly. "Do you want me to apologize?" he added quietly.

"Are you sorry?" she returned.

"I am not," he said, every word deliberate as he stared into her eyes.

That husky statement made her tingle all over with delicious sensations, but he still looked formidable. His lean fingers caught her shoulders and gently moved her away. She looked as devastated as he felt.

Her eyes searched his quietly. She was shaking inside from the delicious crush of his mouth, so unexpected. "What did you mean, about ten years not being a generation?" she asked suddenly.

"You harp on my age," he murmured coolly, but he was still looking at her soft, swollen mouth. "You shouldn't tell Pauline things you don't want me to hear. She can't keep a secret."

"I wouldn't tell her my middle name," she muttered. "She hates me, haven't you noticed?"

"No, I hadn't."

"It would never have been my idea to send the girls to boarding school," she insisted. "I love them."

His eyebrows lifted. Kasie didn't appear to be lying. But Pauline had been so convincing. And Kasie was mysterious. He wanted to know why she was so secretive about her past. He wanted to know everything about her. Her mouth was sweet and soft and innocent, and he had to fight not to bend and take it again. She was nervous with him now, as she hadn't been before. That meant that the attraction was mutual. It made him feel a foot taller.

"Pauline wants to go down to Nassau for a few days with the girls. I want you to come with us," he said abruptly.

She gaped at him. "She won't want me along," she said with conviction.

"She will when she has to start looking out for Bess and Jenny. Her idea of watching them is to let them do what they please. That could be disastrous even around a swimming pool."

She grimaced. It would be a horrible trip. "We'd have to fly," she said, hating the very thought of getting on an airplane. She'd lost everyone she'd ever loved in the air, and he didn't know.

"The girls like you," he persisted gently.

"I'd really rather not," she said worriedly.

"Then I'll make it an order," he said shortly. "You're coming. Have you got a current passport?"

"Yes," she said without thinking.

He was surprised. "I was going to say that if you didn't have one, a birth certificate or even a voter's registration slip would be adequate." He was suspicious. "Why do you keep a passport?"

"In case I get kidnapped by terrorists," she said, tongue in cheek, trying to put aside the fear of the upcoming trip.

He rolled his eyes, let her go and walked to the door. "We'll go Friday," he said. "Don't take much with you," he added. "We'll fly commercial and I don't like baggage claim."

"Okay."

"And stop letting me kiss you," he added with faint arrogance. "I've already made it clear that there's no future in it. I won't marry again, not even to provide the girls with a grown-up playmate."

"I do know that," she said, wounded by the words. "But I'm not the one doing the grabbing," she pointed out.

He gave her an odd look before he left.

She could have told him that she didn't have much to take anywhere, and she almost blurted out why she was afraid of airplanes. But he was already out the door. She touched her mouth. She tasted scotch whiskey on her lips and she was

amazed that she hadn't noticed while he was kissing her. Why
had he kissed her again? she wondered dazedly. The other
question was why had she kissed him back? Her head was
reeling with the sudden shift in their relationship since the
night before. Kissing seemed to be addictive. Perhaps she
should cut her losses and quit right away. But that thought was
very unpleasant indeed. She decided that meeting trouble head-
on was so much better than running from it. She had to conquer
her fear and try to put the past behind her once and for all.
Yes, she would go to Nassau with him and the girls—and
Pauline. It might very well put things into perspective if she
saw Pauline and Gil as a family, while there was still time to
stop her rebellious heart from falling in love.

Kasie's seat was separated from Gil's, Pauline's and the
girls' by ten rows. Gil didn't appear pleased and he tried to
change seat assignments, but it wasn't possible. Kasie was
rather relieved. She was uncomfortable with Gil since he'd
kissed her so passionately.

Pauline was furious that Kasie had been included in the trip.
She was doing everything in her power to get Kasie out of
Gil's life, but nothing was going the way she planned. She'd
envisioned just the four of them in the exquisite islands, where
she could convince Gil that they should get married. He agreed
to her suggestion about the trip more easily than she'd hoped,
and then he said Kasie would have to come along to take care
of the girls. He didn't even mention boarding school, as if he
didn't believe Kasie had suggested it. Pauline was losing
ground with him by the day. She could cheerfully have pushed
Kasie out of the terminal window. Well, she was going to get
rid of Miss Prim over there, whatever it took. One way or
another, she was going to get Kasie out of Gil's house!

They boarded the plane, and Kasie smiled with false bravado
as she passed the girls with a wave and found her window seat.
There was only one seat next to hers. She was watching the
people file in while she fought her own fear. Seconds later, a

tall blond man wearing khakis swung into the seat beside hers and gave her an appreciative smile.

"And I thought this was going to be a boring flight," he chuckled as he stuffed his one carry-on bag under the seat in front of him and fastened his seat belt. "I'm Zeke Mulligan," he introduced himself with a smile. "I write freelance travel articles for magazines."

"I'm Kasie Mayfield," she replied, offering her small hand with a wan smile. "I'm a governess to two sweet little girls."

"Where are the sweet little girls?" he asked with a grin.

"Ten rows that way," she pointed. "With their dad and his venomous secretary."

"Ouch, the jealousy monster strikes, hmm?" he asked. "Does she see you as competition?"

"That would be one for the books," she chuckled. "She's blond and beautiful."

"What are you, chestnut-haired and repulsive?" he chided. "Looks aren't everything, fellow adventurer."

"Adventuress," she corrected. She glanced out the window and noticed the movement of the motorized carts away from the plane. It was going to take off soon. Sure enough, she heard the rev of the engines and saw the flight attendants take up their positions to demonstrate the life vests even as the plane started to taxi out of its concourse space. "Oh, gosh," she groaned, tightening her hands on the arms of her seat.

"Afraid of flying?" he asked gently.

"I lost my family in a plane crash," she said in a rough whisper. "This is the first time I've flown, since I lost them. I don't know if I can...!"

She'd started to pull at her seat belt. He caught her hand and stilled it. "Listen to me," he said gently, "air travel is the safest kind. I've been knocking around on airplanes for ten years, I've been around the world three times. It's all right," he stressed, his voice low and deep and comforting. His fingers contracted around hers. "You just hold on to me. I'll get you through takeoff and landing. Once you've conquered the fear, you'll be fine.''

"Are you sure?" she asked on a choked laugh.

"I walked away from a crash once," he told her quietly. "A week later I had to get on a plane for Paris. Yes," he added. "I'm sure. If I could do it, I know you can."

Her lips parted as she let out the breath she'd been holding. He was nice. He was very nice. He made her feel utterly safe. She clung to his hand as the airplane taxied to the runway and the pilot announced that they were next in line to take off.

"Here we go," her seat companion said in her ear. "Think of *Star Trek* when the ship goes into light speed," he added on a chuckle. "Think of it as being flung up into the stars. It's exciting. It's great!"

She held on tighter as the plane taxied onto the runway, revved up its engines and began to pick up speed.

"We can even sing the Air Force song as we go," he said. "I spent four years in it, so I can coach you if you can't remember the words. Come on, Kasie. Sing!"

Kasie started to hum the words of the well-known song.

The passengers around them noticed Kasie's terror and her companion's protective attitude, and suddenly they all started singing the Air Force song. It diverted Kasie with uproarious laughter as the big airplane shot up into the blue sky, leaving her stomach and her fears far behind.

"I'm very grateful," she told him when they were comfortably leveled off and the flight attendants were getting the refreshment cart ready to take down the aisle. "You can't imagine how terrified I was to get on this plane."

"Yes, I can. I'm glad I was here. Where are you staying in Nassau?" he added.

She laughed. "I'm sorry. I don't know! I didn't realize that until just now. My boss will have all the details in hand, and a driver to meet us when we land. I didn't ask."

"New Providence is a small island," he told her. "We'll see each other again. I'm at the Crystal Palace on Cable Beach.

You can phone me if you get a few free minutes and we'll have lunch."

"Do you go overseas to do stories?" she asked.

He nodded. "All over the world. It's a great job, and I actually get paid to do it." He leaned close to her ear. "And once, I worked for the CIA."

"You didn't!" she exclaimed, impressed.

"Just for a year, while I was in South America," he assured her. "I might have kept it up, but I was married then and she didn't want me taking chances, especially while she was carrying our son."

"She doesn't travel with you?" she asked curiously.

"She died, of a particularly virulent tropical fever," he said with a sad smile. "My son is six, and I leave him with my parents when I have to go away during his school year. During the summer, he goes places with me. He loves it, too."

He pulled out his wallet and showed her several photographs of a child who was his mirror image. "His name's Daniel, but I call him Dano."

"He really is cute."

"Thanks."

The flight attendant was two rows away, with snack meals and drinks. Kasie settled down to lunch with no more reservations. She'd landed on her feet. She wondered what Gil would think if he saw her with this nice young man. Nothing, probably, she thought bitterly, not when he was so wrapped up in Pauline. Well, she wasn't going to let that spoil her trip.

Nassau was unexpected. Kasie fell in love with it on first sight. She'd seen postcards of the Bahamas, and she'd always assumed that the vivid turquoise and sapphire color of the waters was exaggerated. But it wasn't. Those vivid, surreal colors were exactly what the water looked like, and the beaches were as white as sugar. She stared out the window of the hired car with her breath catching in her chest. She'd gone overseas with her parents as a child, but to distant and primitive places. She remembered the terror of those places far better than she remembered the scenery, even at so young an age. Even now, it was hard to think about how she'd lost the parents who'd loved her and Kantor so much. It was harder to think of Kantor...

"Do stop pressing your nose against the glass, Kasie. You look about Jenny's age!" Pauline chided from her seat beside Gil.

"That's funny," Bess said with a giggle, not understanding the words were meant to hurt.

"I've never seen anything so beautiful," Kasie murmured a little shyly. "It really does look like paradise."

Pauline yawned. Gil ignored her and watched Kasie a little irritably as she and the girls enthused over the beach.

"When can we go swimming in the ocean, Daddy?" Bess asked excitedly.

"We have to check into the hotel first, baby," Gil told her. "And even then, the beach is dangerous. Kasie doesn't swim."

"Oh, we can take them with us," Pauline said lazily. "I'll watch them."

It occurred to Gil that he never trusted Pauline with his children. She wasn't malicious, she just didn't pay attention to what they were doing. She'd be involved in putting on sunscreen and lying in the sun, not watching children who could become reckless. Bess was especially good at getting into trouble.

"That's Kasie's job," Gil said, and put a long arm around Pauline just to see the reaction it got from Kasie. It was a constant source of anger that he couldn't keep his hands off Kasie when he was within five feet of her, and he still didn't trust her.

Kasie averted her eyes. Odd, how much it hurt to see Pauline snuggle close to Gil as if she were part of him. Remembering the hungry, masterful way he'd kissed her in the study, Kasie flushed. She knew things about Gil Callister that she shouldn't know. He made her hungry. But he was showing her that he didn't feel the same way. It was painfully obvious what his relationship was with Pauline. Even though she'd guessed, it hurt to have it pointed out to her like this.

She knew then that she was going to have to resign her job when they got back to the States. If he married Pauline, there was no way she could live under the same roof with them.

Gil saw the reaction that Kasie was too young to hide, and it touched him. She felt something. She was jealous. He could have cheered out loud. It didn't occur to him then why he was so happy that Kasie was attracted to him.

"Who was the man you were talking to on the concourse, Kasie?" Gil asked unexpectedly.

"His name was Zeke," she replied with a smile. "He had the seat next to mine."

"I noticed him. He's good-looking," Pauline said. "What does he do?"

"He's a freelance writer for several travel magazines," Kasie told her. "He's down here doing a story on a new hotel complex."

Gil didn't look pleased. "Apparently you made friends quickly."

"Well, yes," she confessed. "I was a little nervous about flying. He talked to me while we got airborne." She grinned. "Didn't you hear us all singing the Air Force song?"

"So that's what it was," Pauline scoffed. "Good Lord, I thought the plane was full of drunks."

"Why were you afraid of flying?" Gil persisted.

Kasie averted her eyes to the girls. "My family died in an airplane crash," she said, without mentioning under what circumstances.

He shifted uncomfortably and looked at his daughters, who were watching for exciting little glimpses of people playing in the surf on the white beaches as they passed them.

"I'm all right now," she said. "the flight wasn't so bad."

"Not with a handsome man to hold your hand," Pauline teased deliberately.

"He *was* handsome," Kasie agreed, but without enthusiasm,

and without noticing that Gil's eyes were beginning to glint with anger. He leaned back, glaring at Kasie.

She wondered what she'd done to provoke that anger. It made her uneasy. Pauline obviously didn't like it, either, and the woman was giving Kasie looks that promised retribution in the near future. Kasie had a feeling that Miss Raines would make a very bad enemy, and deep in her stomach, she felt icy cold.

Chapter 7

It took an hour to get checked into the luxury hotel. The girls played quietly in the marble-floored lobby with a puzzle book Kasie had brought along for them, while Pauline complained loudly and nonstop about the inconvenience of having to wait for a room to be made ready. By the time the clerk motioned them to the desk, Gil was completely out of humor. He hadn't smiled since they got off the plane, in fact. When they were given keys to a two-bedroom suite and a single adjoining room, Pauline's expression lightened.

"Oh, that's nice of you, darling, letting Miss Mayfield have a room of her own."

Gil gave her a look that combined exasperation with impatience. "The girls can't be alone at night in a strange hotel," he said curtly. "Kasie's staying in the room with them, and the other bedroom in the suite is mine. You get the single."

"Why can't I just share with you, darling?" Pauline purred, enjoying Kasie's sudden flush.

Gil looked furious. He glared down at her from his superior height. "Maybe you've forgotten that I don't move with the times," he said quietly.

Pauline laughed a little nervously. "You're kidding. What's so bad about two...friends sharing a room?"

"I'm not kidding," Gil said flatly. He handed Pauline her key and motioned for Kasie and the girls to follow him.

Pauline stomped into the elevator, fuming. She gave Kasie a ferocious glare before she folded her arms over her chest and leaned back against the wall. The bellboy signaled that he'd wait for the next elevator to bring their luggage up, because six other people had jumped into the elevator right behind Pauline.

Gil and Pauline led the way down the hall, with Kasie and the girls following suit.

"At least, you can take me out tonight," Pauline told Gil, "since Kasie's along to baby-sit. Come on, darling, please? They have the most beautiful casino over on Paradise Island, and floor shows, too."

"All right," he said. "Let me get the girls and Kasie settled first, and find out about room service. You will want to have supper up here, won't you?" he asked Kasie stiffly.

"Of course," she said, not wanting to make things worse than they were—if that was possible.

"Good. Kasie can take the girls out to the beach while I check with the concierge about reservations," he added, watching Pauline's face beam. "I'll pick you up at your room at five-thirty."

"But that only gives me an hour to dress," she moaned.

"You'd look beautiful in a pillowcase, and you know it," he chided. "Go on."

"Okay." Pauline walked off to her own room without a word to the girls or Kasie.

Gil opened the door, noting that the bellboy was coming down the hall toward them with the luggage on a rolling carrier. He motioned Kasie and the girls inside.

"The bedrooms both have two double beds," he told Kasie stiffly. "And there's a balcony off the sitting room, if you want to sit outside and watch the surf after the girls get to sleep," he added, indicating the French doors that led onto a small balcony with two padded chairs.

"We'll be fine," she told him.

"Don't let them stay up past eight, no matter what they say," he told her. "And don't you stay up too late, either."

"I won't."

He hesitated at the door to his own room and looked at Kasie for a long moment, until her heart began to race. "You didn't tell me that you lost your family in an air crash. Why?"

"The subject didn't come up," she said gruffly.

"If it had," he replied curtly, "you wouldn't have been sitting alone, despite Pauline's little machinations with the seat assignments."

She was taken aback by the anger in his tone. "Oh."

"You make me feel like a gold-plated heel from time to time, Kasie," he said irritably. "I don't like it."

"I was all right," she assured him nervously. "Zeke took care of me."

That set him off again. "You're getting paid to take care of my children, not to holiday with some refugee from a press room," he pointed out, his voice arctic.

She stiffened. "I hadn't forgotten that, *Mr.* Callister," she added deliberately, aware that the girls had stopped playing and were staring up at the adults with growing disquiet. She turned away. "Come on, babies," she said with a forced smile. "Let's go change into our bathing suits, then we can go play on the beach!"

"All of you stay out of the water," Gil said shortly. "And I want you back up here before I leave with Pauline."

"Yes, sir," Kasie said, just because she knew it made him angry.

He said something under his breath and slammed the door to his own room behind him. Kasie had a premonition that it wasn't going to be much of a holiday.

She and the girls played in the sand near the ocean. On the way outside, Kasie had bought them small plastic buckets and shovels from one of the stores in the arcade. They were happily dumping sand on each other while, around them, other sun-worshipers lay on towel-covered beach chaise lounges or splashed in the water. The hotel was near the harbor, as well, and they watched a huge white ocean liner dock. It was an exciting place to visit.

Kasie, who'd only ever seen the worst part of foreign countries, was like a child herself as she gazed with fascination at rows of other luxury hotels on the beach, as well as sailboats and cruise ships in port. Nassau was the brightest, most beautiful place she'd ever been. The sand was like sugar under her feet, although hot enough to scorch them, and the color of the water was almost too vivid to believe. Smiling, she drank in the warmth of the sun with her eyes closed.

But it was already time to go back up to the room. She hated telling the girls, who begged to stay on the beach.

"We can't, babies," she said gently. "Your dad said we have to be in the room when he leaves. There's a television," she added. "They might have cartoons."

They still looked disappointed. "You could read us stories," Bess said.

Kasie smiled and hugged her. "Yes, I could. And I will. Come on, now, clean out your pails and shovels, and let's go."

"Oh, all right, Kasie, but it's very sad we have to leave," Bess replied.

"Don't want to go." Jenny pouted.

Kasie picked her up and kissed her sandy cheek. "We'll come out early in the morning, and look for shells on the beach!"

Jenny's eyes lit up. She loved seashells. "Truly, Kasie?"

"Honest and truly."

"Whoopee!" Bess yelled. "I'll get Jenny's pail, too. Can we have fish for supper?"

"Anything you like," Kasie told her as she put Jenny down and refastened her swimsuit strap that had come loose.

Above them, at the window of his room, Gil watched the byplay, unseen. He sighed with irritation as he watched the girls respond so wholeheartedly to Kasie. They loved her. How were they going to react if she decided to quit? She was very young; too young to think of making a lifelong baby-sitter. Pauline said she'd been very adamant about sending the girls away to school, but that was hard to believe, watching her with them. She was tender with them, as Darlene had been.

He rammed his hands hard into the pockets of his dress slacks. It hurt remembering how happy the two of them had been, especially after the birth of their second little girl. In the Callister family, girls were special, because there hadn't been a girl in the lineage for over a hundred years. Gil loved having daughters. A son would have been nice, he supposed, but he wouldn't have traded either of his little jewels down there for anything else.

It wounded him to remember how cold he'd been to Kasie before and after the plane trip. He hadn't known about her family dying in a plane crash. He could only imagine how difficult it had been for her to get aboard with those memories. And he'd been sitting with Pauline, talking about Broadway shows. Pauline had said that Kasie wanted to sit by herself, so he hadn't protested.

Then, of course, there was this handsome stranger who'd comforted her on the flight to keep her from being afraid. He could have done that. He could have held her hand tight in his and kissed her eyes shut while he whispered to her...

He groaned out loud and turned away from the window. She was worming her way not only into his life and his girls' lives, but into his heart as well. He hadn't been able to even think about Pauline in any romantic way since Kasie had walked into his living room for the job interview. Up until then, he'd found the gorgeous blonde wonderful company. Now, she was almost an afterthought. He couldn't imagine why. Kasie wasn't really pretty. Although, she had a nice figure and a very kiss-able mouth and those exquisitely tender eyes...

He jerked up the phone and dialed Pauline's extension. "Are you ready to go?" he asked.

"Darling, I haven't finished my makeup. You did say five-thirty," she reminded him.

"It is five-thirty," he muttered.

"Give me ten more minutes," she said. "I'm going to make you notice me tonight, lover," she teased. "I'm wearing something very risqué!"

"Fine," he replied, unimpressed. "I'll see you in ten minutes."

He hung up on her faint gasp of irritation. He didn't care if she wore postage stamps, it wasn't going to cure him of the hunger for Kasie that was tormenting him.

He heard the suite door open and the sound of his children laughing. Strange how often they laughed these days, when they'd been so somber and quiet before. She brought out the best in people. Well, not in himself, he had to admit. She brought out the worst in him, God knew why.

He went out into the big sitting room, still brooding.

"Daddy, you look nice!" Bess said, running to him to be picked up and kissed heartily. "Doesn't he look nice, Kasie?" she asked.

"Yes," Kasie said, glancing at him. He was dishy in a tuxedo, she thought miserably, and Pauline probably looked like uptown New York City in whatever she was wearing. Pauline was like a French pastry, while Kasie was more like a stale doughnut. The thought amused her and she smiled.

"Bess, get the menu off the desk and take it in your room. You and Jenny decide what you want to eat," Gil told them.

"Yes, Daddy," Bess said at once, scooping up the menu and her sister's hand as they left the room.

"Don't let them fill up on sweets," he cautioned Kasie. His pale eyes narrowed on her body in the discreet, one-piece blue bathing suit she was wearing with sandals and a sheer cover-up in shades of blue. Her hair was down around her shoulders. She looked good enough to eat.

"I won't," she promised, moving awkwardly toward the bathroom with the towel she'd been sunbathing on.

"Next time, get a towel from the caretaker down on the beach," he said after she'd put the towel in the bathroom. "They keep them there for beach use."

She flushed. "Sorry. I didn't know."

He moved toward her. In flats, she was even shorter than usual. He looked down at her with narrow, stormy eyes. The curves of her pretty breasts were revealed in the suit and he thought for one insane instant of bending and putting his mouth right down on that soft pink skin.

"Mr. Callister," she began, the name almost choking her as his nearness began to have the usual effect on her shaking knees.

His lean hand moved to her throat and touched it lightly, stroking down to her bare shoulder and then back to her collarbone. "You've got sand on your skin," he observed.

"We had a little trouble making a sand castle, so the girls covered me up instead," she said with an unsteady laugh.

His hand flattened on the warm flesh and he looked into her huge, soft eyes, waiting for a reaction. Her pulse became visible in her throat. His blood began to surge, hot and turbulent, in his veins. His fingers spread out deliberately, so that the touch became intimate.

She wasn't protesting. She hadn't moved an inch. She didn't even seem to be breathing as she looked up into his pale, glittery eyes and waited, spellbound, for whatever came next.

Without saying a word, his fingers slid under the strap that held up her bodice. They inched into the suit and traced exquisite patterns on the soft, bare flesh that had never been exposed to the sun, or to a man's eyes. He watched her lips part, her eyes dilate with fascination and curiosity.

His hand stilled as he realized what he was doing. The girls were right in the next room, for God's sake. Was he losing his mind?

He jerked his hand back as if he'd scalded it and his expression became icy. "You'd better change," he said through his teeth.

She didn't move. Her eyes were wide, curious, apprehensive. She didn't understand his actions or his obvious anger.

But he was suspicious of her. He didn't trust her, and he didn't like his unchecked response to her. She could be anybody, with any motive in mind. She dressed like a repressed woman, but she never resisted anything physical that he did to her. He began to wonder if she was playing up to him with marriage in mind—or at least some financially beneficial liaison. He knew that she wasn't wealthy. He was. It put him at a disadvantage when he tried to puzzle out her motives. He knew how treacherous some women could be, and he'd been fooled once in recent months by a woman out for what she could get from him. She'd been kind to the girls, too, and she'd played the innocent with Gil, leading him on until they ended up in her bedroom. Of course, she'd said then, they'd have to get married once they'd been intimate...

He'd left her before the relationship was consummated, and he hadn't called her again. Not that she'd given up easily. She'd stalked him until he produced an attorney and a warrant, at which point she'd given up the chase.

Now, he was remembering that bad experience and superimposing her image over Kasie's innocent-looking face. He knew nothing about her. He couldn't take the risk of believing what he thought he saw in her personality. She could be playing him for a sucker, very easily.

"You don't hold anything back, do you?" he asked conversationally, and it didn't show that he'd been affected by her. "Are you like that all the way into the bedroom?" he added softly, so that the girls wouldn't hear.

Kasie drew in a long breath. "I wouldn't know," she said huskily, painfully aware that she'd just made an utter fool of herself. "I'll get dressed."

"You might as well, where I'm concerned," he said pleasantly. "You're easy on the eyes, Kasie, but in the dark, looks don't matter much."

She stared at him with confusion, as if she couldn't believe she was hearing such a blatant remark from him.

He slid his hands into his pockets and studied her arrogantly from head to toe. "You'd need to be prettier," he continued, "and with larger...assets," he said with a deliberate study of her pert breasts. "I'm particular about my lovers these days. It takes a special woman."

"Which, thank God, I'm not," she choked, flushing. "I don't sleep around."

"Of course not," he agreed.

She turned away from him with a sick feeling in her stomach. She'd loved his touch. It had been her first experience of passion, and it had been exquisite because it was Gil touching her. But he thought she was offering herself, and he didn't want her. She should be glad. She wasn't a loose woman. But it was a deliberate insult, and she wondered what she'd done to make him want to hurt her.

Her reaction made him even angrier, but he didn't let it show. "Giving up so easily?" he taunted.

She kept her back to him so that he wouldn't see her face. "We've had this conversation once," she pointed out. "I know that you don't want to remarry, and I've told you that I don't sleep around. Okay?"

"If I catch you in bed with that hack writer, I'll fire you on the spot," he added, viciously.

She turned then and glared at him from wet eyes. "What's the matter with you?" she asked.

"A sudden awakening of reason," he said enigmatically. "You look after the girls. That's your job."

"I never thought it involved anything else," she said.

"And it doesn't," he agreed. "The fringe benefits don't include the boss."

"Some fringe benefit," she scoffed, regaining her composure. "A conceited, overbearing, arrogant rancher who thinks he's on every woman's Christmas list!"

He lifted an eyebrow over eyes with cynical sophistication gleaming in them. "Don't look for me under your Christmas tree," he chided.

"Don't worry, I won't." She turned and kept walking before he could say anything worse. Of all the conceited men on earth!

He watched her go with mixed emotions, the strongest of which was desire. She made him ache all over. He checked his watch. Pauline's ten minutes were up, and he wanted out of this apartment. He called a good-night to the girls and went out without another word to Kasie.

When he got back in, at two in the morning, he paused long enough to open Kasie's door and look in.

She was wearing another of those concealing cotton gowns, with the covers thrown off. Jenny was curled up against one shoulder and Bess was curled into the other. They were all three asleep.

Gil ground his teeth together just looking at the picture they made together. His girls and Kasie. They looked more like mother and daughters. The thought hurt him. He closed the door with a little jerk and went back into his own room. Despite Pauline's alluring gown and her spirited conversation, he had been morose all evening.

Pauline had noticed, and knew the reason. She was, she told herself, going to get rid of the competition. It only needed the right set of circumstances.

Fate provided them only two days later. Kasie and Gil were barely speaking now. She avoided him, and he did the same to her. If the girls noticed, they kept their thoughts to themselves. Impulsively Kasie phoned Zeke at his hotel and asked if he'd like to come over and have lunch with her at the hotel, since she couldn't leave the girls.

He agreed with flattering immediacy, and showed up just as Kasie was drying off the girls.

"Surely you aren't going to take them to lunch with you?" Pauline asked, laughing up at Zeke, who attracted her at once. "I'll watch them while you eat."

"Please can't we stay and play in the pool?" Bess asked Kasie. "Miss Raines will watch us, she said so."

"Please," Jenny added with a forlorn look.

"You'll be right inside, won't you?" Pauline asked cunningly. "Go ahead and enjoy your lunch. I'm not going anywhere."

For an instant, Kasie recalled that Gil didn't trust Pauline with the girls. But it was only for a few minutes and, as Pauline had said, they were going to be just inside the nearby restaurant that overlooked the pool.

"Well, all right then, if you really don't mind," she told Pauline. "Thank you."

"It's my pleasure. Have fun now," Pauline told her. "And don't worry. Gil's not going to be back for at least a half hour. He's at the bank."

Kasie brooded over it even while she and Zeke ate a delicious seafood salad. They were seated at a window overlooking the swimming pool, but a row of hedges and hibiscus obscured the view so that only the deep end of the pool could be seen from their table.

"Stop worrying," Zeke told her with a grin. "Honestly, you act as if they were your own kids. You're just the governess."

"They're my responsibility," she pointed out. "If anything happened to them…"

"Your friend is going to watch them. Now stop arguing and let me tell you about this new hotel and casino they're opening over on Paradise Island."

"Okay," she relented, smiling. "I'll stop brooding."

Outside by the pool, Pauline had noticed that Kasie and her companion couldn't see beyond the hedges. She smiled coldly as she looked at the little girls. Jenny was sitting on the steps of the wading pool, playing with one of her dolls in the water.

Closer to Pauline, Bess was staring down at the swimming pool where the water was about six feet deep—far too deep for her to swim in.

"I wish I could dive," she told Pauline.

"But it's easy," Pauline told her, making instant plans. "Just put your arms out in front of you like this," she demonstrated, "and jump in. Really, it's simple."

"Are you sure?" Bess asked, thrilled that an adult might actually teach her how to dive!

"Of course! I'm right here. How dangerous can it be? Go ahead. You can do it."

Of course she could, Bess thought, laughing with delight. She put her arms in the position Pauline had demonstrated and shifted her position to dive in. There wasn't anybody else around the pool to notice if she did it wrong. She'd show her daddy when he came back. Wouldn't he be surprised?

She moved again, just as Pauline suddenly turned around. Her leg accidentally caught one of Bess's. Pauline fell and so did Bess, but Bess's head hit the pavement as she went down. The momentum kept her going, and she rolled into the pool, unconscious.

"Oh, damn!" Pauline groaned. She got to her feet and looked into the pool, aware that Jenny was screaming. "Do shut up!" she told the child. "I'll have to get someone…"

But even as she spoke, Gil came around the corner of the hotel, oblivious to what had just happened.

"Daddy!" Jenny screamed. "Bess falled in the swimmy pool!"

Gil didn't even break stride. He broke into a run and dived in the second he was close enough. He went to the bottom, scooped up his little girl and swam back up with all the speed he could muster. Out of breath, he coughed as he lifted Bess onto the tiles by the pool and climbed out himself. He turned the child over and rubbed her back, aware that she was still breathing by some miracle. She coughed and water began to dribble out of her mouth, and then to gush out of it as she regained consciousness.

"Call an ambulance," he shot at Pauline.

"Oh, dear, oh, dear," she murmured, biting her nails.

"Call a damned ambulance!" he raged.

One of the pool boys saw what was going on and told Gil he'd phone from inside the hotel.

"Where's Kasie?" Gil asked Pauline with hateful eyes as Jenny threw herself against him to be comforted. Bess was still coughing up water.

There it was. The opportunity. Pauline drew in a quick breath. "That man came by to take her to lunch. You know, the man she met on the plane. She begged me to watch the girls so they'd have time to talk."

Gil didn't say anything, but his eyes were very expressive. "Where is she?"

"I really don't know," Pauline lied, wide-eyed. "She didn't say where they were going. She was clinging to him like ivy and obviously very anxious to be alone with him," she added. "I can't say I blame her, he's very handsome."

"Bess could have died."

"But I was right here. I never left them," she assured him. "The girls mean everything to me. Here, let me have Jenny. I'll take care of her while you get Bess seen to."

"Want Kasie," Jenny whimpered.

"There, there, darling," Pauline said sweetly, kissing the plump little cheek. "Pauline's here."

"Damn Kasie!" Gil bit off, horrified at what might have happened. Kasie knew he didn't trust Pauline to watch the girls. Why had Kasie been so irresponsible? Was it to get back at him for what he'd said the night they arrived in Nassau?

When the ambulance arrived, Kasie and Zeke left their dessert half-eaten and rushed out the door. Zeke had to stop to pay the check, but Kasie, apprehensive and uneasy without knowing exactly why, rounded the corner of the building just in time to see little Bess being loaded onto the ambulance.

"Bess! What happened?!" Kasie asked, sobbing.

"She hit her head on the pool, apparently, and almost drowned, while you were away having a good time with your boyfriend," Gil said furiously. The expression on his face could have backed down a mob. "You've got a ticket home. Use it today. Go back to the ranch and start packing. I want you out of my house when I get back. I'll send your severance pay along, and you can thank your lucky stars that I'm not pressing charges!"

"But, but, Pauline was watching them—" Kasie began, horrified at Bess's white face and big, tragic eyes staring at her from the ambulance.

"It was your job to watch them," Gil shot at her. "That's what you were paid to do. She could have died, damn you!"

Kasie went stark white. "I'm sorry," she choked, horrified.

"Too late," he returned, heading to the ambulance. "You heard me, Kasie," he added coldly. "Get out. Pauline, take care of Jenny until I get back."

"Of course, darling," she cooed.

"And get her away from the swimming pool!"

"I'll take her up to my room and read to her. I hope you'll be fine, Bess, darling," she added.

Kasie stood like a little statue, sick and alone and frightened as the ambulance closed up and rushed away, its lights flashing ominously.

Pauline turned and gave Kasie a superior appraisal. "It seems you're out of a job, Miss Mayfield."

Kasie was too sick at heart to react. She didn't have it in her for a fight. Seeing Bess lying there, so white and fragile was acutely painful. Even Jenny seemed not to like her anymore. She buried her face against Pauline and clung.

Pauline turned and carried the child back to her chaise lounge to get her room key. Not bad, she thought, for a morning's work. One serious rival accounted for and out of the way.

Zeke caught up with Kasie at the pool. "What happened?" he asked, brushing a stray tear from Kasie's cheek.

"Bess almost drowned," she said huskily. "Pauline promised to watch her. How did she hit her head?"

"I wouldn't put much past that woman," he told Kasie somberly. "Some people won't tolerate rivals."

"I'm no rival," she replied. "I never was."

Having noted the expression on her boss's face at the airport when he'd said goodbye to Kasie, he could have disputed that. He knew jealousy when he saw it. The man had been looking at him as if he'd like to put a stake through his heart.

"He fired me," Kasie continued dazedly. "He fired me, without even letting me explain."

"Trust me, after whatever she told him, it wouldn't have done any good. Go home and let things cool down," he added. "Most men regain their reason when the initial upset passes."

"You know a lot about people," Kasie remarked as they started up to her room.

"I'm a reporter. It goes with the territory. I'll go with you to the airport and help you change the ticket," he added grimly. "Not that I want to. I was looking forward to getting to know you. Now we'll be ships that passed in the night."

"So we will. Do you believe in fate?" she asked numbly.

"I do. Most things happen for a reason. Just go with the flow." He grinned. "And don't forget to give me your home address! I won't be out of the country forever."

Chapter 8

It didn't take long for Kasie to pack. She wouldn't let herself think of what was ahead, because she'd cry, and she didn't have time for tears. She changed into a neat gray pantsuit to travel in, and picked up her suitcase and purse to put them by the door. But she stopped long enough to find the phone number of the hospital and check on Bess. The head nurse on the floor, once Kasie's relationship to the girls was made clear, told her that the child was sitting up in bed asking for ice cream. Kasie thanked her and hung up. She wondered if the news would have been quite as forthcoming if she'd mentioned that she'd just been fired.

She moved out into the sitting room with her heart like a heavy weight in her chest. She looked around to make sure she hadn't forgotten anything and went into the hall with her small piece of carry-on luggage on wheels and her pocketbook. It was the most painful moment of her recent life. She thought of never seeing the girls and Gil again, of having Gil hate her. Tears stung her eyes, and she dashed at them impatiently with a tissue.

As she passed Pauline's room, she hesitated. She wanted to say goodbye to little Jenny. But on second thought, she went ahead to the elevator, deciding that it would only make matters worse. Besides, Pauline was probably still at the hospital with Gil. She wished she knew what had really happened by the pool. She should never have left the girls with Pauline, despite the other woman's assurances that she'd look after them. Gil had said often enough that she was responsible for them, not Pauline. She should have listened.

Downstairs, Zeke was waiting for her. He put her small bag into the little car he'd rented at the airport and drove her to the airport to catch her flight.

At the hospital, Bess was demanding ice cream. Gil hugged her close, more frightened than he wanted to admit about how easily he could have lost her forever.

"I'm okay, Daddy," she assured him with a grin.

"Does your head hurt?" he asked, touching the bandage the doctor had placed over the cut, which had been stitched.

"Only a little. But ice cream would make it feel better," she added hopefully.

"I'll see what I can do," he promised with a strained smile.

The nurse came in, motioning Pauline and Jenny in behind her. "I thought it might help to let her sister see her," she told Gil confidentially.

"Hi, Bess," Jenny said, sidling up to the bed. "Are you okay?"

"I'm fine," Bess assured her. "But it was real scary." She glared at Pauline. "It was your fault. You tripped me."

"Bess!" Gil warned his daughter while wondering at Pauline's odd expression.

"I did not trip you!" Pauline shot back.

"You did so," Bess argued. "I wouldn't dive in, and you tripped me so I'd fall in."

"She's obviously delirious," Pauline said tautly.

"You told Kasie you'd stay right with us," she continued angrily. "And she told us not to go swimming, but you showed me how to dive and you told me to dive into the pool. And when I didn't, you tripped me!''

Pauline was flushed. Gil was looking vaguely murderous. "She did hit her head, you know," she stammered. "I was telling her how to dive, I didn't tell her to actually do it!''

"You tripped me and I hurt myself!" Bess kept on.

Pauline backed away from Gil. "What do I know about kids?" she asked impatiently. "She said she wanted to learn how to swim. I showed her a diving position. Then I slipped on the wet tiles and fell against her. It was an accident. I never meant to hurt her. You must know that I wouldn't deliberately hurt a child!" she added fiercely.

He was still silent, as the fear for Bess began to fade and his reason came back to him.

Pauline grabbed up her purse. "I was just trying to do Kasie a favor," she muttered. "That reporter wanted to take her to lunch and I told her to go ahead, that I'd watch the kids. Besides, she was just in the restaurant next to the pool!''

Gil felt his stomach do a nosedive. So Kasie hadn't deserted the kids. Pauline had told her to go, and she'd been right inside. He'd fired Kasie, thinking she was at fault!

"I imagine that reporter went home with her," Pauline continued deliberately. "They were all over each other when he came to pick her up. Besides, governesses are thick on the ground. It won't be hard to replace her."

"Or you," he said coldly.

She looked shocked. "You can't mean you're firing me?"

"I'm firing you, Pauline," he said, feeling like a prize idiot. Kasie was gone, and it was as much Pauline's fault as it was his own. He knew she didn't like Kasie. "I need a full-time secretary. We've discussed this before."

She started to argue, but it was obvious that there was no use in it. She might still be able to salvage something of their relationship, just the same, if she didn't make a scene. "All right," she said heavily. "But we might as well enjoy the vacation, since we're here."

His face became hard. He thought of Kasie going back to Montana, packing, leaving. For an instant he panicked, thinking that she might go so far away that he'd never find her.

Then he remembered her aunt in Billings. Surely she wouldn't be that hard to locate. He'd give it a few days, let Kasie get over the anger she must be feeling right now. Maybe she'd miss the girls and he could persuade her to come back. God knew, she wouldn't miss him, he thought bitterly. He'd probably done more damage than he could ever make up to her. But when they got back, he was going to try. Misjudging Kasie seemed to be his favorite hobby these days, he thought miserably.

"Yes," he told Pauline slowly. "I suppose we might as well stay."

Pauline had hardly dared hope for so much time with him. She was going to try, really try, to take care of the girls and make them like her.

"Bess, shall I go and ask if they have chocolate ice cream?" she asked, trying to make friends. "I'm really sorry about accidentally knocking you into the pool."

"I want Kasie," Bess muttered.

"Kasie's gone home," Gil said abruptly, not adding that he'd fired her.

"Gone home?" Bess's face crumpled. "But why?"

"Because I told her to," he said shortly. "And that's enough about Kasie. We're going to have a good time... Oh, for God's sake, don't start bawling!"

Now it wasn't just Bess crying, it was Jenny, too. Pauline sighed heavily. "Well, we're going to have a very good time, aren't we?" she said to nobody in particular.

Mama Luke never pried or asked awkward questions. She held Kasie while she cried, sent her to unpack and made hot chocolate and chicken soup. That had always been Kasie's favorite meal when she was upset.

Kasie sat down across from her at the small kitchen table

that had a gaily patterned tablecloth decorated with pink roses and sipped her soup with a spoon.

"You don't have to say a word," Mama Luke told her gently, and smiled. She had eyes like her sister, Kasie's mother, dark brown and soft. She had dark hair, too, which she kept short. Her hands, around the mug, were thin and wrinkled now, and twisted with arthritis, but they were loving, helping hands. Kasie had always envied her aunt her ability to give love unconditionally.

"I've been a real idiot," Kasie remarked as she worked through her soup. "I should never have let Pauline look after the girls. She isn't really malicious, but she's hopelessly irresponsible."

"You haven't had a man friend in my recent memory," Mama Luke remarked. "I'm sure you were flattered to have a handsome young man want to take you out to lunch."

"I was. But that doesn't mean that I should have let Pauline talk me into leaving the girls with her. Bess could very easily have drowned, and it would have been my fault," she added miserably.

"Give it time," the older woman said gently. "First, let's get you settled in. Then you can help me with the garden," she added with a grin.

Despite her misery, Kasie laughed. "I see. You're happy to have me back because I'm free labor."

Mama Luke laughed, too. It was a standing joke, the way she press-ganged even casual visitors into taking a turn at weeding the garden. She prescribed it as the best cure for depression, misery and anxiety. She was right. It did a lot to restore a good mood.

In the days that followed, Kasie worked in the garden a lot. She thought about Gil, and the hungry way he'd kissed her. She thought about the girls and missed them terribly. She'd really expected Gil to phone her. He knew she had an aunt in Billings, and it wouldn't have taken much effort for him to track her down. In fact, she'd put Mama Luke's telephone number down on her job application in case of emergency.

The thought depressed her even more. He knew where she'd be, but apparently he was still angry at her. God knew what Pauline had said at the hospital about how the accident happened. She'd probably blamed the whole thing on Kasie. Maybe the girls blamed her, too, for leaving them with Pauline, whom they disliked. She'd never felt quite so alone. She thought of Kantor and grew even sadder.

Mama Luke came out into the garden and caught her brooding. "Stop that," she chided softly. "This is God's heart," she pointed out. "It's creation itself, planting seed and watching little things grow. It should cheer you up."

"I miss Bess and Jenny," she said quietly, leaning on her hoe. She was dirty from head to toe, having gotten down in the soil to pull out stubborn weeds. There was a streak of it across her chin, which Mama Luke wiped off with one of the tissues she always carried in her pocket.

"I'm sure they miss you, too," the older woman assured her. "Don't worry so. It will all come right. Sometimes we just have to think of ourselves as leaves going down a river. It's easy to forget that God's driving."

"Maybe He doesn't mind back seat drivers," Kasie said with a grin.

Mama Luke chuckled. "You're incorrigible. Almost through? I made hot chocolate and chicken with rice soup."

"Comfort food." Kasie smiled.

"Absolutely. Stop and eat something."

Kasie looked at the weeding that still had to be done with a long sigh. "Oh, well, maybe the mailman has some frustrations to work off. He's bigger than I am. I'll bet he hoes well."

"I'll try to find out," she was assured. "Come on in and wash up."

It was good soup and Kasie had worked up an appetite. She felt better. But she still hated the way she'd left the Callister ranch. Probably everybody blamed her for Bess's accident. Especially the one person from whom she dreaded it. "I guess Gil hates me."

The pain in those words made Mama Luke reach out a gentle hand to cover her niece's on the table. "I'm sure he doesn't," she contradicted. "He was upset and frightened for Bess. We all say things we shouldn't when our emotions are out of control. He'll apologize. I imagine he'll offer you your job back as well."

Kasie shifted in the chair. "It's been a week," she said. "If he were going to hire me back, he'd have been in touch. I suppose he still believes Pauline and thinks he's done the best thing by firing me."

"Do you really?" Her aunt pursed her lips as her keen ears caught the sound of a car pulling up in the driveway. "Finish your hot cocoa, dear. I'll go and see who that is driving up out front."

For just a few seconds, Kasie hoped it would be Gil, come to give her back her job. But that would take a miracle. Her life had changed all over again. She was just going to have to accept it and get a new job. Something would turn up somewhere, surely.

She heard voices in the living room. One of them was deep and slow, and she shivered with emotion as she realized that she wasn't dreaming. She got up and went into the living room. And there he was.

Gil stopped talking midsentence and just looked at Kasie. She was wearing old jeans and a faded T-shirt, with her hair around her shoulders. He'd missed her more than he thought he could miss anyone. His heart filled with just the sight of her.

"I believe you, uh, know each other," Mama Luke said mischievously.

"Yes, we do," Kasie said. She recalled the fury in his pale eyes as he accused her of causing Bess's accident, the fury as he fired her. It was too painful to go through again, and he didn't look as if he'd come to make any apologies. She turned away miserably. "If you'll excuse me, I have to clean up," she called over her shoulder.

"Kasie…!" Gil called angrily.

She kept walking down the hall to her room, and she closed and locked the door. The pain was just too much. She couldn't bear the condemnation in his eyes.

Gil muttered under his breath. "Well, so much for wishful thinking," he said almost to himself.

"Come along and have some hot cocoa, Mr. Callister," Mama Luke said with a gentle smile. "I think you and I have a lot to talk about."

He followed her into the small, bright kitchen with its white and yellow accents. She motioned him into a chair at the table while she poured the still-hot cocoa into a mug and offered it to him.

"I'm Sister Luke," she introduced herself, noting his sudden start. "Yes, that's right, I'm a nun. My order doesn't wear the habit. I work with a health outreach program in this community."

He sipped cocoa, feeling as if more revelations were in store, and that he wasn't going to like them.

She sipped her own cocoa. He was obviously waiting for her to speak again. He studied her quietly, his blue eyes troubled and faintly disappointed at Kasie's reception.

"She's still grieving," she told Gil. "She didn't give it enough time before she started back to work. I tried to tell her, but young people are so determined these days."

He latched on to the word. "Grieving?"

"Yes." Her dark eyes were quiet and soft as they met his. "Her twin, Kantor, and his wife and little girl died three months ago."

His breath caught. "In an airplane crash," he said, recalling what Kasie had said.

"Airplane crash?" Her eyes widened. "Well, I suppose you could call it that, in a manner of speaking. Their light aircraft was shot down—"

"What?" he exploded.

She frowned. "Don't you know anything about Kasie?"

"No. I don't. Not one thing!"

She let out a whistle. "I suppose that explains some of the problem. Perhaps if you knew about her background..." She leaned back in her chair. "Her parents were lay missionaries to Africa. While they were working there, a rebel uprising occurred and they were killed." She nodded at his look of horror. "I had already taken my vows by then, and I was the only family that Kasie and Kantor had left. I arranged to have them come to me, and I enrolled them in the school where I was teaching, and living, at the time. In Arizona," she added. "Kantor wanted nothing more than to fly airplanes. He studied flying while he was in school and later went into partnership with a friend from college. They started a small charter service. There was an opportunity in Africa for a courier service, so he decided to go there and set up a second headquarters for the company. While he was there, he married and had a little girl, Sandy. She and Lise, Kantor's wife, came and stayed with Kasie and me while Kasie was going through secretarial school. Kantor didn't want them with him just then, because there was some political trouble. It calmed down and he came and rejoined his family. He wanted to bring everyone home to Africa."

She grimaced. "Kasie didn't want him to go back. She said it was too risky, especially for Lise and Sandy. She adored Sandy..." She hesitated, and took a steadying breath, because the memory was painful. "Kantor told her to mind her own business, and they all left. That same week, a band of guerrillas attacked the town where he had his business. He got Lise and Sandy in the plane and was flying them to a nearby town when someone fired a rocket at them. They all died instantly."

"My God," he said huskily.

"Kasie took it even harder because they'd argued. It took weeks for her to be able to discuss it without breaking down. She'd graduated from secretarial college and I insisted that she go to work, not because of money, but because it was killing her to sit and brood about Kantor.''

He wrapped both hands around the cocoa mug and stared into the frothy liquid. ''I knew there was something,'' he said quietly. ''But she never talked about anything personal.''

''She rarely does, except with me.'' She studied him. ''She said that your wife died in a riding accident and that you have two beautiful little girls.''

''They hate me,'' he said matter-of-factly. ''I fired Kasie.'' He shrugged and smiled faintly. ''John, my brother, isn't even speaking to me.''

''They'll get over it.''

''They may. I won't.'' He wouldn't meet her eyes. ''I thought I might persuade her to come back. I suppose that's a hopeless cause?''

''She's hurt that you misjudged her,'' she explained. ''Kasie loves children. It would never occur to her to leave them in any danger.''

''I know that. I knew it then, too, but I was out of my mind with fear. I suppose I lashed out. I don't know much about families,'' he added, feeling safe with this stranger. He looked up at her. ''My brother and I were never part of one. Our parents had a governess for us until we were old enough to be sent off to school. I can remember months going by when we wouldn't see them or hear from them. Even now,'' he added stiffly, ''they only contact us when they think of some new way we can help them make money.''

She slid a wrinkled hand over his. ''I'm sorry,'' she said gently. She removed her hand and pushed a plate of cookies toward him. ''Comfort food,'' she said with a gleeful smile. ''Indulge yourself.''

''Thanks.'' He bit into a delicious lemon cookie.

''Kasie says you love your girls very much, and that you never leave them with people you don't trust. She's hating herself because she did leave them against her better judgment. She blames herself for the accident.''

He sighed. "It wasn't her fault. Not really." His eyes glittered. "She wanted to have lunch with a man she met on the plane. A good-looking, young man," he added bitterly. "Pauline admitted causing the accident, but I was hot because Kasie was upset about flying and I didn't know it until it was too late. She was sitting all by herself." His face hardened. "If I'd known what you just told me, we'd have gone by boat. I'd never have subjected her to an airplane ride. But Kasie keeps secrets. She doesn't talk about herself."

"Neither do you, I think," she replied.

He shrugged and picked up another cookie. "She looks worn," he remarked.

"I've had her working in my garden," she explained. "It's good therapy."

He smiled. "I work cattle for therapy. My brother and I have a big ranch here in Montana. We wouldn't trade it for anything."

"I like animals." She sipped cocoa.

So did he. He looked at her over the mug.

"Kasie mentioned she was named for the mercenary K.C. Kanton." She raised an eyebrow amusedly. "That's right. I'm not sure how much she told you, but when Jackie, her mother, was carrying her, there was a guerrilla attack on the mission. Bob, my brother-in-law, was away with a band of workers building a barn for a neighboring family. They'd helped a wounded mercenary soldier hide from the same guerrillas, part of an insurgent group that wanted to overthrow the government. He was well enough to get around by then, and he got Jackie out of the mission and through the jungle to where Bob was. Kasie and Kantor were born only a day later. And that's why she was named for K.C. Kanton."

"They both were named for him," he realized. "Amazing. What I've heard about Kantor over the years doesn't include a generous spirit or unselfishness."

"That may be true. But he pays his debts. He'd still like to take care of Kasie,'' she added with a soft chuckle. ''She won't let him. She's as independent as my sister used to be.''

It disturbed him somehow that Kasie was cherished by another man who could give her anything she wanted. ''He must be a great deal older than she is,'' he murmured absently.

''He doesn't have those kind of feelings for her,'' she said quietly, and there was pain in her soft eyes. ''He missed out on family life and children. I think he's sorry about that now. He tried to get her to come and stay with him in Mexico until she got over losing her twin, but she wouldn't go.''

''One of her other character references was a Catholic priest.''

She nodded. ''Father Vincent, in Tucson, Arizona. He was the priest for our small parish.'' She sighed. ''Kasie hasn't been to mass since her brother died. I've been so worried about her.''

''She mentioned taking the girls with her to church,'' Gil said after a minute. ''If I can get her to come back to work for me, it might be the catalyst to help her heal.''

''It might at that,'' she agreed.

Gil took another cookie and nibbled it. ''These are good.''

''My one kitchen talent,'' she said. ''I can make cookies. Otherwise, I live on TV dinners and the kindness of friends who can cook.''

He sipped cocoa and thought. ''How can I get her to go back with me?'' he asked after a minute.

''Tell her the girls are crying themselves to sleep at night,'' she suggested gently. ''She misses Sandy even more than her twin. She and the little girl were very close.''

''She's close to my girls,'' he remarked with a reminiscent smile. ''If there's a storm or they get frightened in the night, I can always find them curled up in Kasie's arms.'' His voice seemed to catch on the words. He averted his eyes toward the hallway. ''The light went out of the house when she left it.''

She wondered if he even realized what he was saying.

Probably not. Men seemed to miss things that women noticed at once.

"I'll go and get her," she said, pushing back her chair. "You can sit by my fishpond and talk with the goldfish."

"My uncle used to have one," he recalled, standing. "I haven't had one built because of the girls. When they're older, I'd like to put in another one."

"I had to dig it myself, and I'm not the woman I used to be. It's only a little over a foot deep. One of my neighbors gave me his used pond heater when he bought a new one. It keeps my four goldfish alive all winter long." She moved to the door. "It's just outside the back door, near the birdbath. I'll send Kasie out to you."

He went out, his hands in his pockets, thinking how little he'd known about Kasie. It might be impossible for them to regain the ground they'd lost, but he wanted to try. His life was utterly empty without her in it.

Mama Luke knocked gently at Kasie's door and waited until it opened. Kasie looked at her guiltily.

"I was rude. I'm sorry," she told the older woman.

"I didn't come to fuss," Mama Luke said. She touched Kasie's disheveled hair gently. "I want you to go out and talk to Mr. Callister. He feels bad about the things he said to you. He wants you to go back to work for him."

Kasie gave her aunt a belligerent look. "In his dreams," she muttered.

"The little girls miss you very much," she said.

Kasie grimaced. "I miss them, too."

"Go on out there and face your problem squarely," Mama Luke coaxed. "He's a reasonable man, and he's had a few shocks today. Give him a chance to make it up to you. He's nice," she added. "I like him."

"You like everybody, Mama Luke," Kasie said softly.

"He's out by the goldfish pond. And don't push him in," she added with a wicked little smile.

Kasie chuckled. "Okay."

She took a deep breath and went down the hall. But her hands trembled when she opened the back door and walked outside. She hadn't realized how much she was going to miss Gil Callister until she was out of his life. Now she had to decide whether or not to risk going back. It wasn't going to be an easy decision.

Chapter 9

Gil was sitting on the small wooden bench overlooking the rock-bordered oval fishpond, his elbows resting on his knees as he peered down thoughtfully into the clear water where water lilies bloomed in pink and yellow profusion. He looked tired, Kasie thought, watching him covertly. Maybe he'd been away on business and not on holiday with Pauline after all.

He looked up when he heard her footsteps. He got to his feet. He looked elegant even in that yellow polo shirt and beige slacks, she thought. He wasn't at all handsome, but his face was masculine and he had a mouth that she loved kissing. She averted her eyes until she was able to control the sudden impulse to run to him. Wouldn't that shock him, she thought sadly.

He looked wary, and he wasn't smiling. He studied her for a long time, as if he'd forgotten what she looked like and wanted to absorb every detail of her.

"How are the girls?" she asked quietly. "Is Bess going to be all right?"

"Bess is fine," he replied. "She told me everything." He grimaced. "Even Pauline admitted that she'd told you to go and have lunch with what's-his-name, and she'd watch the girls. She said she slipped and tripped Bess. I imagine it's the truth. She's never been much of a liar, regardless of her faults," he returned, his voice flat, without expression. "They told me you phoned the hospital to make sure Bess was all right."

"I was worried," she said, uneasy.

He toyed with the change in his pocket, making it jingle. "Bess wanted you, in the hospital. When I told her you'd gone home, she and Jenny both started crying." The memory tautened his face. "For what it's worth, I'm sorry that I blamed you."

She'd never wanted to believe anything as much as that apology. But it was still disturbing that he'd accused her without proof, that he'd assumed Bess's accident was her fault. She wanted to go back in the house. But that wouldn't solve the problem. She had to try and forget. He was here and he'd apologized. They had to go from there. "It's all right," she said after a minute, her eyes on the fish instead of him. "I understand. You can't help it that you don't like me."

"Don't...like you?" he asked. The statement surprised him.

She toyed with the hem of her shirt. "You never wanted to hire me in the first place, really," she continued. "You looked at me as if you hated me the minute you saw me."

His eyes were thoughtful. "Did I?" He didn't want to pursue that line of conversation. It was too new, too disturbing, after having realized how he felt about her. "Why do you call your aunt Mama Luke?" he asked to divert her.

"Because when I was five, I couldn't manage Sister Mary Luke Bernadette," she replied. "She was Mama Luke from then on."

He winced. "That's a young age to lose both parents."

"That's why I know how Bess and Jenny feel," she told him.

His expelled breath was audible. "I've made a hell of a mess of it, haven't I, Kasie?" he asked somberly. "I jumped to the worst sort of conclusions."

She moved awkwardly to the other side of the fishpond and

wrapped her arms around her body. "I wasn't thinking straight. I knew you didn't trust Pauline to take care of the girls, but I let myself be talked into leaving them with her. You were right. Bess could have drowned and it would have been my fault."

"Stick the knife right in, don't be shy," he said through his teeth. His blue eyes glittered. "God knows, I deserve it."

Her eyes met his, wide with curiosity. "I don't understand."

She probably didn't. "Never mind." He stuck his hands into his pockets. "I fired Pauline."

"But…!"

"It wasn't completely because of what happened in Nassau. I need someone full-time," he interrupted. "She only wanted the job in the first place so that she could be near me."

The breeze blew her hair across her mouth. She pushed it back behind her ear. "That must have been flattering."

"It was, at first," he agreed, "I've known Pauline for a long time, and her attention was flattering. However, regardless of how Bess fell into the water, Pauline didn't make a move to rescue her. I can't get over that."

Kasie understood. She'd have been in the pool seconds after Bess fell in, despite the fact that she couldn't swim.

His piercing blue eyes caught hers. "Yes, I know. You'd have been right in after her," he said softly, as if he'd read the thought in her mind. "Even if you'd had to be rescued as well," he added gently.

"People react differently to desperate situations," she said.

"Indeed they do." His eyes narrowed. "I want you to come back. So do the girls. I'll do whatever it takes. An apology, a raise in salary, a paid vacation to Tahiti…"

She shrugged. "I wouldn't mind coming back," she said. "I do miss the girls, terribly. But…"

"But, what?"

She met his level gaze. "You don't trust me," she said simply, and her eyes were sad. "At first you thought I was trying to get to you through the girls, and then you thought I wanted them out of the way. In Nassau, you thought I left them

alone for selfish reasons, so that I could go on a lunch date.''
She smiled sadly. "You have a bad opinion of me as a governess. What if I mess up again? Maybe it would be better if
we just left things the way they are.''

The remark went through him like hot lead. He hadn't
trusted Kasie because she was so mysterious about her past.
Now that he knew the truth about her, knew of the tragedies
she'd suffered in her young life, lack of trust was no longer
going to be a problem. But how did he tell her that? And,
worse, how did he make up for the accusations he'd made?
Perhaps he could tell her the truth.

"The girls' last governess was almost too good to be true,''
he began. "She charmed the girls, and me, until we'd have
believed anything she told us. It was all an act. She had marriage in mind, and she actually threatened me with my own
children. She said they were so attached to her that if I didn't
marry her, she'd leave and they'd hate me.''

She blinked. "That sounds as if she was a little unbal-
anced.''

He nodded, his eyes cold with remembered bitterness. "Yes,
she was. She left in the middle of the night, and the next morning the girls were delighted to find her gone.''

He shook his head. "She was unstable, and I'd left the kids
in her hands. It was such a blot on my judgment that I didn't
trust it anymore. Especially when you came along, with your
mysterious past and your secrets. I thought you were playing
up to me because I was rich.''

It hurt that he'd thought so little of her. "I see.''

"Do you? I hope so,'' he replied heavily, and with a smile.
"Because if I go back to Medicine Ridge without you, I
wouldn't give two cents for my neck. John's furious with me.
He's got company. Miss Parsons glares at me constantly. Mrs.
Charters won't serve me anything that isn't burned. The girls
are the worst, though,'' he mused. "They ignore me completely. I feel like the ogre in that story you read them at
bedtime.''

"Poor ogre," she said quietly.

He began to smile. He loved the softness of her voice when she spoke. For the first time since his arrival, he was beginning to think he had a chance. "Feeling sorry for me?" he asked gently. "Good. If I wear on your conscience, maybe you'll feel sorry enough to come home with me."

She frowned. "What did Mama Luke tell you?" she asked suddenly.

"Things you should have told me," he replied, his tone faintly acidic. "She told me everything, in fact, except why you don't like the water."

She stared down into the fishpond, idly watching the small goldfish swim in and out of the vegetation. "When I was five, just before my parents were…killed," she said, sickened by the memory, "one of my friends at the mission in Africa got swept into the river. I saw her drown."

"You've had a lot of tragedy in your young life," he said softly. He moved a step closer to her, and another, stopping when he was close enough to lift a lean hand and smooth his fingers down her soft cheek. "I've had my own share of it. Suppose we forget the past few weeks, and start over. Can you?"

Her eyes were troubled. "I don't know if it's wise," she said after a minute. "Letting the girls get attached to me again, I mean."

His fingers traced her wide, soft mouth. "It's too late to stop that from happening. They miss you terribly. So do I," he added surprisingly. He tilted her chin up and bent, brushing his lips tenderly over her mouth. His heavy eyebrows drew together at the delight that shafted through him from the contact. "When I think of you, I think of butterflies and rainbows," he whispered against her mouth. "I hated the world until you came to work for John. You brought the light in with you. You made me laugh. You made me believe in miracles. Don't leave me, Kasie."

He was saying something, more than words. She drew back

and searched his narrow, glittery eyes. "Leave...you?" she questioned the wording.

"You don't have an ego at all, do you?" he asked somberly. "Is it inconceivable that I want you back as much as my girls do?"

Her heart jumped. She'd missed him beyond bearing. But if she went back, could she ever be just an employee again? She remembered the hard warmth of his mouth in passion, the feel of his arms holding her like a warm treasure. She hesitated.

"I don't seduce virgins," he whispered wickedly. "If that wins me points."

She flushed. "I wasn't thinking about that!"

He smiled. "Yes, you were and that's the main reason I won't seduce you."

"Thanks a lot."

He cocked an eyebrow. "You might sound a little more grateful," he told her. "Keeping my hands off you lately has been a world-class study in restraint."

Her eyes widened. "Really?"

She was unworldly. He loved that about her. He loved the way she blushed when he teased her, the way she made his heart swell when she smiled. He'd been lonely without her.

"But I'll promise to keep my distance," he added gently. "If you'll just come back."

She bit her lower lip worriedly. She did need the job. She loved the girls. She was crazy about Gil. But there were so many complications...

"Stop weighing the risks," he murmured. "Say yes."

"I still think..."

"Don't think," he whispered, placing a long forefinger over her lips. "Don't argue. Don't look ahead. We're going to go home and you're going to read the girls to sleep every night. They miss their stories."

"Don't you read to them?" she asked, made curious by a certain note in his voice.

"Sure, but they're getting tired of *Green Eggs and Ham.*"

"They have loads of other books besides Dr. Seuss," she began.

He glowered at her. "They hid all the other books, including *Green Eggs and Ham,* but at least I remember most of that story. So they get told it every night. Two weeks of that and I can't even look at ham in the grocery story anymore without gagging…"

She was laughing uproariously.

"This is not funny," he pointed out.

"Oh, yes, it is," she said, and laughed some more.

He loved the sound. It reminded him of wind chimes. His heart ached for her. "Come home before I get sick of eggs, too."

"All right," she said. "I guess I might as well. I can't live here with Mama Luke forever."

"She's a character," he remarked with a smile. "A blunt and honest lady with a big heart. I like her."

"She must like you, too, or she wouldn't have threatened to have you break down my bedroom door."

He pursed his lips. "Nice to have an ally with divine connections."

"She does, never doubt it," she told him, laughing. "I'll just go throw a few things into my suitcase."

He watched her go with joy shooting through his veins like fireworks. She was coming back. He'd convinced her.

Now all he had to do was make her see him as something more than an intolerant, judgmental boss. That was not going to be the easiest job he'd ever tackled.

Kasie kissed Mama Luke goodbye and waited while she hugged Gil impulsively.

"Take care of Kasie," her aunt told him.

He nodded slowly. "This time, I'll do better at that."

Mama Luke smiled.

They got into his black Jaguar and drove away, with Kasie

leaning out the window and waving until her aunt was out of sight.

Gil watched her eyes close as she leaned back against the leather headrest. "Sleepy?"

"Yes," she murmured. "I haven't slept well since I came back from Nassau."

"Neither have I, Kasie," he said.

Her head turned and she looked at him quietly. It made her tingle all over. He was really a striking man, all lean strength and authority. She'd never felt as safe with anyone as she did with him.

He felt her eyes on him; warm, soft gray eyes that gave him pleasure when he met them. Kasie was unlike anyone he'd every known.

"Did Pauline finish keying in the herd records to the computer before she left?" she asked, suddenly remembering the chore that had been left when they went to Nassau.

"She hasn't been around since we came home," he said evasively. "I think she's visiting an aunt in Vermont."

She traced a line down the seat belt that stretched across her torso. "I thought you were going to marry her."

He had a good idea where she'd heard that unfounded lie. "Never in this lifetime," he murmured. "Pauline isn't domestic."

"She's crazy about you."

"The girls don't like her."

She pursed her lips. "I see."

He chuckled, glancing at her while they stopped for a red light. "Besides, after they found out that I'd fired you, they made Pauline's life hell. Their latest escapade was to leave her a nice present in her pocketbook."

"Oh, dear."

"It was a nonpoisonous snake," he said reassuringly. "But she decided that she'd be better off not visiting when the girls were around. And since they were always around..."

She shook her head. "Little terrors," she said, but in a tone soft with affection.

"Look who's talking," he said with a pointed glare.

"I've never put snakes in anybody's purse," she pointed out. "Well, not yet, anyway."

He gave her an amused glance. "Don't let the girls corrupt you."

She smiled, remembering how much fun she'd had with the little girls. It made her happy that they wanted her back. Except for her aunt, she was alone in the world. She missed being part of a whole family, especially on holidays like Christmas.

The light changed and he pulled back out into traffic. Conversation was scanty the rest of the way home, because Kasie fell asleep. The lack of rest had finally caught up with her.

She was jolted awake by a firm hand on her shoulder.

"Wake up. We're home," Gil said with a smile.

She searched his blue eyes absently for a moment before the words registered. "Oh." She unfastened her seat belt and got out as he did.

The girls were sitting on the bottom step of the staircase when the door opened and Kasie walked in with Gil.

"Kasie!" Bess cried, and got up to run and throw herself into Kasie's outstretched arms.

"Bess!" Kasie hugged her close, feeling tears sting her eyes. She was so much like Sandy.

Jenny followed suit, and Kasie ended up with two arms full of crying little girls. She carried them to the staircase and sat down, cuddling them both close. Her face was wet, but she didn't care. She loved these babies, far more than she'd realized. She held them and rocked them and kissed wet little cheeks until the sobs eased.

"You mustn't *ever* leave us again, Kasie," Bess hiccuped. "Me and Jenny was ever so sad."

"Yes, we was," Jenny murmured.

"Oh, I missed you!" Kasie said fervently as she dug into her pocket for a tissue and wiped wet eyes all around.

"We missed you, too," Bess said, burying her face in Kasie's shoulder while Jenny clung to her neck.

Gil watched them with his heart in his throat. They looked as if they belonged together. They looked like a family. He wanted to scoop all three of them up in his arms and hold them so tight they'd never get away.

While he was debating that, John came down the hall and spotted Kasie. He grinned from ear to ear. "You're back! Great! Now maybe Mrs. Charters will cook something we can eat again!"

"That's not a nice way to say hello," Kasie chided with a smile.

"Sure it is! What good is a man without his stomach?" John asked. He moved closer to Kasie and the girls and bent to kiss Kasie's wet cheek. "Welcome back! It's been like a ballpark in January. Nobody smiled."

"I'm happy to be back," Kasie said. "But what about all those herd records that need putting into the computer?" she asked, realizing that Gil never had answered her when she'd questioned him about them.

"Oh, those. It turns out that Miss Parsons is a computer whiz herself," he said to Kasie's amusement. "She's got everything listed, including the foundation bloodlines. And remember that Internet site you suggested? It's up and running. We're already getting three hundred hits a day, along with plenty of queries from cattlemen around the country!"

"I'm so glad," Kasie said sincerely.

"So are we. Business is booming. But the babies have been sad." He glanced at his older brother meaningfully. "We missed you."

"It's nice to be back," Kasie said.

"Are we ever going to have lunch?" John asked then. "I'm fairly starved. Burned eggs and bacon this morning didn't do a lot for my taste buds."

"Mine, either," Gil agreed. "Go tell Mrs. Charters Kasie's

back and is having lunch with us," he suggested. "That might get us something edible, even if it's only cold cuts."

"Good thinking," John said, smiling as he went out to the kitchen.

"Our eggs wasn't burned," Bess pointed out.

"Mrs. Charters wasn't mad at you, sweetheart," Gil told her. "You two need to run upstairs and wash your hands and faces before we eat."

"Okay, if Kasie comes, too," Bess agreed.

Kasie chuckled as both girls grabbed a hand and coaxed her to her feet. "I gather that I'm to be carefully observed from now on, so I don't make a run for the border," she murmured to Gil.

"That's right. Good girls," Gil said, grinning. "Keep her with you so she doesn't have a chance to escape."

"We won't let her go, Daddy," Bess promised.

They tugged her up the staircase, and she went without an argument, waiting in their rooms while they washed their hands and faces.

"Daddy was real mad when we came home," Bess told Kasie. "So was Uncle Johnny. He said Daddy should go and get you and bring you home, but Daddy said you might not want to, because he'd been bad to you. Did he take away your toys, Kasie and put you into time-out?"

"Heavens, no," she said at once.

"Then why did you go away?" the child insisted. "Was it on account of Pauline said you left us alone? We told Daddy the truth, and Pauline went away. We don't like her. She's bad to us when Daddy isn't looking. He won't marry Pauline, will he, Kasie?"

"I don't think so," she said carefully.

"Me and Jenny wish he'd marry you," Bess said wistfully. "You're so much fun to play with, Kasie."

Kasie didn't dare say anything about marriage. "You can't decide things like that, sweetheart," she told Bess. "People don't usually marry unless they fall in love."

"Oh."

The child looked heartbroken. Kasie went down on her knees and caught Bess gently by the waist. "What do you want to do after we have lunch?" she asked, changing the subject.

"Could we swim in the pool?"

She'd forgotten that the family had a swimming pool. "I suppose so," she said, frowning. "But it's pretty soon after your accident, Bess. Are you sure you want to?"

"Daddy and me went swimming the day after we came home," Bess said matter-of-factly. "Daddy said I mustn't be afraid of the water, after I fell in, so he's giving me swimming lessons. I love to swim, now!"

So some good had come out of the accident. That was reassuring. "Let's go down and eat something. Then we have to wait a little while."

"I know. We can pick flowers while we wait, can't we? There's some pretty yellow roses in a hedge behind the swimming pool," Bess told her.

"I love roses," Kasie said, smiling. "But perhaps we'd better not pick any until someone tells us it's all right."

"Okay, Kasie."

They went downstairs and Kasie helped Mrs. Charters set the table. She was welcoming and cheerful about having Kasie back again. John talked easily to Kasie and the children. Gil didn't. He picked at his food and brooded. He watched Kasie, but covertly. She wondered what was going on in his mind to make him so unhappy.

He looked up and met Kasie's searching eyes, and she felt her stomach fall as if she was on a roller coaster. Her hands trembled. She put them in her lap to hide them, but her heartbeat pounded wildly and her nervousness was noticeable. Especially to the man with the arrogant smile, who suddenly seemed to develop an appetite.

Chapter 10

For the next few days, Gil seemed to watch every move Kasie made. He was cordial with her, but there was a noticeable difference in the way he treated her since her return. He was remote and quiet, even when the family came together at mealtimes, and he seemed uncomfortable around Kasie. She noticed his reticence and understood it to mean that he was sorry for the way he'd treated her before. He didn't touch her at all these days, nor did he seem inclined to include her when he took the girls to movies and the playground, even though he asked her along. But she always refused, to the dismay of the children. She excused it as giving them some time alone with their father. Gil knew that wasn't the truth. It made matters worse.

John left Thursday for a conference that Gil had been slated to attend, and Gil stayed home. Kasie noticed that he seemed unusually watchful and he was always around the ranch even when he wasn't around the house. He didn't explain why. Kasie would have loved thinking that it was because he was interested in her, but she knew that wasn't the reason. There was more distance between them now than there had ever been before.

Mrs. Charters mentioned that there was some uneasiness

among the cowboys because of a threat that had been made. Kasie tried to ask Gil about it. He simply ignored the question and walked away.

He was missing at breakfast early one Monday morning. The girls were sleeping late, so Kasie walked into the dining room and found only John at the table.

"Pull up a chair and have breakfast," he invited with a grin. "I have to move bulls today, so I'm having seconds and thirds. I have to keep up my strength."

"If you keep eating like that, you could carry the bulls and save gas," she said wickedly. "I thought you had to go to Phoenix to show a bull this week?"

He averted his eyes. "I thought I'd put it off for another couple of weeks." He sipped coffee and studied Kasie quietly. "There's a new movie showing at the theater downtown. How would you like to pack up the girls and go with me to see it?"

Her eyes lit up. "I'd love to," she said at once.

He grinned. "Okay. We'll go tomorrow night. I, uh, noticed that you don't like going to movies with my brother, even if the girls go along."

"I just thought he'd like some time alone with them," she hedged. "After all, I'm just the governess."

He poured himself more coffee before he replied. "That's a bunch of hogwash, Kasie."

She drew in a long breath. "He makes me uncomfortable," she said. "I always feel like he's biding his time, waiting for me to make another mistake or do something stupid."

He chuckled. "He doesn't lie in wait to ambush you," he said softly. "He meant it when he apologized, you know. He was sorry he misjudged you. Believe me, it's a rare thing for him to make a mistake like that. But he's had some hard blows from women in recent years."

"I felt really bad about what happened," she said with a wistful sadness in her eyes. "I should have remembered that he never trusted Pauline to look after the girls. I'd met this man on the plane, and he invited me to lunch. I liked him. He kept me from being afraid on the way to Nassau.''

John's face sobered, and she realized that Gil must have told him about her past. "I'm sorry about your brother and his family,'' he said, confirming her suspicions. "Gil and I haven't really been part of a family since our uncle died.''

"Don't you ever go to see your parents?'' she asked curiously.

"There was a time when they offered an olive branch, but you know Gil,'' he said soberly. "He's slow to get over things, and he refused to talk to them. Maybe they did neglect us, but I never thought it was malicious. They had kids before they were ready to have them. Lots of people are irresponsible parents. But you can't hold grudges forever.'' He frowned. "On second thought, maybe Gil can.''

She smiled and reached across the table to lay her hand over his. "Maybe one day you can try again. It would be nice for the girls to have grandparents.''

"The only ones they have left are our parents. Darlene's died years ago.'' He caught her hand in his and held it tight. "You make the hardest things sound simple. I like myself when you're around, Kasie.''

She laughed gently. "I like you, too,'' she said.

"I never believed you had anything to do with Bess getting hurt,'' he said somberly. "Anyone could see how much you care about the girls.''

"Thanks. It's nice to know that at least one grown-up person in your family believed I was innocent,'' she said, oblivious to the white-faced, angry man standing in the hall with an armload of pale pink roses. "It hurt terribly that Gil thought I'd ever put the girls at risk in any way, least of all by neglecting them. But it wasn't the first time he's accused me of ulterior motives. I should be used to it by now. I think he's sorry he rehired me, you know,'' she added sadly, clinging to his hand. "He looks through me when he isn't glaring at me.''

"Gil's had some hard knocks with women,'' John repeated,

letting go of her hand. "Just give him time to adjust to being wrong. He rarely is." He picked up a forkful of eggs. "If it's any consolation, he roared around here for two weeks like every man's nightmare before he went after you. He wanted you to have enough time to get over the anger and let him explain his behavior. He would have gone sooner, he said, but he wasn't sure he could get in the front door."

She remembered her lacerated feelings when she'd arrived at her aunt's house. "It would have been tricky, at that," she agreed. "He was the last person on earth I wanted to see when I first came back from Nassau."

Footsteps echoed out in the hall and a door slammed. Kasie frowned.

"Sounds like Gil's going to bypass breakfast again this morning," John remarked as he finished his eggs. "He doesn't have much of an appetite these days."

"I'll just check and make sure it isn't the girls," Kasie said.

"Suit yourself, but I know those footsteps. He only walks that way when he's upset. God help whatever cowboy he runs into on his way."

Kasie didn't reply. She walked into the hall and there, on the hall table, was an armload of pink roses with the dew still clinging to the silky, fragrant petals. It took a few seconds for her to realize that Gil must have heard every word she'd said. She groaned inwardly as she gathered up the roses. Well, that was probably the end of any truce, she thought. He'd think she couldn't forgive him, and that would make him even angrier. Unless she missed her guess, he was going to be hell to live with from now on.

She took the roses to the kitchen and found a vase for them, which she filled with water before she arranged the flowers in it. With a sigh, she took them upstairs to her room and placed them on the dresser. They were beautiful. She couldn't imagine what had possessed Gil Callister to go out and cut her a bouquet. But the gesture touched her poignantly.

Sure enough, when Gil came in early for supper, he was

dusty and out of humor. He needed a shave. He glared at everybody, especially Kasie.

"Aren't you going to clean up first?" John asked, aghast, when he sat down to the table in his chaps.

"What for?" he muttered. "I've got to go right back out again." He reached for his coffee cup, which Mrs. Charters had just filled, and put cream in it.

"Is something wrong?" John asked then, concerned.

"We've got a fence down." His eyes met his brothers. "It wasn't broken through. It was cut."

John stared at the older man. "Another one? That makes two in less than ten days."

"I know. I can't prove it, but I know it was Fred Sims."

John nodded slowly. "That makes sense. One of the cowboys who was friendly with him said Sims hasn't been able to find another job since we fired him."

Gil's pale blue eyes glittered. "That damned dog could have bitten my babies," he said. "No way was he going to keep it here after it chased them onto the porch."

"Bad doggie," Jenny agreed.

Bess nodded. "We was scared, Daddy."

"Sims is going to be scared, if I catch him within a mile of my property," Gil added.

"Don't become a vigilante," John cautioned his older brother. "Call the sheriff. Let him handle it. That's what he gets paid to do."

"He can't be everywhere," Gil replied, eyes narrowed. "I want all the cowboys armed, at least with rifles. I'm not taking any chances. If he's brazen enough to cut fences and shoot livestock, he's capable of worse."

Kasie felt her heart stop. So that was why he'd been around the ranch so much lately. The man, Sims, had threatened vengeance. Apparently he was killing cattle as well as cutting fences to let them escape. She pictured Gil at the end of a gun and she felt sick all over.

"I'll make sure everyone's been alerted and prepared for

danger," John agreed. "But you stay out of it. You're the one person around here that Sims would enjoy shooting."

"He'd be lucky to get off a shot," Gil replied imperturbably. He finished his meal and wiped his mouth. "I've got to get back out there. We haven't finished stringing wire, and it's not long until dark."

"Okay. I'll phone the vet about those carcasses we found. I want him to look for bullet wounds."

"Good idea."

Gil finished the last sip of his coffee in a grim silence that seemed to spread to the rest of the family. The girls, sensing hidden anger in the adults around them, excused themselves and went upstairs to play in their room while Mrs. Charters cleaned away the dishes. John went to make a phone call.

Gil got to his feet without looking at Kasie and started toward the front door. Kasie caught up with him on the porch. It was almost dark. The sky was fiery red and pink and yellow where the sun was setting.

"Thank you," she blurted out.

He stopped and turned. "For what?"

His hat was pulled low over his eyes, and she couldn't see the expression in them, but she was pretty sure that he was scowling.

She went closer to him, stopping half an arm's length away. "For the roses," she said hesitantly. "They're beautiful."

He didn't move. He just stood there, somber, quiet. "How do you know they were meant for you?" he drawled. "And how do you know I brought them?"

She flushed scarlet. She didn't know for sure, but she'd assumed.

He averted his eyes, muttering under his breath. "You're welcome," he said tersely.

"That man, Sims," she continued, worried. "The day you fired him, John said that he had a mean temper and that he carried a loaded rifle everywhere with him. You...you be careful, okay?"

She heard the soft expulsion of breath. He moved a step closer, his lean hands lifting her oval face to his. She could see the soft glitter of his blue eyes in the faint light from the windows.

"What do you care if I get myself shot?" he asked huskily. "I'm the one who sent you packing without even giving you the chance to explain what happened in Nassau."

"Pauline didn't like me," she said. "And you trusted her. I was just a stranger."

"Not anymore, Kasie," he said gruffly.

"I mean, you didn't know anything about me," she persisted. She searched his eyes, feeling jolts of electricity flow into her at the exquisite contact. "I was upset and I behaved badly when you came to Mama Luke's. But deep inside, I didn't blame you for not trusting me."

His lean hands tightened on her face. "I've done nothing but torment you since the first day you came here," he bit off. "I didn't want you in my life, Kasie," he whispered as he bent toward her. "I still don't. But a man can only stand so much...!"

His mouth caught hers hungrily. His arms swallowed her up against him, so that not an inch of space separated them. For long, achingly sweet seconds, they clung to each other in the soft darkness.

He drew away from her finally and stood just looking at her in a tense, hot silence. His hands were firm around her arms, and she swayed toward him helplessly.

She felt her knees go shaky, as if they had jelly in them instead of bone and cartilage. "Look, I'm very old-fashioned," she began in a choked tone.

"I almost never make love to women on the floor of the front porch."

She stared at him dimly, only slowly becoming aware that he was smiling and the words were both affectionate and teasing.

A tiny laugh burst from her swollen lips, although the kiss had rattled her.

"That's better," he said. His eyes narrowed. "How do you feel about my brother?"

Her mind refused to function. "How do I what?"

"Feel about John," he persisted coolly. "When I asked you why you wanted this job, you said it was because John was a dish. I know you had a crush on him. How do you feel now?"

She was at a loss to know what to say. "I like...him," she blurted out. "He's been kind to me."

"Kinder than I have, for damned sure," he agreed at once. "And he believed you were innocent when I didn't."

She frowned. "You explained why."

His hands tightened on her arms and his lips flattened. "He's younger than I am, single and rich and easygoing," he said harshly. "Maybe he'd be the best thing that ever happened to you."

Her eyes widened. "Thank you. I've always wanted a big, strong man to plan my future for me."

He let her go abruptly, angry. "You said it yourself. I'm a generation older than you with a ready-made family."

She couldn't make head or tail of what he was saying. Her mind was spinning as she looked up at him.

"Maybe you're what he needs, too," he added coldly. "Someone young and optimistic and intelligent."

"Are you going to buy the ring, too?"

He turned away. "That wasn't funny."

"I don't want to marry your brother. Thanks, anyway."

He kept walking.

She ran after him. "That man Sims has got a gun," she called. "Don't you dare go out there and get shot!"

He paused on the top step and looked back at her as if he had doubts about her sanity. "John's going out with me as soon as he finishes his phone calls."

"Great!" she exclaimed angrily. "I can worry about both of you all night!"

"Worry about my daughters," he told her bluntly. "That's your only responsibility here. You work for me, remember?"

"I remember," she replied irritably. "Do you?"

"Stay in the house with the girls until I tell you otherwise. I don't want any of you on the porch or in the yard until we settle this, one way or another."

He did think there was danger. She heard it in every word. "I won't let anything happen to Bess and Jenny. I promise."

He glared at her. "Can you shoot?"

She shook her head. "But I know how to dial 911."

"Okay. Keep one of the wireless phones handy, just in case."

She moved toward him another step, wrapping her arms tight around her body. "Have you got a cell phone?"

He indicated the case on his belt. That was when she noticed an old Colt .45 strapped to his other hip, under the denim shirt he was wearing open over his black T-shirt.

Her breath caught. Until that minute, when she saw the gun, it was a possibility. But guns were violent, chaotic, frightening. She bit her lower lip worriedly.

"I'll be late. Make sure you lock the doors before you go upstairs. John and I have keys."

"I will," she promised. "You be careful."

He ignored the quiet command. He took one long, last look at her and went on down the steps to his pickup truck, which was parked nearby.

She stood at the top of the steps until he drove away, staring after him worriedly. She wanted to call him back, to beg him to stay inside where he'd be safe from any retribution by that man Sims. But she couldn't. He wasn't the sort of man to run from trouble. It wouldn't do any good to nag him. He was going to do what he needed to do, whether or not it pleased her.

She got the girls ready for bed and tucked them in. She read them a Dr. Seuss book they hadn't heard yet. When they grew drowsy, she pulled the covers over them and tiptoed to the door, pausing to flick off the light switch as she went out into the hall.

She left the door cracked and went on down the hall to her own room. She got ready for bed and curled up on her pillows with a worn copy of Tacitus's *The Histories.* "I wonder if you ever imagined that people in the future would still be reading words you wrote almost two thousand years ago," she murmured as she thumbed through the well-read work. "And nothing really changes, does it, except the clothes and the everyday things. People are the same."

Her heart wasn't in the book. She laid it aside and turned off the lights, thinking how it would have been two thousand years ago to watch her husband put on his armor and march off to a war in some foreign country behind one of the Roman generals. That made her think of Gil and she gnawed her lip as she lay in the darkness, waiting for some sound that would tell her he was still all right.

It was two o'clock in the morning before she heard a pickup truck pull up at the bottom of the steps out front. She threw off the covers and ran to the window, peering out through the lacy curtain just in time to see Gil and John climb wearily out of the truck. John had a rifle with the breech open under one arm. He led the way into the house, with Gil following behind.

At least, thank God, they were both still alive, she thought. She went back to bed and pulled the covers up to her chin. Relieved, she slept.

She'd forgotten John's invitation to the movies, but he hadn't. And he looked odd, as if he was pondering something wicked, when he waited for her to come down the stairs with the girls.

Kasie was wearing a pretty dark green silk pantsuit with strappy sandals and her hair around her shoulders. She smiled at the little girls in their skirt sets. They looked like a family, and John was touched. He went forward to greet them, pausing to kiss Kasie's cheek warmly.

Gil, who was working in the office, came into the hall just in time to see his brother kissing Kasie. His eyes splintered with unexpected helpless rage. His fists clenched at his side. She wouldn't leave the house with him, but here she was dressed to the nines and all eager to jump into a car with his brother.

John glanced at him warily and hid a smile. "We're off to the movies! Want to come?"

"No," Gil said abruptly. He avoided looking at Kasie. "I've got two more hours of work to finish in the den."

"Let Miss Parsons do it and come with us," John persisted.

"I gave Miss Parsons the day off. She's visiting a friend."

"Let it wait until tomorrow, then."

"No chance. Go ahead and enjoy yourselves, but don't get too comfortable. Watch your back," he said tersely, and returned into the study. He closed the door firmly behind him.

John, for some ungodly reason, was rubbing his hands together with absolute glee. Kasie gave him a speaking glance, which he ignored as he herded them out into the night.

The movie was one for general audiences, about a famous singer. John didn't really enjoy it, but Kasie and the girls did. They ate popcorn and giggled at the funny scenes, and moaned when the heroine was misjudged by the hero and thrown out on her ear.

"That looks familiar, doesn't it?" John murmured outrageously.

"She should hit him with a brickbat," Kasie muttered.

"With a head that hard, I don't know if it would do any good," he said, and Kasie thought for a minute that it didn't sound as if he were referring to the movie. "But I have a much better idea, anyway. Wait and see."

She pondered that enigmatic remark all through the movie. They went home, had dinner and watched TV, but it wasn't until the girls went up to bed and the study door opened that

Kasie began to realize what John was up to. Because he waited until his brother had an unobstructed view of the two of them at the foot of the staircase. And then he bent and kissed Kasie. Passionately.

Kasie was shocked. Gil was infuriated. John winked at Kasie before he turned to face his brother. "Oh, there you are," he told Gil with a grin. "The movie was great. I'll tell you all about it tomorrow. Sleep well, Kasie," he added, ruffling the hair at her temple.

"You, too," she choked. She could barely manage words. John had never touched her before, and she knew that it hadn't been out of misplaced passion or raging desire that he'd kissed her. He'd obviously done it to irritate his big brother. And it was working! Gil looked as if he wanted to bite somebody.

He moved close to Kasie when John was out of sight up the steps, whipping out a snow-white handkerchief. He caught her by the nape and wiped off her smeared lipstick.

"You aren't marrying my brother," he said through his teeth.

"Excuse me?"

"I said, you aren't marrying John," he repeated harshly. "You're an employee here, and that's all. I am not going to let my brother become your meal ticket!"

She actually gasped. "Of all the unfounded, unreasonable, outrageous things in the world to say to a woman, that really takes the cake!" she raged.

"I haven't started yet," he bit off. He threw the handkerchief down on the hall table and pulled her roughly into his arms. "I've never wanted to hit a man so badly in all my life," he ground out as his mouth went down over hers.

She couldn't breathe. He didn't seem to notice, or care. His mouth was warm, hard, insistent. She clung to his shirtfront and let the sensations wash over her like fire. He was insulting her. She shouldn't let him. She should make him stop. It was just that his mouth was so sweet, so masterful, so ardent. She

moaned as the sensations piled up on themselves and left her
knees wobbling out from under her.

He caught her closer and lifted her against him, devouring
her mouth with his own. She felt her whole body begin to
shiver with the strength of the desire he was teaching her to
feel. Never in her life had she known such pleasure, but even
the hungry force of the kiss still wasn't enough to ease the
ache in her.

Her arms went up and around his neck and she held on as
if she might die by letting go. He groaned huskily as his body
began to harden. He wanted her. He wanted to lay her down
on the Persian carpet, make passionate love to her. He
wanted...

He dragged his mouth from hers and looked down at her
with accusation and raging anger.

"I'm mad," he growled off. "You aren't supposed to enjoy
it."

"Okay," she murmured, trying to coax his mouth back
down onto hers. She had no will, no pride, no reason left. She
only wanted the pleasure to continue. "Come back here. I'll
pretend to hate it."

"Kasie..."

She found his mouth and groaned hoarsely as he gave in to
his own hunger and crushed her against the length of his tall,
fit body. It was the most glorious kiss of her entire life. If only
it would never end...

But it did, all too soon, and he shot away from her as if
he'd tasted poison. His eyes glittered. "If you ever let him kiss
you again, I'll throw both of you out a window!"

She opened her mouth to speak, but before she could manage words, the front doorbell rang.

It was one of the cowboys. Two more head of cattle had
been shot, and the gunman was still out near the line cabin.
One of the cowboys had him pinned down with rifle fire and
needed reinforcements. It took Gil precisely five minutes to
call John, load his Winchester and get out the door. He barely

took time to caution Kasie about venturing outside until the situation was under control. She didn't even get a chance to beg him to be careful. She went upstairs, so that she'd be near the girls, but she knew that this was one night she wouldn't sleep a wink.

Chapter 11

Kasie lay awake for the rest of the night. When dawn broke, she still hadn't heard Gil come into the house. And once she'd thought she heard a shot being fired. Remembering how dangerous the man Sims was supposed to be made her even more uneasy. What if Gil had been shot? How would she live? She couldn't bear the thought of a world without Gil in it.

She got up and dressed just as Mrs. Charters went into the kitchen to start breakfast. John and Gil were nowhere in sight.

"Have they come in at all?" she asked Mrs. Charters.

"Not yet," the older woman said, and looked worried. "There were police cars and sheriff's cars all over the place about two hours ago," she added. "I saw them from my house."

"I thought I heard a shot, but I didn't see anything," Kasie said, and then she really worried.

"You couldn't have seen them, it was three miles and more down the road. But I'm sure we'd have heard if anything had happened to Gil or John."

"Oh, I hope so," Kasie said fervently.

"I'll make coffee," she said. "You can have some in a minute."

"Thanks, Mrs. Charters. I'm going to go sit on the front porch."

"You do that, dear."

The ranch was most beautiful early in the morning, Kasie thought, when dawn broke on the horizon and the cattle and horses started moving around in the pastures. She loved this part of the day, but now it was torment to sit and wonder and not be able to do anything. Had they found Sims? Was he in custody or still at large? And, most frightening of all, was the memory of that single gunshot. Had Gil been hurt?

She nibbled at her fingernails in her nervousness, a habit left over from childhood. There didn't seem to be a vehicle in the world. The highway was close enough that the sound of moving vehicles could be heard very faintly, but at this hour there was very little traffic. In fact, there was none.

She got up from the porch swing and paced restlessly. What if Gil had been shot? Surely someone would have phoned. John would, she was certain. But what if the wound was serious, so serious that he couldn't leave his brother's side even long enough to make a phone call? What if…!

The sound of a truck coming down the long ranch road caught her attention. She ran to the top of the steps and stood there with her heart pounding like mad. It was one of the ranch's pickup trucks. She recognized it. Two men were in the cab. They were in a flaming rush. Was it John and one of the hands, come to tell her that Gil was hurt, wounded, dying?

Dust flew as the driver pulled up sharply at the front steps. Both doors flew open. Kasie thought she might faint. John got out of the passenger side, whole and undamaged and grinning. Gil got out on the other side, dusty and worn, with a cut bleeding beside his mouth. But he was all in one piece, not injured, not shot, not…

"Gil!" She screamed his name, blind and deaf and dumb to the rest of the world as she came out of her frozen trance and dashed down the steps, missing the bottom one entirely, to rush right into his arms.

"Kasie..." He couldn't talk at all, because she was kissing him, blindly, fervently, as if he'd just come back from the dead.

He stopped trying to talk. He kissed her back, his arms enfolding her so closely that her feet dangled while he answered the aching hunger of her mouth.

She was shaking when he lifted his head. His eyes were glittery with feeling as he searched her eyes and saw every single emotion in her. She loved him. She couldn't have told him any plainer if she'd shouted it.

John just chuckled. "I'll go drink coffee while you two...talk," he murmured dryly, bypassing them without a backward glance.

Neither of them heard him or saw him go. They stared at each other with aching tenderness, touching faces, lips, fingertips.

"I'm all right," he whispered, kissing her again. "Sims took a shot at us, but he missed. It took two sheriff's deputies, the bloodhounds and a few ranch hands, but we tracked him down. He's in jail, nursing his bruises."

She traced the dried blood on his cheek. "He hit you."

He shrugged. "I hit him, too." He smiled outrageously. "So much for pretending that you only work for me, Kasie," he said with deliberate mischief in his tone.

She touched his dusty hair. "I love you," she said huskily. Her eyes searched his. "Is it all right?"

"That depends," he mused, bending to kiss her gently. "We discussed being old-fashioned, remember?"

She flushed. "I wasn't suggesting..."

He took her soft upper lip in both of his and nibbled it. "This is the last place in the world that you and I could carry on a torrid affair," he pointed out. "The girls can take off doorknobs if they have the right tools, and Mrs. Charters probably has microphones and hidden cameras in every room. She always knows whatever's going on around here." He lifted his head and searched her eyes. "I'm glad you love children, Kasie. I really don't plan to stop at Bess and Jenny."

She flushed softly. "Really?"

"We should have one or two of our own," he added quietly. "Boys run in my family, even if Darlene and I were never able to have one. If we had a son or two, it would give Bess and Jenny a chance to be part of a big family."

Her eyes grew dreamy. "We could teach all of them how to use the computer and love cattle."

He smiled tenderly. "But first, I think we might get married," he whispered at her lips. "So that your aunt doesn't have to be embarrassed when she tells people what you're doing."

"We wouldn't want to embarrass Mama Luke," she agreed, bubbling over with joy.

"God forbid," he murmured. He kissed her again, with muted passion. "She can come to the wedding." He hesitated and his eyes darkened. "I'm not sure about my brother. I could have decked him for kissing you!"

"I still don't know why he did," she began.

He chuckled. "He told me. He wanted to see if I was jealous of you. I gave him hell all night until Sims showed up. He laughed all the way back to the ranch. So much for lighting fires under people," he added with a faint grin. "I'll let him be best man, I guess, but he's going to be the only man in church who doesn't get to kiss the bride!"

She laughed. "What a wicked family I'm marrying into," she said as she reached up to kiss him. "And speaking of wicked, we have to invite K.C.," she added shyly.

He froze, lifting his head. "I don't know about that, Kasie..."

"You'll like him. Really you will," she promised, smiling widely.

He grimaced. "I suppose we each have to have at least one

handicap," he muttered. "I have a lunatic brother and you're best friends with a hit man."

"He's not. You'll like him," she repeated, and drew his head down to hers again. She kissed him with enthusiasm, enjoying the warm, wise tutoring of his hard mouth. "We should go and tell the babies," she whispered against his mouth.

"No need," he murmured.

"Uncle John, look! Daddy's kissing Kasie!"

"See?" he added with a grin as he lifted his head and indicated the front door. Standing there, grinning also, were John, Bess, Jenny, Mrs. Charters, and Miss Parsons.

The wedding was the social event of Medicine Ridge for the summer. Kasie wore a beautiful white gown with lace and a keyhole neckline, with a Juliet cap and a long veil. She looked, Gil whispered as she joined him at the altar, like an angel.

Her excited eyes approved his neat gray vested suit, which made his hair look even more blond. At either side of them were Bess and Jenny in matching blue dresses, carrying baskets of white roses. Next to them was John, his brother's best man, fumbling in his pocket for the wedding rings he was responsible for.

As the ceremony progressed, a tall, blond man in the front pew watched with narrowed, wistful eyes as his godchild married the eldest of the Callister heirs. Not bad, K.C. Kantor thought, for a girl who'd barely survived a military uprising even before she was born. He glanced at the woman seated next to him, his eyes sad and quiet, as he contemplated what might have been if he'd met Kasie's aunt before her heart led her to a life of service in a religious order. They were the best of friends and they corresponded. She would always be family to him. She was the only family he had, or would ever have, except for that sweet young woman at the altar.

"Isn't she beautiful?" Mama Luke whispered to him.

"A real vision," he agreed.

She smiled at him with warm affection and turned her attention back to the ceremony.

As the priest pronounced them man and wife, Gil lifted the veil and bent to kiss Kasie. There were sighs all around, until a small hand tugged hard at Kasie's skirt and a little voice was heard asking plaintively, "Is it over yet, Daddy? I have to go to the bathroom!"

Later, laughing about the small interruption as they gathered in the fellowship hall of the church, Kasie and Gil each cuddled a little girl and fed them cake.

"It was nice of Pauline to apologize for what she did in the Bahamas," Kasie murmured, recalling the telephone call that had both surprised and pleased her the day before the ceremony.

"She's really not that bad," Gil mused. "Just irresponsible and possessive. But I still didn't want her at the wedding," he added with a grin. "Just in case."

"I still wish you'd invited your parents," Kasie told Gil gently.

"I did," he replied. "They were on their way to the Bahamas and couldn't spare the time." He smiled at her. "Don't worry the subject, Kasie. Some things can't be changed. We're a family, you and me and the girls and John."

"Yes, we are," she agreed, and she reached up to kiss him. She glanced around them curiously. Mama Luke intercepted the glance and joined them.

"He left as we were coming in here," she told Kasie. "K.C. never was one for socializing. I expect he's headed for the airport by now."

"It was nice of him to come."

"It was," she agreed. She handed a small box to Kasie. "He asked me to give this to you."

She frowned, pausing to open the box. She drew out a gold necklace with a tiny crystal ball dangling from it. Inside the ball was a tiny seed.

"It's a mustard seed," Mama Luke explained. "It's from a Biblical quote—if you have even that amount of faith, as a mustard seed, nothing is impossible. It's to remind you that miracles happen."

Kasie cradled it in her hand and looked up at Gil with her heart in her eyes. "Indeed they do," she whispered, and all the love she had for her new husband was in her face.

The next night, Kasie and Gil lay tangled in a king-size bed at a rented villa in Nassau, exhausted and deliciously relaxed from their first intimacy.

Kasie moved shyly against him, her face flushed in the aftermath of more physical sensation than she'd ever experienced.

"Stop that," he murmured drowsily. "I'm useless now. Go to sleep."

She laughed with pure delight and curled closer. "All right. But don't forget where we left off."

He drew her closer. "As if I could!" He bent and kissed her eyes shut. "Kasie, I never dreamed that I could be this happy again." His eyes opened and looked into hers with fervent possession. "I loved Darlene. A part of me will always love her. But I would die for you," he added roughly, his eyes blazing with emotion.

Overwhelmed, she buried her face in his throat and shivered. "I would die for you," she choked. She clung harder. "I love you!"

His mouth found hers, hungry for contact, for the sharing of fierce, exquisite need. He drew her over his relaxed body and held her until the trembling stopped. His breath sighed out heavily at her ear. "Forever, Kasie," he whispered unsteadily.

She smiled. "Forever."

They slept, eventually, and as dawn filtered in through the venetian blinds and the sound of the surf grew louder, there was a knock on the door.

Gil opened his eyes, still drowsy. He looked down at Kasie, fast asleep on her stomach, smiling even so. He smiled, too, and tossed the sheet over her before he stepped into his Bermuda shorts and went to answer the door.

The shock when he opened it was blatant. On the doorstep were a silver-haired man in casual slacks and designer shirt, and a silver-haired woman in a neat but casual sundress and overblouse. They were carrying the biggest bouquet of orchids Gil had ever seen in his life.

The man pushed the bouquet toward Gil hesitantly and with a smile that seemed both hesitant and uncertain. ''Congratulations,'' he said.

''From both of us,'' the woman added.

They both stood there, waiting.

As Gil searched for words, there was movement behind him and Kasie came to the door in the flowered cotton muu-muu she'd bought for the trip, her long chestnut hair disheveled, smiling broadly.

''Hello!'' she exclaimed, going past Gil to hug the woman and then the man, who both flushed. ''I'm so glad you could come!''

Gil stared at her. ''What?''

''I phoned them,'' she told him, clasping his big hand in hers. ''They said they'd like to come over and have lunch with us, and I told them to come today. But I overslept,'' she added, and flushed.

''It's your honeymoon, you should oversleep,'' Gil's mother, Magdalene, said gently. She looked at her son nervously. ''We wanted to come to the wedding,'' she said. ''But we didn't want to, well, ruin the day for you.''

''That's right,'' Jack Callister agreed gruffly. ''We haven't been good parents. At first we were too irresponsible, and then we were too ashamed. Especially when Douglas took you in and we lost touch.'' He shrugged. ''It's too late to start over, of course, but we'd sort of like to, well, to get to know you and John. And the girls, of course. That is, if you, uh, if you…'' He shrugged.

Kasie squeezed Gil's hand, hard.

"I'd like that," he said obligingly.

Their faces changed. They beamed. For several seconds, they looked like silver-haired children on Christmas morning. And Gil realized with stark shock that they were just that— grown-up children without the first idea of how to be parents. Douglas Callister had kept the boys, and he hadn't approved of his brother Jack, so he hadn't encouraged contact. Since the elder Callisters didn't know how to approach their children directly, they lost touch and then couldn't find a way to reach them at all.

He looked down at Kasie, and it all made sense. She'd tied the loose ends up. She'd gathered a family back together.

She squeezed Gil's hand again, looking up at him with radiant delight. "We could get dressed and meet them in the restaurant. After we put these in water," she added, hugging the bouquet to her heart and sniffing them. "I've never had orchids in my life," she said with a smile. "Thank you!"

Magdalena laughed nervously. "No, Kasie. Thank *you.*"

"We'll get dressed and meet you in about fifteen minutes, in the restaurant," Gil managed to say.

"Great!" Jack said. He took his wife's hand, and they both smiled, looking ten years younger. "We'll see you there!"

The door closed and Gil looked down at Kasie with wonder.

"I thought they might like to visit us at the ranch next month, too," Kasie said, "so they can get to know the babies."

"You're amazing," he said. "Absolutely amazing!"

She fingered the necklace K.C. had given her at the wedding. "I like miracles, don't you?"

He burst out laughing. He picked her up and swung her around in an arc while she squealed and held on to her bouquet tightly. He put her down gently and kissed her roughly.

"I love you," he said huskily.

She grinned. "Yes, and see what it gets you when you love

people? You get all sorts of nice surprises. In fact," she added with a mischievous grin, "I have all sorts of surprises in store for you."

He took a deep breath and looked at her with warm affection. "I can hardly wait."

She kissed him gently and went to dress. She gave a thought to Gil's Darlene, and to her own parents, and her lost twin and his family, and hoped that they all knew, somehow, that she and Gil were happy and that they had a bright future with the two little girls and the children they would have together. As she went to the closet to get her dress, her eyes were full of dreams. And so were Gil's.

* * * * *

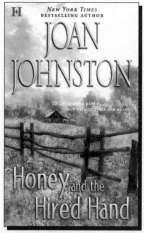

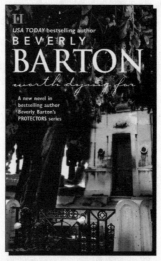

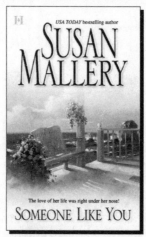